I Killed Zoe Spanos

Also by Kit Frick

See All the Stars
All Eyes on Us

I killed Zoe Spanos

A NOVEL BY

KIT FRICK

MARGARET K. McELDERRY BOOKS
New York London Toronto Sydney New Delhi

MARGARET K. McELDERRY BOOKS
An imprint of Simon & Schuster Children's Publishing Division
1230 Avenue of the Americas, New York, New York 10020

MARGARET K. McELDERRY BOOKS is a trademark of Simon & Schuster, Inc.
For information about special discounts for bulk purchases, please contact Simon & Schuster Special Sales at 1-866-506-1949 or business@simonandschuster.com.
The Simon & Schuster Speakers Bureau can bring authors to your live event. For more information or to book an event, contact the Simon & Schuster Speakers Bureau at 1-866-248-3049 or visit our website at www.simonspeakers.com.
Book design by Debra Sfetsios-Conover and Irene Metaxatos
The text for this book was set in Garamond.
Manufactured in the United States of America
First Edition
10 9 8 7 6 5 4 3 2 1
Library of Congress Cataloging-in-Publication Data
Names: Frick, Kit, author.
Title: I killed Zoe Spanos / Kit Frick.
Description: First edition. | New York : Margaret K. McElderry Books, [2020] | Audience: Ages 14 up | Audience: Grades 10–12 | Summary: Working as a nanny in the Hamptons before starting college, Anna learns of her weird connection to a missing girl, but after she confesses to manslaughter a podcast producer helps reveal life-changing truths.
Identifiers: LCCN 2019025732 (print) | ISBN 9781534449701 (hardcover) | ISBN 9781534449725 (eBook)
Subjects: CYAC: Missing persons—Fiction. | Nannies—Fiction. | Podcasts—Fiction. | Hamptons (N.Y.)—Fiction. | Mystery and detective stories.
Classification: LCC PZ7.1.F75478 Iaah 2020 (print) | DDC [Fic]—dc23
LC record available at https://lccn.loc.gov/2019025732

For Osvaldo. Last night, I dreamt
we went to Manderley again.

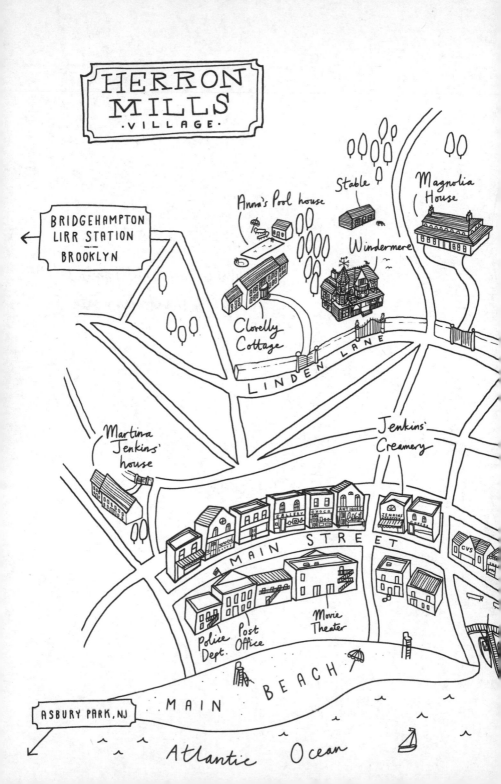

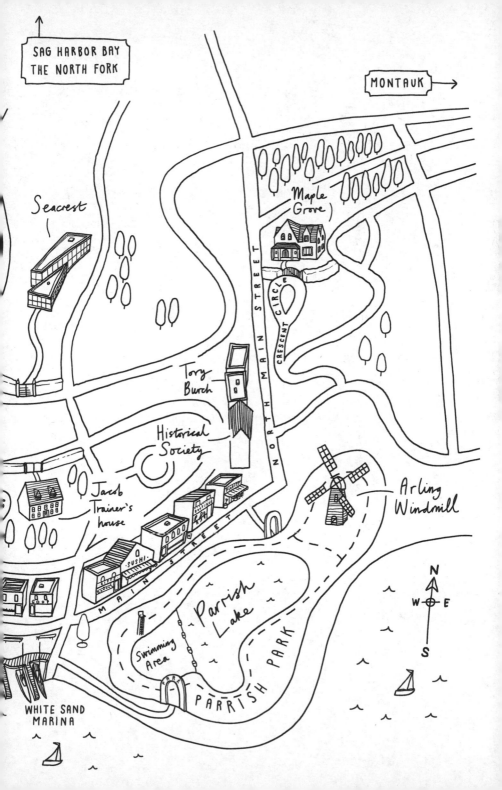

PART I

The Village

It's very difficult to keep the line between the past and the present.
Do you know what I mean?

—Edith "Little Edie" Bouvier Beale, *Grey Gardens*

1

August

Herron Mills Village Police Department,
Long Island, NY

"ANNA? WE'RE RECORDING."

The camera pans up from a long crack in the linoleum floor to rest on the hunched-over frame of a girl. She's perched on the edge of a wobbly metal chair, cutoff shorts touching the smallest possible strip of a once-blue fabric seat. Her tank top is a bright shock of red in the colorless room. She tightens her arms around her waist, as if trying to make herself smaller or cover the red with the bloodless wash of her skin. Her head is tilted forward, gaze trained on her shoes, and a thick curtain of tangled black hair falls in front of her face.

"Do you understand, Anna? The camera is on." A white time stamp in the bottom left of the screen notes that it's August 5, 9:02 p.m.

"Yes."

"Okay then." The voice coming from behind the camera is female, but it's not kind or nurturing or any of those attributes we assign to women like a requirement or curse. Detective Holloway's words have a jagged edge, chiseled from stone, then left raw. She faces the lens and states the date and time, that this is an interview with Anna Cicconi, a minor who is not, at present, under arrest. Then she turns to Anna. "Go ahead and repeat what you just told Assistant Detective Massey and me."

The third person in the room is barely visible in the camera frame. AD Massey is in his late twenties and not used to sitting for so many hours on end. He fidgets in a rolling chair behind a small desk, kitty-corner to Anna, letting his senior partner take the lead. Over the past six hours, he has mostly stayed on the sidelines, making the occasional run to the vending machine for soda and slightly stale corn chips. Observing. Taking down notes.

There are no parents, no lawyers. The girl's father is unreachable, has been unreachable for years. Someone called the girl's mother, but not until after Anna placed herself at the scene where the body was found. Gloria Cicconi is on her way here now, but the drive across Long Island will take her over two hours, and she had to arm-twist her neighbor into lending her the car first. They told the girl they'd called right away, but no one actually did. Maybe it was a mistake, a wire crossed. Maybe it was on purpose. Maybe the girl should have refused to speak to the detectives until her mother arrived. Maybe things would have gone differently with Gloria's leonine presence in the room. But that's not how it happened.

Anna is used to doing things on her own. She has learned not to depend on adults to either take her to task or dig her out when she fucks up. Which has been often. She has grown accustomed to her mother's display of hollow disinterest in her failures. Why should she expect this time to be different?

The detective steps out from behind the camera, confident now that it's doing its job, and takes a seat in the empty chair beside Anna. In the shot, she looks close. Too close for comfort. You can see the girl shift slightly to her right. "Go ahead," she repeats. "What you just told us."

"About Zoe?" She lifts her head, hair parting to reveal chapped lips, sharp blue-green eyes sinking into dark circles, her already pale face almost ghostly in the white LED lights, one of the Herron Mills Village PD's recent station upgrades.

"Why don't you start at the beginning." It's not really a question. Detective Holloway extends her hand toward Anna, then seems to think better of it, and drops it down to the chair's metal arm. "On New Year's Eve."

"Okay." There's a catch to Anna's voice, a scraped-out quality. On the recording, it sounds like she has a cold, but really, it's because she's been talking to the police for hours already, before anyone decided to press record. They've been through quite a dance, the girl and Detective Holloway. It was midafternoon when Anna got here, shaken but brimming with a resolve that quickly wavered inside the station walls. Now, if there were any windows in this room, she'd know it's been dark outside for more than an hour.

"We started the night at Kaylee's. Early, like six thirty. She's five blocks down from my mom's place, in Bay Ridge."

"That's in Brooklyn?"

"Yeah. Yes. In Brooklyn. We, um . . . we started a lot of nights at Kaylee's. Her dad's gone too, and her mom works nights. We'd drink there for a couple hours, then go out. Meet up with Starr and everyone. There are a few bars around that know us, or we'd get on the train, head down to Coney Island. Go dancing."

"And that's where you went on New Year's Eve? To Coney Island?" Detective Holloway's face is still smooth for a woman of forty. But mascara clumps in the corners of her eyes and a stale film is beginning to coat her tongue and teeth. They've been at it since three, and she's eager to finish this. Place the girl under arrest.

"Yeah, but not out dancing. I never made it farther than Starr's place. She's older, like twenty-two? Starr kind of took Kaylee and me under her wing last year, until she moved down to Orlando."

"When was that?"

"Soon after New Year's. Starr got a job at one of the parks."

"Okay. But that night, it was you, Kaylee, and Starr at her apartment in Coney Island."

"And a couple other people. Kaylee's sort-of boyfriend, Ian. And this guy Mike we know from around."

"Around?"

"Like, around Brooklyn. Not from school." Anna tugs at a thread on her cutoffs until it snaps free from the denim.

"I see. And what time did you leave Starr's apartment?"

For a moment, Anna is quiet. She leans forward, elbows pressed into bare knees, hair falling back across her eyes. She looks younger than her seventeen years, made small by the camera's greedy eye and the imperial presence of adults in uniform.

"It must have been nine or nine thirty."

"Must have been, or it was?" The detective's voice is sharp.

Anna's voice, in turn, is a low mumble, the words snagged in her hair. "I don't really remember. But if I got a ride out to Herron Mills, and got there by midnight, I must have left around then. Or even earlier if I took the train."

The detective lets out a low breath. "Fine. Then what do you remember?" She sits back in her seat but keeps her hand on the arm of Anna's chair.

"We were on the balcony at Windermere. The long one that wraps around the front of the house, on the third floor."

"Who's we, Anna?"

"Me and Kaylee. And Zoe."

"Just the three of you?"

"Just the three of us."

"And where were the Talbots?"

"In the city, at their friend Doreen's, I think. Not home."

Detective Holloway stares at Anna for a moment. The girl holds her gaze. "Fine, continue."

"We were drinking whiskey. Glenlivet, the good stuff. Better than Kaylee and I could ever buy back home." Something bitter, so slight you might miss it, slips in, then out of her words. "Caden always kept a bottle stashed in this unused stall in the Windermere stable. I guess that's where we got it."

"You guess or you remember?"

"I guess. I just remember we were passing the bottle around, up on the balcony."

"And who was drinking beer?" the detective asks.

"What?" Anna's chin jerks up, hair parting once again. For a quick moment, she meets the older woman's eyes. Then her gaze drops to the pale glint of her knees.

"Before, you told me you were drinking whiskey and beer."

"I did?" On the recording, you can see Anna press her lips between her teeth. She runs her tongue over the cracked, flaking skin. "I guess so," she says after a moment. "I'd been drinking for hours—it's not very clear. I guess there was also beer."

"Tell me about how Zoe fell," Detective Holloway says. She lifts her hand from the arm of the chair and places it lightly on Anna's shoulder. Anna doesn't seem to notice, doesn't react. Her eyes are unfocused, but when she speaks, her voice is clearer than it's been all night.

"The railing's kind of low. Only up to your thigh? We were messing around, the three of us. I remember Kaylee pinching me, like she was trying to keep me awake. I guess I was pretty out of it. And I remember Zoe laughing. She had one of those infectious laughs, like silver. It made you feel all warm inside."

"And how did she fall, Anna?" Detective Holloway squeezes the girl's shoulder, not quite gently.

"Oh." Anna looks up for a moment, not at the detective, but straight into the camera. It's like she's remembering, for the first time, where she is. What she came here to say. "Kaylee went inside. I think she was getting us a snack. Zoe and I stayed on the balcony. I remember twirling, our arms crossed in an X between us, holding hands. We were twirling and laughing and it was fun until I started to feel sick. I think I let go of her hands."

"You think? You need to be honest, Anna." Her words slice the air. Anna flinches, just slightly.

"I remember she hit the balcony rail. It was too low. Her knees buckled, and then it was like she was flying."

"Cut the pretty language," Detective Holloway snaps. "Just tell the truth."

"She fell backward, onto the lawn." Something wild dances in Anna's eyes, then fades, her pupils sinking once again into dark, exhausted circles. For a moment, everyone is silent. Anna clasps her hands tight in her lap. "By the time I got down there . . . I don't really remember seeing her body. I just remember the way it hit me like this cold, empty dread—she's really gone, and it's my fault. And I couldn't find her bag; it was missing. I don't know why that seemed important."

AD Massey stands abruptly, chair rolling back and hitting the wall. Anna and Detective Holloway look up at him, as if they've both just remembered he's there. "Did you push her?" His voice is thin but loud.

Anna draws in a sharp breath. "No."

"I'm going to ask you one more time." He takes three steps, closing the distance between them. Standing, he towers over Anna, all lean muscle and pants that are too big in the hips and too short at the ankle. The camera captures him from the shoulder down, a headless menace. "Did. You. Push. Her?"

"N-no." For the first time, Anna trips over her words. "We were twirling. I let go of her hands."

Detective Holloway glares sharply up at her junior partner. He takes one step back.

"What happened then, Anna?" she asks.

"I guess I drove her out to the lake."

"You drove Zoe. Alone."

"Yes."

"In what car?"

Anna stares down at her hands, as if they might hold the answer. "I don't remember. Maybe Zoe's. Maybe a car from the Windermere property. Everyone has cars out here. And Mrs. Talbot isn't much for keeping things locked."

Detective Holloway grunts, part sound and part breath. "What *do* you remember, Anna?"

Anna draws in a lungful of air. "I remember the water. It was gray and dull, like an old car with the paint worn off. I remember kneeling on the bank, staring out across the surface after she was down there. I remember how cold it was that night, how the wind was sharp and wet against my cheeks. Most of all, I remember the guilt, how it crushed the air out of my lungs."

The detective is silent for a moment, taking Anna's words in. "Let's take a step back," she says finally. "How did you sink her body in the motorboat?"

Anna tugs at her lower lip with her teeth. "I don't remember that part."

"Think harder." Detective Holloway's voice is sharp.

"With buckets of water?"

"And what else?"

The girl pauses, considering. "With rocks?"

The two detectives exchange a glance.

"Okay. What rocks?"

Anna is silent for a moment. She chews a flake of skin from her lip and grinds it between her front teeth.

"From Windermere, I guess. Maybe I found some large

rocks on the grounds, and I put them in the trunk." She fidgets, rolling a new thread from her cutoffs between her thumb and forefinger, as AD Massey jots something down on the legal pad in front of him.

Detective Holloway clears her throat. She stands, changing the air in the room. "Tell me more about your relationship with Zoe." Her voice is softer now, cajoling. "How did you know her?"

"We were friends," Anna supplies unhelpfully. She's mumbling again, holding something back.

Detective Holloway clasps her hands behind her back, exudes patience. "Had you known each other long?"

The question is so simple. But Anna doesn't want to answer, or she doesn't know how.

"Let me rephrase. How did you and Zoe meet?"

"I think . . ." Anna's voice trails off. "It'll be easiest if I show you. On my phone."

This is new. Detective Holloway's eyes light up. She nods toward her partner, who retrieves Anna's phone from a small plastic basket on the room's one desk. "What am I looking for?" he asks.

"Messenger. Bottom of the first screen? It's like a little lightning bolt."

AD Massey grunts, then taps open the app. He crouches next to Anna, holds her phone out between them.

"Scroll down a ways," Anna says. "Here, it's probably easier if I . . ." She looks up to Detective Holloway for permission.

Anna takes her phone gently from the junior detective's hands, then starts scrolling back through months of chats. "Here." She stabs her finger at a conversation from December—two messages from Zoe Spanos dated 12/10 and 12/28.

For a moment, the room is completely silent while the detectives pore over the notes from a dead girl. Anna barely breathes.

After her phone is taken away, the messages thoroughly dissected, then logged into evidence, after AD Massey has returned to his rolling chair and Detective Holloway is seated again at Anna's side, only then does Anna draw in a full, deep breath.

"Is there anything else you'd like to tell us?" the detective asks.

For a moment, Anna is silent. Then, she turns to look the older woman in the eye. "We both loved that Tennyson poem. Do you know it? 'The Lady of Shalott?'"

At the edge of the frame, you can see AD Massey slowly stand. His senior partner gives him a glance. *Hold on.*

"Tell me about the poem, Anna," she says.

"She lives in this castle on an island, near Camelot. And she's cursed to sit at a loom and weave only what she sees in this mirror, which is kind of a reflected window to the world around her." She pauses. "I'm not explaining this right."

"It's okay," Detective Holloway prompts. "Keep going."

"Um, so the lady watches this newlywed couple in the mirror, and wants what they have. They're real; all she has is a shadow of real life. And then she sees Sir Lancelot, and she turns and looks directly out the window, which triggers the curse. She's doomed, but she leaves her castle and finds a boat and sets sail to Camelot, even though she knows she'll die before she gets there. The boat becomes her grave."

For so long you might think it's a mistake, the only sound

on the recording is the *scritch-scritch* of AD Massey's uniform pants rubbing together at the seams as he shifts uncomfortably from side to side.

"And so you found a boat for Zoe?" Detective Holloway asks. Her voice is a song now, the jagged edge smoothed away entirely.

"Maybe I thought it's what she would have wanted. Maybe I was trying to make things right."

"Make things right?" The detective repeats Anna's words back to her.

"In some small way. After what I'd done. It was an accident, but . . . I killed Zoe Spanos."

THEN

June

Two months earlier . . .
Bridgehampton LIRR station,
Long Island, NY

I DON'T KNOW why I expect the station to be right on the ocean. Train doors sliding open to the thin cry of seagulls. The mist of salt air. Sand kicked up by the sea breeze to nip at my skin. *Welcome.*

It's nothing like that. When I step onto the platform at Bridgehampton, train doors closing behind me, my flip-flops land on a dirty strip of concrete. In front of me is a matchbox of a station. Through the windows, I can see a couple benches, a single ticket machine. Along the length of the platform, a green-painted railing stretches for yards in both directions, overlooking not the ocean, but a parking lot.

I adjust my shades across the bridge of my nose and squint into the low-hanging sun. All around me, passengers stream down the ramp to the parking lot, clamber into waiting cars and taxis and shuttles. It's Monday. I can't even imagine what this place looks like on a Friday, the tourists and "summer people" here to claim the weekend, make the Hamptons their own.

I'm not here to summer. I'm here to work. I've only met Emilia and Paisley Bellamy once, and suddenly I'm not sure I'll recognize them. There are stylish mothers with their equally stylish kids everywhere, mixed in with the couples, the businesspeople, the groups of girlfriends. I look for Paisley's fine blond hair, the delicate slope of her nose and chin. Her mother's chestnut bob, tennis player's physique. First day on the job, and I'm already floundering, the familiar dread of arriving to class on time but unprepared settling in my stomach like a stone.

From somewhere in the depths of my backpack, I can hear my phone buzz. I'm already regretting this respectable sundress, its lack of pockets. I've been told I will need to "dress for dinner," but I hope my regular summer uniform of cut-offs and tank tops will be permissible around town. Otherwise I'm going to be recycling the same four dresses until I get my first paycheck.

I roll my unwieldy purple suitcase across the platform and prop it against the railing, shrug my backpack around to the front to dig for my phone. It's new, a graduation gift from Mom, gold case still sparkly and screen not yet scratched. I should take good care of it—it's the nicest thing I own—but chances are I won't.

The texts aren't from Emilia Bellamy, or Tom, the husband I haven't yet met. They're from Kaylee.

I can't believe you abandoned me.

We JUST graduated like ten
seconds ago.

What am I supposed to do with myself
all summer?

Anna, hello?

A guilty twinge in my chest says I should have given Kaylee more of a heads-up about my summer plans, but I knew she'd react like this. I close out of my messages and make sure my ringer is cranked all the way up in case the Bellamys call. By now, the platform has cleared out, and most of the parking lot too. I hope I'm in the right place. That I got the meeting time right. It would be just like me to fuck this all up, which is exactly why I'm here. To get out of Bay Ridge. Away from Kaylee. Away from myself. In two months, I'll be a first-year at SUNY New Paltz while Kaylee starts community college in Brooklyn. We'll both be starting new lives, or at least I will. But I can't wait another two months. I need this fresh start now.

I'm debating calling Emilia when a shiny black Lexus SUV pulls into the lot below. A man's tan arm and face lean out of the window, peer up at me. "Anna Cicconi?" he asks. He's handsome in a dad way, or at least he's what I imagine a young, successful dad would look like. I used to have one of those. When I was a kid, he was always working. Now I barely remember his face.

I give him a small, awkward wave. "Mr. Bellamy?"

"Call me Tom," he says, motioning me over. Backpack over one shoulder, purple monster wheeling behind me, I make my way down the ramp.

It's a quick ten minutes from the train station into Herron Mills, one of the many ocean-side towns dotting the south-eastern shore of Long Island like jewels on a sandy crown. To my surprise, we pass as much farmland as we do art galleries and private homes on our drive toward the shore. The sun flares low and hot and orange against the tree line. I squint into it, trying to take it all in. I haven't seen the water yet, but this is definitely not Brooklyn.

"First time in the Hamptons?" Tom asks.

I turn my head toward him, tearing my eyes from the hedgerows and entrance gates that obscure what promise to be jaw-dropping houses from public view. "Yeah. Yes. I think so, anyway."

My interview for the nanny position took place last month, in Manhattan. I met Emilia and Paisley on the terrace café at MoMA, and the three of us spent the afternoon together. Emilia paid for my iced tea but not my entry to the museum. They probably have a membership. I guess little things like fourteen-dollar student tickets don't cross your mind when you're rich. In my lap, my hands clench and unclench.

"Then let me give you the lay of the land," Tom says. His teeth flash white and straight against his tan skin. The weather just warmed up last week; I wonder how he's had the chance to spend so much time in the sun. "The Hamptons stretch along the East End of Long Island. Twenty or so hamlets and villages in all. We're on the South Fork, the branch of the peninsula that meets the Atlantic. To our north is the bay, then the North Fork."

"Got it." I *did* look at Google Maps. Maybe not until I was packing this morning, but still. I'm hoping for more local history, less geography, but I don't want to be impolite.

"Herron Mills is one of the oldest villages, so you'll see a real mix of architecture, everything from Dutch colonial to very modern. And Restoration everything. Clovelly Cottage is English country traditional, so it blends in with the older architecture on Linden Lane, but it's a 2011 construction. We've made a few updates over the years, but we bought it turnkey because Emilia needed to be settled before Paisley came. Barely made it too; we closed in late February and she went into labor three weeks later."

I nod and pretend I'm following more than every second word out of Tom's mouth. Clovelly Cottage, I've gathered from my exchanges with Emilia, is the name of the Bellamys' home. Because of course these people name their houses. They've been here eight years if they moved in the year Paisley was born. Everything else, I guess I'll figure it out when we get there.

"Where did you move from?" I ask.

"Upper West. Great commute, but Emilia didn't want to raise a family in the city." He shrugs. "Everything's a trade-off."

Tom slows down as we turn onto Main Street. Everything's Tory Burch and Ralph Lauren and what looks like a small house converted into a pop-up shop for Gwyneth Paltrow's lifestyle line. It's like they took a slice of Fifth Avenue and plopped it down on a quaint, tree-lined village street with brick sidewalks and an abundance of benches and parking.

"This isn't the most direct route home, but I wanted you to see downtown before it gets dark. I'm sure Paisley will drag you into town tomorrow. Or to the beach."

I close my eyes for a second and hope for the beach. I can hear my phone chirping again, surely another series of pissed-off texts from Kaylee, and reach into my backpack to turn the ringer down.

We take another couple turns off Main Street, and then Tom's steering us onto Linden Lane. He slows down again. "This first house is Seacrest. Belongs to the Fulton-Barrs, our newest neighbors. Jeffrey and Arvin had it designed by Michael Kent, which you can see in the angles and use of glass." I tilt my head to peek out the window. The house is set back on the property and concealed partly by a privacy hedge. Only the second floor is visible from the road, or what I assume to be the second floor, because Seacrest is all sweeping glass windows and sharp angles that make no structural sense. I can't tell if the building is actually futuristic or more like a model of what some architect in the seventies thought the future would look like.

"Hideous, right?" Tom laughs, and I'm so relieved, I laugh too. "Seven point two million. It's what we call a starter home around here."

I swallow to keep my jaw from dropping open. A *starter home?*

"This next one's Magnolia House. 1920s construction, still in great condition. Kyra and Jacques take excellent care of the place. Can't see much from the road, but it's the largest property on the block, a full five acres. Real beauty. And this"— Tom slows the car to an almost stop, and I crane my neck to get a good look—"is Windermere. Owned by the Talbot family since the estate's construction in 1894. Real shame how they've let the place go these past few years."

What was once a privacy hedge has grown to soaring and unsteady heights along the side of the road. Through gaps where the shrubbery has parted, made flimsy in its reach for the sky, I can catch glimpses of a stone drive leading to a large, wood-shingled house with vines creeping up the walls and white-painted columns. The house is three stories, plus what looks to be a steepled attic up top. A long balcony terrace wraps around what I can see of the third floor, and an unused porch swing and several rocking chairs populate a front porch on the ground level. It's beautiful and creepy all at once. Gothic. Through the leaves, I think I see the front door open, a tall shape step onto the porch. But before I can be sure, we're driving on, and Windermere is swallowed again in a curtain of green.

"Who lives there?" I ask.

"Meredith Talbot's the sole owner now; her husband left her widowed about fourteen years ago. Their son Caden's home from Yale this summer, looking after things."

I raise my eyebrows. Yale, naturally. The thought of having someone close in age nearby is nice, but I'm sure he has more important things to do than befriend the nanny next door. Before I can give Caden Talbot too much thought, we've pulled up in front of what must be Clovelly Cottage, and Tom is pressing the remote to open the entry gate. Two sturdy wooden panels on stone pillars part to swing soundlessly inward on their hinges, and we drive on through.

For a moment, all I can see are lush green trees to my right and a long line of flowering bushes to my left, in full powder-pink bloom in front of still more trees. As we curve around the end of the long, pebbled drive, a building slowly emerges.

"This," Tom says, "is your home for the summer. Welcome to Clovelly Cottage."

What stands before us is hardly a cottage. It's not even a house. Clovelly Cottage is nothing short of a mansion. I can see at once what Tom meant by the building blending in with the older architecture in the area. The estate is clearly in pristine condition, but it doesn't look like something built in 2011. Unlike the oddly angled Seacrest down the street, Clovelly Cottage is perfectly symmetrical and very grand. The front of the house displays two clear wings joined by a rectangular midsection with a curved front entry. The house is painted a dusky rose, one shade darker than the flowering bushes we passed on the ride in. It looks like it belongs in the English countryside, surrounded by windy moors and horse-drawn carriages, which I guess is the point. English country traditional, Tom called it.

He steers us around a stone fountain big enough to fulfill a child's swimming fantasies and shifts the car into park in the circular band of driveway abutting the front door. With the house to my right, I can see that, beyond the fountain, the trees and flowering bushes give way to a private tennis court, its crisp turf and netting concealed entirely from the road. My palms feel clammy all of a sudden, and I wish again for pockets I could shove them into.

"Do you play?" Tom asks, catching me looking.

I shake my head, no. My hair falls forward into my face, and I lift my arms to tame it, grateful for something to do with my hands. I thought about cutting it after graduation, a new look to go with the new Anna, but I love my hair too much to crop it off. It's my best feature.

"Well, maybe you'll pick it up. We have plenty of spare rackets. I'm sure Paisley would be thrilled to have a new opponent."

I nod gamely and wonder if I'll have any time to squeeze in some practice before getting my butt handed to me by an eight-year-old. I don't tell Tom I've never held a tennis racket in my life.

"Come on," he says, swinging his door open and stepping out onto the drive. "Paisley is dying to see you. She's been chattering nonstop all day. One of the many reasons I don't make a habit of working from home." Tom explains that I'm unlikely to see him much during the week, from this point forward. Monday through Thursday, he stays in an apartment in the Financial District. He's only home today to meet me, then he'll disappear into the city before I'm awake tomorrow.

I swing my door open too and grab my backpack from the floor while Tom pops the trunk and effortlessly hefts the purple monster from the back. The sun has dipped now behind the house, and I prop my sunglasses back on top of my head to get a better look. It's *stately*. I guess that's the right word. The house embodies the same mix of classic beauty and money that seems to seep out of the Bellamys' pores.

"Emilia wasn't kidding," Tom says, appearing suddenly next to me. "You really do look just like her."

Before I can ask who she is, the front door bursts open and Paisley runs out and down the three stone steps to the drive, fine blond hair and eponymous green paisley sundress streaming behind her. Emilia stands in the open doorway in pressed linen pants, a pale blue blouse, and a matching linen blazer. She gives me a smile and neat wave. Paisley comes to a sudden halt before her father and me, clearly conflicted about who to wrap her arms around first.

"Hey, angel," Tom says, crouching down to pull his daughter into a quick hug, then spinning her to face me. "You remember Anna, right?"

"Hi, Paisley." I crouch down too, then stick out my hand. She takes it solemnly in hers and gives me a firm shake.

"It's lovely to see you, Anna," she says, her voice too small and lilting for the formality of her words.

My lips part into a grin. She's as precocious and charming as I remember. I'm going to be the best version of myself for this little girl, all summer long. It's the promise I made when I took this job. To the Bellamys, but mostly to myself. This is my new leaf. Anything short of flawless is not an option.

"Well, it's lovely to see you too." I give her hand a small squeeze, then push myself back up. "You want to show me inside?"

Half an hour later, we've nearly completed the Clovelly Cottage tour, although Paisley pulls me from room to room so fast, I'm sure I've missed everything. Emilia attempts to supplement Paisley's commentary—this is the best room for playing pretend; this is the window through which she saw three baby bunnies once—with a litany of design details, but before she can finish, Paisley's impatient and tugging me toward the next tour stop.

I learn that the kitchen counter is navy soapstone from a local stone yard, which mirrors the navy ceiling. It's a high gloss paint that Emilia calls "brilliant," to match the effect of the stainless steel and navy detailing throughout. My gaze lingers a moment too long on the glass-front cabinet displaying the Bellamys' impressive collection of top shelf booze. Heat rushes to my cheeks, and I tear my eyes away before Tom or Emilia catch me staring. I hope.

The living room is something called "double height," which I take to mean it extends for the height of two floors. The family room, which houses Paisley's complete Disney princess DVD collection, is outfitted with a "beachy" natural fiber rug in a color that matches Emilia's linen pants and blazer. The "character grade" oak throughout gestures toward a turn of the century home. Tom points to the imperfections on the hallway floor as we crest the top of the stairs to the second level, which he notes have been retained intentionally to give the floors an older feel. Christ. Next-level privilege at its finest.

The house has six bedrooms and four full baths on the upper floor, plus a fully finished lower level complete with a game room and wine cellar with white, glazed-brick walls like you'd find in a French bistro in the city.

Outside, on what Tom calls an "adequate" two point two acres of land that look vast to me, are the tennis court we saw before and a detached garage to the side of the house. Around the back is the most beautiful swimming pool I've ever seen. Guess Paisley doesn't need to splash around in the fountain. The water spills off the long end facing the tree line in what Emilia calls an "infinity edge." There's a hot tub on one end and a pool house on the other, which Emilia explains is a fully equipped guest cottage with its own bedroom, bathroom, and kitchen—and will be my home for the summer.

"You're welcome, of course, to take one of the guest bedrooms instead," she offers. "It's entirely up to you, if you'd prefer to be in the main house. But we thought you might like a little privacy."

"Some separation between work and life, at least at night," Tom adds. "We know this job can be a bit . . ."

". . . consuming," Emilia finishes for him. "Lindsay, our last au pair, was with us for four summers. She loved the job, but she always did appreciate having her own space out here."

Paisley squeezes my hand, and I bite my lip at Emilia's use of the term *au pair*. It's how they listed the job, what she said during our interview. I looked it up; technically, you're only an au pair if you come to work from a different country, in a specific kind of exchange agreement. But Brooklyn may as well be a different country. There's plenty of money in New York City, but there's nothing like this. The wide-open green space. The quiet. The stars just starting to glint like tiny flashbulbs in the sky. The stench of privilege is everywhere, but beneath it, there's something undeniably peaceful. I can be a new person here. Responsible, *better*. I can feel it.

"This will be perfect," I say. "Thank you."

Paisley points up, and I follow her gaze. "That's Ursa Major," she says, tracing the stars with her fingertip. "And Ursa Minor."

"You're into astronomy?"

She nods. "I'm learning all the constellations. But it's easier to practice in the winter, when it gets dark early."

As if on cue, bright lights blink on all around the pool, and the water shimmers and shifts in the yellow glow. It's a quarter after eight and just getting dark.

"Why don't you drop your things inside, and then we'll eat," Emilia says. "We usually sit down to dinner much earlier, but tonight we wanted to wait until you arrived. Mary's making salmon and new potatoes."

My stomach rumbles. I was too nervous to eat lunch, and some chips and half a crushed granola bar on the train were hardly a meal. "That sounds great."

"Good," Paisley says, releasing my hand for the first time since we stepped outside and tilting her head back to look me straight in the eyes. "Because it's almost my bedtime, and I'm starving."

I smile down at her, and I know I made the right choice this summer, despite my mother's empty protests that she needed me at home for reasons she couldn't define, despite Kaylee's decree that I've abandoned her. If she wants to give anyone shit for leaving, it should be Starr. She's been in Orlando for months now, and without her around to match my best friend's thirst for the next party, next high, next adventure, all the pressure to keep up with Kaylee has fallen to me. On nights we're not drinking, it's pills pilfered from my mom's stash or vaping with Mike and Ian. Before Starr left, I used to hole up at home and recharge for days at a time. But with just Kay and me, there's been something frenetic in the air, charged and ready to spark. The last months of senior year were a hazy, thrilling blaze—but they were also exhausting.

Now that I'm here, I barely miss Bay Ridge. I dig my nails into my palms and try not to think about the unopened bottle of Roca Patrón in the Bellamys' kitchen. I am going to be the best nanny—au pair—Paisley's ever had. The old skin I couldn't shed fast enough is as good as gone, cast off in a dirty heap outside the Atlantic Terminal back in Brooklyn. That girl can't touch me here; I'm different already.

3

June

Herron Mills, NY

WE SPREAD OUT our blanket on the white sand, and immediately Paisley vaults into the water. "She's a strong swimmer," Emilia assured me over breakfast, before dropping us off for the day. Her arms were impressively toned in a sleeveless silk V-neck, and her skin had a dewy, well-moisturized glow. I wondered if she always looked this polished at 8:00 a.m. "You have to keep an eye on her, but you don't have to get in."

Which is a good thing, because even lathered up with SPF 50, the sun will burn me to a crisp in no time. Like her father, Paisley is already tan, something my skin just doesn't do. I position myself on my stomach in full shade beneath the Bellamys' red-and-white-striped beach umbrella, chin propped on my hands to get a clear view of Paisley splashing around in the surf. The beach is small—another surprise—long, but narrow, and it's easy to keep her in sight. In under five minutes, Paisley's found a friend, a tall, red-haired girl. They seem to know each other, presumably from school. I catch snippets of their conversation, something about sand crabs and *Moana*.

I take a deep breath in, and my lungs fill with the salt air I've been craving since I was offered the position last month. Here, finally, is my fine sea mist. My thin gull cries. Blue water lapping at white sand. It's crowded, but in an exclusive, permit-only kind of way, nothing like the busy city beaches Kaylee and I used to haunt on long summer afternoons.

Under the umbrella, I free my hair from its elastic and let it blow free, then plop an oversize sun hat on my head. Can't be too careful. I accepted Emilia's offer of a couple magazines to bring along, but I'm too nervous to take my eyes off Paisley. What if she runs off when I'm reading about this summer's hostessing trends? I'm reassured to see lifeguards stationed every few yards, but it's my first day nannying. I'm not taking any risks.

I keep my eyes trained on Paisley but can't stop my mind from wandering. The Bellamys' lives seem so effortless. Tom does whatever makes him his millions in the city while Emilia runs her graphic design business from her home studio. They're both pursuing their passions; they have this beautiful kid and a beautiful house minutes from the beach. It's everything I never had growing up in Bay Ridge with Mom. She's a tech at a medical lab part time, but they can't give her enough hours, so she cleans apartments too. The work hurts her back, so she takes too much Oxy, Demerol, Vicodin . . . the stream of pills is endless. I used to be thankful she was too out of it to care when the school complained about my spotty attendance record. When the cops brought me home for partying, again. When I'd pocket a few pills for Kaylee and Starr and me. Until I kind of started wanting her to care.

At least she stuck around, kept me fed, got me through high school. I have to give her that. But I think if I had as much money as the Bellamys, I'd move somewhere new to settle down. Herron Mills is beautiful, but I'd go somewhere far away from NYC, where no one would have to spend four nights a week in an apartment in the city, where the whole family could stay together.

I fantasize about Nashville, San Diego, Seattle. Any of the cities that might house my father, who got as far away as possible as soon as I started kindergarten. Guess he didn't want to raise a child in the city either. Or at all.

My gaze skates across the shoreline in front of me, and for a moment, I can't find Paisley. In my mind's eye, I see her floating facedown too far out, where the water is dark and choppy, blond hair framing her small head like a halo. The sun is beating down on the umbrella overhead, but I'm suddenly cold. I'd had my eyes locked on her, but then . . . somewhere around Vicodin and cop cars I must have lost my focus. I'm about to scramble to my feet and start shouting her name when, a few yards to the left, Paisley and her friend burst out of the ocean and onto the beach, holding hands and shrieking. In a minute, they're kneeling on the sand, sifting for shells. I let out a slow, shaky breath.

"Z?" My head jerks up. A couple feet in front of me, a boy is leaning over, hands propped on knees, head tilted to the side to peer under my umbrella rim. He's a year or two older than me, scrawny but muscular, wearing red lifeguard trunks with the *Herron Mills Guard* insignia sewn on in white. He's blocking my view of Paisley. I roll off my stomach and shove myself up to a sitting position. With Paisley back squarely in my sight, I tug my shades down to the tip of my nose and squint at him.

"Do I know you?" I ask. He's another redhead, hair buzzed short and freckles dusting his nose. I'm pretty sure I don't know him.

"Oh." He takes a step back, then sinks into a squat, one freckled hand pressed to his chest. After a minute, he scrubs it across his face and blows a long stream of air through his lips. "Christ, I'm sorry. I thought you were someone else." He looks like he's seen a ghost.

I slip my sunglasses back on and gather my hair in my hands, taming it again with an elastic. "That's okay. I'm Anna. I'm nannying for the Bellamys this summer?"

"Oh sure," he says. "That's my little sister Paisley's playing with. I'm Kyle." He extends his hand toward me, and I have to reach out to grasp it. "Welcome to Herron Mills."

"You're a guard?" I ask, for lack of anything better to say.

"On my break. I was just raiding the cooler." He grins, then motions toward Paisley and his family with his chin. "Come on over, I'll introduce you."

I grab a gauzy swimsuit cover from my bag and slip it over my shoulders. Paisley has joined Kyle's family on their recliners a few feet over, and it hits me that I probably should have made a point to introduce myself to her friend's parents on my own. What if they turned out to be creeps? What if Emilia asked me who Paisley met up with at the beach today, and

I didn't even know her friend's name? My stomach clenches with the queasy certainty that I got this job by mistake, that despite my best intentions, I have no idea what I'm doing. I'm going to mess this up just like I mess everything up. New, improved scenery, same old Anna.

But before I can shrivel into a puddle of shame, Kyle is introducing me. "Everyone, this is Anna . . ."

"Cicconi," I supply. "Paisley's nanny."

I smile wide and shake the hands of the Paulson-Gosses, who introduce themselves as Hilary and Elizabeth. Raychel, Paisley's friend, raises her fist for me to bump.

"Want some?" Paisley extends a bag of sweet potato chips toward me.

"I think those are probably Raychel's chips," I say because it sounds like something a responsible nanny would say. "Shouldn't you ask her?"

"It's fine," Raychel says. "We're all about sharing."

I'm still full from Emilia's breakfast spread, which involved about four more components than I'm used to at home, but I take a few chips to be polite.

Kyle swoops in for a fistful, then checks his chunky waterproof wristwatch. "I'd better get back. It was nice meeting you, Anna." He grabs a can of soda from the cooler at his moms' feet, and then he's gone.

"How are you finding Herron Mills, Anna?" Hilary asks. She's tall and willowy like her kids and shares their red hair and freckled complexion.

"I just got into town last night, so I haven't had much of a chance to explore. But it's lovely so far."

Elizabeth, petite and curvy in a navy blue one-piece, explains that they're taking a few days of "family stay-cation," which I guess is what you do when you live at the beach. I look out, eyes skating across the water, and I'm struck suddenly by an intense wave of nostalgia. *The fine white froth of the surf against the shore. The ocean's wide maw. The narrow ribbon of sand.*

Mom and I aren't exactly travelers; I've never been on a beach vacation. And the beaches in Brooklyn don't look anything like this. Still, there's something about this specific stretch of sand that's so familiar, I could swear I've been here before. For a moment, it's like I'm standing inside a past version of myself, scanning the water through her eyes, reliving a day I've already experienced. I can almost remember. It's at the edge of my vision, just outside the frame.

"Paisley will have to take you to Jenkins'." Elizabeth's voice punches through my reverie, yanking me back to the present. To a place where the logical part of my brain says I've never set foot before today. "That's the ice-cream shop on Main, family-owned for two generations now."

"If you'll have access to a car, there's the aquarium in Riverhead," Hilary adds.

"And the Big Duck!" Paisley squeals.

I shake off the last gritty silt of my almost-memory, tell myself it was a trick of the light against water. Then I tuck my hands into my armpits and flap them up and down like wings until Paisley and Raychel explode in a fit of giggles. Goofing off I can do. Adventures I can do. It's responsibility that doesn't come so easy. I make a promise to myself to work harder.

That evening, after grilled lamb chops and pea-greens salad on the back porch with Emilia and Paisley, I stretch out on a recliner by the pool and listen to the soft lap of the water spilling over the infinity edge in an endless black cascade. *Hush, hush.* It's just begging me to draw it. My sketchbook is still packed, but I'll dig it out tonight when the darkness prods me inside. There's so much beauty out here. Both the natural kind and the kind that comes with scads and scads of money. I want to capture it all.

My days officially end after dinner, which is served at six thirty. Emilia and Paisley have mother-daughter time after the plates are cleared, and she takes care of the nighttime routine. I know it's a pretty good arrangement; I should be grateful for so much time off. But tonight, staring down the end of my first full day in Herron Mills, I could use something to keep me busy. Someone to talk to. I can't remember the last time I was totally on my own so early in the evening—no Mom, no Kaylee or whatever guy I was hooking up with at the time. Their chatter filling my ears, filling the hours before school would start up again, and I'd drag myself through another day.

The sticky summer air makes me miss Kaylee, in spite of myself. Sometimes, if we had money, we'd go to a movie or grab a slice of pizza. But most summer nights we'd fill our water bottles with vodka and grapefruit juice and lots of crushed ice and sit out on her fire escape, painting our toenails and surfing YouTube for funny videos until we got bored. Then we'd go to a bar, get older guys to buy us drinks. Go to Starr's, go dancing where we could get in for the pretty girl discount, no ID, no questions asked. Last July was the first time the cops brought me home. It happened two more times over winter break. That I remember.

The back of my mouth waters, and I can't tell if the idea of holding a cold drink in my hand is making me thirsty or ill. I want it and I don't want it all at once. I don't even *like* drinking that much, not past the first few sips when the booze still tastes like possibility and the promise of escape. New night, new faces, new Anna. It's always a letdown. The next morning, I'm always the same. I kept it together enough to keep my grades up. Get into a decent college. But those last few months of senior year . . . I tell myself that's why I'm here. I have something better to do this summer, someone better to become. Still, the night's damp heat and the empty hours yawning before me make my palms itch at my sides, my lips turn dry.

I rummage in my bag for my phone, something to keep my hands busy. Mistake. I have three new messages from Kaylee since we got back from the beach, and I still haven't responded to her texts from yesterday. I sigh and type out a quick reply, something about how busy my job is keeping me and how much I miss her. I promise to call soon, then sign off with a beach umbrella emoji.

I know she's going to be pissed; it's a bullshit reply. But I can't get sucked into Kaylee's drama right now, no matter how much I miss her. I need to learn how to be by myself, give this new, better Anna a shot. A girl who can spend a quiet summer evening by the pool with a paperback or sketchbook for company. A girl who doesn't need guys to buy her drinks, doesn't need to drink at all.

My phone rings, and I brace myself for Kaylee's rancor. But it's not Kaylee.

"Hi, Mom."

"So you are alive."

"I just got here yesterday. I was going to call this weekend."

It's distinctly unlike my mom to act, well, this maternal. She's never been the "call me when you get there" type.

"I got you that new phone for a reason."

"I know."

"You can come home. If you change your mind."

"I'm fine," I assure her. "It's really nice here. Paisley's cute, the Bellamys are nice. I've got this." My voice is filled with conviction. Fake it till you make it.

"I'm sure you do. It's not that I don't trust you, Anna."

"What is it then?" But as soon as the words are out of my mouth, I get it. This is my first time away from home. The first time she's had to worry. She probably *should* have done some worrying when I was still in Brooklyn, but at the end of the night, I always came home. She's known about New Paltz for a while now, but I kind of sprang this job on her. I didn't give her much time to mentally prepare.

"I'm sorry," I say before she has a chance to respond. "I'll try to call more."

"You really like it there? In Herron Mills?"

"Yeah, it's great. I'm going to save a lot for the fall. Me being here, this is a good thing, Mom."

She sighs. "I'm sure it is, doll. I just miss you."

I listen to a story about one of her coworkers at the lab, then promise to text her pictures from Clovelly Cottage and the beach. When we hang up, I lean my head back against the recliner and let the fading light wash over my skin. The back of the house faces west, and the sun is the same brilliant orange orb behind the tree line it was at this time yesterday. It's beautiful. I tell myself to relax, focus on the girl I want to be. *Just breathe.*

4

Pathways Juvenile Center,
East New York, Brooklyn

"GIRL, YOU ARE DAMN LUCKY."

"Um, hi?"

"I cannot believe they've got you at Pathways. When Ryan Denny's grow house got busted sophomore year, they held him at fucking Rikers."

On the other end of the line, Anna lets Kaylee's words sink in. She adjusts the phone's sticky plastic receiver against her ear and glances at the guard stationed down the hall. Watching. Over the past two weeks, she's rarely considered herself lucky. She's back in Brooklyn, but this place could be anywhere. She's never felt so far from home.

"Yeah, lucky me." Anna shifts her weight, left foot, then

right, and her Pathways-assigned sneakers *squish* against the concrete floor.

That night with Detective Holloway and AD Massey feels like another lifetime. In the fourteen days following her arrest, she's been charged; processed; admitted; screened for medical, dental, and mental health; assessed for trauma; and assigned a case worker named Aubrey, a flighty woman only a few years older than Anna who doesn't seem cut out for the juvenile justice system. Anna should be home, packing for SUNY New Paltz. The semester will start next week, without her. A trial date hasn't even been set.

"But you're also totally delusional. You know that, right?"

This isn't the first time Anna has considered the possibility that something may be off-balance with her "mental health and wellness," as the counselors here like to say. At night, in her cot, she closes her eyes and sends a mental searchlight around the inside of her head, scanning for a sign, a clue, a patch of rot. But her mind stays inscrutable. And she passed her intake screening. No one has said a peep about mental illness, at least not to her face. Either she has everyone fooled, including herself, or her memories of that night are real.

"Maybe," she concedes to Kaylee. "But I know what I remember. What I did."

"Murder, Anna?" Kaylee squeaks. "You seriously think you killed some girl out in the Hamptons?"

Anna holds the receiver away from her ear until silence settles on the other end. She shifts her weight back and forth, back and forth, listening to the *squish-squish* of her sneakers. "Not murder, manslaughter," she says softly.

"And the difference is?"

In the past two weeks, Anna has become an expert. "They're charging me with manslaughter in the second degree. It means I recklessly caused her death." And then concealed her body, a second felony. The two charges combined carry eight to twenty years in prison. Anna turns eighteen in December. If convicted, they probably will send her to Rikers Island. There's been talk of shuttering the notorious jail complex for years, but it won't be fast enough for Anna.

"Your memories are shit," Kaylee says, shattering Anna's thoughts, a rock into a sheet of glass. "You told them I was *with you* that night. Are you trying to punish me for what happened on the beach? Is that what this is about?"

It takes a minute for Anna to register what Kaylee's asking. Her mind travels back a month and a half, to the Fourth of July, on the beach on Montauk. The last time she and Kaylee were together. "It was just a party. And I was never mad; I thought you were." This isn't about that, not even close. Isn't really about Kaylee at all.

"You want to sink your own ship, fine." Kaylee can't see Anna flinch at her poor choice of words. "But leave me the hell out of it. All this time, I thought you were too messed up that night to remember anything. But apparently, you were much more messed up than I realized."

"What do you—?"

"Listen to me, Anna. If you remember anything real, you have to know what happened—whatever happened—it wasn't our fault."

Anna tries to swallow, but her mouth is all sand and grit. "I said you were inside when she died," she manages. "I told them you didn't have anything to do with hiding her body."

"No shit I didn't. Because I wasn't in the Hamptons, Anna. And neither were you. I don't know how you got things so freaking scrambled. Mom and I had the cops here earlier this week, you know that? Wanted to have a little chat about my account of New Year's Eve."

Anna sucks in a sharp breath. "What did you tell them?"

"The truth, obviously. Well, the parts that mattered. That I never left Brooklyn. *We* never left Brooklyn."

"But—" Anna wants it to be true. But she knows better now.

"No, you listen. The story you told police, the one they wanted me to confirm? Girl, you are way off, so let me jog your memory. We were at Starr's. Everyone wanted to go dancing, but you were passed out on the couch. Mike and I got you in a cab, and you were home before ten. Got it?"

One more piece clicks into place for Anna. Kaylee got her in a cab. But Kaylee's not telling the whole truth, because she got in that cab too. She was with Anna at Windermere. Anna remembers the three of them on the balcony together. Zoe's silvery laugh in Anna's ear. Kaylee pinching her cheek, holding back her hair. The freezing bite of the night wind rolling in off the ocean.

"Do you have a lawyer, Anna?" Kaylee asks, voice taut with exasperation.

"Of course I do."

"And what does he say?"

"*She* says I shouldn't have talked to the police without my mom present. Without hiring her first."

Kaylee's sigh is so loud Anna swears she can feel it blow

through the phone line. "Well, I guess it's too late for that now."

From down the hall, the guard jerks her chin at Anna, taps her fingers to her wrist. *Wrap it up.*

"I have to go."

"Tell them to stop sniffing around my place. Deep in your heart, Anna Cicconi, you know no good is going to come of this."

"I really have to go."

"What you need is to get your head on straight. Tell them you were wrong; you didn't do it. Make that lawyer of yours get the charges dropped."

But Anna did do it. How else can she explain everything she remembers about Herron Mills, about Zoe? She's not sure if it really was manslaughter. What she remembers sounds a lot like an accident. But they told her Zoe didn't drink, ever, not with the medication she was on. So it must have been Anna who got her drunk that night. Anna's bad influence. Anna who behaved *recklessly*. It sounds a lot like the person she used to be. The person she was with Kaylee.

The guard starts to walk in her direction. She puts the receiver back in its cradle without saying goodbye.

"Excuse me?" Anna asks. "The update I requested to my approved visitors list. Do you know if it went through?"

"Can't add anyone who isn't family." The guard ushers Anna away from the phone bank. "You know the rules."

"But Aubrey said Pathways might make an exception, since family's just my mom, and she can't—"

"Take it up with the office, honey." She motions to the inmate at the front of the line. "Next!"

THEN

June

Herron Mills, NY

MY THIRD EVENING at Clovelly Cottage, I post up by the pool with my sketchbook and charcoals as soon as dinner is cleared. While the light is still good, I want to capture the way the water looks like it's vanishing clean into the landscape, inky and alchemical. I draw the pool first, then the lush yard behind, thin blades of grass fanning out to meet a robust bank of pristinely manicured trees. I brought my watercolor pencils and some oil paints too. Maybe once I've gotten a few sketches down, I'll play around with painting the pool's silvers and navies, the emeralds and laurels of the lawn, the way the sky is a soft powder blue until the first tendrils of orange and pink sluice across it like melting sherbet.

It gets dark too fast. By eight thirty, the pool lights have cast the patio in a bright wash of yellow, and the world beyond the water is pure black. The back of my throat itches, and I cough into the crook of my arm, but the itch only gets worse. Summer nights mean dark bars where the air-conditioning can't compete with the body heat. Long walks on never-quite-empty beaches with Starr and Kaylee, the world soft and pill-blunt around us. Fumbling, boozy hookups that were better as stories after than they were in the moment. Summer means never sitting still. I don't want to be back in Brooklyn, not exactly, but I don't know what to do with myself when I'm not working. Last night, I had unpacking to keep me busy once the stars came out. But tonight, I'm fully settled into the guest cottage / pool house, and at least three hours stretch between me and a reasonable bedtime.

Inside, I place my sketchbook on the small table by the window and wonder if I should have taken a room in the main house instead. The cottage is as big as the apartment I share with my mom in Bay Ridge, and the privacy is nice, but it's almost too quiet out here. I slip out of respectable sundress number three and back into my cutoffs and tank top and consider heading inside to see if Emilia wants some company. But that would be weird, right? It's probably close to Paisley's bedtime. I'd be interrupting.

I dig out my phone and spend some time on ModCloth searching for dresses with pockets, then scroll through Instagram, catching up on the south Brooklyn summer, the parties I'm missing, the rowdier beach with its diverse medley of sunbathers, so different from the mostly white, all-moneyed crowd at the main beach in Herron Mills. In one photo, Mike tackles Kaylee and her hair flashes like strands of spun gold across the brassy brown of his arms. In another, Kaylee's posed on her stoop with our friend Vic from school and Wanda, another girl we go out with sometimes.

I click over to Starr's account to see if she's posted anything new, but there's nothing, not that she ever posted much from Brooklyn either. We used to talk on Messenger, so I open the app, send her a quick note, something I haven't done since the spring. It stung when she skipped town without saying goodbye. She'd told Kaylee her plans, and Mike, but I guess I didn't rank. Now she's not responding to my messages either. I tell myself it's not personal, that she got the fresh start I'm looking for now. We had fun, but I know her life in Brooklyn wasn't great. Twenty-two, no college, shitty job waiting tables at an all-night diner in Brighton Beach. Estranged from her ultraconservative family in Arizona, a string of boyfriends who didn't stick around long. She always loved Disney. I tell myself it's not about me.

By nine, cabin fever has officially set in. My fingers dance across the screen, itching to open my messages, text Kaylee. My phone has been trenchantly quiet all day. Either Kaylee has given up on me or she's serving up a bitter taste of my own medicine. Knowing my best friend, it's surely the latter.

I press my phone facedown into my comforter and shrug on a hoodie. Then I spritz some bug spray on my legs, grab one of the several mini-flashlights from the glass bowl on the kitchen counter, and head out into the night.

My star-lit tour of the Clovelly Cottage grounds is surprisingly brief. Maybe Tom was right, two point two acres isn't quite as massive as it initially seemed. I hug the tree line, crossing behind the pool, then pass the detached garage and gurgling fountain on my way toward the tennis court. But when I'm there, I can't figure out how to turn on the lights, and the rackets appear to be locked in the storage shed anyway.

I abandon my plan of privately smacking balls in the general direction of the net and trudge down the pebbled drive toward the road instead. The LED beam casts a thin white veil over the bushes as I pass—azaleas, according to Emilia— their pink flowers fluttering in the breeze with a ghostly glimmer that makes me shiver, despite the still-warm air. I zip my hoodie all the way to my throat.

Out on Linden Lane, I think about turning right, stealing a glimpse of the houses on the longer stretch of street Tom and I didn't cover on our way in. But my feet are drawn instead toward Windermere, sneakers pulling me next door, toward its neglected grounds. When I get to the wrought iron entrance gate, all vine-covered rails and scrolls and flourishes, the first thing I notice is how much closer the house is to the road than Clovelly Cottage or the other, newer houses in Herron Mills. Here, standing in the slice of driveway that isn't entirely obscured by the unfettered growth of the privacy hedge, I have a clear view of Windermere through the gaps in the gate.

The porch light is on, bathing the unused swing and blue-painted rocking chairs in soft, pale light. I switch my flashlight off and tuck it in my pocket, lean into the shadows surrounding the pillar on which the gate hinges. Tom said that Windermere was built in 1894, which must make it one of the older original homes in the area. I try to imagine this swath of the Hamptons before Seacrest or Magnolia House or Clovelly Cottage. The landscape must have seemed unlimited, nothing but farmland and sky. There would have been no need for hedges or tall banks of trees to keep the estate's secrets veiled from nosey neighbors. And Linden Lane was probably barely traveled, the silence even deeper than it is tonight.

"Hello?"

I rocket back from the pillar, skin buzzing with something that feels like electricity or fear. *"Hello?"* The word passes through my lips, more demand than question, as if I'm not the one skulking in shadow, gawking at someone else's house after dark.

On the other side of the gate, a figure steps into the driveway from somewhere on the front lawn, a part of the property blocked from my view. He's slim and not too tall, maybe five feet ten. His hands are shoved in jeans pockets, and a silver watchband glints on one wrist.

"Are you lost?" he asks. I squint into the glow of the porch light, trying to get a good look at his face, but I can see only that his skin is a soft shade of brown, and he's my age, maybe a bit older. My heartbeat slows to a slightly elevated thud. This must be Caden Talbot, the Yalie.

"I'm Anna," I say. "The nanny at Clovelly Cottage?"

"Oh right." He leans leisurely against the pillar, his body pressed against the stone in a mirror image of my stance a moment ago. "Emilia mentioned she'd hired someone new."

"I'm sorry I was staring." My words slip out on a hot rush of breath. "I'm not a creeper. Well, not usually."

As my eyes strain to compose something photo-realistic from his backlit silhouette, an itchy sensation crawls down my spine. This boy is a stranger, but for a slippery moment I can see our lives intertwining, our darkest secrets and deepest fears laid bare in the still night air.

He grins, and just as suddenly, the itchy feeling is gone, and along with it my pseudo-psychic inklings. I'm clearly lonely, and maybe a little bored.

"It's okay," he says. "Windermere is something to behold. I'm Caden, by the way." He sticks his hand through a scroll in the gate, and I take it in mine, forcing myself to behave like the friendly stranger I am. It's warm and smooth, and he smells just slightly of sage and vanilla. Everything about him seems well cared for, in sharp contrast to the house in the background.

"I just got in on Monday," I tell him. "I'm still getting to know the area."

"After dark?"

I shrug. I can feel the darkness wrapped around my skin like a cloak. "There's not a lot to do at night. I was restless."

"Yeah, me too." He gestures toward the lawn to my left, beyond my line of sight. "We used to have a koi pond. Now it's mostly frogs and weeds. I was thinking about how I might clean it up."

"After dark?" I throw the question back at him.

He laughs, a warm, easy sound that makes my skin flush beneath my hoodie. "I do my best thinking at night. Besides, I'm stuck here right now."

"At home?"

"Yeah. My mom gets kind of freaked out when I leave Windermere at night."

I can feel my eyebrows arch up my forehead, but Caden must not be able to see the face I'm making in the dark. A college boy with a curfew? I've been basically leashless in the city for as long as I can remember. I can't fathom staying home at night to please my mother, even if home was on multiple acres.

"How old are you?" The words are out of my mouth before I can bite them back.

He laughs again, but it's cooler this time. "Nineteen. My mom hasn't been doing great. That's why I'm home this summer."

"Oh, sorry." Now I feel like a jerk. "You're at Yale?"

"Just finished my second year. Emilia tell you about me?"

"Tom gave me the Linden Lane tour when we were driving in."

He grunts softly, and I strain to get a better look at his face, but he's still backlit in the porch light. "You in school?" he asks.

"Just graduated. I start at SUNY New Paltz in the fall."

He says something about liking the New Paltz area, how he has a friend studying theater there. He recommends a place to go hiking, and I make a mental note for September. I wonder for a moment if he's going to open the gate, invite me inside. Maybe this is the start of something, or the sequel to a memory idling deep beneath the surface. But then a light blinks on on the third floor of the house, and a filmy shadow darkens the window. Caden turns to follow my gaze up, toward Windermere.

"I should go in," he says, voice suddenly brisk.

I don't want this conversation to be over. I haven't gotten a chance to ask about his mom, what's wrong with her, why he can't leave. But I can see his body closing up, shoulders hunching inward, and I know it's not the right time.

"It was nice meeting you?"

He's already backing away from the gate. He gives me a small wave before he turns.

"See you around, Anna."

Back in the guest cottage, I dig out my watercolor pencils from my bag. Sketchbook spread out on the bed, I draw a slender boy with light brown skin and a silver wristwatch. His arm and side are propped gracefully against a stone pillar crawling with vines, and one foot is crossed over the other where the pillar meets the drive. In my drawing, he's turning to look at a brightly lit window in the house behind him, and his face is lost in shadow.

June

Herron Mills, NY

PAISLEY WANTS ICE CREAM. I raise my eyes from my bowl of granola and yogurt to peer at Emilia across the breakfast table, ready for her to tell her daughter she'll have to wait until after dinner. But Emilia just nods and digs in her wallet for cash before slipping into her office and closing the door. While I load our dishes into the sink, Paisley chatters excitedly about Jenkins' Creamery, the much-lauded shop on Main Street that has withstood the luxury brand takeover for two generations. In the few days I've been in town, I've already had it recommended to me three times. I insist we wait until eleven, when the shop opens, then we set off on foot, leaving Emilia to her client work and the midmorning sunshine that spills through the east-facing windows at the front of Clovelly Cottage like yards and yards of buttery gauze.

When we reach the end of the drive, Paisley tugs my hand, pulling me right, away from the shortest route to town.

"This way," she insists. "It's prettier."

I let myself be dragged, momentarily mourning the fact that I won't get to steal another glimpse of Windermere, possibly see Caden in daylight. Last night, he trailed me across a series of dreams I otherwise can't remember, the features on his face shifting and rearranging into something out of Picasso's cubist period. I can vividly see the outline of his body, the way he turned to meet his mother's gaze in the upstairs window. But his face is a mystery to me, an endless jumble of possibilities that won't let my artist's brain rest until I see him again.

I tell myself that's all it is. The painter in me in need of artistic resolution.

Caden and Windermere quickly fade into birdsong and Paisley's bright chatter as we walk the other way down Linden Lane, Paisley giving me her own version of a tour, which centers around which families have kids, how old they are, and who's here and who's renting out their house for the summer while they flit around Europe or Japan.

Pretty nice set of options. I press my lips between my teeth.

"Do you have friends on your street in Brooklyn?" Paisley asks.

"Sure, although we've moved a few times. When I was your age, I had two really good friends on our block, Krista and Jayla. Our parents called us Triple-A."

Paisley wrinkles her nose at me, fine lines creasing her soft skin.

"Because our names all ended in *A*? Krist*a*, Jayl*a*, Ann*a*?"

"It would be better if your names all *started* with *A*," Paisley declares, then pulls me around the corner, off Linden Lane and onto a connecting street that will take us into town. Paisley clearly knows where she's going, but I checked the route on my phone before we started, just in case. The streets here form a wide, irregular grid, spaced far apart to accommodate the properties in between, and even on this slightly longer route, we'll make it to Jenkins' by eleven fifteen. They'd better have coffee ice cream.

When we turn onto Main, I'm surprised by how busy the street seems for a Thursday morning. Shop doors open and close, and sidewalk café tables are filled as we pass, the empty peace of the residential streets replaced by a low-key bustle.

"Doesn't anyone work around here?" I mutter, instantly regretting the twinge of contempt in my voice. Paisley responds with complete solemnity.

"Not the summer people. They're here on vacation. Mommy and Daddy are working."

"Of course they are," I say, steering Paisley around an overexcited Jack Russell straining on his leash. "That's why you've got me."

Inside Jenkins', we stand before a giant, wall-mounted menu that looks like a chalkboard, but its descriptions are so vivid and smudge free, I wonder if it's actually paint. The shop is empty, aside from Paisley and me. Behind the counter, a man in a white smock is crouched down, fiddling with something behind the case of hard ice cream. The menu boasts twelve flavors, all homemade, and an array of toppings. There's also a soft ice-cream machine with levers for chocolate, vanilla, and twists, and a selection of two sorbets. In the very center of the menu, inside a box with jagged edges like a bright blue starburst, is the shop's featured flavor: Chocolate Caramel Popcorn.

"I want two scoops of Peanut Butter Cup," Paisley says, but her words wash over me. I'm still fixed on the menu board, that bright blue box advertising something I'd never usually order. But I can taste the flavor at the back of my mouth, coating my tongue like a memory. *Chocolate Caramel Popcorn.* I stare until my eyes lose focus, until the words squiggle and pulse against the blackness like a lighthouse in a storm. Suddenly I'm a little light-headed, and I lean my hip against the glass to keep my balance.

"Always get a waffle cone," Paisley advises, and I force myself to tear my eyes away from the menu, focus on her. "Mr. Jenkins fills the bottom with hard chocolate so the ice cream doesn't leak."

"Shop secret," says the man behind the counter, his deep, earthy voice snapping me back to reality. He straightens up and leans slightly forward, over the glass, to give Paisley a grin. "But your friend will find out soon enough."

He's in his fifties, I'd guess, ruddy cheeks studded with black points of stubble. His crisp white smock reads *Lou Jenkins* in curvy embroidery. I raise my eyes to meet his, which are hazel and creased with kind lines. In that moment, his expression changes, geniality sliding away into something between awe and dread.

"Zoe?" he splutters.

Before I can figure out how to respond, Paisley cuts in, her voice like a chime. "This is Anna Cicconi. She's from Bay

Ridge, in Brooklyn, New York. Anna is my au pair for the summer."

Lou Jenkins takes a small step back, taking me in. He runs his hand across his face, in a gesture that makes my mind skip back to the other day on the beach, Kyle the lifeguard peering under the umbrella, his hand tracing the same bewildered route across his eyelids and cheeks. *Christ, I'm sorry. I thought you were someone else.*

"Who's Zoe?" Nerves bunch in a tight knot in my stomach. I gather my hair back self-consciously, slip an elastic from my wrist, and twist it up into a messy knot on top of my head.

"Zoe Spanos disappeared last January," Paisley supplies. "No one knows what happened to her."

"That's horrible. From Herron Mills?"

"She grew up here," Lou explains. His face has not yet regained its formerly jovial glow, but at least he's stopped looking at me like I'm a ghost. "She was in college, home on winter break. She went out on New Year's Eve, and her family hasn't heard from her since."

"And I look like her?" I ask, the need to name the elephant in the room burning hot in my throat.

Paisley nods eagerly, like this is a game we're all playing and not some highly cryptic coincidence. "I think it's mostly your hair. And your face."

I laugh, the tension bubbling up, then bursting like the sharp crack of gum against my lips. "Just my hair and face?"

Lou tilts his chin to the side. "With your hair up, there's less of a resemblance. And she has more of an olive complexion. But you two could be sisters." He smiles. "I'm sorry, I didn't mean to make you uncomfortable. Everyone in Herron Mills has been a little on edge since Zoe disappeared."

I do the mental math back to New Year's Eve. That was nearly six months ago. I don't know a whole lot about missing girls, but I'm pretty sure the odds she'll show up alive after this much time must be pretty slim.

"Can I get you ladies some ice cream?" Lou asks, a burst of energy filling his voice like he's clutching some invisible steering wheel, directing us onto a new course. "Or maybe a coffee or tea?"

Paisley gives him her order, and while the rational part of my brain says to ask for black coffee, which is probably the only thing I can stomach after that exchange, I hear myself ordering a scoop of the Chocolate Caramel Popcorn.

"Waffle cone?" Lou asks.

"Just a cup," I reply, then assure Paisley I'll order a cone next time, if she promises future trips to Jenkins' can be scheduled for after lunch.

Outside, the street is drenched in crisp white sunlight, and the strange encounter in the shop rolls off my shoulders like the last wisps of stale morning fog off the East River. Paisley and I post up on a wooden bench about a block down from Jenkins' to eat and people watch. The ice cream tastes like chocolate Easter eggs and the popcorn from those big tins they sell at Target around the holidays. It tastes like childhood. It tastes amazing.

"Want to try?" I offer.

"That's okay," Paisley says. "I've had it before. It's their most popular flavor. Dad says that Mr. Jenkins says that his dad invented it. The original Mr. Jenkins. I prefer peanut butter."

"Heya, Paisley." We look up to find two girls around my age stopped on the sidewalk in front of our bench. One is wearing a red-and-white checkered sundress that looks vintage and a pair of Mary Jane flats the color of cherry pie filling. Her glossy brown hair is bone straight and pulled back in a neat ponytail, and her skin is a soft fawn brown. The other girl is dressed like me, denim shorts and a tank top. She's only five feet three or four, but she's all muscle. A swimmer, or maybe a gymnast. Her hair is cropped into a feathery pixie cut that emphasizes the surprising plumpness of her cheekbones and cool olive of her skin. A pair of large gold hoop earrings, the metal helixed into a delicate twist at the base of each hoop, dangle from her ears.

"Hey, Aster!" Paisley holds out her cone for me to take and jumps up to give the shorter girl a hug. I can feel two sets of eyes trained on me, their faces narrowing into the same apprehensive scrutiny I saw play across Lou's face a few minutes ago.

"I'm Anna," I supply quickly, eager to nip those looks in the bud. I shove up to my feet. "Paisley's nanny."

"Martina Green." The girl in the vintage dress sticks out her hand, then drops it when she realizes mine are both filled with ice cream.

Her friend rolls her eyes. "She's Martina *Jenkins*. 'Green' is like a stage name or something."

Martina flashes Aster a flinty glare. "It's my professional name," she says, as if that clarifies anything. She can't be any older than I am. What kind of profession could possibly require a name change? The ice-cream profession? Jenkins' must be her family's shop. I wonder fleetingly if she's a print model. She doesn't look quite tall enough, but she's obviously into fashion, and she has that slightly edgy Urban Outfitters look.

I must be making a face because Martina sighs, as if resigning herself to an explanation that makes her tired. "I'm going to be a journalist, and my mother doesn't like the idea of attaching the family name to my investigative work. She's old school like that."

"Like TV news and stuff?" I ask.

"For now, I'm editor in chief of my school paper. And I run a podcast series. Well, ran." She offers Aster a weak smile, then drops her eyes to the sidewalk.

For a moment, everyone is quiet, and I wonder how many uncomfortable exchanges one morning can possibly hold.

"The podcast is about Zoe," Paisley explains in a reverent voice, her chin tilted up toward me. "Aster and Zoe are sisters, and Martina's going to find out what happened to her."

Aster and Zoe. *A* to *Z*. I glance back at the shorter girl, noting how little she resembles me, or vice versa. Which means she must not look much like Zoe either, but of course not all siblings look alike. I remember Lou saying something about Zoe having an olive complexion, though, and as the sun glints off Aster's gold hoops and olive shoulders, it strikes me that they're probably Greek. Spanos.

"I did my best," Martina says. "I'm so sorry, Aster."

Aster wraps one toned arm around Martina's shoulders and gives her friend a jostling squeeze. "It's the police who dropped the ball, not you," she says, voice kind. My gaze comes to rest on the raw, red lines of sadness that have settled along the rims of her eyes. She looks like she's been living ten seconds away from tears for months.

Martina leans down to kiss the top of her friend's head, and Aster's lips soften into a smile. "Okay, no more Zoe talk before lunch," she says, straightening up. "Do we still have time for sushi before your shift?" Her eyes flicker toward the ice-cream shop.

Martina digs her phone out her pocket—of course *her* dress has pockets—and turns on the screen. "Plenty. Dad can hold down the fort for another hour."

The girls wave and say it was nice to meet me, and I hand Paisley back her melting cone. She takes a big lick. "Zoe used to babysit me when she was in high school," she says. "Aster's three years younger. She was my babysitter after Zoe went to college."

"I thought you had Lindsay," I say. "Wasn't that your last au pair?"

"Lindsay was only in the summers," Paisley says. "Like you. I'd have Zoe and Aster on the weekends, or if Mom and Dad went out on a date night. Zoe was super nice, but I think Aster was my favorite babysitter."

"Why's that?" Paisley works at her cone, and we start ambling slowly down Main Street.

"Because she's brave. This one time, before school let out last June, I told her about this boy Markus who was teasing me. My teacher wasn't doing anything to stop it, so Aster came up with this whole plan to get back at him. Markus was having a pool party, for his birthday, so the night before, we snuck around to the back of his house and dumped buckets of water mixed with yellow food coloring into his pool. It looked like it was full of pee." Paisley giggles.

"That doesn't sound very mature, but it definitely sounds fun."

Paisley grins, but then her smile drops. "Aster's had to be really brave this year, and her parents too. That's what my mom says. Because Zoe's probably not coming back."

I toss the remains of my melted ice cream in a trash bin, the nostalgia factor fading into sugary soup. I reach out for Paisley's hand, and she slips it into mine. "Why didn't you tell me I look like the missing girl?"

Paisley shrugs and takes another lick. "Everybody loves Zoe. I don't see why it's a big deal."

I guess it isn't, but I resolve to order a few more sun hats along with my pocket dresses, as soon as I get paid. I'm not sure I'm up for an entire summer of weird looks and mistaken identities.

"Did you listen to her podcast?" I ask.

"Mom won't let me. She says it's 'too adult.'" Her voice forms air quotes around the words.

"Oh. That sucks."

Paisley chomps down on her waffle cone, channeling the unfairness of childhood into the bite.

"But she might be right." I shrug. "Sounds like scary stuff."

"Yeah." For a minute, she stares down at our feet, sandals keeping pace on the sidewalk together. "Do you think she'll come back, Anna?"

A thin blade of worry glides up my rib cage and settles between my lungs. Is there a right answer to that question? What would Emilia say?

"I don't know." My voice is quiet. "I hope so."

☙ ❦ ☙

In the pool house that night, I google Zoe Spanos. The results fill my phone screen, dozens of news articles from last winter and spring about the nineteen-year-old girl who disappeared from Herron Mills without a trace. I click on the first one, and the photos of Zoe make my breath catch. She does, as promised, look a hell of a lot like me. Same messy cascade of black hair, same high-set cheekbones and big, toothy smile. But her skin is creamy olive where mine is pasty white, her eyes yellow-flecked brown where mine are a sharp blue-green. She has what looks like a splotchy brown birthmark near the center of her collarbone, where my skin is bare. Resting against it, in most of the photos, is a delicate gold chain with the initials *ZS*.

Me, but not me. The similarities are striking; they prick at the corners of my eyelids, making me squint and then open wide until I see myself, then don't again. I remember in ninth grade, this new kid Bryan told me I reminded him of his friend from home. He held out his phone across the cafeteria table, showed me a picture of a stranger that was like looking into a fun-house mirror. It's that feeling all over again.

I quickly scan through the other search results, looking for a podcast. I try again with *Martina Green podcast* in the search bar, and I'm directed to four episodes of *Missing Zoe* on SoundCloud. There's a thumbnail picture of Martina wearing a pair of black cat-eye glasses and burgundy lipstick, her hair styled in the same ponytail I saw today. The podcast description promises in-depth investigative reporting with a single goal: to uncover what really happened to Zoe last New Year's Eve. A chilly finger of curiosity tinged with fear zips down my spine, and I slip my earbuds in.

TRANSCRIPT OF *MISSING ZOE*
EPISODE ONE: SHE'S (NOT) A LITTLE RUNAWAY

[ELECTRONIC BACKGROUND MUSIC]

ADULT MALE VOICE: It's not illegal to disappear.

YOUNG FEMALE VOICE: If Zoe was there, I would have known. Zoe never showed up that night.

ADULT FEMALE VOICE: Nine-one-one, what's your emergency?

SECOND ADULT MALE VOICE: My name is George Spanos, and my daughter Zoe is missing.

[END BACKGROUND MUSIC]

MARTINA GREEN: Today is Tuesday, February eleventh, and Zoe Spanos has been missing for six weeks to the day. Last Friday, the Herron Mills Village PD declared Zoe a runaway, and that's why I'm here, talking to you. Because if you know Zoe, you know she didn't run away.

Zoe Spanos is missing. And we're missing Zoe.

[*MISSING ZOE* INSTRUMENTAL THEME]

MARTINA GREEN: Hi, I'm Martina Green, and you're listening to the first episode of *Missing Zoe*, a multipart podcast series about the disappearance of Zoe Spanos, a nineteen-year-old resident of Herron Mills, New York, on the night of December thirty-first or morning of January first this year.

You can probably tell from my voice that I'm not your typical true crime podcast host. I'm a junior at Jefferson High School in Herron Mills. That's on the East End of Long Island, one of those quaint beach towns you might visit one summer for the ocean, the lobster rolls, the relaxed pace of village life. For many, Herron Mills is a destination, an escape. But for others, like Zoe and me, it's home.

Let's begin by taking a quick stroll through Herron Mills. Consider this your welcome tour.

ALFRED HARVEY: You might notice there's been a bit of a commercial boom around here lately. [CHUCKLES.]

MARTINA GREEN: There's no greater expert on the textured history of Zoe's hometown than village historian Alfred Harvey. We spoke in his office at the Herron Mills Village Historical Society.

ALFRED HARVEY: But it retains rich elements of its agrarian past in the surrounding farmland and the farm-to-table restaurants that have cropped up. And of course the windmills.

MARTINA GREEN: And there's a long-standing artistic history as well?

ALFRED HARVEY: Of course. The village was initially settled in the sixteen hundreds and incorporated in 1873. Artists and writers began to flock to the Hamptons, including Herron Mills, in the late nineteenth century. They came for the quiet, the rural beauty, the light. The culture of creation is part of the fabric of the landscape out here. Nowadays, when people hear "the Hamptons," they hear wealth, celebrity, privilege. But that's only part of the story. On the bay side, in Sag Harbor, there's been a thriving African American community since World War Two. The Shinnecock Reservation in Southampton is home to between six and seven hundred tribal members. There's much more to the Hamptons than exclusivity and wealth.

MARTINA GREEN: When you're a resident of Herron Mills, you know everyone. I've known Zoe since I was a baby; her sister Aster is my best friend. I'm telling you this in the interest of full disclosure. I'm not an unbiased reporter, an outsider looking in. I'm not someone with a twenty-year career in journalism behind me, although I hope I will be someday. But I don't think that's what we need to find Zoe. I think we need an insider. Someone who knows this community, knows the people, isn't afraid to ask the tough questions the police don't seem interested in exploring.

ASSISTANT DETECTIVE PHILIP MASSEY: It's not illegal to disappear.

MARTINA GREEN: I spoke to Assistant Detective Philip Massey, one of the officers on the Zoe Spanos case, over the phone.

AD MASSEY: I can't comment specifically on the Spanos case, but in general, you're an adult, it's perfectly legal to leave your life behind. Start a new one. Might be hurtful or unkind, but there's no law you have to tell anyone where you're going.

MARTINA GREEN: Why can't you discuss Zoe specifically? Didn't your office close the investigation last week?

AD MASSEY: As our office stated publicly last Friday, there is strong evidence to suggest Miss Spanos willingly left Herron Mills on the night of December thirty-first last year. That's all I can say. It's still an open investigation.

MARTINA GREEN: The investigation may still technically remain open, but it's clear that local police have wound down their search. Yes, Zoe is nineteen. Yes, that means she's an adult in the eyes of law enforcement, allowed to step willingly away from her sophomore year at Brown, from her holiday at home with her family and friends, and start over somewhere new. No note. No explanation. No news, six weeks later.

But I don't buy it, and that's why I'm here. I'm angry, and that's why I'm here.

So, let's go back to late December of last year. For those of you who have been following Zoe's case, none of this will come as new information. Everything I'm about to recap was widely reported on the news during the days and weeks that followed Zoe's disappearance. But it's important to start with the facts we can agree upon, the things that are known. And to examine critically the way in which law enforcement approached the case once Zoe was reported missing.

Before she disappeared, Zoe had been home from Brown for

about two weeks, spending time with her family. Several Herron Mills residents saw Zoe around town.

JUDITH HODGSON: She spent a few afternoons at the library. Nothing unusual about that. Zoe always was very serious about her studies.

MARTINA GREEN: That was Judith Hodgson, reference librarian at the Herron Mills Public Library. I personally saw Zoe twice, once at the grocery store, where she was helping her mom with the shopping, and again on the day after Christmas, when Aster and I spent the afternoon together at the Spanos house. Zoe was baking cookies in the kitchen. We talked for a few minutes about the marine bio internship she'd done in California over the summer and the advanced research course she'd be taking in the spring.

PROFESSOR DAVID BRECHER: I was looking forward to working with Miss Spanos this spring. She made quite a case to get into my class. I have a firm policy about restricting admission to upperclassmen. But Miss Spanos had completed the prerequisites early, and she showed a great deal of promise.

MARTINA GREEN: Professor David Brecher spoke with me on the phone from his office at Brown. Why would Zoe campaign to get into that course if she wasn't planning to return to school? There was nothing in Zoe's behavior that pointed to a girl making plans to sever ties, to vanish into the night.

Fast forward to New Year's Eve, a Tuesday: Zoe left the house around nine o'clock. She told her parents that she was meeting friends at a nearby house party thrown by Jacob Trainer, a

Jefferson alum from Zoe's class. Multiple sources, including Zoe's friend Lydia Sommer, confirm she never made it to that party.

LYDIA SOMMER: I texted her a few times that night—no response. Which wasn't like Zoe at all.

MARTINA GREEN: Is it possible that she went to Jacob's with someone else? That you might have missed her?

LYDIA SOMMER: No way. If Zoe was there, I would have known. Someone would have seen her. It was almost all Jefferson alum at that party. We all knew each other. Zoe never showed up that night.

MARTINA GREEN: The next morning, Mr. and Mrs. Spanos woke to the realization that Zoe had not returned home. If you read the comments on the news articles that ran in the following days or dive into the Reddit thread about Zoe's case, you'll see that many people were immediately critical of their parenting, but let's remember: Zoe is nineteen and a sophomore in college. Her parents were used to her living away from home, where she'd been an A student at an Ivy League college. And as the police have been so quick to emphasize, Zoe is an adult. Her parents knew where she was going, to a party within walking distance from their home. She hadn't had a curfew since high school. Let's stop blaming the Spanos family. They didn't do anything wrong.

In fact, they did exactly what they should have done. The morning of Wednesday, January first, when Zoe wasn't responding to phone calls or texts, Mr. Spanos called nine-one-one.

911 DISPATCHER [RECORDING]: Nine-one-one, what's your emergency?

MARTINA GREEN: It was New Year's Day, and local police had been dealing with their share of calls throughout the night and into the morning: two separate car accidents on Grove and Ocean Avenue, noise complaints, vandalism, a stolen boat—we're going to get back to that in a minute—littering, trespassing, you name it. If you're going to go missing, New Year's Eve is probably just about the worst time to do it.

Or the best time to disappear, if you believe the police.

GEORGE SPANOS [RECORDING]: My name is George Spanos, and my daughter Zoe is missing. We're at Forty-Five Crescent Circle, Herron Mills, New York. She didn't come home last night.

MARTINA GREEN: Nine-one-one dispatch transferred Mr. Spanos to the local police. We don't have access to that recording, but according to TV interviews that ran in the following week, they told Mr. Spanos to check local hospitals and call around to Zoe's friends and their parents. They told him that Zoe had probably spent the night at a friend's house, and perhaps her phone battery had died. They told him to do his due diligence, but to try not to worry. Zoe wasn't a minor. She was responsible and bright. What the police suggested was a perfectly plausible scenario. The most likely scenario. It made sense. But it was wrong.

The Spanoses made those calls. Zoe had not been admitted to any hospital on Long Island. No one had seen her. She had not been to Jacob Trainer's party. She hadn't called anyone to say she wasn't going to make it. She hadn't responded when three separate friends, including Lydia Sommer, checked in via phone or text between 11:35 p.m. and 1:17 a.m.

Zoe Spanos walked out of her house in Herron Mills around nine o'clock on New Year's Eve and vanished into thin air.

On the morning of Thursday, January second, when Zoe had still not come home or contacted anyone to say she was okay, the police finally started searching. A pair of officers went door to door in the neighborhood. Zoe was declared a missing person, her photo and description shared with local news. The police worked with the Spanos family to organize a search party for the morning of January fourth, to comb the woods behind the Spanos property. But by the fourth, they had uncovered something else.

Remember that missing boat I mentioned earlier? On the morning of January first, Mrs. Catherine Hunt of Herron Mills reported her small motorboat missing from its post at the White Sand Marina, one of two local marinas where residents can purchase docking permits.

CATHERINE HUNT: I assumed it was kids, partying in the area. It was New Year's, after all. But then on Thursday afternoon, I heard on the news that there might be a connection between my boat and the missing girl. It was shocking.

MARTINA GREEN: When the boat had not turned up two days later—and an investigation into Zoe's cell phone records determined that the last GPS activity on her phone could place her within a hundred-foot radius of the marina at 2:12 on the morning of January first—the police put two and two together.

But here's where I think they got their math mixed up. The search went ahead as planned on the morning of the fourth, but with a fraction of the expected turnout. I was there. Zoe's family was there. There were maybe thirty of us total, friends of Zoe's home from college, neighbors, family friends. Searchers did not find anything in the woods.

At the same time, the Herron Mills PD arranged for the ocean floor to be dragged in and around the White Sand Marina. Dozens of onlookers—who should have been searching—showed up there instead.

CATHERINE HUNT: It seemed, at the time, like the divers might find something that day. The marina isn't large. I'm sure they did a thorough job. But if she made it out of the marina, onto the open ocean . . .

MARTINA GREEN: The initial working theory was that Zoe had arrived to the marina early Wednesday morning, released Mrs. Hunt's boat from its post or more likely found it already liberated by New Year's revelers who had taken their party elsewhere, and that she tried to take the boat out and drowned.

The Spanos family was horrified, but police overturned that theory lightning-fast with a new one: Zoe didn't drown. She took the boat, and she literally sailed away into the night.

AD MASSEY [RECORDING]: We've now concluded an initial investigation into Miss Spanos's financial records and can report that the 2:12 data activity on her Verizon-registered cell phone was a PayPal transaction. The purchase from Miss Spanos's account was for a one-way bus ticket from Asbury Park to

Philadelphia for the evening of January first. Miss Spanos's phone was turned off after the transaction went through, and no further activity has been registered.

MARTINA GREEN: We're hearing a clip of AD Massey from Channel Four news, which aired on the night of January seventh. That's right, listeners. The police actually think Zoe Spanos attempted to motorboat across the Atlantic to the Jersey shore, to board a bus to Philadelphia. And that she succeeded.

Maybe it's possible, for an experienced boater, which Zoe was not. The police have latched onto the fact that Zoe was majoring in marine biology like it's some kind of proof she was an expert in all things nautical. News flash: College-level research knowledge of the giant squid does not equal experience with boating or aquatic navigation.

Maybe it would have been a plausible escape route for a desperate person. But here's the thing: While the purchase is indisputable, the fine folks at Greyhound Lines cannot confirm that Zoe actually got on that bus. This clip is also from Channel Four, from the evening of January ninth.

GREYHOUND SPOKESPERSON [FEMALE]: We have no record that the ticket purchased by Zoe Spanos was scanned. Our scanner was working and in use, and we've turned our records over to the police. It is highly unlikely that Zoe Spanos boarded the 317 line on the night of January first.

MARTINA GREEN: If Zoe's phone was turned off following that PayPal transaction, how did she navigate Mrs. Hunt's motorboat to New Jersey? The police theory would require a good deal of advanced planning on Zoe's part. It would also require a good deal of stupidity and desperation, neither of which describe Zoe at all.

So, what *do* we know about Zoe?

Fact one: Zoe had access to her parents' car. If she wanted to get to Asbury Park, or Philadelphia for that matter, she could have driven herself there.

Fact two: Zoe also had access to the LIRR. If she was concerned about being charged with grand theft auto, she could have easily hopped on a train.

Fact three: If Zoe was really trying to run away, leave no trace, why would she create an obvious digital trail with the PayPal transaction? She had access to plenty of cash, yet did not withdraw any from her bank account before she disappeared. Additionally, none of Zoe's accounts have been accessed since.

Fact four: Zoe had no reason to run away from her life. This has been the sticking point for police, the motive they can't produce. But they don't need to produce a motive, because Zoe's supposed choice to run away isn't a crime.

Over the course of the past six weeks, police have proposed an unlikely string of theories: that Zoe didn't make it all the way to Asbury Park, drowned somewhere out in the Atlantic. (Which would actually seem the most logical scenario, if you believe that Zoe would have attempted to make the boat trip in the first place, which I firmly do not.) That Zoe made it to Asbury Park but then rerouted. That she met up with friends with a car. That she purchased the bus ticket to deliberately lead us off track. What friends in New Jersey? And where is the boat?

As of last Friday, search efforts in Asbury Park, Philadelphia, and along Zoe's supposed oceanic route have officially wound down. From what we can tell in Herron Mills, they unofficially wound down a lot sooner than that. We've been told there's no way to clearly trace her path. That without communication from Zoe, who clearly does not want to be found, it's like searching for a needle in a haystack.

So, I'm here to ask the questions the police won't. Because Zoe Spanos had no reason to run away, and certainly not in the way the police think she did. I'm here to propose that there's no connection between Zoe and that missing boat. Yes, she—or her phone—was in the vicinity of the marina that night. She—or someone who had access to her phone—purchased that bus ticket. But that's where the connection between Zoe and the boat ends.

Something happened to Zoe Spanos on New Year's Eve, and someone knows what it was. Someone knows where Zoe is.

Zoe, I hope you're alive. I hope you're still out there. There are a lot of people at home who are missing you. And no matter what the police think, I, Martina Green, am going to try my hardest to uncover the truth and bring you home.

[CODA TO *MISSING ZOE* INSTRUMENTAL THEME]

7

September

Herron Mills, NY

MARTINA WAITS PATIENTLY to be connected to Anna Cicconi at the Pathways Juvenile Center. Her phone is on speaker on the kitchen table, ready to record. She picks at a plate of cold tostones, the sole remnants from last night's dinner still waiting in the fridge when she got home. Dad must have taken the rest with him to Jenkins'. She thinks about microwaving the leftover plantains, but she's too hungry to wait. She reaches for the salt.

She had wanted to go to Brooklyn, to visit Anna in person, but the center's visitation policy is inflexible. Only immediate family, and further, only adults. Martina is neither, boxed out. Not that Mami would have let her go anyway. She doesn't approve of the podcast, would certainly never approve of her daughter visiting a criminal in a detention center. But Martina would have gone anyway, if Pathways had let her. Martina is seventeen, newly a senior at Jefferson. She'll be applying to colleges soon, moving away, hopefully to the city to double major in journalism and sociology at NYU. She's almost an adult. What Mami doesn't know won't kill her.

Martina cringes inwardly and thanks her lucky stars she didn't say that out loud, in hearing distance of the neighbors. It has been a full month now since Anna's arrest. The revelation that Zoe is really dead has barely settled in for Martina, for anyone. Even though her body, or what was left of it, has been found. Even though her family confirmed her identity and the dental records sealed the deal. The family can't have a funeral yet, not if they want a body to bury. The autopsy results still haven't come in. It's not like on TV, postmortems moving lightning fast, cases being closed by the end of the sixty-minute episode.

It still seems impossible to believe they found her in Catherine Hunt's missing motorboat—albeit at the bottom of nearby Parrish Lake, not submerged in the Atlantic Ocean. Martina was wrong about the boat. But not about the most important thing: Zoe wasn't trying to run away. Someone put Zoe's body in that boat. Someone sank it to the bottom of the lake. Someone who might be Anna.

Martina knows that she confessed, understands that things don't look great for the girl she'd only just gotten to know this past summer. But just like with the police's bogus theories about Zoe the Runaway, there are lots of things that don't add up for Martina about Anna's confession. Officially, the details won't be made public until the case goes to trial, but everyone seems to know what Anna told police. Secrets don't stay secret for long in Herron Mills, and Anna's friend Kaylee spread this one like wildfire. She told anyone who would listen exactly how wrong Anna's story is, but hearing Kaylee say it just made everyone believe: How Anna got Zoe drunk before she fell from the Windermere balcony that night. How Anna drove her body to the lake, hid it in the boat. Martina pops another piece of plantain in her mouth.

"Martina Jenkins?"

She swallows quickly. "Yes, speaking."

"You have ten minutes with Ms. Cicconi. Understood?"

Martina hears a soft scuffling sound on the other end of the line. Then Anna's voice breaks through.

"Martina?"

"Hey. Okay if I record this?"

There's a momentary pause. "Sure. Everything's recorded on this end anyway."

"I'm sorry I didn't call sooner. I was . . . angry, at first. And really sad. And then there was like a three-step approval process, just to get a phone call."

"Yeah. They love their approval processes around here." Anna makes a sound that's almost a laugh, but not quite.

"I wanted you to know I'm working on another episode of the podcast."

"Oh. What for?"

Martina takes in a deep breath, gets ready to say the words she's been rehearsing since school let out. "I think there are still a lot of unanswered questions about that night. I think . . . I'm not sure you could have done what you said you did. Or maybe I'm just not understanding, and I want to understand. I'd like to speak with you, Anna. Again."

"Like an interview?"

"Exactly. I'd schedule it through Pathways, just like this. Would you be open to that?"

Martina is very aware of the formality of her words. All the ease she'd begun to feel with Anna over the summer, the beginning of what felt like a real friendship, is buried beneath the weight of what happened to Zoe, the place where Anna is locked up, the circumstances surrounding this phone call.

"I think I would," Anna says finally. "I think I'm starting to have some questions too. About that night."

"We both want the same thing," Martina says carefully. "Just to know what happened. To get some real answers for Aster and her parents."

Most of all, even more than she wants to uncover something important, something that will get her into NYU in spite of her miserable track record with standardized tests—and she wants NYU *a lot*—Martina wants answers for her best friend. The *real* answers. She watched the discovery of Zoe's body steal the last flash of hope from Aster's eyes. She saw her best friend crumble. Martina can't get Zoe back for Aster. No one can. But she's going to try her hardest to bring Aster a little bit of peace. Answers—solid, definitive—let you sleep at night.

"Will you help me?" she asks.

"Yeah," Anna says. "Yes."

Martina exhales.

Then, Anna's voice drops. "Can I ask you one thing?"

"Sure."

"Has Caden . . . said anything? About me?"

Martina chews on the inside of her cheek. Growing up,

she used to feel a tenuous kind of connection to Caden, even though he was three years ahead of her in school. When you live in a town as white as Herron Mills, you notice the one or two (in her case, two) other biracial kids at your school. Maybe you aren't close friends, but you exchange glances. Keep tabs. But Caden has been less than cooperative over the past six months. Any connection she used to feel is gone.

"He's back at Yale," she says finally. "I haven't seen him."

"Right," Anna says quickly. "Of course."

"I'll schedule the call," Martina confirms, and the girls say their goodbyes.

Alone again in her kitchen, Martina punches the phone's red end call button. Anna should be in college herself by now. Martina wonders if she'll still get to go, sometime. Or if she'll end up getting her degree in prison. She eyes the remaining tostones and decides she's not really hungry anymore.

She'd rather think about college than the question of if Anna really did it. But of course that's exactly what she needs to figure out. For Aster, and Zoe. For the whole Spanos family. For herself. Because once again, the police have latched onto the available explanation. They have their suspect, their confession. Their easy answer. Even though Martina can spot at least three gaping holes in what she's heard of Anna's story. Holes she's sure the police have decided to conveniently ignore in the interest of closing the case.

Martina has seen every true crime documentary available on Netflix and Investigation Discovery. Has listened to enough episodes of *The Vanished* and *Criminal* and *True Crime Garage* to develop a healthy distrust of law enforcement. She's watched footage of detectives cajoling confessions out of minors without their parents in the room. She's listened to heartbreaking testimonies from the wrongfully convicted and stories of police departments and sheriff's departments bungling investigations due to lack of resources or lack of communication or lack of expertise or the plain willful conviction that they've got their man.

At the same time, Martina's gut says that Anna is lying. Maybe she's innocent. Or maybe whatever happened that night was much worse than the story she told police. She wants to trust Anna, but Anna never told Martina about the messages from Zoe on her phone. What else has Anna been hiding? Maybe her confession doesn't add up because Anna is manipulating the details. In the grand scheme of things, a charge of second-degree manslaughter looks a lot better than murder.

Martina makes the same silent promise she made back when she recorded the first episode of *Missing Zoe* last February. She's going to do her best to find out what happened to her best friend's sister. She's going to put her interests in journalism and true crime reporting to work, to get answers to the questions the detectives should be asking. If Anna is innocent, she's going to use what small platform she has to try to ensure justice isn't falsely served. But if she's guilty, she's going to root out the truth for the Spanos family, uncover the real story beneath Anna's murky confession.

8

THEN

June

Herron Mills, NY

IT'S RAINING. A hard, drenching cascade that seems to barrel from the clouds in fully formed sheets. It pummels the Clovelly Cottage roof, the grounds, goads the pool's infinity edge into a gushing waterfall. It's only ten thirty, and Paisley is bored with Quiddler and Ticket to Ride. I suggest *Moana*, then *Happy Feet*, then *Matilda*. Paisley is not in the mood. Paisley wants to *do* something.

It's clearly not a beach day, and unlikely to clear up into a town day any time soon. I can hear Emilia in her office, on what sounds like an intense phone call about deliverables and reliable vendors for high-end printed something or other. I'm on my own to figure out a fun indoor activity.

I promise Paisley that if she puts the board games away,

I'll have a surprise planned for the morning by the time she's done. She gives me a look like she sees right through me, but agrees with a dainty handshake. I slink out of the family room, totally unsure how I'm going to deliver on my promise. I try to remember what my mom did with me when I was Paisley's age. Mostly, she sent me out to run around with the neighborhood kids or parked me in front of the TV. She worked a lot. We definitely couldn't afford a nanny.

But sometimes we baked together. On weekend mornings, we'd mix up batter for pancakes or banana bread or mini blueberry muffins. Over the holidays, she'd break out the Pizzelle iron, and we'd bake batch after batch of the thin Italian waffle cookies that both my parents were raised on. I put my money on Paisley's sweet tooth and wander into the Bellamys' immaculate, navy-ceilinged kitchen, hoping their cook, Mary, won't mind too much if we make a mess before she gets in to start the dinner prep at three.

It doesn't take long to find the basics: flour, sugar, butter, eggs, milk. There's a revolving tray of every spice imaginable nestled in one tall cabinet along with cocoa powder, semisweet chips, baking powder, vanilla, and a host of other ingredients. We're in business.

I'm resting my arms on the counter, scrolling through recipe options on my phone, when Paisley comes in.

"Found you." She surveys the ingredients surrounding my elbows. "Cookies?" she asks, face lighting up. I breathe an inward sigh of relief.

"Or brownies, maybe. I'm looking at recipes now."

"Let's make peanut butter and jelly cookies," Paisley says.

I'm typing her request into the search box when Paisley

points to a beautiful cream stone box resting at the back of the counter, beside a built-in butcher block. "It's in the recipe box."

"Ah." I set my phone down and lift the lid, which is heavy and cool to the touch. I didn't realize people kept real recipe boxes anymore, but based on the cramped scrawl and yellowed edges surrounding most of the index cards, I'd be willing to guess these have been passed down from a previous generation. Inside, everything is organized neatly by category—fish, poultry, appetizers, etc. I flip through to dessert.

The recipe for peanut butter and jelly cookies is right up front. Unlike its fellows, this card is pink, and the recipe itself has been typed out and pasted on. There's an oily smudge in the top left corner, probably dried peanut butter.

Paisley expertly locates the stand mixer and remaining ingredients, I preheat the oven, and we get to work. The batter is easy—just eggs, sugar, peanut butter, and vanilla. Paisley presses her thumb into the center of each cookie to make a small impression, which we fill with apricot or strawberry or raspberry jam from an assortment of little pots in the fridge. By lunchtime, we have three batches cooling, a fourth in the oven, and two more ready to go. We may have gone a bit overboard, but I'm sure Paisley has friends who'd be willing to take some fresh-baked cookies off our hands.

I task Paisley with returning cold ingredients to the fridge, then begin loading dishes in the dishwasher. The rain has abated to a dull gray drizzle, and if the sun ever comes out, we can spend the afternoon making deliveries around the neighborhood.

Installed on the patio beneath the overhang, munching cookies and the shrimp and watercress sandwiches Mary has left us for lunch, Paisley and I make our game plan for the afternoon. She knows exactly which families are likely to be home, within walking distance, and free from peanut allergies. I guess that's common knowledge among elementary schoolers. As we stand to take our plates inside, the first few tentative rays of sunlight filter down to the glistening surfaces of the lawn and pool. The air is heavy with moisture, but the clouds above are white and rapidly clearing. The rain is done.

The only paper plates I can find in the kitchen are the fancy kind decorated with a floral pattern and thin gold band around the rim. I'm a little hesitant to open the package, but Emilia's office door is still firmly shut, and worst-case scenario, I'll replace them. I leave a note for Emilia on the kitchen table along with a couple dozen cookies. As I'm plating the rest and covering them with plastic wrap, Paisley wanders away from the table and reaches across the stove top to fiddle with the buttons. I whip around.

"Whatcha doing, Paisley?"

She turns, looking guilty. "It got left on," she says. "I didn't want you to get in trouble."

"Oh." My shoulders slump. I leave the cookies and walk over to Paisley, squatting down in front of her. "Hey, I'm sorry. That was my bad, not yours. Next time just tell me if I screw something up, okay?"

She nods. "Deal."

I give her shoulder a squeeze, then press the oven's off button firmly with my thumb. I tell myself it's not a big deal. It's not like the house was going to burn down while we went out for a couple hours. But if Emilia had noticed, or Mary, they might not agree. My stomach churns, and I have to force my eyes away from the well-stocked liquor cabinet above my head.

Five minutes later, the plates of cookies are stacked in a tote bag along with a couple water bottles and sunscreen, and Paisley and I are off. The air along the driveway is even stickier than it was on the patio, and by the time we reach the road, my skin is coated in a thin sheen of sweat. The clouds have mostly cleared, and the sun is out in full blazing force, turning the petals of the rain-soaked azaleas into shiny pink mirrors as we pass. Damp tendrils of hair cling to the back of my neck, and I run my fingers along my bare wrist, searching for an elastic that isn't there. I take the sunscreen out of my bag and make Paisley stop so I can coat both our faces and arms before we continue on.

Paisley has four stops planned on our route, the first of which is two houses down on Linden Lane, in the same direction we walked yesterday into town. Claudia, Paisley explains to me as we buzz at their gate and wait to be let in, is less than a year older but a grade ahead due to how their birthdays fall. She used to be Paisley's best friend until last spring, when Claudia confided in her that she was getting teased for hanging out with a second grader. There's a crackling at the intercom and we introduce ourselves. As the gates swing open, Paisley wrinkles her nose. "She's been extra nice to me since school let out. Like when no one from her grade is around, she thinks things can just go back to normal."

"Well, it's nice of you to bring her cookies. Eventually she's going to realize that good friendships are much more important than the opinions of some girls who don't know what they're talking about."

"And if she doesn't?"

"And if she doesn't, it's her mistake. You deserve people in your life who are going to have your back."

Paisley is still beaming up at me when the door opens to reveal a plump woman with frosted, spiky blond hair. She's dressed in all black save for a giant red statement necklace, and her eyes are heavily made up with black liner and mascara. She looks like she belongs in the West Village, not the Hamptons.

"Paisley!" she exclaims while I twist my hair behind me and tuck it down the back of my tank top in an effort to minimize what I'm starting to think of as the Zoe-factor. I keep my sunglasses on.

"Hi, Mrs. Cooper." Paisley turns her smile toward the woman, who is presumably Claudia's mom.

"I'm Anna," I say, extending my hand. "Paisley's nanny."

Mercifully, there's no shock of recognition on the older woman's face, no hand reaching to scrub across her eyes, no awkward double take. She takes my hand in hers, and I notice her nails are painted the same deep red as her necklace.

Mrs. Cooper graciously accepts Paisley's offering of cookies, explaining that Claudia will be at a riding lesson until four. "We're still on for tomorrow afternoon?" she asks.

I stare blankly.

"The girls have a pool date," she says after a minute. "Just drop Paisley off at two. I thought Emilia might have mentioned it."

Paisley nods and gives my hand a tug. "We talked about it at breakfast," she reminds me.

"Oh, of course," I murmur. *We did?* "We're on," I say with a smile. I need to get my head together.

The rest of our route takes us off Linden Lane and away from Main Street, deeper into residential Herron Mills. Two of the three families are home, and we spend an hour or so at the Paulson-Gosses, Paisley and Raychel running around upstairs in a house that I'm relieved to see more closely resembles a regular suburban dwelling while Elizabeth and I chat about my college plans—yes, I'll be living in the dorms; no, I haven't yet picked out a major—over sweating glasses of iced green tea in the kitchen.

When I catch Elizabeth glancing at the microwave clock, I call for Paisley upstairs and explain we still have another stop or two to make, even though this was the end of the line. Outside, Paisley and I make our way quickly back to Clovelly Cottage. We're both hot and sweaty, and the oven's temperature display flashes across my eyelids every time I blink. *So careless.* We'll take a dip in the infinity pool, wash the afternoon off our skin.

By four thirty, we're both showered and changed for dinner, towels and swimsuits drying on the pool deck. I duck into the kitchen for some baby carrots and hummus and find Mary, a tall, plump woman in a tailored white chef's jacket with black buttons, hard at work on something that smells like garlic and white wine. My mouth waters.

"Dinner's at six thirty," she reminds me, and I promise we won't fill up on snacks.

She glances at the heaping plate of cookies still sitting on the kitchen table. "I see Paisley introduced you to her favorites."

"We may have gone a bit overboard," I admit. "Please help yourself." I remember the fourth paper plate still sitting in my tote in the entryway, and suddenly I get an idea.

"Hey, Paisley." I slip out of the kitchen and into the family room, where Paisley is dressed in a matching white cotton short and top set on the couch, watching some kid's show I don't recognize. I place the hummus and carrots on the coffee table in front of her. "Want to take that last plate of cookies next door?"

She wrinkles her nose at me. "The Andersons are in Lucerne until August," she says.

"The other next door. The Talbots."

Beneath her summer tan, the color drains out of Paisley's face. "To Windermere?" she asks, voice suddenly soft and filled with breath. She shakes her head back and forth, almost violently, fine blond hair whipping in still-wet ropes against the back of the couch.

I frown. I'm not sure what's going on with Paisley, but I've never seen her act like this. "Right, to Windermere," I say. "I'm sure the Talbots like cookies."

"No way." Paisley draws her knees into her chin, and I can see the feathery blond hairs prickle along her arms and legs. She lowers her voice to a whisper and looks straight into my eyes. "It's haunted."

I sit down on the couch next to her, smoothing my sundress over my knees and trying not to laugh. Windermere has clearly seen better days, and I can see why a kid might be creeped out by the overgrown vegetation hiding the house from the road. It does look a bit like something out of a gothic fairy tale. "It's not haunted," I assure her. "It just needs a little TLC. And Caden seems really nice."

Paisley nods, her chin bobbing against her knees, still

clutched against her chest. "Yeah, Caden's nice," she agrees. "But I'm not going over there." She turns back to face the TV screen, and I can see I've lost her.

I glance at Emilia's office door. Still closed. She might not approve, but running out for a few minutes seems like it would be okay. Mary's here, after all. I poke my head into the kitchen to ask if she can keep an eye on Paisley for a little while.

Cookies retrieved from my tote, I set off again down the drive toward the road, then hang a left, back toward Windermere.

At the gate, it takes me a minute to locate a buzzer through the crawling vines. When I do find a small cream button nestled into a flat panel on one of the stone pillars, it looks more like a regular doorbell than the sophisticated intercom boxes installed at the entrances to Clovelly Cottage and the other houses on our route today. I press my finger against it and a dull light glows beneath the plastic, instilling in me a dubious confidence that somewhere inside the house, a chime is ringing.

I wait for a minute that becomes three. Up the drive, I can see two cars parked near the house, an older sports car and something long, expensive-looking, and black. Someone is home. I wonder if there used to be an intercom, if the speaker is broken. If pressing the bell did anything at all. I slip my foot out of my sandal and run my big toe up and down against the back of my calf, scratching at one of several mosquito bites that have swelled into itchy red welts, despite my best efforts with bug spray.

Kaylee would laugh if she saw me now. Every summer,

no matter what I do, mosquitos flock to me and leave her completely unscathed. I picture her at the beach with Ian, the guy she's been low-key on-again, off-again with all senior year, packing up their stuff as the sun begins its slow dip toward the ocean. With a swell of guilt, I realize I still haven't called her. I resolve to pick up the phone soon, no matter what.

Just as I'm debating pressing the bell again or giving up and heading back, the front door swings open, and Caden steps onto the porch. As he walks toward me, I'm surprised to see he's dressed up. Gone are the jeans and plaid shirt, replaced with pressed khaki slacks, an olive button-down tucked in at the waist, and brown dress shoes. I guess they dress for dinner at Windermere too. As he approaches the gate, I can see him squinting at me through the rails and scrolls. There's a falter in his step; he must not recognize me from the other night.

"It's Anna," I call out. "Paisley's nanny."

He keeps walking, then pauses on the other side of the gate, not saying anything in return. His face finally comes into focus, and something unlatches inside my chest. Caden, in daylight. His features are delicate but not sharp. Gentle. Except for his eyebrows, which form two bold brush strokes across his forehead. Beneath them, his eyes are surprisingly hard. They narrow, taking me in, and whatever had come loose inside me before tightens again. Anna in daylight is clearly not what he'd hoped for.

I can feel my cheeks burn red, and realizing he still hasn't said a word, I hold up the plate of cookies, wondering if I can slide them through the gate and run. "Paisley and I baked," I offer, cursing the tremble in my voice.

Caden presses something on the other side of the pillar,

and the gate creaks and slides on its track, disappearing into a slot in the stone. He motions toward the house with his chin. "Come on."

As we walk up the drive toward Windermere, cookies still clutched in my hands, I can feel Caden's eyes trained on my face. I make myself look anywhere but at him. To our left is the pond he mentioned restoring; the lawn around it has been freshly mowed, and there's a large pile of weeds and debris on the bank closest to the gate. My eyes skate across the lawn up to the house itself, which is still majestic in stature and has not been long enough neglected to have fallen into serious disrepair. If they would bring someone in to hack down the vines and clean up the landscaping, that would be 90 percent of the job, but I keep my lips pressed tightly together. Not my business.

"You look different without your hoodie," Caden says finally as we near the porch. He pauses, so I pause too, and I make myself turn to face him. We're both standing on the first step, suspended between the drive and the porch. Our bodies are suddenly close together. I'm in his space, but I didn't mean to be. I want to take a step back, but can't decide if that would be even more awkward. Before I can make up my mind, he reaches one hand slowly toward me and gently lifts a dark lock of hair between his fingers. "Raven," he says.

Above us, I hear a flutter and series of cries, and then I do take a step back, off the stairs, feet returning to the drive. Caden drops his hand and shoves it in his pocket. I look up in time to see a cloud of black feathers lift off from the third-floor balcony, twenty birds or more taking to the sky.

"Ravens," Caden says again, and I wonder if I misunderstood him the first time. "My mother keeps birds. Parakeets mostly, sometimes canaries. The wild birds can smell the feed; they're always around."

There's something stiff about his voice, his posture. Not at all like the other night, his casual lean against the pillar, the easy conversation. I get the sense he's being polite, and my stomach clenches. I keep my eyes trained on the balcony, and as the ravens disperse against the sky, I'm hit with a powerful wave of vertigo. It strikes hard and fast, the balcony tilting toward me, or the driveway rippling to waves beneath my feet.

I pitch forward. I'm falling.

I grasp at the house with my free hand, try to steady myself as Windermere careens around me, falling, everything falling. I shut my eyes and let the wall's brown shingles take solid shape against my hand until the vertigo passes, and the world rights itself again. I draw a deep breath in.

"You okay?" Caden is squinting at me, concerned.

"Just dizzy for a sec. I think I looked up too fast." It sounds good, but I'm not sure what that was. I've never been great with heights, but staring up from below has never been a problem. Something about that balcony tipped the world off-kilter.

Caden nods, satisfied, then turns abruptly and walks up the stairs to the front door. "You'd better come in, since you're here," he says, swinging the door wide. Immediately, I hear barking, and we're met by a midsize brown and white dog, some kind of spaniel.

"That's Jake," Caden says, ruffling the dog's floppy ears. "He's friendly."

I join Caden on the porch and let Jake sniff my hand, which he promptly fills with his warm muzzle. Jake's coat is shiny and he looks well cared for, but as I crouch down to pet him,

I have to hold my breath. He smells. Really smells.

I straighten up and take a step toward the house, and that's when it hits me that the smell isn't coming from Jake. It's coming from inside Windermere.

In the entryway, the mysterious odor is immediately identifiable. The hall is absolutely teeming with birds—and bird droppings. There are cages hanging here and there, others propped on various pieces of once-beautiful furniture, but the doors have been unlatched, and the birds seem to have free rein of the place.

My mouth must be hanging open because Caden says, "You're here all summer, right? You were going to see it sooner or later."

I snap my jaw shut and try to breathe through my teeth.

"My mother isn't well," he says. "I think I mentioned the other night." He gestures loosely toward a portrait of a pretty young woman with fair skin and glossy brown hair hanging at the base of a tall, gently curving staircase to my left. The banister, once a grand thing, is dusty and coated with bird shit. "She was in her late twenties or early thirties when that portrait was done. The man in the painting next to her was my father. Died when I was a little kid. I don't really remember him."

Both of Caden's parents appear to be white, and I wonder if he was adopted. It doesn't seem like the right time to ask.

"I'm sorry," I say. "About your dad."

Caden shrugs but doesn't say anything.

"And that your mom is sick," I add. I feel like an intruder in their home. It was clearly beautiful once; the furnishings in the entry hall look old and sturdy and probably very expensive. A dust-covered tapestry lines one wall, and to my left, beyond the staircase, is what appears to be a formal living room or parlor. The curtains are drawn across floor-to-ceiling windows, and the room is swallowed in musty darkness. Did he invite me inside to gawk? Or is this some sort of test of my character? If it is, I'm not sure I'm passing.

"I brought cookies," I say again, holding out the little plate. "We baked way too many. I hope you like peanut butter."

Caden's thick eyebrows arch suddenly toward the ceiling, and he looks at the plastic-wrapped plate in my hand for the first time. Without warning, he reaches out and takes it from me, a little too sharply.

"What are these?" he asks.

"Um, peanut butter and jelly cookies?" A dark cloud passes over his face, and I feel a lump take shape in my throat. "I thought, um, we used three different kinds of jam," I start to ramble. "But if you don't like them, I'm sure we'll do more baking later."

"Please take them back." Caden's voice is cold. He holds the plate out toward me, his arm stiff and eyes hard. I try to swallow, but my mouth is completely dry.

"Okay, sure." I grasp the cookies, wishing I had a bag I could shove them into. I've done something horribly, irrevocably wrong. Made some mysterious faux pas. Jake brushes against my legs, and I pat the top of his head, more to reassure myself than anything else.

"You should go," Caden says as I'm already turning toward the door, ready to leave Windermere and never return. Maybe Paisley was right. This place *is* haunted. Not by the dead, but by the flinty secrets of the living.

I stumble down the porch steps and back to the gate, which

Caden has mercifully left open as if he knew my stay inside the Windermere grounds would be brief. I turn the corner onto Linden Lane and sprint toward Clovelly Cottage, punching in the code at the end of the drive with trembling fingers. I mess it up the first time, then make myself stop a moment, take a breath. Down the road, just past Claudia Cooper's house, Tom's Lexus is parked on the street. He's standing outside, leaning against the SUV's driver's side door, and raking his fingers through his hair. I raise my hand to wave, but he doesn't see me. He's clearly involved in a very intense phone call that doesn't seem close to ending anytime soon, so I get my shit together and punch in the gate code again.

Instead of going in through the front door, I duck around the side of the house and cross behind the pool, waving feebly to Mary and Paisley, who are carrying glasses and a stack of plates out to the table on the porch, then slip into my cottage. I jam the plate of cookies into the trash, then collapse on the bed, tears filling my eyes.

I swipe them away, angry at myself for letting Caden get to me. He was the rude one, stormy and harsh for no good reason. I didn't do anything wrong. Did I?

The clock on my phone says there's still an hour until dinner. I need to move, to get this funk out of my system. I won't have time to shower again, but I don't care. I slip out of my sundress and into my one athletic outfit and sneakers, then grab my phone and earbuds and start jogging back around the house, down the drive. When I turn onto Linden Lane, the street is empty where Tom's Lexus was parked a few minutes ago. Instead of music, I pull up my podcasts and hit play on the second episode of *Missing Zoe.*

TRANSCRIPT OF *MISSING ZOE*
EPISODE TWO: THE BOYFRIEND THEORY

[ELECTRONIC BACKGROUND MUSIC]

YOUNG FEMALE VOICE: They were "that couple," you know?

YOUNG MALE VOICE: I thought something might have happened, but I didn't want to ask. But then Zoe was with Caden at the gospel choir's winter concert right before break, and everything seemed fine. That was the last time I saw her.

[END BACKGROUND MUSIC]

MARTINA GREEN: Hi, listeners, and welcome back. Today, I've got the second episode of *Missing Zoe* for you. But if you didn't catch Episode One, you should probably start there to learn about Zoe Spanos, the young woman who vanished without a trace from her Herron Mills hometown last New Year's Eve, and why we're discussing her case here. Go ahead and listen; I'll be here when you get back.

[BRIEF PAUSE]

Okay, everybody ready? Today is Tuesday, February eighteenth, and it's been seven weeks to the day since Zoe disappeared. Zoe Spanos is still missing. And we're missing Zoe.

[*MISSING ZOE* INSTRUMENTAL THEME]

MARTINA GREEN: If you know Zoe personally or if you've been following the media coverage of her case, you may have noticed that I left out something—or rather, someone—important in last week's episode: Zoe's long-time boyfriend, Caden Talbot.

And that's because I'm going to devote the majority of this episode to Caden and his relationship with Zoe. If you follow true crime media at all—or read murder mysteries or missing girl stories or watch *Law & Order* or *CSI*—you know that the husband or boyfriend is the first person the police bring in when a woman goes missing or is the victim of a violent crime.

In July 2017, the Centers for Disease Control and Prevention released a report that showed over half of women killed in the United States are victims of intimate partner violence. I spoke with Judith Corrado Smith, assistant director for Communication at the CDC, over the phone from her Atlanta, Georgia, office. Here's what she had to say:

JUDITH CORRADO SMITH: Our study looked at 10,018 murders of women in eighteen states from 2003 through 2014. Of those deaths, fifty-five percent were intimate partner violence related. We say "intimate partner violence related" because crimes committed by a family member or friend of the victim's partner are included within this classification, however in ninety-three percent of the intimate partner murder cases we examined, the perpetrator was a current or former romantic partner of the victim.

Strangers perpetrate just sixteen percent of all homicides where a woman is the victim. The popular narrative of a random killing by a mysterious stranger may be great fodder for urban legends and ghost stories, but it's just not a likely scenario.

MARTINA GREEN: While tales of stranger danger certainly haunt our cultural psyche, today's crime dramas and murder mysteries also frequently explore the narrative that the CDC's study confirmed: In real life as in fiction, there's a very good chance that the husband-slash-boyfriend did it.

But let's take a step back. You're probably asking: Does Martina Green believe that Caden Talbot was responsible for Zoe's disappearance—or that he may have even killed her? The short answer is no, I don't believe this to be true. We have no evidence that Zoe is dead, nor do I think it likely that Caden was the perpetrator of violence against her.

CAROLINE FOX-RIGG: I can't speak to his mental state; I'm not a mental health care practitioner. But in terms of personality? Caden was never anything but a kind, conscientious member of our Jefferson community. Very bright, one of our academic superstars. Especially in the humanities, although he held his own in my class too. And he was very devoted to Zoe.

MARTINA GREEN: That's Miss Fox-Rigg, a chemistry teacher at Jefferson High School. You'll hear more from her in our third episode.

The more complicated answer to the question of "why look so hard at Caden" is this: Because the police latched on so quickly to their Zoe-as-runaway theory, I don't believe they did their due diligence in this regard. And this was a grave oversight, because whether or not he had anything to do directly with Zoe's disappearance, Caden is the one person in Zoe's life most likely to be in possession of valuable information in her case—information that may seem trivial or unrelated, but which could be extremely useful to police.

ASSISTANT DETECTIVE PHILIP MASSEY: Both Caden and Meredith Talbot were identified as persons of interest early in our investigation. They are not suspects. As the investigation remains open, I cannot comment further on our interactions with the Talbots.

MARTINA GREEN: You might remember AD Massey from our first episode as an officer on Zoe's case. While the detective would not delve into particulars, to the best of my knowledge, Caden Talbot and his mother Mrs. Meredith Talbot were each brought in for questioning only once by police following Zoe's disappearance.

I tried to get Caden to speak with me for this episode, but those requests were declined. I'll keep pressing for future episodes. While police have refrained from further exploring what I'm calling the boyfriend theory, it's my belief that buried somewhere in the contours of Zoe and Caden's relationship lies the key that will unlock the mystery to what happened on New Year's Eve.

Let's start at the beginning, with some background on the Talbot and Spanos families. I checked in again with village historian Alfred Harvey, for a dose of family history.

ALFRED HARVEY: The Talbots are old Herron Mills. The family has been in the area since the late eighteen hundreds—shortly after Herron Mills was incorporated as a village. They're one of the few families in the area who have been here since the beginning and still have a presence.

MARTINA GREEN: What can you tell us about the recent generations of Talbots?

ALFRED HARVEY: Well, Laurence and Faye were the fifth generation at Windermere, the family's Linden Lane estate. They were born to parents Daniel and Martha in 1968 and 1971, respectively. Daniel and Martha relocated to London in the early nineties, leaving Windermere in their son Laurence's care. Faye lives in the Boston area with her wife Carla, and to the best of my knowledge, the two have never shown an interest in taking over management of the estate.

Laurence Talbot, known to his friends and colleagues as Larry, was a very successful art dealer until his death in 2006. Stomach cancer, he was only thirty-eight. Laurence left Windermere to his wife, Meredith, and son, Caden, who inhabit it today.

MARTINA GREEN: And the Spanos family?

ALFRED HARVEY: There's less to tell. George and Joan Spanos are much newer to Herron Mills. They moved to our village from Queens, New York, in 1995, when George established his landscape architecture practice in the East End. Joan was then an assistant editor and is now the editor in chief of *Wayfare + Ramble*, a New York City–based travel magazine. As your listeners will know, they have two daughters, Zoe and Aster.

HARRIET BENYON: At three years apart, you'd think things might have been competitive between them, but it was never really like that.

MARTINA GREEN: You're hearing from Harriet Benyon, a friend of Aster's—and mine—from school. While I could talk all day about the Spanos sisters, I wanted you to be able to hear a perspective apart from my own.

HARRIET BENYON: They fought sometimes, they were normal siblings. I wouldn't exactly describe them as best friends; they each had their own groups. But even though Aster was younger, she was always taking care of Zoe. I remember one of the first times I went over to their place. I think Aster and I were eleven and Zoe was fourteen. We were watching this movie about witches, and Aster held Zoe's hand through all the scary parts. That's a pretty good metaphor for their relationship. Her sister's disappearance has been really hard on Aster. I mean, obviously. But she feels like she let her guard down, like she should have been there personally to stop anything bad from happening to Zoe.

ELLE COLERIDGE: George and Joan? They're typical Herron Mills parents.

MARTINA GREEN: Again, I wanted to bring you an outside take. So now you're hearing from Elle Coleridge, another classmate of Aster's and mine. Elle is the president of Jefferson's DECA and FBLA chapters, and she and Aster are both on swim team.

Elle, can you tell us what you mean by "typical Herron Mills parents"?

ELLE COLERIDGE: Oh. Well, you know. Busy. Career-focused. Big ambitions for their kids. They were thrilled when Aster made captain this year. Aster's a little short for a swimmer, but she's a total powerhouse. It's usually George in the bleachers at meets; I think Joan's in the city a lot for work.

MARTINA GREEN: Do you get the impression they aren't around enough for their daughters?

ELLE COLERIDGE: No, I'm not saying that. I think like most parents around here, Mr. and Mrs. Spanos are balancing demanding jobs with raising a family. It's like there are a lot of expectations placed on modern parents, especially mothers, to be everything all the time. It's just not realistic. They're good parents. Everyone saying they dropped the ball, trying to shove responsibility off on the family—it's gross. You know no one has ever solved the Long Island Serial Killer murders, and that's mostly because those girls were escorts, and no one reported them missing. For years, law enforcement didn't care. It's so sad. I'm not saying LISK had anything to do with Zoe, but this is a case where her family cares deeply. I can't even look at Reddit anymore. What we need is a real lead, so people will stop passing judgment on the family, as if letting their college-aged daughter go to a New Year's party was some kind of sin.

MARTINA GREEN: Indeed.

Let's turn now to Caden and really dig into that relationship. Zoe and Caden have known each other practically since infancy; their friendship turned romantic in early high school, and they began dating during the summer following ninth grade. Zoe has always been much beloved by Mrs. Talbot; in turn, the Spanos family doted on Caden.

At school, they were the couple everyone was rooting for, the couple everyone secretly wished they could be. And their relationship didn't just look picture-perfect from the outside. As anyone who has ever been in high school knows, relationships are very much on display within school walls. Whether you've been part of a high school couple or observed others, you know what sort of microscope those relationships are under. I spoke on the phone with Di MacAdam, former Jefferson senior class president, from her dorm room at Skidmore.

DI MACADAM: Zoe and Caden were . . . [PAUSE.] Wow, I'm still just so shocked, I'm sorry. [ANOTHER PAUSE.] Okay, Zoe and Caden. They were "that couple," you know? And they didn't even care about being popular. They were nominated for Homecoming Court a couple times, but they turned that stuff down. They had friends, but they mostly kept to themselves. I think that's why everyone loved them so much. They weren't big on PDA; they didn't rub their relationship in anyone's face. But they were clearly very much in love. She was always so sweet to him, and when she talked, you could tell he really listened.

MARTINA GREEN: Would you consider either of them close friends?

DI MACADAM: I was closer to Caden. He was on student council all four years, so we spent a lot of time together planning events and sitting in student gov meetings, that sort of thing. He was really serious about Zoe. One time, I remember he asked for my opinion on a gift for her. He was picking out a necklace; he wanted to make sure it was something she would actually wear. And it was beautiful, a delicate chain with her initials in gold. Perfect.

In our Senior Superlatives, they were voted "Couple Most Likely to Actually Get Hitched," which tells you something, you know? The fact that they were totally rock solid through graduation and beyond is pretty unusual. I mean, how many couples do you know who make it all the way through high school? But that's just who Caden and Zoe were.

They were in their own happy little orbit.

MARTINA GREEN: The summer before starting college, Caden and Zoe were stronger than ever. I saw Zoe a lot that summer. I was often over at the Spanos's home with Aster. Zoe was getting ready to begin her first year at Brown, and Caden was set to begin his at Yale. You might think the decision to attend separate colleges would have sounded Zoe and Caden's death knell, but nope. Zoe said they didn't even apply to the same colleges because they didn't want to be defined by their relationship. They each applied to schools within driving distance in the northeast, so they could see each other often, yet focus on establishing their own lives and academic pursuits. Talk about mature.

I spoke on the phone with Kelly Ann Bate, Zoe's first year roommate at Brown. Kelly Ann was walking between buildings on campus when we talked, so you'll hear some background chatter and wind in the audio. Sorry about that. I'll post a transcript of this part of the episode online with the show notes for reference.

KELLY ANN BATE: I'd say Zoe was gone one, maybe two weekends a month our first year. And Caden was here on campus about the same. They'd stay in this little B & B nearby. She was always really respectful of the fact that we shared a room.

[LOUD SOUNDS OF LAUGHTER AND SHOUTING.] More than I can say for some people at Brown. I'm sure it was a transition, being in college and figuring out how that factored into their relationship, but they made it work. Zoe didn't seem to have a problem blending her relationship into her world here. [WIND GUST.] They'd come to basketball games, eat with us at the Ratty. They probably saw each other three weekends a month, all in all, and they were always on the phone.

MARTINA GREEN: And what about the fall semester of sophomore year?

KELLY ANN BATE: I'm not totally sure. [WIND GUST.] We weren't roommates anymore, so I didn't notice as much when Zoe was gone for the weekend. And you know, Zoe and I were friendly, but we had our own groups. I saw Caden on campus a couple times last fall, for sure. But Zoe had a single; I bet they were holed up there a lot. She did this marine bio internship in California over the summer, so they were probably ready for some one-on-one time.

MARTINA GREEN: I also spoke on the phone with Tim Romer, a friend of Caden's at Yale.

TIM ROMER: Zoe? Yeah, she was around a lot our first year. A couple times a month? She made an effort to get to know me, all of Caden's friends really. Other people's girlfriends from home didn't do that. I always liked Zoe; she could hang.

MARTINA GREEN: And this fall?

TIM ROMER: Nah, she wasn't around so much. Caden was really busy with the radio station, and he's been doing this research project with Professor Eaton. She's the chair of our African American Studies Department. She usually only works with grad students, so it's kind of a big deal. I thought something might have happened, but I didn't want to ask. But then Zoe was with Caden at the gospel choir's winter concert right before break, and everything seemed fine. That was the last time I saw her.

MARTINA GREEN: It's my hunch—and this is only a hunch—that the key to unlocking what happened to Zoe Spanos lies in the events of that fall semester of sophomore year—the fall leading up to her disappearance. What was Zoe doing when she wasn't visiting Caden at Yale? Were they really just busy, or did Zoe meet new people that fall? Who were they, and how much did Caden know? Did the police even bother to ask?

I doubt they did, and here's why. According to their own accounts, Caden Talbot and his mother were not in Herron Mills on the night of December thirty-first last year.

The Talbots regularly spend Christmas week in the city with close family friends on the Upper West Side. Aster did not wish to be recorded for this episode, but she did confirm that the Talbots were among the first people Mr. Spanos called on the morning of January first, when Zoe had not come home. According to Aster, the Talbots had initially planned to return from the city in time for Zoe and Caden to spend New Year's Eve together. Zoe had been excited about their plans, which included attending Jacob Trainer's house party together. But at the last minute, the Talbots' trip home was delayed to the following day.

Mrs. Talbot did not feel up to traveling that afternoon.

So when Mr. Spanos called on the morning of January first, the Talbots were allegedly still in the city. Caden told Mr. Spanos that he had last heard from Zoe around two o'clock that afternoon, when the two had exchanged text messages about the change in plans. Caden and Mrs. Talbot returned to Windermere the afternoon of January first and spoke with police on the afternoon of the second. The final text message exchange between Caden and Zoe was entered into evidence, and is on record with the Herron Mills PD.

It's here where I believe local police first dropped the ball in this case. Because Caden and Meredith Talbot were allegedly not in Herron Mills the night that Zoe vanished, they were not further interviewed by police. Were their alibis investigated? Confirmed? This remains unclear.

Here's what I do know: Meredith was able to account for Caden's whereabouts up until 10:30 on the night Zoe disappeared; then she went to bed. He was next seen at 6:30 a.m., when Doreen Winn-Carey, the family friend with whom they were staying, passed by the couch where he was sleeping on her way to the bathroom. Not only were their alibis restricted to this closed triangle of Doreen, Meredith, and Caden, but the eight hours between 10:30 p.m. and 6:30 a.m. remain unaccounted for. I guess their story was good enough for the Herron Mills PD, though.

To reiterate, I am not suggesting that Caden—or his mother—perpetrated violence against Zoe or were even directly involved in her disappearance. But I do not believe we can so easily rule them out. And at the very least, I believe that Caden knows

information—about that fall, about that night, about Zoe's life—
that could lead us to find her.

Caden, if you're listening, I'd love to talk to you, on or off the
record. Please get in touch.

[CODA TO *MISSING ZOE* INSTRUMENTAL THEME]

9

THEN

June

Herron Mills, NY

I AM NOT at my best during dinner—but fortunately, neither is anyone else. We're half finished by the time Tom arrives to the table, dressed down and looking a bit flustered. He gives Emilia a kiss, murmuring something about a rough Friday at the office and getting stuck late in a meeting. She's clearly pissed. I take a big gulp of water and keep my mouth shut. He's been back since at least five, but it's none of my business what he's been up to.

My mind is somewhere else entirely: with Caden and Zoe. As we eat, I stumble over every question Tom asks about my first week at Clovelly Cottage. Mary's garlic roasted chicken sticks in my throat. My lips are thick and sluggish; they struggle to form the words that would prove I'm all right, perfectly normal, fine just fine. Fortunately, Paisley comes to my rescue, happy to recount our various excursions around town in elaborate, lively detail. She mercifully leaves out the bit about me leaving the oven on and then abandoning her to Mary's watch for much longer than a few minutes this evening.

The air around me buzzes with the truth. Caden is Zoe's. Caden *loves* Zoe. And now Zoe is gone, leaving Caden to his lonely summer in Herron Mills. Laying low and avoiding the watchful eyes of the village that rooted me out at once, caring for a mother who is unwell in some way that has led to Windermere's steep decline. Caden, avoiding the town's pity. Maybe their accusations too.

My thoughts stay stubbornly lodged at Windermere all day Saturday, while Emilia tasks each of us with an array of housekeeping jobs and errands in preparation for the "small garden party" the Bellamys will host in honor of Tom's thirty-eighth birthday on Sunday. In the afternoon, I drop Paisley off at the Coopers' for the girls' pool date, then drive Emilia's car to the florist on Main Street to pick up a missing bouquet from the Bellamys' order.

Back at Clovelly Cottage, I peek at the guest list. There are 103 affirmative RSVPs. Caden and Meredith Talbot's names are included among a small list of guests who have not responded to the invitation. I breathe a small sigh of relief.

As I cart lawn furniture from the shed to the yard behind the pool, I perfect my inward cringe. What must Caden have thought of me? Poking around Windermere twice in three days. My uncanny resemblance to his missing girlfriend. My failed attempt at a neighborly gift, which he probably saw as a thinly veiled attempt to gain admission to Windermere. And wasn't that exactly what it had been? I'd wanted an excuse to see him. To be invited inside. To insert myself into his life. I hadn't known what I was doing, but I'd done it all the same. No wonder he'd shoved the cookies back into my hands once he'd gotten a clear look at my face.

Under an hour into Sunday's party, I'm at a complete loss. I'm technically on nanny duty as usual, but Paisley is running around with Raychel and a small gaggle of their friends, and they don't need much in the way of supervision. I almost wish they did; it would give me a reason to stay far away from the bar set up beside the hot tub.

The pool deck is swarming with well-heeled guests sipping chic cocktails I've never heard of with names like Negroni and Paloma. I back away, onto the grass. The last thing I want is to get snared in a web of small talk with the Bellamys' friends. I can feel their eyes roving across my skin, even though I've pinned my hair up under a broad-rimmed sun hat in my best attempt to look un-Zoe-ish.

I'm not entirely sure it's working. The more I listen to Martina's podcast, the more I learn about Zoe and her strange disappearance, the more I wonder what I'm doing here. It can't be a coincidence—this job, my mysteriously missing doppelgänger. But I don't have the first clue what any of it means.

On the front lawn, I slip into the shade of the long white tent that has been set up kitty-corner to the fountain and tennis court and fill a small plate with purple carrots and mushroom tartlets. Most of the guests are mingling by the pool; this side of Clovelly Cottage is almost deserted, save for the kids, who are turning cartwheels across the tennis court. I park myself at a tall, round cocktail table in the shade where I can rest my elbows and keep an eye on Paisley.

"What a charming sundress." The compliment is laced with something like pity or scorn. I spin around. The speaker is a tall, older woman with a body shaped like a bowling pin. She leans primly against the lip of the fountain, an actual parasol propped on the drive in front of her. Slender arms sprout from narrow, sloped shoulders. A trim waist swells abruptly into ample hips and thighs beneath a fluttering skirt. She is dressed head-to-toe in white.

"Thank you?" I'm not sure how she snuck up on me. From where I'm standing, I have a clear view of the drive. And if she'd already been around back at the pool, I'm sure I would have noticed her among the other, younger guests in their effortless summer dresses and pressed linen suits.

She leans forward, using her parasol as a cane, and takes three steps toward me. I can't tell if she's fifty or seventy-five. "Take off your hat," she demands. When I hesitate, she makes an impatient gesture in the air with her hand. "Well, go on."

Slowly, I slip my sun hat off and place it on the cocktail table. She's surly but authoritative, and I feel oddly compelled to obey her. Beneath my hat, a few bobby pins have come undone. Loose bits of hair fall limply down my shoulders and back.

"Hrmph." She's standing next to me at the table now, uncomfortably close. I get the sense she's appraising me like a slightly damaged antique overvalued at auction. "Not as striking as I'd been led to believe, but I do see a sickly sort of resemblance. Mostly in the cheekbones and hair."

It hits me all at once who this woman must be. She looks

like the painting, but much older. "Mrs. Talbot?" I venture.

She takes a small step back to extend one pale hand. Unlike everyone else I've encountered in Herron Mills, her skin decidedly lacks an early summer tan. "Yes," she replies.

I take her hand in mine, and a small shiver runs through me. It's very cold, and her grip is tight.

"I'm Anna," I manage to choke out. "But I guess you knew that already."

"Anna Cicconi, the au pair." She releases my hand from her grasp. This time, I recognize the note in her voice: judgment.

Just then, a thin wail rises from the tennis court. A chubby girl with curly brown hair is on the ground, clutching what looks like a freshly skinned knee—Paisley's erstwhile best friend, Claudia.

"Anna!" Paisley shouts, waving wildly even though I'm only a few yards away.

"You'd better go." Mrs. Talbot's voice pitches into a thin sneer that says plainly what she thinks of my nannying skills. I want to protest that I'd been watching them until she showed up, that Claudia isn't even my responsibility, but I feel babyish in the shadow of her glare. Silenced.

Without saying anything, I rush off toward the girls on the court. I know where the Bellamys keep the first-aid kit. It's only a scraped knee; I'll get Claudia fixed up in no time. I can be good at this job. I've got this.

"And, Anna," Mrs. Talbot says as Paisley slips her hand into mine, pulling me over to inspect Claudia's wound. I turn my head to face her once more. "I won't expect to see you at Windermere again. We don't need anything . . . stirred up."

She doesn't wait for me to respond. Parasol propped over

her shoulder, making me wonder if its previous use as a cane was entirely performative, she spins on her heel and starts off across the lawn, toward the deep thicket of trees that separate Clovelly Cottage from Windermere. I see then how she arrived so stealthily on the grounds. She didn't come up the drive at all, but simply slipped through the trees between the properties.

I whip back around and scoop a wailing Claudia into my arms. With instructions to Paisley to take the other girls to the pool deck where their parents can see them, I head across the drive toward the front door.

At a few minutes after six, as Tom and Paisley splash together in the pool and the guests are starting to depart for their Sunday dinners and end-of-the-weekend rituals, I find myself standing alone at the bar with Emilia. One thin dress strap has slipped down a tan shoulder and her neat bob looks windswept. She gives our order to the bartender—a Negroni for her, seltzer and lime for me—and I notice that her speech is just slightly slurred.

I take a deep breath. If I'm about to offend her, maybe she'll be less likely to hold it against me now. Maybe she won't remember tomorrow.

"Can I ask you a question?"

Her eyes focus somewhere in the area of my nose. "Of course, Anna."

"It's about the job," I begin.

"Oh." She frowns. "Has it not been what you've expected?"

"It has," I rush to say. "Everything's been great. What I mean is, I'm hoping you would tell me why I was hired."

"Ah." Emilia plucks our drinks from the bar and takes a seat on a lounge chair. She hands over my seltzer, and I perch on a wicker seat beside her. In the pool, Tom tosses Paisley into the air, and she squeals. "It was Paisley's choice, really. We interviewed three candidates in the spring. We were supposed to see two more after you, but we canceled those appointments. Paisley was set on you."

"Do you know why?" I press.

"Well." Emilia folds her lips together, as if not sure how much to say. "I'm sure someone has pointed out by now your resemblance to Zoe Spanos?"

I nod eagerly. My heart speeds up, a quick *rat-a-tat* in my chest. This is what I've been waiting for. Someone to tell me that none of this is a coincidence. That I'm here for a reason.

"It's such a tragedy," Emilia says. "She was one of Paisley's favorite babysitters. I think, truthfully, when she saw how much you looked like Zoe, she was won over immediately. And you've been great with her, of course. Tom and I know we made the right choice."

She smiles reassuringly, but I'm not sure what I feel. I'm here *because* of Zoe. Because we look alike, and that strange bit of happenstance struck the fancy of a little kid. All those strange looks, awkward conversations. Not coincidence after all, not really.

"You might have warned me," I say, I hope not rudely. I take a big gulp of seltzer through my straw.

"I'm sorry." Emilia's face clouds over. "You're right, we should have. I didn't know how to bring it up, honestly. I was afraid you might not take the job."

"Do George and Joan—" I start to ask. I want to know

if Zoe's parents know about me. What if I run into them in town? But before I can finish my question, Emilia cuts me off.

"What about Joan?"

"Oh, I . . ." I'm hit with the presumptuousness of my question. Martina's podcast made me feel for a second like I was on a first-name basis with everyone in the Spanos family, the same way characters on TV start to feel like friends. Emilia looks at me sharply, then her eyes wander to Tom, still in the pool. Mentioning Mrs. Spanos clearly pushed some kind of button, and I forget why I even brought her up. "Nothing, never mind."

Emilia's face relaxes. "We didn't only hire you because of that, you know. You interviewed well. You were fantastic with Paisley during our trial run at MoMA. Don't think I let Paisley entirely steer the ship." She laughs and leans back in the chaise, hair fanning out against the back of the chair.

"Right, of course not." But it's clear now. I got this job because of the missing girl. It doesn't explain everything I've been feeling—the rush of nostalgia at the beach, the odd moment at the ice-cream shop, the wave of vertigo peering up at the balcony at Windermere. But it's something. A rational explanation for the way in which my fate and Zoe's have oddly intertwined.

Mary is off tonight, and I'm instructed to help myself to party leftovers in the kitchen if I get hungry later. I feel the opposite of hungry. No, that's not quite right. I feel hollow and like nothing could ever make me solid again. As soon as the last guests have departed and it seems socially acceptable, I slip into the pool house and latch the door behind me.

Tearing off my hat and sundress, I turn the hot water all the way up, filling the bathtub. I need a long, long soak. I feel more than just sweaty and hot. I feel violated somehow, and at the same time, like I'm the one who's done something wrong. I'm an interloper in Herron Mills, in Caden Talbot's world. Even though I didn't mean to be. Even though the Bellamys invited me in.

I slip into the bathtub, gritting my teeth until my skin adjusts to the scalding water. I don't have bubble bath, so I pour some shower gel beneath the tap until it forms a few lackluster suds. My phone is propped on the edge of the tub. I've barely had it for two weeks, and there's already a scratch on the top left corner of the screen.

I think about putting on music. I should put on music. But my finger traces the scratch, then navigates to my podcasts. I don't want to listen anymore. But I need to know. I press play on Episode Three.

Martina Green is struggling. I turn the volume all the way up and sink down in the bath, breathing in the steam. The third episode of *Missing Zoe* is dedicated to interviews with the people closest to Zoe, but by the last week of February, eight weeks after she vanished, Caden has still declined Martina's interview requests, and the Spanos family is, understandably, not ready to speak to a teen podcast producer about the very open wound left by the disappearance of their beloved daughter and sister.

It's palpable in the interviews that Martina does get—with a teacher from their high school, a couple of friends, and the volunteer coordinator at the animal shelter where Zoe used to walk dogs and clean cages during high school—that with every passing week, the likelihood that Zoe will return alive and unharmed has diminished.

I do the mental math. It's June 28. That means it's been almost eighteen weeks since Martina recorded this episode and twenty-six weeks total since Zoe disappeared. It will be six months on Tuesday. There's still one episode of *Missing Zoe* remaining, but I know she hasn't been found. After Episode Four, Martina's trail went cold.

I listen to Zoe's teacher talk about her academic promise. How she excelled in math and science, how she was a student leader, involved in multiple clubs and activities. How it came as no surprise when Zoe landed the internship in California the summer after her first year at Brown, when those spots were typically reserved for juniors. I listen to her friends talk about her bright and easygoing personality, how she loved animals and baking, how she planned something thoughtful for all her friends' birthdays, without fail, every single year. She didn't drink, brought huge pitchers of her own juice blends to parties, which somehow everyone thought was endearing, not dorky. She loved Caden. She loved her family. She had the most volunteer hours in her graduating class.

It's a nice character study of Zoe. It's clear that everyone liked her. All the episode seems to prove is how unlikely it is that Zoe Spanos had any enemies in Herron Mills. Martina ends the episode on a hopeful note that she'll still get to talk to Caden, to Aster, to George and Joan Spanos. That she'll uncover information the police discarded or didn't think was important about the fall leading up to that night, the night itself. But I saw the way Martina looked at Aster on Main

Street earlier this week. It was a look of failure. A look I know really well.

By the end of the episode, the water has turned lukewarm and my fingers have puckered into prunes, but I don't want to get out. "I'm sorry," I whisper out loud, although I'm not quite sure why. I'm sorry we look alike? I'm sorry you're gone, and I'm here, in Herron Mills, where you should be? I'm sorry I stepped unwittingly into your life? *I don't know, I don't know, I don't know.*

"I'm sorry," I say again. The urge to apologize is strong, the need clawing at my throat like angry talons. "I'm so sorry, Zoe."

I stumble out of the tub and dry myself off. Wrapped in my robe with my hair twisted in a towel on top of my head, I sit in the center of the bed and open Google. I type *Zoe Spanos* into the search bar and click through the first few results. Most links take me to news articles from January about Zoe's disappearance, then a few more recent posts with paltry, unsatisfying updates. There are a couple older hits from the Jefferson website and the school paper's online archive. Most compelling of all, there's an open-access web forum set up by Zoe's college friends where people from all facets of her life—Brown, Jefferson, Herron Mills, and beyond—have posted everything from theories to photos to open messages for Zoe.

I read everything. Then I read through her LinkedIn profile, her intern bio from last summer on the research center's website, even a long article about Brown's fund-raising campaign for a new campus lab that quotes Zoe only once, but I somehow read through to the end. By the time my phone warns me it's reached 15 percent battery life, it's almost midnight. Eyes stinging and skin crawling with the persistent sensation that there's something ever so slightly familiar about everything I just found, I reach for my charger, then force myself to turn off the light.

10

NOW

September

Herron Mills, NY

MARTINA SITS ON the family room couch with Mami, suffering through the commercial break before the eight o'clock news. Pampers. Coleridge Audi. A new drug treatment for fibromyalgia. She wishes her dad were here to cut the tension in the room with his warm smile and quick laugh, but he's at the shop, closing up for the night. Martina has two siblings, both brothers, both older, both no longer living at home, so it's just Martina and Mami tonight. Mami thinks her daughter's interest in the Zoe Spanos case is unhealthy. Morbid. But even Mami can't tear her eyes away from the screen tonight because the autopsy report for Zoe is about to be released. All of Herron Mills is watching.

Martina fidgets with her phone, shoots Aster a quick text.

You OK?

It joins the chain of five others Martina has sent her best friend today. They're all unread. Martina last heard from Aster early this morning; she was in the car with her parents, on their way to meet with someone from the medical examiner's office. Martina thought she might get the news straight from Aster, but she didn't come to school today, and she's been silent since this morning's text: Autopsy results are in. We have to drive all the way to Hauppauge. I feel sick and Mom literally threw up before we got in the car. IDK if I can handle this.

Whatever the report said, Zoe is still dead. It's not a good day.

Still, Martina curls her hands into fists beneath her thighs, keeps her eyes trained on the screen as the local newscaster, a brightly rouged woman with a frosty blond bob seated behind a desk in the NBC New York newsroom, opens the segment.

"Breaking news in Suffolk County tonight. Autopsy results were released this morning to George and Joan Spanos, parents of Zoe Spanos, who disappeared on her way to a house party in the Long Island village of Herron Mills last New Year's Eve. The missing girl's body was found submerged in a small boat in Parrish Lake last month, just over two miles from her home. Channel Four has the latest."

The words NEW INFORMATION flash in silver block letters across the screen as the newscaster introduces a young reporter with a thin smile and wire-rimmed glasses to match standing inside the busy front hall of an administrative building somewhere in Suffolk County. On the couch beside Martina, Mami clasps and unclasps her hands in her lap.

"Thanks, Cady. What we know right now is that autopsy results were released to the victim's family earlier today, but they have not yet been made public. We're expecting a representative from the medical examiner's office to give a statement shortly."

The camera cuts to a wooden podium in a room not quite as packed with reporters as Martina would have hoped. Across the front of the microphone-studded podium hangs a gold and black seal with the figure of an ox surrounded by the words SUFFOLK COUNTY SEAL * NEW YORK * FREEDOM AND INDEPENDENCE. Above it hangs a cardboard identification card for Daniel Medina, Supervisor, Medical Forensic Investigations.

The Jenkins women grit their teeth through three local news stories until Daniel Medina is ready to speak. When he comes to the podium, he has a prepared statement in hand. Martina leans toward the screen as he rustles the papers before him. Mami raises one hand to her lips.

Daniel tells the room that the forensic medical investigators and pathologists could not determine a cause of death due to the advanced state of decomposition in which Zoe's body was found. Hot bile floods the back of Martina's throat, and Mami whimpers, clasps her hands in her lap. But what they can confirm is shocking: Zoe Spanos did not have any broken bones when she died. Which means Anna's story about Zoe falling to her death from the third floor balcony of Windermere?

Impossible.

Martina's pulse begins to race.

Martina fidgets in her desk chair in the back of the chemistry lab, which Miss Fox-Rigg has kindly agreed to let her use for her interview. *The* interview. She can't be home for this, can't risk Mami walking through the door while she's recording. While she's supposed to be at an SAT study session she's currently blowing off. Besides, the lab has the best acoustics. For the next hour, it's all hers.

She checks her phone, again. 3:56. In four minutes, she'll put through the call to Pathways. She wonders how much Anna knows, how much she's been told. She has to know at least as much as has been made public over the last forty-eight hours. Her lawyers would be keeping her up to speed. In the past day, Anna's mother has hired two more, a real legal team. It's been all over the news.

Martina pulls up Pathways in her contacts and presses the green call button on her phone. Her recording equipment is all set to go. She's ready.

"Martina?"

"Anna, hi."

"Before we start, can you do me a favor? They monitor everything we do online here, and there's an address I need you to look up for me. . . ." Anna's voice trails off.

"Sure," Martina says. She agrees to look it up before they end the call.

"I'm going to start recording now, okay?" Martina tries to keep her voice steady, calm. Professional. She digs her nails into her palm.

"Yeah. Yes."

Martina draws in a deep breath. She had so much she'd planned to ask Anna today, but the autopsy news has blown everything out of the water.

"The answer is, I don't know," Anna says before Martina

has a chance to speak. Then Anna laughs, a hollow, tinny sound funneled through the miniature speaker on Martina's phone.

"What?" Martina is caught off-guard.

"Sorry, it wasn't funny. It's a quote from an old movie. They don't have anything from this century in this place." Anna clears her throat. "You were going to ask what really happened that night. Now that the autopsy results have come in. You were going to ask how Zoe died, if she didn't fall from that balcony."

"Right," Martina says, regaining her composure. "Is there anything you can tell me? Anything you remember?"

"Honestly, no. I remember being on the balcony. With Zoe. I remember falling. I thought she fell."

"And what do you think now, Anna?"

"I don't know what to think. I've been here a whole month. I've had nothing but time to think." A pause. Then, Anna starts to sing. "'Time keeps on slippin', slippin', slippin' into the future!'" In the lilt of Anna's voice, Martina detects a tinge of something that sounds like hysteria. She clears her throat.

"I should have it all figured out by now," she continues, "but it seems like I never knew what I was talking about."

Anna's words are podcast gold. She just admitted to lying to police. Didn't she? Martina makes an effort to steady her voice, to tamp the giddiness down. "Are you saying you weren't responsible for Zoe's death? Or that she didn't die in the way you told police?"

There is a long pause, and for a moment, Martina wonders if she's lost Anna. If she's still on the other end of the line. When Anna finally speaks, she doesn't answer Martina's question.

"My lawyers say this is good news. They didn't want me to do this interview, but I don't really care. I need to know what happened. I *really* need to know. And I think you're going to figure it out, Martina. I trust you."

Martina steadies her palms against the desk. She's glad she's alone, that no one can see the way her eyes flash and shimmer, how she can barely force her feet to stay planted on the floor. She tries another angle.

"The night you spoke with Detective Holloway and Assistant Detective Massey, August fifth. Were you telling the truth?"

Anna draws in a deep breath. "I told them what I remembered, and those memories haven't gone away. But I was under a lot of stress that night. More than I realized. Did you know I was in that interview room for seven hours? Eventually I just wanted the questions to stop. So I told them what I remembered, and my brain filled in the blanks. Or they filled them in for me."

"What kind of blanks?"

"There's this gap after the Windermere balcony. I don't remember driving to Parrish Lake, or putting Zoe in that boat. I never remembered any of that. I remember being by the water, though, after. Knowing she was down there, that I could never get her back. I told the police I must have taken her body to the lake because it fit. Because they told me I must have done it. At the time, it seemed like the answer to a question I'd been chasing all summer."

"Why did you confess, Anna?"

"I don't know how to explain it. . . . I remembered feelings, scraps of things. I had all these scraps, and nowhere to fit them. And then, after what Caden said, suddenly they all shifted into place. It was the only story that made sense."

"Did you kill Zoe Spanos?"

For a moment, the sound of Anna's breathing is the only sign that she's still there. That she hasn't hung up like Martina still fears she might.

"I do not believe I killed Zoe Spanos, or concealed her body."

Blood rushes to Martina's head, and she focuses on her phone's black screen. "And do you have any idea who did? Anything that could help the investigation move forward?"

"I think," Anna says slowly, "it's time for Caden Talbot to speak to the police."

PART II

The Stable

We can never go back again, that much is certain.
The past is still too close to us.

—Daphne du Maurier, *Rebecca*

THEN
June

Riverhead & Herron Mills, NY

PAISLEY WANTS TO do the Penguin Encounter at the Long Island Aquarium, so on Monday morning, Emilia calls to book two tickets for the one-thirty group, then hands over the keys to her car. I've driven it a couple times, little errands around Herron Mills, but it's about forty-five minutes to Riverhead, and the pending drive makes my nerves spike. I've had my license for a year now, but I don't have much highway experience. Plus, this time, I'll have Paisley with me. I hide my jitters beneath a big smile, reminding myself I learned to drive in Brooklyn. I can handle Long Island.

The drive is undeniably beautiful. While Paisley entertains herself in the back with Emilia's iPad, I will the scenery to soothe my nerves as we coast from the South to North Fork:

lake shores, vineyards, farmland, and the largest golf course I've ever seen. But I can't relax. My palms are slippery with sweat on the wheel, and every electronic chime from Paisley's game makes me flinch.

About halfway there, the puffy clouds above us darken, and rain splatters the windshield. It's barely more than a drizzle; the sun is still shining through the clouds. But my entire body tenses. As raindrops patter against the roof and the road becomes wet and black beneath us, all I can imagine is losing control, tires skidding across the highway, our small car colliding with oncoming traffic. My vision fills with smoke, blood, broken glass. I twist around, seat belt biting into my neck, and a small whimper escapes my lips: Paisley's broken body is slumped across the backseat. Through the smashed window, dark water rushes in, filling the car, my nose, my lungs.

"You okay, Anna?" Paisley is asking.

I breathe. The water retreats.

"Fine," I manage. Twist back around, focus on the road. I flex my fingers against the wheel, unknot the cramps. *What was that?* Paisley's fine. We're both fine. Heart still hammering, I drive at five miles under the speed limit until the sky clears up and we leave the rain behind.

Google Maps directs me into the parking lot, and we spend the remainder of the morning at the indoor exhibits—everything from alligators to sand sharks to marmosets—while we wait for our scheduled time with the penguins. And I'm still fine. No more dark visions. No panic knotting inside my chest.

By the time we meet our penguin expert and guide at the AQUATIC ADVENTURES sign, the morning's drive feels like it happened to another girl. Max Adler is tall and muscular, with a mop of brown hair, and looks like he spends a lot of time in the sun. He's young, maybe early twenties, and very enthusiastic about the African penguins with whom we're about to get up close and personal. Paisley, who has been chattering nonstop about the little black and white waddlers since we got here, suddenly gets quiet and tugs on my hand. I crouch down next to her.

"What's up?" I whisper.

"Does he have to be our guide?" she asks in my ear.

I frown. "I think so, yeah. Do you know him?" We're missing the rundown of the rules and regulations, and I give Max half a smile to show I'm paying attention. When our eyes meet, he pauses just long enough to garner some curious glances from the rest of the tour group. Then he seems to collect his thoughts, and continues.

"I've seen him around," Paisley whispers.

Unsure what that means but fairly certain we're in no immediate danger from the penguin guy, I give her hand a reassuring squeeze and straighten up. Max finishes his overview, then leads us toward the Penguin Pavilion. As soon as we're inside the exhibit, Paisley visibly relaxes. The squat little birds are adorable—swimming, sunning themselves, and napping in little hutches nestled along the back wall. We learn that the average lifespan of the African penguin is fifteen to thirty years, and that the birds at the Long Island Aquarium were imported illegally into the US from South Africa, where they had been captive bred. They've been living in the pavilion since the US Fish and Wildlife Service intervened in 2004.

Another staffer, Molly, takes over to explain penguin care and handling, and that everyone in the group will get to meet a fluffy, heart-melting little penguin chick, which is totally worth every penny of Emilia's money. As we wait for our personal meet-and-greet, Max walks over to us, and I can feel Paisley stiffen again beside me.

He stretches out his hand, and I take it. "Enjoying your encounter?" he asks. I'm not much into people's vibes or auras, but everything about Max is signaling friendly and warm. Two dimples crease his cheeks, and I wonder if he's even younger than I originally thought. After this weekend's epic failure with Caden, I need a distraction. I throw Paisley a worried glance as she steps half behind me.

"We are," I say. Molly is calling for the next set of volunteers to meet the chick, and I usher Paisley over.

"Seems like a pretty great gig," I say when she's joined Molly at the Penguin Preschool gate. "How'd you get into the penguin game?"

"Just graduated from Brown, ecology and evolutionary bio. I'm taking some time before applying to grad programs." Max goes on to explain how the job isn't just tours and animal care, how he's also heading up a research project at the aquarium and collecting data for some schmancy-sounding scholar. But all I hear is Brown. Biology. Suddenly the way he caught my eye earlier starts to make a familiar kind of sense, how he singled me out to talk just now.

"So you knew Zoe Spanos?" I ask point-blank.

Max stops midsentence, suddenly out of words.

"I look like her, I know," I go on. "You're a friend of Zoe's? That's why Paisley recognized you?"

"Oh," Max says, finding his voice again. "I knew Zoe a bit from school. I'd see her around the labs. She was two years behind me, though, so we weren't in classes together or anything." He pauses for a moment. "Who's Paisley?"

"My friend." I gesture toward Penguin Preschool. "She seemed to know you."

"Huh." Max looks genuinely perplexed. "I don't think so. Zoe's from Herron Mills, right? I live out on Montauk. Kind of close, but Zoe and I didn't really hang out off campus."

I don't know why he'd lie about that, so I just shrug. The fact that he knew Zoe from Brown is a bit of an odd coincidence, but given everything the past week has thrown at me, it barely registers on the weirdness scale. Maybe Paisley mistook him for someone else.

"Dunno." Max shrugs. "For what it's worth, I don't think you two look that much alike. Zoe was so serious; she always seemed like she was in a hurry." I wonder if he knows he's talking about her in the past tense. If it's because he thinks she's dead, or simply because she wasn't on campus last semester, has become a part of his past. "Being friendly with the visitors is just part of the job," he continues, and I push Zoe out of my mind. "Swear it's nothing more than that."

"Then you should probably mingle," I say. "I have a penguin chick to meet."

At the end of our "encounter," Paisley and I pose for photos with the birds, and Max holds out a business card with an address and phone number scrawled on the back. "This Saturday, if you're free, a few friends and I are having a little get-together on the beach for the Fourth. Beer, fireworks, nothing fancy. I'd love to see you there, um . . . ?"

"Anna," I supply.

"I'd love to see you there, Anna."

"Do you invite all Penguin Pavilion visitors?" I ask, and Max blushes.

"No, this is a personal invitation." Heat pricks my chest, and for the first time in days, I feel genuinely good about myself. Part of me would love a day at the beach, cold beer, no responsibilities.

"I'd love to, but I can't. I'm taking a break from partying this summer, and besides"—I nod toward Paisley, who is saying her goodbyes to her new penguin friends—"I'm working."

"Okay." Max shrugs. "In case your schedule changes." He presses the card into my hand, and even though I know I won't use it, I slip it into my back pocket. After a week filled with nothing but strange reactions from everyone I've met, I have to admit that a little friendliness and flirting is refreshing.

I spend Monday night on the phone, giving my mom the Herron Mills highlights reel, minus any mention of Zoe Spanos. She finally seems to have settled into the reality of my absence; no need to let her know the real reason I got this job. When Mom lets me go, I bite the bullet and try to patch things up with a very incensed Kaylee, then reward my moderately successful efforts with the online shopping spree I've been promising myself. By the end of my second week here, I'll have something new to wear to dinner—and several new sun hats to supplement my wardrobe.

On Tuesday, I pick up Raychel from the Paulson-Gosses and take the girls for a day at the beach. I can feel my life in Herron Mills slipping into a regular, if still unsettling, routine. I do some after-dinner sketches at the pool—Max, Paisley with the penguins, then Caden again, his face coming to life on the page, even though I tell myself I'd rather forget it. By the time the sun has sunk low behind the tree line and the lights on the pool deck have sprung into action, he's all I can think about.

He made it very clear he didn't like me showing up at Windermere last Friday. And Mrs. Talbot flat-out told me not to come back. But I can't shake the connection I felt the first night we met. Before he got a good look at my face.

The need to explain myself swells in my chest. If I could just make Caden understand how much I didn't know, how I wasn't trying to be insensitive. I need one more chance.

Armed with the knowledge that I might only make matters worse, I slip on sneakers and the same hoodie I was wearing the first time I walked over to Windermere and grab the flashlight from the kitchen counter. I think about following Mrs. Talbot's lead and walking straight through the trees onto the Windermere grounds, but I can't imagine that would help my case. Instead, I walk around to the front of Clovelly Cottage, noting the light glowing in the family room. Emilia and Paisley are blacked out in silhouette on the couch, the TV flickering in front of them.

I'm close to the end of the driveway when I notice someone standing at the entry gate. I raise the flashlight, and a slim figure holds up his arm in front of his eyes, shielding them from the light. He looks like he was about to ring the buzzer.

"Caden?" I ask.

"Anna? Sorry to just show up, I didn't have your number."

I lower the flashlight beam to the ground. "It's . . . not a problem."

At the gate, I key in the combination and stand back while

the doors do their thing. Soon, Caden and I are standing face to face, shrouded in darkness once again.

"Still restless?" he asks. I can feel him studying my face in the dark.

"I was going to take a walk," I hedge, not ready to admit my intended destination. It doesn't seem possible that I read things wrong at Windermere, but . . . I decide to just let this play out.

"I feel bad about the way things went down on Friday. I was in a weird space."

"It's okay. I get it."

"Do-over?" he asks, and I nod, probably too eagerly.

"I can't go far. But if you'll have me for company, we could hang out in the stable?" He steps through the open gates, onto the drive.

"Stable?" By now, I'm certain I've explored every inch of the Clovelly Cottage grounds, and there are definitely no horses.

"At Windermere. But it's faster if we cut through the trees, and less chance my mother will see us."

I let Caden lead the way back up the drive and across the grass. Inside the Bellamys' house, the lights in the family room have gone dark. We cut through the thick copse of trees where I watched Mrs. Talbot disappear on Sunday, flashlight beam bouncing across the ground in front of our feet. It may be pitch dark, but it's only nine o'clock, and again I'm reminded of Caden's curfew. Which maybe makes a bit more sense now that I know about Zoe. If your son's girlfriend vanished without a trace, you'd do everything you could to keep him close. Even if it was mostly for yourself. As twigs and pine needles snap and crack beneath our feet, it strikes me with a shiver that whatever or whoever came for Zoe last New Year's Eve probably has no respect for curfews or parental best intentions.

My mind flashes suddenly to an image of a girl who looks a lot like me, but out of focus, falling, body twisting in a long white party dress with a pale yellow sash. She's young, and a diminutive version of my features—or Zoe's—are frozen in terror on her face. I drop the flashlight to the ground, and the beam flickers out.

Caden stops. "Anna?"

I crouch down and scramble to put my hands on the flashlight in the dark, to make the image go away. My fingers find pine needles and rocks, my mind still snared by the vision or memory. Zoe falling from some great height. Zoe, dead.

Caden's standing over me, the light of his phone screen casting a watery glow on the woodsy floor. We spot the flashlight at the same time and both reach for it.

"I'm sorry," he says, as I draw my hand sharply back.

"No, I'm sorry." I grasp the flashlight and push myself up to standing. "You'd better take this." I hold it out to him. "Butterfingers."

Part of me burns to tell Caden what I just saw. But if I'm imagining things, I won't be doing myself any favors by spilling my "vision" to him. And if what I saw was somehow real, I'm not sure what that means. The possibilities range from unsettling to flat-out terrifying, so I shove them back into the dark where they belong.

The incident in the car yesterday, and now this. Something very creepy is going on with my brain, and a small voice at the back of my head says if I know what's good for me, I'll keep my thoughts to myself.

We start walking again, and in a minute, we're through the trees and standing in tall, unkempt grass. The few windows on this side of the estate are dark. Caden turns right and guides me along the edge of Windermere, back toward the grounds behind the house.

Soon, a barnlike structure that must be the stable comes into view. On the far side, I can see a riding pen. It's hard to be sure in the dark, but as we approach, something tells me this piece of Windermere is better cared for than the house itself.

Caden takes hold of the handle and swings a heavy wooden door wide. As if reading my mind, he says, "Charlie's the one person she lets on the grounds. Helps us with the horses. She loves to ride, but they need a lot of care."

We step inside the stable, and I look down to find Jake pressing against Caden's legs, tongue lolling happily to one side of his spaniel mouth. Caden reaches down to scratch the top of his head. My nostrils are flooded instantly with the sweet tang of hay, the rich, earthy scent of leather, and the smell of the horses themselves, which is distinctly animal. It smells like the country.

"This is Jackie O." Caden gestures toward the tall brown mare in the first stall. "And this is Pike." Pike is just a bit smaller, and his coat is a dappled white and gray. Caden reaches into Pike's stall to rub his nose, and I take a step back.

He watches me with amusement. "I thought all girls were into horses."

"Don't they teach you anything about not making binary assumptions at that fancy college of yours?" I ask.

Caden laughs. "My bad. But Pike's very friendly, promise."

I look around the rest of the stable. There are six stalls in all, but the other four appear to be empty. There's a locked door at the back, which is probably where they keep saddles and feed and whatever else gets stored in a horse stable. Both the top and bottom panels of the door to the last stall on the right are closed and latched. Caden heads back toward it, Jake on his heels, and in a minute, the bottom panel is open, and Caden is rustling around inside.

"Drink?" he asks, emerging with a bottle of whiskey and two cans of Coke.

I hesitate. "Just the Coke," I say finally. "I'm not really drinking right now."

He hands it to me, and I'm surprised to find the can is icy cold.

"You have a fridge back there?"

Caden grins. "Windermere can be . . . intense. My mother only ever comes out to ride in the mornings, so the stable's empty a lot. Sometimes I need a place to kick back."

I'm tempted to tell him about my run-in with Mrs. Talbot at Tom's birthday party. But things are actually not weird with Caden right now. Easy. Relaxed. Like they were that first night. I don't want to rock the boat. He closes the stall door and sits on the floor with his back against it. I follow suit across the aisle, cracking open my Coke, and Jake flops down on the stable floor between us. I can justify keeping quiet about Mrs. Talbot, but I do need to tell Caden about Zoe. That I know she was his girlfriend. *Is* his girlfriend? That I get why my sudden presence next door must have caught him off-guard.

I watch him take a long swig of soda, then pour a thin

stream of whiskey into the can. It's Glenlivet, the good stuff. Kaylee's always been more of a whiskey drinker than I have. I prefer tequila, gin, rum. He makes a few small circles with the can, mixing the whiskey in. My mouth waters slightly, and I tear my eyes away.

"I know about Zoe," I spit out before I can lose my nerve. Caden's eyes snap up to meet mine. "My first week here was a little strange. I got a few looks."

"I bet." Caden smiles thinly and takes a sip of his drink.

"But then I met Lou Jenkins at the ice-cream shop. He filled me in."

I watch the corners of Caden's mouth tug down. He reaches forward and ruffles his hand through Jake's fur.

"Not a fan?" I ask.

"I've got nothing against Lou. Or his ice cream. But his daughter's a bit much."

"I met her," I say. "Martina, right?"

"So you know about the podcast?"

"I've listened to most of it," I admit. "I have one episode left. Seems like she ran out of leads."

"Martina and everyone else." Caden takes another sip. "She wouldn't let up about interviewing me. Which, I get. But what did she think I was going to tell her that I hadn't already told police? She had this whole theory I was sitting on some critical piece of information. Believe me, if I knew something that could help find Zoe, I would have gone straight to the cops."

I raise the can to my lips and take a long, fizzy sip. I believe him.

"And it's not . . ." His voice trails off, gaze shifting to the can in his hands. It looks like he wants to say something else.

"Not what?" I prompt.

"Nothing. You wouldn't understand."

I shift against the stable floor, sitting up straight. "Try me?"

Caden presses his lips together and studies me, considering. "Any guy in a relationship with a missing girl is going to get looked at by the police. That's fine, they eliminated me from the investigation. But when you're black, you don't get eliminated by the public, no matter what the cops say. Martina's podcast . . . It doesn't matter that she tried to be careful, make it clear she didn't think I directly harmed Zoe. She planted the seed that I was suspicious, hiding things. It's easy enough to assume the boyfriend did it. But the black boyfriend?" He raises the can to his lips.

"Have people . . ." I swallow. Caden's right. I can't understand what the past few months must have been like for him. Sympathize, sure. But I'll always have my whiteness to shield me from the kind of scrutiny he can't escape.

"Been outwardly racist?" he finishes for me. I nod. "It's more like what people haven't done. Herron Mills fancies itself liberal. Woke. No one's going to come right out and accuse me to my face. But I've been home for weeks now. There hasn't exactly been a stream of visitors to check on my mom and me, see how we're doing. No one's going out of their way to extend their support, like they are to Zoe's family. I'm not saying it's Martina's fault; it would have happened anyway. But she definitely didn't help."

"I'm really sorry. That's so shitty, and—" I feel shame pooling in my stomach. That Caden had to spell it out for me.

"Anna. You don't have to apologize for them, or for listening to the podcast. It's fine." He takes another long swallow from his can.

"Okay. It's just, I feel like by being here, I'm making things even worse. I thought it was a bizarre coincidence, how much we look alike, but it turns out it's really not. Emilia let Paisley get involved in the hiring process. I'm sure I only got the job because of her."

Caden laughs, and the mood in the stable lifts, air particles rearranging. His laughter is light and warm like the first night. "Figures," he says. "Paisley loved Zoe. Zoe would bring her over here all the time when she was babysitting. When we were in high school, Paisley had the run of the Windermere grounds. She loved Jake and the horses and the pond out front. The place was in better shape then. My mom was in better shape."

I don't know what surprises me more: the vision of Windermere in all its glory or the knowledge that Paisley used to spend time here. A lot of time. But before I can dwell on either point, Caden surprises me again.

"We were engaged," he says. "Most people don't know that." He stares down into his drink. Jake lets out a very human-sounding sigh and readjusts himself on the stable floor. "I'm getting tired of guarding our secret. And you're not from around here, so."

"I won't tell," I promise.

"I like you, Anna. I'm sorry about last Friday. I didn't expect you to look so much like her. And those cookies . . ."

"What about the cookies?" My grip on the can tightens, and I'm glad to have something to hold on to.

"It was Zoe's signature recipe, peanut butter with all sorts of fancy jellies and jams. She used to bake all the time."

"Paisley suggested them," I breathe, thinking of the pink index card among its yellowed companions in the Bellamys' cream stone box. Zoe's recipe.

"Sure, makes sense. I overreacted." He reaches out to tap his can lightly against mine in a belated cheers. "No harm done."

"So you were engaged?" I ask, steering the topic away from my witless blunder and back to Caden's secret. A secret even Martina Green didn't seem to uncover.

"Since the summer after high school," he says. "Only my mother knew, and Zoe's little sister, Aster."

"We've met," I say. "She was hanging out with Martina in town last week."

Caden nods, then leans his head back against the stall door. A cloudy, unfocused look steals across his eyes. "It wasn't like we didn't want to tell people. After I proposed, after she said yes, I wanted to tell literally everyone. I thought I might explode with the secret. But we knew what people would think. We were so young, we still had four years of college ahead of us. We weren't planning to get married until after we graduated. But still, we knew people would either judge us for it or place all these expectations on our relationship. So we kept it private."

"Makes sense," I say. "Is it hard now?" I flinch and grip the can until the metal dents. "Sorry, that was a brainless question. Of course it's hard. What I mean is, do you wish people knew?"

"I think it's better," he says, the cloudy look gone from his eyes. He tilts the can back and drains the rest in one long gulp.

"I've already been cast as the grieving boyfriend or the most likely suspect, depending on who you ask. If people knew we were engaged, it would only raise the stakes, aim even more attention my way. It's like everyone's sure she's dead."

"But you're not?" I strain to keep my voice neutral.

"It's just a hunch," Caden says. "I don't know any more than anyone else, no matter what Martina thinks. But we were together for a long time. I don't have the first clue where Zoe went, or why. But if she were dead, I'd know. I'm sure of it." Jake's ears train back toward Caden, but he keeps his muzzle pressed between his paws.

There's a sharp insistence to Caden's words that cuts through the heartache. I drop my eyes to the stable floor. I want to believe him. That Zoe is still alive. That her disappearance is as much a mystery to Caden Talbot as it is to everyone else. I raise my eyes again, search for his, but he's not looking at me anymore. His eyes are closed and his jaw is set in a hard line. A muscle in his left cheek twitches once.

TRANSCRIPT OF *MISSING ZOE*
EPISODE FOUR: FAMILY TIES

[ELECTRONIC BACKGROUND MUSIC]

YOUNG MALE VOICE: The cops? Nah, never heard from them.

OLDER MALE VOICE: From the beginning, the police were nonchalant. They should have started looking right away.

YOUNG FEMALE VOICE: Maybe she has a whole new life, somewhere amazing.

[END BACKGROUND MUSIC]

MARTINA GREEN: Today, we're back with the fourth episode of *Missing Zoe*. Sorry I ghosted you for a few weeks there. To say that arranging the interviews for this episode has been a challenge would be an understatement. I have so much respect for the Spanos family, and I absolutely understand their reservations about speaking in a public way about Zoe's disappearance and the police investigation. But I'm glad they decided to participate in this conversation, and I'm so excited about what I have to share.

Today is Tuesday, March twenty-fourth, and it's been twelve weeks to the day since Zoe disappeared. Zoe Spanos is still missing. And we're missing Zoe.

[*MISSING ZOE* INSTRUMENTAL THEME]

GEORGE SPANOS: Eighty-two days. That's how long she's been gone. The longest we've ever gone without hearing from Zoe was maybe ten days, and that was during her first set of college finals. We used to talk every weekend. Sometimes she'd call again during the middle of the week, just to tell us some story that couldn't wait, or ask a question about oven temperatures or laundry.

ASTER SPANOS: Adulting.

GEORGE SPANOS: What?

ASTER SPANOS: That life stuff she was always asking you and Mom about. Zoe isn't always the best at that kind of thing.

MARTINA GREEN: On Friday, I spoke with Mr. George Spanos, Zoe's father, and Aster Spanos, Zoe's younger sister, in their Herron Mills home, Maple Grove. They both seemed tired, a little frayed around the edges. It was the end of a long week. Aster had just come home from swim practice; Mr. Spanos was still answering emails when I arrived. Zoe's mother, Ms. Joan Spanos, declined to be interviewed for this episode.

GEORGE SPANOS: From the beginning, the police were nonchalant. We cooperated with them fully, checking hospitals, friends' houses. Of course we did. But they should have started looking right away. It could have made a difference.

MARTINA GREEN: After the second episode aired, I received some questions from listeners about your interactions with Caden and

Meredith Talbot on the morning of January first. I stated that you called Caden that morning, and that he told you that he was still in New York City with his mother. Is that correct?

GEORGE SPANOS: It is. When we spoke, Caden told me that he had last corresponded with Zoe sometime in the afternoon of December thirty-first. He had been planning to meet her that night for the party at the Trainers' house, but Meredith was unwell. He let Zoe know that they'd be returning on the first instead.

MARTINA GREEN: And those messages were verified?

GEORGE SPANOS: Joan and I didn't see them, but we're told that Caden cooperated with police, and that the texts have been entered into evidence. I believe the detectives additionally have record of the Talbots' EasyPass transactions from January first. I really don't doubt Caden in this.

ASTER SPANOS: We just *love* Caden.

MARTINA GREEN: Was that sarcasm, Aster?

ASTER SPANOS: What? No. Forget it.

MARTINA GREEN: I'd really love to hear what you have to say.

ASTER SPANOS: Fine, it's just, I think you're right. What you said in your "boyfriend theory" episode. Even if Caden's story checks out—which, by the way, does no one else think it's odd that he didn't call or text Zoe at midnight?—I think they let him off too easy. It was New Year's. Did he really just sit around in his mom's friend's apartment all night? [PAUSE.] I don't know. Maybe Caden had nothing to do with this. But the fact of the matter is, Zoe has this whole world outside Herron Mills now. Did the police talk to anyone at Brown, or Yale? Did they even try to look at the big picture?

MARTINA GREEN: Aster raises an important point here about the lack of qualitative detective work undertaken by the Herron Mills PD during the course of their investigation. They seemed focused solely on the quantitative facts of that night—the GPS phone data, the missing boat, the Greyhound ticket purchase. I spoke again with Caden's friend Tim Romer and Zoe's former roommate, Kelly Ann Bate, to be sure.

TIM ROMER: The cops? Nah, never heard from them. Far as I know, they didn't come up to Yale. Caden's one of my best friends. We don't exactly have the best record when it comes to diversity and inclusivity here in New Haven. Cops asking questions, sniffing around the black kids on campus? It would've gotten back to me.

KELLY ANN BATE: No detectives came here, at least not that I'm aware of. It's not like she was anywhere near Brown when it happened, so I never gave it much thought. Campus was closed for break. But I guess you're right, her friends might know things about her life that could be relevant to police. Stuff from fall semester that could have shed some light on where Zoe went, if she did run away. Now that I think about it, it's strange that no one asked questions.

MARTINA GREEN: Unfortunate, yes, but maybe not that strange. Regrettably, as media coverage has shown time and again, it's not uncommon for three-dimensional detective work to slide or be deliberately eschewed when police are certain about a theory or suspect. I can't speak to the inner workings of the Herron Mills PD specifically, but based on the public cases I've studied, this kind of debilitating, narrow focus is shockingly common. I'll link to some examples in the show notes.

GEORGE SPANOS: They were convinced from the start that Zoe ran away.

MARTINA GREEN: That's George Spanos again.

GEORGE SPANOS: The Greyhound ticket, sure, it looks like she was planning to go somewhere. And I can't account for that. But Zoe had a good life. She was happy. She loved Brown, she had so many friends. Maybe she was a little bored at home over break. There isn't a whole lot going on in Herron Mills in the winter, and her boyfriend had been in the city all week. Maybe she was planning to visit someone in Philadelphia for a few days, and she just hadn't told us yet. It's possible. But stealing that boat? Running away? It's [BLEEP] absurd.

ASTER SPANOS: Dad.

GEORGE SPANOS: I'm sorry. I am. Joan and I, we've been doing our best to keep things together for twelve weeks now. We trusted the police to do their job—what else could we do? But under what circumstances would Zoe cut off all communication with us, with Caden, with her friends? Under what circumstances would she not withdraw any money from the bank, or use her credit card? We've kept the accounts open, just in case . . . in case she needs them. [MUFFLED SOBBING.]

MARTINA GREEN: Indeed, after twelve weeks, there has still been no activity on any of Zoe's accounts, which indicates that Zoe's abduction—if that is what happened—was not financially motivated.

GEORGE SPANOS: [CLEARS THROAT.] It is my deepest hope that my daughter is still alive. Zoe, if you're listening, if you did leave us willingly, it's okay. We're not angry with you. We just want to know you're okay.

But I think, at this point, we have to consider the alternative. Because if Zoe didn't run away, it means she's been abducted, or worse. And that person is still out there. [VOICE RISING.] If Holloway and Massey and the rest of them would do their [BLEEP BLEEP] jobs, we might all sleep a little easier. Because this isn't just about my daughter. This is about the safety of our entire community. [BLEEP.] I'm sorry. I think I have to stop.

MARTINA GREEN: I'm still at Maple Grove. Aster and I have relocated to her bedroom on the second floor. She's sitting on the edge of her bed and working a conditioning treatment into her hair.

ASTER SPANOS: There are things I can't say in front of my dad. Dad, if you're listening to this episode, which I honestly doubt, I'm sorry.

MARTINA GREEN: What kind of things?

ASTER SPANOS: What my dad said? About it being absurd that Zoe would run away? I don't think that's entirely true.

MARTINA GREEN: You think the police are right? That Zoe ran away?

ASTER SPANOS: I don't know. But last fall, she wasn't happy. Not like she was over the summer, when she was out in California. Not like she was last year. I don't think my parents noticed. Not anything against them, it's just Zoe was always cheerful on the phone. She put up a good front, but . . . When she came home for Thanksgiving, something wasn't right. She was just . . . off. She stayed in her room a lot, wouldn't tell me what was going on. It wasn't like her.

MARTINA GREEN: Was Caden home for Thanksgiving? Did Zoe spend time with him?

ASTER SPANOS: He was. Zoe went over to Windermere maybe twice that weekend. She swore nothing was wrong, but I'm her sister. I could tell.

MARTINA GREEN: You think something wasn't right in their relationship? That they were fighting, or having problems?

ASTER SPANOS: I never saw them fighting. Maybe it was something else entirely. She wouldn't talk to me about it. When she came home for winter break, she was quiet. She really loved

Christmas, always went totally overboard with baking cookies and making these super thoughtful presents. This year was no exception. So I can see why my parents thought everything was normal. But as soon as Christmas was over, she kind of retreated to her room again. She said she was getting a head start on the reading for this upper level course she was taking in the spring. Maybe she was.

MARTINA GREEN: While Assistant Detective Massey would not speak to me about the contents of Zoe's computer, which was searched in the days following her disappearance, the Herron Mills PD did return the laptop to the Spanos family, which serves as a strong indication that they didn't find anything relevant in her search history or files. If Zoe was devising an elaborate escape plan from her room in the days after Christmas, she left no trace of it on her laptop.

ASTER SPANOS: If I'm being really honest, I hope the police are right. I hope Zoe did run away.

MARTINA GREEN: Why's that?

ASTER SPANOS: Maybe she has a whole new life, somewhere amazing. Like, Buenos Aires or Monte Carlo. Don't get me wrong, I'd give her hell for doing this to us if she ever comes home. But consider the alternatives. If she didn't run away . . .

MARTINA GREEN: Aster and I concluded our conversation there. The point she raises is an interesting one. I've spent this entire podcast series pushing against the police's runaway theory.

And I think that's warranted—my thinking hasn't changed. But in a strange way, like Aster, I hope I'm wrong. I hope the police are right, and Zoe did simply, however implausibly, run away. That she has a fabulous new life now, and wherever she is, she's listening to this and laughing at all of us.

But I really don't think so.

If you have any information about Zoe Spanos, no matter how insignificant it may seem, please contact the tip line that has been set up by the Spanos family: 631-958-2757.

As for me, there are more interviews I'd like to conduct. More angles to this story that I'd like to explore. I'm not sure when our next episode will air, but you can be certain I haven't stopped digging. Until next time, I'm Martina Green, and this is *Missing Zoe.*

[CODA TO *MISSING ZOE* INSTRUMENTAL THEME]

July

Herron Mills, NY

JUNE MELTS INTO July without warning. The week unspools, each day a glistening pearl on an invisible thread: sunny and bright, but not too hot. Perfect. On Wednesday, we post up at our usual spot at the beach. While Paisley collects shells, my mind travels back to the night before with Caden in the Windermere stable. Before I made my way back to Clovelly Cottage, we exchanged numbers. Those ten little digits burn in my phone. I stretch out under the umbrella and think about texting him, but I can't come up with anything good to say.

By Thursday, Paisley's itching to go somewhere new, so we drive to a giant water park not too far from the aquarium. Emilia grants us permission to miss family dinner, so we stay at the park all day and fill up on popcorn chicken strips and cheesy fries on the boardwalk before dragging ourselves back to the car, exhausted, when the park closes at six.

I'm in my pj's and about to open the book I've been reading at the beach—a story that's set half in New York City and half in the world of a dark, ruthless fairy tale—when my phone chimes.

Movie night?

I entered him into my phone as CT. Not Caden, or something cute like Boy Next Door. Just CT. As if a part of me knows he shouldn't be there. Not when his heart belongs to Zoe, and with Zoe still missing.

You want to go into town? What's
playing?

I've seen the little Herron Mills movie theater, but haven't yet been inside. The temperatures are sure to spike into the nineties before long, and then Paisley and I will find our way there for whatever Disney and Pixar are offering up this summer.

More like stay in than go out.

My fingers hover over my phone screen. I'm sure Caden assumes I have a laptop, but I don't. A computer for college is at the top of the list of things I'm saving up for this summer. I'm trying to figure out what to say when his next message appears.

> There's a film room downstairs
> at Windermere. Come over
> same way as last time and I'll
> meet you around back.

Ten minutes later, I'm dressed and stomping through the trees again. Tonight, there are no cryptic visions of girls in white dresses or clutching fingers of panic. It's not even dark yet; the sky beneath the branches is laced with shadow, but the last dregs of sunshine still filter through. My brain is focused on more mundane concerns: If this is a date. If I want it to be.

Caden meets me at the edge of the trees with a sheepish grin.

"Sorry about the uninspired destination," he says. "I know it's not the same as going into town, but I can offer a massive selection of horror and classic musicals on Blu-ray."

"Horror and old musicals?" I ask, following him through the tall grass that surrounds Windermere toward a large stone patio. The area has been recently weeded, and the patio furniture looks wiped down and somewhat new, unlike the haphazard array of rocking chairs and end tables gathering cobwebs on the small front porch. The contents of Caden's summer days are still largely a mystery to me, but it's clear he's been plugging away at projects around the estate, probably whatever he can manage without engaging Mrs. Talbot's attention.

"I like movies that capture human extremes. There's something equally fascinating about big song and dance numbers and gratuitous displays of gore."

"That is very weird," I say.

"Welcome to my brain."

Caden unlocks the back door and swings it wide. I hold my breath and brace myself for more birds and their detritus, but the room in front of me is surprisingly airy and clean. It's a parlor or living room of some sort, sparsely furnished with a couch, coffee table, and bookshelves that aren't exactly new, but definitely aren't antiques like the pieces that populate the front hall. To my left, I can see what looks like a kitchen through a pass-through in the wall.

"Servants' quarters," Caden says, answering my thoughts. "Or they were at one time. This wing of the house has been pretty much out of use for a couple generations." I spot a thick stack of library books and an empty Coke can on the coffee table. *From Slavery to Freedom*; *A People's History of the United States*; *Women, Race, and Class*; *The Grey Album*. Looks like Caden has been turning the unused wing into a library this summer.

"No Jake?"

Caden shrugs. "He's sleeping upstairs, I think. This way." He motions me toward a waist-high gate cordoning off a narrow spiral staircase at the back of the servants' parlor / reading room, then leans over to undo the latch. As he holds the gate open, I peer down. There's a railing, but the stairs look a bit perilous. I straighten up and press my palm against the wall, floor heaving up at me in waves at the base of the stairs.

"You go first," I say.

"Not a fan of heights?"

"Not so much."

"Sorry, wish there was an elevator or something, but this is it." Caden starts down the stairs, not even bothering to hold the rail.

"I'll be fine," I say through gritted teeth. I keep one hand pressed against the wall and the other firmly attached to the railing and look straight ahead as I make my way down.

When I reach the bottom, my breath hitches in my throat. Caden wasn't kidding about this being a film room. Instead of the flat screen I expect to find hanging before me, there's a real movie screen. Caden presses a button on the wall, and a digital projector extends slowly from the ceiling. Six rows of vintage-looking theater seats with red velvet cushions are bolted to the floor, and along one wall is the largest display of Blu-rays I've ever seen. Tucked in a back corner is a half-used roll of paper towels and a bucket of cleaning supplies. The air smells faintly of antiseptic. Caden cleaned for me.

"Wow. This is seriously fancy."

"My dad designed it," Caden says. "There's a whole closet filled with film reels, but the projector's busted. He was a huge movie buff. My parents used to hold screenings here, invite all their friends."

I close my eyes, try to imagine a different Windermere. Grand, bustling, filled with people. "That must have been really cool."

Caden shrugs. "They used to do all sorts of entertaining at Windermere. The screenings were small, but my parents were known for throwing these legendary parties. The whole town would come, plus friends from the city. But I barely remember any of that."

"Why's that?" I ask, walking over to examine the wall of Blu-rays. In addition to the promised profusion of musicals and horror, there's everything from recent comedies and Marvel movies to a large selection of biopics and a limited edition Lord of the Rings box set.

"Dad died when I was five. I guess my mom didn't feel much like entertaining after that."

"Oh right." I can't remember if Caden told me that his dad died from stomach cancer or if I heard it on one of Martina's podcasts. I press my lips between my teeth, trying to trace the information back to its source before I say something I have no right to know. "Yeah, that makes sense."

I think back to the stack of library books on the coffee table upstairs. "Was it weird?" I blurt out before I can stop myself. "Growing up here with white parents?"

"Huh." Caden flops down in the back row and props his feet up on the seat in front of him. "What made you ask that?"

"It's just, it's not very diverse." I gesture around the film room, but I mean all of Herron Mills. "Like you were saying the other night."

At home in Brooklyn, my friends and I talk about race and class stuff a lot. Students of color make up well over half of our high school, and none of us are even close to rich. But this feels different from talking to my friends. Maybe because Caden and I aren't much more than strangers. Maybe because of what he told me in the stable. Maybe because he's a boy, and instead of flirting, getting him to buy me drinks, telling myself I don't care when his hands rove like clumsy mitts across my skin, I actually want to get to know him.

"Well," he says slowly, "in retrospect, yes. Now, I can't not be constantly aware of the whiteness and privilege here. Even before Zoe disappeared, it could be suffocating. But when I was little, I didn't understand a lot about being biracial." I abandon the wall of movies and perch on a seat two rows up, back turned toward the screen so I can face him. "My birth mom's white; she was seventeen when I was born. Birth dad's black, but they didn't stay together. So even though it was an open adoption, he's not in my life.

"And Mom didn't really know how to teach me about black culture. She was a great parent, don't get me wrong. Her health wasn't always like it is now. But yeah, it was weird. There was a lot I didn't understand growing up about race, from either a personal or a cultural perspective. A lot of experiences I'm still putting into context."

"Is it different at Yale?"

"Different, yeah. But Yale's a weird place. New Haven is only thirty percent white and over sixty percent African American and Latino. But at Yale, under six percent of the students are black. When you're black, you feel that tension."

I nod slowly, remembering what his friend Tim Romer said on the podcast about police sniffing around black kids on campus. Then I think how weird it is that I know things about Caden's life that he hasn't told me, how invasive, and I keep my mouth shut.

"How are your parents taking it?" Caden asks, changing the subject. "You nannying out here for the summer?"

"My mom was pretty weird about it at first. Took her a bit, but she seems to be adjusting to her baby being away." I grin. "Haven't seen my dad since I was four, so I doubt he cares."

"Mmm, No Dad Club." Caden smiles thinly.

"Yeah, guess so."

"Cut your mom some slack," he says. "You her only?"

"Yeah."

He shrugs, and I know he's thinking about his own mother, his decision to spend the summer here, when I'm sure he could be off doing some amazing internship or studying abroad or whatever other Yalies do for the summer.

"Speaking of moms," I say, reaching behind me to twist my hair into a thick rope down the center of my back, "I met yours last weekend."

Caden raises his eyebrows. This is awkward, but if we're going to be friends, I don't want Mrs. Talbot lurking between us like an unpleasant secret. Might as well rip the Band-Aid off.

"During Tom's birthday party, she stopped over to tell me to stay away from you."

Caden clasps his hands behind his head and lets out a long sigh. "So she did see you that night," he says. "When you brought the cookies. I thought I saw her looking out her window while we were walking up the drive."

My mouth twists into a lopsided frown.

"It's okay," he says. "The thing you have to understand about my mother is, she loved Zoe. They were really, really close. And Mom has schizophrenia; she was diagnosed in her twenties. No one knows exactly how schizophrenia develops, but since there are likely genetic factors, my parents decided to adopt. Anyway, she has great doctors and she's been on a treatment plan my whole life, but when Zoe disappeared, her negative symptoms spiked big time."

I'm quiet a minute, letting that all sink in. I don't know a lot about schizophrenia, except that it can be very serious and difficult to treat. "That sounds really hard."

"It can be," Caden says. "I love my mom. She's a really wonderful woman. She's also really difficult to live with. And Windermere . . ." His voice trails off, and he looks around the film room. "We needed small repairs, painting, when I was in high school. She kept putting it off. She stopped letting anyone on the grounds when I moved to New Haven. And then she got the birds. I was so into my life at college, I guess I just ignored it my first year. I wanted to pretend everything was fine at home, she was fine. But by last Christmas, it was getting hard to ignore. And when Zoe disappeared, things escalated."

"That's why you're home."

"That's why I'm home." Caden unclasps his hands and lets them fall into his lap. "So, Anna Cicconi, now that we've covered every inch of my life, tell me something about yours."

He's right, I've been doing nothing but asking personal questions all evening. It's almost nine, and we haven't even picked out a movie yet. Before I can steer things back toward the Blu-ray wall, though, I need to give him something in return. A piece of my past. A little bit of truth about the girl I've been.

"Before I came out here, I wasn't exactly in control of my life. Remember the other night in the stable, I told you I was taking a break from drinking?"

He nods.

"My friend Kaylee and I, we spent most of last semester partying. I was fucking up a lot, and I kind of started to hate myself. The person I was when I was drinking."

"And who was that?" Caden asks. I take a deep breath, debating how much to show him. I might be killing any chance of us getting together, if that was ever even a possibility. But more than a boyfriend, I realize I want a friend. Someone my age, who I can talk to. Someone who might understand something about living with a past that's hard to let go.

"The old me? She hooked up with guys she didn't remember the next morning. Blacked out. Woke up on strangers' couches. Got brought home in the back of a cop car on more than one occasion." I pause, waiting for him to say something. Judge me. "My friend Starr, she's been on her own since she was sixteen. I used to think I wanted what she had, total freedom." I shrug. "But freedom gets old. My mom works two jobs. She doesn't have time to babysit me. I think part of me was just trying to get her attention."

"And did it work?"

"Not really." I laugh. "But I got sick of myself."

"And that's why you're here?" he asks, throwing my earlier question back at me.

"When you're in charge of a kid, you can't screw up. So far, I'm keeping it together." *Barely*, I almost add. I don't say the other thing, the thing he knows already. That in a twisted way, I'm here because of Zoe. But there's no point in dwelling on that. No matter why I got the job, the fact is, I'm good at it, most of the time. I'm going to be good at college too. I can feel it. I've been out here less than two weeks. There's still plenty of time to become a new person.

"I believe in you, Anna Cicconi," he says, using my full name again. I smile. "Now, are you feeling more haunted house, possessed child, witches, or slasher?"

"Um, maybe we should save scary movies for another night? I'm kind of in the mood for something light."

"Good call," he says. "This did get a bit deep." He leaps up from his seat and deftly pulls several movies from the wall. I review the options—a mix of musicals and comedies—and land on *Singin' in the Rain*.

"Solid choice," he commends, then gets the tech set up in

the back. Soon, the MGM lion fills the screen, and Caden slips into the seat beside me. I kick off my shoes and pull my knees up to my chest, very aware of his hand on the armrest between us. He keeps it there for the entire film, doesn't make a single move to brush it against my arm or curl his fingers toward mine. If things were different, I might be disappointed. He's cute, and smart, and weird in a good way.

But he's also very much not available. Not really. I remind myself that his fiancée is missing. He's home taking care of his mother, who has a serious mental illness. What Caden needs is a friend, not a summer fling. And the new Anna wants more than that too. I'd be lying if I said I didn't want to slip my hand over his on the armrest, rest my head in the dip between his neck and shoulder. But I think this is the start of a real connection, not some hookup. I keep my arms wrapped tight around my knees and resolve to keep the boundaries firm between us.

That night, I dream I'm back at Windermere again. The estate glimmers in moonlight, ethereal and grand. The walls are free of vines and the sturdy columns that stretch from the ground to the third-floor balcony extend like pale white pillars toward the sky. No peeling paint. No dust or cobwebs to sully the rocking chairs on the front porch. The grass is manicured and lush with the glistening residue of late afternoon rain, and in the front of the property, shielded from the road by a stately and freshly trimmed hedge, is the koi pond. Their lithe orange and white bodies gleam just below the surface, then vanish, swift and stealthy, far into the water's black depths.

I'm looking down on the estate from above, and then I'm on

the balcony, sitting all the way at the edge, legs pressed through the wooden rails and dangling down, down in the night. In the dream, the height doesn't scare me at all. My fingers dance across the top of the railing like it's a set of piano keys.

I'm not alone. On the balcony next to me sits a girl, a year or two older, with olive skin and the same unbridled mane of thick black hair spilling down her back. She wears a dress so yellow it's almost gold, and one gold sandal dangles from the tips of her toes.

"You're going to lose that," I hear myself saying.

She laughs, and the sound shimmers in the summer night. Her head tilts back until I can see her teeth flash, two rows of pearls in the moonlight. My eyes travel down to the bright golden gleam of the initials *ZS* dangling against the birthmark on her collarbone. She swings her leg, one swift kick, and releases her sandal into the sky. It rises in a hasty arc, then surges soundlessly to the thick carpet of grass below.

When I draw my eyes back to the balcony, I'm alone. I glance down at my body, and a gold-yellow dress now hugs my skin where shorts and a worn T-shirt used to be. One of my feet is bare, and suddenly the ground seems very far below. I draw my legs back through the slats in the balcony railing and pull my knees in to my chest.

I wake with a jolt, grope for my phone.

It's almost three. After a few minutes of staring at the ceiling, eyes adjusting to the darkness, I know I'm not going to get back to sleep. I swing my legs over the side of the bed, grab my hoodie, then make my way out of the cottage and onto the pool deck.

Night-lights dance along the water's edge. It's cool out here, but not uncomfortable. Curled up on one of the loungers, I pull up Messenger, open my latest exchange with Starr. Still no reply. I start to type.

> Thinking about you tonight. What do the stars look like from the Magic Kingdom? ☆

A drink would help me get back to sleep. I crane my neck, stare behind me through the windows into the Bellamys' dark kitchen. Almost as much as I want a drink, I want to know more about Zoe. But I'm all out of podcast episodes, and I'm not sure what's left to google. I open up Instagram and type her name into the search. Her profile is still up, but the photos stop in December. Scrolling backward, it's mostly landscape shots of the beach in winter, then Providence in the fall, bright bursts of changing leaves and Zoe's startled reflection captured in a puddle. Further back to California, tangerine sunsets and seagulls soaring above a marina. I have to scroll back to last spring to find many pictures of Caden, but there they are, the two of them together at Yale, then at Brown, faces glowing in selfie after selfie. I click out of the app.

Fighting sleep, I open Google and search for Windermere. There's more than I expected to find. Apparently it's been landmarked by the Herron Mills Village Historical Society, so there are a couple articles on the estate over the generations, a blog run by a Hamptons history buff with a small entry on Windermere including some cool memorabilia like a photograph of an invitation to a ball on the grounds in 1906 and photos of the house in 1927 and again in 1968.

An image search pulls up a couple more recent photos, from the early 2000s. This is what the house would have looked like when Caden was growing up there. It looks fresh, vibrant, like it did in my dream.

My eyes shutter closed, and soon I'm drifting off again, back to the Windermere balcony, back to the dream. This time, Caden is with me. He's sitting behind me on the balcony, sliding his arms around my waist. His lanky legs are bent on either side of my body. With fingers that feel like cotton candy or clouds, he brushes my tangle of hair to one side and rests his chin on my shoulder.

His lips brush my neck, feathery at first, then more insistent. I let my spine relax into his chest, tilt my head until my lips find his. Soft and warm with the night air. We fit together, new and familiar all at once. His fingers move from my hair to my shoulder, then play lightly across my throat, down to my collarbone. They stop. He pulls away, eyes fixed on the bare gleam of my chest, above the neckline of my camisole. Instinctively, my fingers rise to meet my skin, travel like soft brush bristles across it.

"Your necklace," he says. "It's gone."

And then Caden is gone too, and I'm alone on the balcony again. Behind me, vines start creeping up the shingles. A crack appears along one windowpane. I grasp for the railing in front of me, but the wood is pulpy and rotten. It disintegrates beneath my touch, and I pitch forward, gasping. I think I'm going to fall, but just then, a flock of ravens descends, the force of their wing beats driving me backward, away from the edge. I roll over, curl into myself. The first sharp jab of a beak meets my flesh.

13

September

Herron Mills, NY

You need to stop.

Martina is in class. Her phone should be in her locker, not in her backpack, and her backpack certainly shouldn't be open beneath her desk, barely concealing the glowing screen. But she can't be disconnected right now. It's physically impossible. Her entire body is buzzing; the world online suddenly more real and vividly alive than anything happening within the Jefferson walls. She almost skipped school today, but Mami would have killed her—metaphorically, obviously metaphorically—and then what use would she be to anyone? Realistically, Mami would have grounded her, taken her phone. A fate much worse than sitting through Mr. Cohu's 9:00 a.m. lecture on the Crimean War.

Her eyes stay fixed on the text, its four words a caution or threat. The fifth episode of *Missing Zoe* posted yesterday afternoon—the first in nearly six months, the first since Zoe is no longer missing. But her death remains a mystery, now even more than when her body was found in August. Because Anna's role in it no longer seems to fit quite so neatly, just as Martina has been suspecting since Anna confessed. And now everyone knows the truth about how little Anna really remembers from that night—in Anna's own words.

The episode covered a lot of ground, everything from the discovery of Zoe's body in Parrish Lake on up to the autopsy bombshell last week. Martina included audio from interviews with multiple sources, as she always does, but it's the interview with Anna that's been getting all the buzz. Suddenly, *Missing Zoe* has skyrocketed from a modest 300 average downloads per episode to 7,700 downloads of Episode Five alone.

It's been less than twenty-four hours. Martina can't stop checking her stats. People are still downloading, talking, reblogging. Her audience is no longer limited to her Jefferson classmates, her neighbors in Herron Mills, the people who have grown reticently accustomed to her podcasting efforts over the seven months since the police stopped looking and she started digging. Suddenly, strangers are listening. Nationwide. And they're going back and listening to the series from the beginning.

Martina's mentions are exploding with tags in strangers' opinion pieces and hot takes and theories. Anna Cicconi has been incarcerated for six weeks, and the interview with Martina is the first she's given. She's had a few days to process it, but now it's really hitting: Martina got an exclusive with Zoe's confessed killer. And that interview is changing the way people are thinking about Anna, thinking about the case. She's innocent at best, a calculating liar at worst. Perhaps much worse than the accidental killer she confessed to being.

The interview is inviting acclaim and vitriol in equal measure, which people feel the need to express to Martina directly. In addition to her Twitter feed, people are finding their way into her inbox, her DMs, her texts. Mostly, she's been ignoring them. Well, reading, but not responding. It's not like she could write back even if she wanted to; until three fifteen, she's trapped inside Jefferson. But this latest text is harder to ignore. Because it's from Anna's friend Kaylee. Before she can think of an appropriate response, the texts start up again.

> What the hell were you thinking? Her
> lawyers are flipping the fuck out. Her
> mom too.

> Anna's still not telling the truth about
> NYE. WE WERE NEVER IN HERRON MILLS.
> WE'VE NEVER MET ZOE.

> Get that through your head. This
> interview isn't helping.

Martina takes a deep breath and zips her backpack all the way closed before she gets caught. What was she thinking? She was thinking that Anna hasn't gotten a voice, not since the police took that half-assed confession filled with "I must haves" and "maybes" and "I don't remembers." She was thinking that if Anna is convicted for a lesser crime—or for crimes she didn't commit at all—Zoe's family won't get justice, not really. Either she'll get off too easy, or the Spanoses will get to see *someone* locked away, but not the right someone. And that's not justice at all.

But she was also thinking about herself, her resolve to find the truth, her piss-poor PSAT scores, and the half-complete application to NYU saved on her laptop. For the first time since she spoke to Anna, she allows herself to consider the teensy, tiny possibility that the interview could hurt Anna's case. Maybe she should have advised Anna to listen to her lawyers, keep her head down. Maybe she was only being selfish. The prosecution might twist Anna's words, use them against her. Airing the interview felt right, but maybe it was also just a bit irresponsible. Maybe Martina was thinking more about herself than she was about Anna.

The day inches forward, the dismissal bell still hours away. By lunch, Episode Five has hit fifteen thousand downloads, almost doubling in the three hours since Martina slid into her seat in AP Euro. Her classmates are talking about her, but that's nothing new. The whole country is talking about her. Martina lets the rapidly escalating download count ease her doubts: The interview is bringing new, much-needed attention to the case. Airing it was the right thing to do.

Her high is brought to a crashing low when Aster slams her cafeteria tray down on the table in front of her. Her swim-toned muscles spark like live wires beneath her skin. "I can't believe you."

Martina inhales the bite of turkey sandwich she'd been chewing, eyes glazing with tears. "What?" she sputters, half voice and half cough.

"Don't 'what' me. You know what." Her best friend sounds convincingly like Mami.

"I thought . . ." Martina's face is twisted with hurt and confusion. "Things are finally moving forward. We're actually getting somewhere, for the first time."

"Fuck that," Aster says. "Suddenly everyone's sympathetic toward Anna? She confessed, and now she's just taking it all back. Because of you."

People are staring. Martina feels their eyes on the back of her neck. She lowers her voice.

"I didn't tell her what to say. You saw the autopsy report. That story Anna told police wasn't real, Aster. It couldn't have happened that way."

Aster stiffens in her seat on the cafeteria bench. Her cheeks are flushed red. Martina notices with a start that the gold hoop earrings she gave Aster sophomore year—the earrings she never takes off except to swim and sleep—are gone, her best friend's ears naked in the fluorescent cafeteria light. The message is clear: *Fuck you.*

"It doesn't mean she didn't do it," Aster says. "Some other way."

"I agree!" Martina almost shouts. She kept her role in the interview unbiased, she knows she did. If people came out of the episode thinking Anna is innocent, that's the conclusion they're drawing. She didn't lead them one way or the other.

"Doesn't seem that way," Aster spits.

Martina doesn't know what to say. She thought Aster would get it. The release of the autopsy report, Anna's admission that she doesn't remember what happened that night, they're both steps in the right direction. The direction that leads toward uncovering the truth, whatever that truth might be.

"I'm sorry," she says finally. "I just want justice for your family."

"And how's that going to happen now?" Aster spits. "Anna's going to get off."

"What if she didn't do it, Aster?" Martina's voice is one notch above a whisper and one notch below a hiss. "Don't you want to know who did?"

Aster gives Martina an exasperated glare. "Because the police are following so many other leads. There are so many killers lurking in the shadows of Herron Mills." Her fingers grip the edge of the table between them. "If Anna gets off, that's it. Don't you get it? She's using the autopsy to generate doubt. She probably lied about how Zoe died from the beginning, on purpose. Because she knew the results would come back and disprove what she said. She's playing you, Martina. She's manipulating all of us."

Martina is shocked into silence. She doesn't believe what her best friend is saying, that Anna is running some kind of long con. That this is all part of a master plan. But what is abundantly clear is that Aster believes it. Her whole family must believe it. Because Aster is right about one thing—there are no other suspects, no other leads. Not yet anyway. If Anna is released, it doesn't guarantee justice will be served. But now, maybe the police will broaden the investigation. Maybe they'll look closer at Anna—and beyond her too. The prospect of a wrongful conviction seems like the worst possible outcome, and it's more likely now that won't happen.

For the first time, she realizes her friend doesn't see it that way. Anna has become the Spanos family's only hope. For answers, truth, justice. It doesn't make sense; they're not thinking clearly. But that's what's happening. She's read Aster's behavior all wrong in the week since the autopsy results came back. The withdrawn looks at school, the texts she hasn't responded to, the claims she's too busy to hang out. Aster hasn't been mulling over what the report might mean in the same way that Martina has. She's been fuming. Because she's *sure* Anna's lying. And now she thinks Martina has turned the public's sympathy toward Anna, snatched justice away from them.

Martina is silent for a long time. Her appetite is gone. She chews absently on the tip of her long ponytail, a nervous childhood habit she hasn't indulged in years. Before she can come up with something, anything to say, she looks across the table and realizes that Aster is gone.

14

THEN

July

Herron Mills, NY

THE SUN WAKES ME early Friday morning. I'm still out by the pool, where I must have fallen asleep, and my thigh is red and sore where a long splinter from the lounge chair jabbed through my skin in the night. I'm barely out of the shower and dressed when Emilia knocks on the door of the pool house to remind me that Paisley's leaving in an hour and we need to finish getting her ready for her trip.

My mind spins. *Paisley's trip?*

I play along until I get to the main house. When Emilia ducks into her office, I casually ask Paisley where she's going. It turns out she's spending the Fourth in the Catskills with the Paulson-Gosses, and I'm going to have a few days off over the holiday weekend. I try to act unsurprised, but Paisley is clearly onto me.

"We talked about it at MoMA," she whispers. "And Mom went through the summer schedule last week, remember?"

"Sure." I grin, a flimsy disguise. "I just forgot which weekend, that's all."

Forty minutes later, I'm standing out front with Emilia, getting Paisley settled in the van with Raychel, Kyle, and their moms and wondering what I'm going to do with myself for almost four whole days. Paisley doesn't return until Monday night. It's more time than I know what to do with. When Emilia has checked Paisley's luggage for sunscreen and vitamins for the third time, Elizabeth clears her throat and assures her that Paisley will be fine, that they'll call when they get there. Emilia relents and presses the button on the van door. We both wave as Hilary navigates around the fountain and down the Clovelly Cottage drive.

Back inside, I lean against the soapstone counter in the kitchen, helping myself to a yogurt from Emilia's breakfast spread and accidentally eavesdropping on her phone conversation with Tom. They're spending Saturday and Sunday in Amagansett with friends, something I was also supposed to know. She wants him to leave the office early, try to beat the holiday weekend rush. My mind trips back to last Friday, to Tom's car parked in front of the Coopers' house two hours before he joined us for dinner. I'd forgotten all about that, but now I wonder what time he usually gets home for the weekend.

I rinse out my bowl in the sink and wander out to the pool deck. My fingers twitch against my phone in my back pocket, but it's too early to text Caden. It hasn't even been a full twelve hours since I left the film room. *Since we kissed*, I catch myself thinking. But Caden didn't kiss me. It felt so real, but that was definitely my imagination running wild. I press my fingers into my temples. Much as I want to see him again, I could probably use a little break from Windermere. A day to clear my head. Maybe I'll take a swim. Read my book. Walk into town with my sketchbook and post up on a bench for a while.

Before I can decide, two things happen at once: my phone vibrates, and Emilia calls out to me from inside the house. "Anna, package!"

My new clothes. I hurry through the main house, to the front door, to collect the box from the UPS driver.

Back in the pool house, I try on everything I ordered. Three sundresses and a long blue skirt, all featuring pockets. Two new tops. Two floppy sun hats. I'm so wrapped up in my own private fashion show, I forget about my unread text until my phone buzzes again.

> Forgot to tell you we're away this
> weekend. Mom's friends in the city.

> Movie night was fun, let's do it again
> when we're back.

Huh. I stare down at the screen, disappointment unfurling slowly inside my chest.

> Absolutely. Have fun!

Who leaves the Hamptons to go to the city for the Fourth? Suddenly these four days of freedom seem unbearably long. My phone pings again.

Unlikely. 🙃

I hang my new dresses in the closet and decide a trip into town is what I need. I'll do some sketching, maybe grab lunch at that sushi place Martina and Aster mentioned last week. Make a day of it.

I'm on the last chapter of my book and three bites into my tuna avocado roll when my phone lights up. I lift it from the table, hoping for an update from Caden, maybe even news that they're not leaving until tomorrow, but no such luck.

Guess where I am.

I take the bait.

Brighton Beach boardwalk, the cafe
with the black and white checkered
tablecloths. 🌞

Kaylee's reply is a selfie. I squint to make sense of the background. Train seat, flash of green outside the window. Definitely not the subway. She's on the LIRR.

I get into Bridgehampton at
2:15. Pick me up.

It's not a question. Christ, I didn't even remember I had the Fourth off. But suddenly our conversation comes flooding back: Emilia must have told me during the interview, just like Paisley said, because when Kaylee was reaming me out for taking this job, I mentioned this weekend, dangled it like an olive branch. The memory was there, and then gone. And now it's back again. My stomach does a little flip.

My mind has been a jumble these past few weeks, but Kaylee's is a steel trap when it comes to promises. She could have texted me to confirm, but why ruin the surprise? I grimace into my miso soup and wonder how long she's planning to stay.

Two hours later, I'm parked in the station lot in Emilia's car, waiting for Kaylee's train. I apologized profusely to Emilia for the last-minute houseguest, but she was thankfully distracted by her own weekend plans and didn't seem to care as much as I thought she might. Then again, she hasn't met Kaylee.

When the train pulls in at 2:24, I find myself white-knuckling the steering wheel, even though the car is turned off. Maybe it's better I didn't know she was coming. I would have spent all week being anxious; instead, all that anxiety has been compressed into the last two hours. Without Kaylee, responsibility hasn't exactly come easy, but I've been managing. Doing my best. Who will I be with her here to remind me? I grit my teeth and throw open the car door.

I hear Kaylee almost before I see her. "Excuse me, coming through, on a mission here." She's jostling through a crowd of people at the mouth of the ramp, amber-gold strands of waist-length hair flying out behind her, purple duffle as big as she is slung over one shoulder. It came with my suitcase. Kaylee borrowed it for a school trip in ninth or tenth grade, and it became part of her permanent collection.

She's wearing a tiny pair of white shorts and a bright orange bandeau tank that shows off her sun-bronzed arms and a neon green belly ring. That's new. She stops abruptly in the middle of the ramp, forcing her fellow travelers to part around her in a sea of grumbles. Her hand shoots into the air in a frantic wave, as if I could have possibly missed her. "Anna!"

"Hey, Kaylee!" I force my lips to part into a big toothy grin and wave back. "Come on, you're holding up the show."

She rushes the rest of the way down the ramp, and before I know what's happening, Kaylee is wrapped around me in a tangle of arms and hair and summer breeze body mist. I stiffen for just a beat, then let my body sink into the familiar comfort of my best friend. I can't help it. Despite everything, I've missed her.

If Kaylee's still mad at me, she doesn't let on. From her perch in the passenger's seat, she fills me in on everything I've missed over the past two weeks, which isn't a whole lot. She got her belly button pierced on the day I left, a graduation present to herself. I'm a little bit jealous. Kaylee's eighteen already. I've never really minded being the baby of our class, but I won't turn eighteen until almost the end of my first semester of college. It's not that I want a neon belly ring specifically, but I wouldn't mind getting a tattoo at the end of the summer. Something to commemorate my time in Herron Mills, or the start of fall. My new leaf.

As I navigate slowly through the increasing crush of holiday weekend traffic, Kaylee chatters on about Mike's current hookup and this new Hawaiian-themed bar that's going in on Seventy-Fourth and Fifth. I wonder if an autumn leaf would be too clichéd, maybe on my ankle?

"Turn here," Kaylee says, pointing toward an upcoming side road. She has her phone out, directions pulled up on the screen. Her silver hoop earrings flash in the sun.

"Where are we going?" I ask, but I'm already making the turn.

"Supply run. There's a liquor store in point five miles."

I narrow my eyes behind my sunglasses but keep driving. Starr used to keep us stocked in booze before she moved, but we don't have Starr or her ID here in the Hamptons.

"They're gonna card. It's a holiday weekend."

"It'll be fine," Kaylee says. "You worry too much."

And Kaylee doesn't worry nearly enough, but I figure if they do card us, it won't be the worst thing. Let Kaylee be mad at the store. We'll just have to figure out some boozeless activity to keep us occupied.

Suddenly, Kaylee is tugging on my sleeve. "Pull over, pull over!"

I hit the brakes and steer us to the side, startled. The car behind me honks, then swerves around us while I fumble with Emilia's hazards. Kaylee flings her door open and leaps onto the sidewalk.

"Becca, holy shit!" She wraps her arms around a petite Chinese girl with a nose ring and hot pink streaks in her hair. She's standing on the sidewalk with a lanky white guy in a possibly ironic muscle shirt and board shorts. They're both carrying shopping bags. "When did this *happen*?" Kaylee squeals, releasing the girl from her hug and running her fingers through her hair.

I join them on the sidewalk, and the girl introduces her boyfriend to us as Zeb. "I'm Anna." I stick out my hand to Zeb, then offer it to the girl.

She giggles and raises a hand to cover her mouth. "I remember," she says.

Kaylee narrows her eyes at me. "You remember Becca, right? Her hair was blue in the winter."

I squint at the girl's face. Becca. She doesn't look remotely familiar. "Sure," I say. "It looks so different with the pink."

Becca giggles again, and Zeb says something about having to get the groceries back to their beach house before the ice cream melts. Kaylee promises to text Becca later, and soon we're back in Emilia's car, en route to the liquor store.

"I don't remember her," I confess to Kaylee. "How do you—?"

"Really?" Kaylee shoots me an odd look. "I mean, it's been a few months, but she was at all of Wanda's parties last winter. I feel like you and Becca had a marathon conversation about some boring shit like acrylic paints once."

"She's an artist?"

"Here, here, turn in."

I steer the car into the liquor store lot. "We know her from Brooklyn?" I ask, pulling into an open spot.

"Where else?"

Inside, Kaylee grabs a small shopping cart and takes off past the wine displays and toward the aisles of hard alcohol like she owns the place. By the time I catch up, she has our cart stocked with a bottle of Jose Cuervo, a bottle of Bacardi white, and a yellow-green jug of margarita mix.

"Have you been here before?"

Kaylee tilts her head to one side and squints at me. "It's a liquor store, Anna. They're all the same. See if you can find us some pineapple juice and seltzer in the back?"

I nod and do as instructed. While I'm pulling a six-pack of little pineapple juice cans from the cold case, I hear a throat clear behind me. I straighten up, prepared to move out of the way.

"Anna?"

I spin around. "Penguin guy."

"I prefer penguin expert," Max says, grinning. He brushes a piece of floppy brown hair out of his eyes, and it falls right back.

"Of course." I grin back. He's even cuter out of his aquarium uniform, and unlike Caden, he's unlikely to come with baggage of the missing fiancée variety. But despite myself, I can't help wishing it were Caden standing before me, eyes and smile glittering in the neon liquor store lights.

My gaze drops down to the giant shopping cart parked in front of him. It's filled to the brim with cases of beer and a few bottles of vodka and gin. "You do your shopping in Herron Mills often?"

He laughs. "Not really. Just finished up at the aquarium, and this is the best liquor store on the way back to Montauk. Most places don't have both the hard stuff and a great beer selection."

"Right," I say, "the party."

As if on cue, Kaylee wheels our significantly smaller cart around the corner and pulls up next to Max and me. "Party?"

"This is Kaylee," I say. "Kaylee, Max."

She sticks out her hand, eyes flashing bright, and he takes

it in his. *She can have him,* I tell myself. *You didn't want him anyway.* The bigger issue is Max's party on Montauk. I'd put it immediately out of my mind after he invited me; it feels like a lifetime has passed between Monday and today. Drinking with Kaylee in the pool house tonight is one thing. We're unlikely to get into that much trouble, just the two of us. But a Fourth of July party on the beach . . . As Max gives Kaylee the details, my stomach churns.

"I thought you had to work," Max says, and I realize he's speaking to me.

"I did," I say. "I mean, I thought I did. But Paisley's with friends for the weekend."

"That's settled then." Max reaches into Kaylee's cart and transfers our bottles over into his. "These are on me. Meet you in the parking lot?"

"I told you not to worry," Kaylee says when we're outside with our bags of seltzer and pineapple juice. I watch Max through the big store window, unloading case after case of beer onto the conveyor belt and chatting with the white-haired man behind the register. He definitely would have carded us.

"Pretty convenient," I concede, wondering if Herron Mills really has the best liquor store between Riverhead and Montauk. On the other hand, it's not like Max followed us. The contents of his cart indicate he was definitely in the store already when we pulled up. There's nothing to be paranoid about.

A few minutes later, Max is handing our tequila and rum over to Kaylee and I'm trying not to be embarrassed that he so clearly knew we were underage. I remind myself it doesn't matter. He's too old for me, and I'm not into him anyway.

Kaylee doesn't look embarrassed at all. We stay to help him load up his trunk, then hop back into Emilia's car with a promise we'll see him tomorrow. At the very least, I tell myself, anything that happens will be four towns away from Herron Mills.

I make Kaylee promise to be on her best behavior while the Bellamys are around. She rolls her eyes, but agrees to keep the booze stashed in the pool house until they go to bed. We spend the rest of the afternoon at the pool, eating chips and reading the *People* magazines Kaylee brought from Brooklyn. As expected, by the time I hear Emilia leave to go meet Tom, the sun is starting its dip toward the tree line. They must get dinner out, because by the time their cars pull back into the garage, it's after ten, and they go straight up to the second floor.

When their light goes out, we make margaritas and splash around in the pool. I take a small sip, then a bigger one. Our drinks glow like neon Kool-Aid in the pool lights, and Kaylee calls them "belly-ring green." I have to admit, I'm having a great time. My whole body feels warm and loose. It's like I'm glowing.

"Have we been here before?" I ask when I'm two drinks in and my skin is buzzing with tequila and the warm night air. I don't know why Kaylee would lie to me, but that girl Becca, and the way she seemed to know her way around town today . . .

"Like, in another life?" Kaylee giggles. "Sure, probably."

"No, seriously." I don't know how to ask this without sounding profoundly uncool. Kaylee drinks as much as I do, more, but she never blacks out. She already thinks I'm a lightweight. "Herron Mills, the Hamptons. Did we ever come out here?"

"What, no." Kaylee sets her cup down on the side of the pool. Her face is suddenly serious. "Why would you ask that?"

"Forget it," I say. I dive under and swim toward Kaylee, wrap my arms around her legs underwater. She yelps as I drag her down with me, and we both come up gasping for air.

15

July

Montauk, NY

ON SATURDAY AFTERNOON, we pack the mixers and unopened bottle of rum, and I request a Lyft to take us to Bridgehampton station. Emilia and Tom left around nine thirty; I listened to them load up the Lexus while Kaylee and I were still lounging around in bed. Max said to come anytime after noon; the party is an all-day kind of thing. Kaylee would have had us out of the house an hour ago, but I insisted on cooking us a big brunch and then thoroughly cleaning the Bellamys' kitchen before we left. Who knows if there'll be anything to eat besides potato chips once we get there. By two, Kaylee's eager to hit the road, and I've run out of excuses to hang back.

When the LIRR's path syncs up with the highway, I gape at the line of cars outside. The traffic on Route 27 is epic. The train is packed, but the highway is one giant gridlock. It's like the whole world is driving to Montauk today. The train deposits us at the station, and I request another Lyft to take us to the beach, trying not to think about how much this weekend is cutting into my college fund. Kaylee texts Max from the car, and he gives us vague directions toward the patch of sand where we'll find him and his crew.

Once we're out of the car and burning the soles of our feet on the hot, white sand, I'm surprised—again—by how different the beach here is from the one in Herron Mills. We're only twenty miles further east, but here at the tip of the East End, there's a bit of an end-of-the-world vibe. The beach is rockier, wilder. We pound the sand toward Max's coordinates, steep bluffs crested with a thick tangle of grass to our left and white-capped waves teeming with surfers to our right. I watch Kaylee taking it all in; the beachgoers are young, beautiful, rich. This is the place to be. She tosses back her hair and rolls her shoulders, pink bikini straps flashing beneath a gauzy white beach cover with shiny silver tassels. She probably thinks my whole summer has been like this.

Max and his buddies aren't that hard to locate; fortunately, there's a bright red food truck nearby, and Kaylee spots Max tossing a Frisbee around with a couple other guys in the hot midafternoon sun. We spread out our beach towels and I lather myself up with today's second layer of sunscreen while Kaylee runs off to get in on the Frisbee toss. I was hoping Max's crew might have an umbrella or tent I could post myself under, but it's all blankets and towels and unadulterated sunshine for miles. My new hats arrived just in time; the one I'm wearing today is pale blue and enormous, the brim casting a lip of shadow around my shoulders.

Unless I find some actual shelter, though, I'm still going to fry. I'm twisted around and looking behind me, wondering if the sand below the bluffs will get any shade by late afternoon, when something wet and very cold bumps against my knee. I yelp and whirl around.

"Kaylee!"

But it's Max, pressing a can of Sixpoint against my skin and grinning, all sea salt and mischief.

"Sweet Action?" he asks. "We have cider too, and I think someone brought wine coolers."

"This is perfect." I accept the beer and crack open the tab, telling myself I'm officially off the wagon until Kaylee leaves. It's not like I'm working, and the thought of being the only sober person at this party isn't exactly appealing. "We brought some rum and mixers. Or I guess technically you did."

"Thanks, we'll get them in the coolers." He motions over a bearded, slightly potbellied friend, who introduces himself as Sam and whisks our tote away. My eyes follow Sam across the beach and land on Kaylee. She's standing with a beanpole of a guy with John Lennon sunglasses and a very prominent Adam's apple. Whatever he's saying, he keeps cracking himself up. Kaylee's smiling politely and drilling her boredom into the Frisbee with her fingertips.

"Anna?"

"Huh?" Whatever Max just said, I missed it.

"Just making sure you're having a good time."

"Thanks, definitely." I flash him a tight smile. I'm not really feeling the Max Adler vibe today, if I ever was. It's like as soon as I told myself Kaylee could have him, it really hit that he's at least four years older than me—and mostly, he's not Caden. "I think I need to check on Kaylee."

Four hours later, it's as hot as ever, but the sun is mercifully beginning to fade. Despite constant sunscreen reapplication efforts, my shoulders are definitely pink. I've spent most of the afternoon talking to Max's sister and her friend, who are home from their first years at Vassar and Northwestern, respectively. They're nice enough and seem more interested in geeking out about the latest Cassandra Clare novel than drinking, and so we've been getting along just fine. They push up from the sand and head toward the coolers to forage for snacks, with the promise to bring me back something salty.

Kaylee is a couple yards down the sand, somewhere between lit and full-on wasted, and I'm more than happy to hang back while she hangs off Max's shoulders and garners the glares of two nearby brunettes. At some point, Becca and Zeb arrived with a NY Islanders cooler and a giant inflatable beach ball, which has been slowly making its way down the beach. Kaylee must have texted them. I should probably go over and say hey, but I still can't remember a single previous interaction with Becca before yesterday's run-in, and besides, they seem to have made themselves totally at home with Max's friends. Everyone fits in here better than I do.

My scalp is sweating under my sun hat, so I let it hang down my back and shake my mane loose. A wave of exhaustion washes over me. It's probably all the UV rays, I think, lying back on my towel and pulling my hat over my eyes as a large white cloud drifts across the sun and I'm finally blanketed in shade.

ℒ ℱ ℒ

When I wake up, I'm hot and cold all at once. I'm not sure how long I was sleeping, but the white cloud is gone, replaced by a chill in the air and the last gasp of a gorgeous sunset over the water. I blink at it hazily through the hat's pale blue mesh. The right side of my body is warm—body heat warm. I wiggle my fingers and find them locked with someone else's.

"Zoe?" It's a man's voice.

I pull the hat off my face and twist around. Max is sprawled on Kaylee's towel next to me, but Kaylee is nowhere in sight. His hand is clasped in mine, and the side of his body is pressed up against my arm and leg.

"You're awake," he says. His words are thick and slippery, like mercury sliding around in an old thermometer. He's very, very drunk.

I twist my hand out of his. "You called me Zoe."

"What?" He stares down at his hand, as if he's not quite sure where mine went. Then he flops onto his side and squints at me.

"Forget it." I shove myself up onto my knees and rummage around in my bag for a T-shirt. Gooseflesh prickles my skin, which is a deep rose pink. When we get home, I'll match Emilia's azaleas. Perfect. "Where's Kaylee?" I ask, tugging the T-shirt over my head and fishing back in the bag for my shorts.

"Who?"

"Seriously? Kaylee, my friend. You were flirting all afternoon."

Max's face splits open into a wide, sloppy grin. "Just jokes," he says, but I'm not sure I buy it. I narrow my eyes at him.

"Hey, lighten up. I don't know where she is. Sam and Shiri

went in for a dip a little while ago; I think I saw her go with them."

I scan the shoreline, but the sun is slipping away, and it's hard to make out who's who among the throng of bodies splashing around in the surf.

I start to turn back toward Max, but before I can even get my head all the way around, his mouth is on mine, and we're kissing. More accurately, he's kissing me, all rough, sun-chapped lips and too much tongue.

"Stop!" I push him off me and swipe my arm across my lips. It comes away smeared with spit.

"What's wrong?" His voice is all innocence spiked with male privilege. As if whatever's wrong, he's here to save me from it, not the other way around.

"I'm not into this." I gesture in the air between us. "Sorry," I add, even though I'm not. I stand up, cutoffs in hand, and step into them. Suddenly I want to be wearing much more than a two-piece. If I had a trench coat, I'd put that on too.

"What the fuck?" Max's face is twisted into something ugly.

"We're only here because of Kaylee," I say, snatching my towel from the sand and wrapping it around my shoulders like a cape. Max holds up his arm to shield his face from flyaway sand.

"Jesus, Anna."

"It looked like you two hit it off."

"Look." Max shoves himself up to a slightly unsteady standing position. "I invited *you* to this party."

"Yeah, well, that doesn't mean something's going to happen between us. Excuse me." I turn away from him and start walking toward the ocean, toward the mass of people who might be Kaylee. It's going to be dark soon; time for fireworks. I just want to find her and get out of here.

Kaylee finds me first. "Hey." She's standing suddenly beside me, hand wrapped around my wrist like a claw.

"I was looking for you."

"What was that?" she hisses. "With Max."

"That was Max being a drunken asshole." Guess she was watching us. Fantastic.

"You kissed him," she accuses.

"*He* kissed *me*," I clarify. "And I told him to get lost."

"You knew I liked him," she pouts, as if this was my fault, as if I didn't just tell Max the same thing two minutes ago. And suddenly it clicks. This is why I needed a break from Kaylee this summer. Not just because of the partying. When I'm with her, I'm this girl. The girl who lets herself get dragged to parties she didn't even want to go to, who lets herself get sunburned, who gets towed down into spats over boys who aren't even close to worth it. I feel petty and skin-crawly and pissed at Kaylee and pissed at myself for becoming this girl all over again.

I take a deep breath.

"I know," I say, my voice soft. "I'm really sorry. I don't know why he did it." I glance then at the ocean. Swimming probably isn't allowed after sundown, but no one seems to be regulating. The water is filled with slick, dusky bodies splashing and floating in the surf.

"Do you want to go in?" I ask, a peace offering. Something about the sight of all those shapes in the dark water makes my stomach twist, but I want to end this day with Kaylee on a good note. And we always take a dip before leaving the beach—it's tradition.

Kaylee glances at the ocean, then takes a step back, away from the darkness seeping over the surf. Away from the bodies made faceless in the near-dark. "I'm not really feeling it," she says. Her voice is tight.

"Fine," I sigh, relieved in spite of myself. Suddenly I want to get as far away from the water as possible.

"I'm hungry," she whines, tugging at my arm. She hasn't forgiven me, but she's going to drop it, at least for now.

"Me too. Did Becca and Zeb leave?"

She nods. "A while ago."

"Then let's get out of here. I saw a pizza place near the station."

We collect the rest of our stuff and Max ignores us entirely as we start back down the beach toward the exit. Real classy. I notice Kaylee look over her shoulder once, then twice, and my heart squeezes for her.

Back on the train, Kaylee is silent. We eat our slices and smear the grease on thin paper napkins. When we pull into the station before Bridgehampton, Kaylee balls up her beach towel and presses it against the window, then props it beneath her head like a pillow.

"We're almost there," I say.

"I'm not getting off."

"What do you mean?"

"I bought my return ticket to Brooklyn," she says. "I'm not getting off at Bridgehampton."

I lean the back of my head against the seat and stare up at the train ceiling. It looks dirty in that way soap can't fix. I want Kaylee to go home, but not like this.

"I'm not into him," I say. "Not even a little bit."

"Whatever, I'm over it." Clearly a lie. "I have to be back first thing tomorrow anyway; Mom needs me." Possibly true, but who knows. Kaylee never did tell me how long she was planning to stay. The train starts to pull in at Bridgehampton, and I gather up my things.

"You sure?" I ask, even though I already know the answer.

"Positive," she says through tight lips, eyes still fixed out the window.

"I'll call you," I promise.

"Yeah."

I feel like shit. I sling my bag over my shoulder, strap biting into my sunburned skin, and make my way toward the exit.

16

THEN

July

Herron Mills, NY

I STAY IN bed as long as I can stand myself. My skin burns, then itches, then burns, and I stink of stale sweat and sunscreen and pizza grease. At twelve thirty, the longest I've slept in since probably last summer, I finally drag myself into the bathroom and turn the shower on. I should have taken one before crawling into bed all sandy and gross last night, but why not end a day of bad decisions on one more mistake? Besides, I have no plans today and the Bellamys won't be home until tomorrow. Guess I'm spending the afternoon doing laundry.

After I'm clean and my skin is slathered in aloe vera courtesy of the pool house bathroom closet, I strip my sheets and stuff them in my laundry bag along with everything else I've been needing to wash. Kaylee's abandoned duffel bag glares at me from the corner of my room, and I paw through it. For such a big bag, she didn't pack a lot. Just magazines, a Luna bar, and a few clothes I can return at the end of the summer. I shove it under my bed.

In the main house, I get the first load going and wander out onto the pool deck with some toast and a glass of orange juice. From across the grounds, a high-pitched drone fills the air. Someone's mowing their lawn. It sounds like it's coming from Windermere, but that can't be right.

I open my messages and scroll through my last texts with Caden. He'd said they were going to the city for the weekend; it's not quite two on Sunday afternoon, which seems a little early for them to be back. But maybe. My fingers hover over the screen, then I change my mind and switch off my phone. If he's really mowing the lawn, he won't hear his phone anyway. I'll just pop over and see if their car's in the drive.

I take the long way around the front of the house and down Linden Lane to Windermere. When I peer through the scrolls in the entry gate, Mrs. Talbot's big black car is still gone, but the sports car, which I've since learned belongs to Caden, is there along with a gray pickup with mud-caked tires. ANDER-SON & CO. is painted on the side in burgundy lettering. I'm sure they only took one car to the city, but for a moment, I'm puzzled. If the Talbots aren't home, how did this work vehicle get through the gate? After a minute, it occurs to me that this must be Charlie, the guy who cares for the horses. Of course they'd still need to be fed and exercised and whatever else one does with horses while the Talbots are gone.

I push away from the gate, determined not to get caught peeking at Windermere uninvited twice in two weeks. It's cooler today, and while I'm outside, I figure I might as well take a walk. I'm not consciously waiting for Charlie to finish up and leave. As I stroll casually down to the end of Linden Lane, past Magnolia House and Seacrest, that monstrosity of metal and glass, and then back around the other way, I'm not actively planning to slip through the trees and over to Windermere as soon as Charlie's truck is gone. But by my third loop of the street, when it's getting on three and the truck is lumbering away, that's exactly what I do.

I find myself walking along freshly mowed grass on the side of Windermere. Caden must have pounced on their trip to get the job done. It looks a lot nicer back here now; you can actually see the work Caden's been doing on the back patio, and instead of sprouting haphazardly from weeds, the stable looks purposeful and bright. I gravitate toward it, thinking I could go for a whiskey and Coke. I'm still on vacation until tomorrow. No one to judge me but me.

I wonder for a moment if the stable will be locked, trying to picture how Caden let us in in the dark the other night. But the doors are secured by a simple wooden bar that lifts right up.

"Hi, Jackie O. Pike." I nod toward both horses, who are busy chewing feed inside their stalls. Jackie O. lifts her head and gives me a soft snort, but neither seems too bothered to see me in their domain. I head to the back of the stable, toward the unused stall with Caden's whiskey stash. I swing open the bottom panel of the stall door, as I watched Caden do the other night, and crouch down to climb inside. My eyes take a minute to adjust to the dimmer light, then focus on the mini-fridge in the corner. Inside, I find several cans of Coke and a box of Thin Mints. The cookies are tempting, but I leave them alone and grab a can.

My eyes dart around the rest of the stall. On the floor against the side wall are three bottles of Glenlivet, two unopened and one half filled. But it's the small table against the back wall that catches my eye. It's old and wobbly and looks like a nightstand from a child's bedroom set. On top rests a single envelope. Curiosity piqued, I set my Coke down on top of the fridge and swing open the stall's top panel to get some more light inside, then walk over to get a better look.

It's a square greeting card envelope, made out to ZOE in neat block letters. My breath catches. I spin it over, but of course, it's sealed.

I place the envelope back down and slide open the nightstand's single drawer. Inside is a black flash drive with bright yellow polka dots. Otherwise, the drawer is empty. I look behind my shoulder, paranoid, as if my snooping might summon Caden from Manhattan. Or Zoe, from wherever she may be. Possibly from beyond the grave.

My fingers close around the flash drive. A heat that feels like adrenaline spiked with something much stronger floods my veins. My desire for a drink is gone; a new scrap of information about Zoe is a far better drug. I close my eyes, riding the high, and theories start to whirr. If Caden has a letter for her stashed in the stable, he must still believe she's out there somewhere. That she's going to come back for it. Or maybe this is some kind of simple shrine. A birthday card he never got the chance to give her and a flash drive with his favorite pictures of them together. Whatever it is, it's obviously private. It obviously has nothing to do with me.

I grab both items, shut the stall doors behind me, and slip out of the stable and back through the trees to Clovelly Cottage. Pike gives me a little whinny on my way out.

In the main house, I place the pilfered items on the kitchen counter as my heart rate slows to almost normal. I'll change my laundry over, then I'll decide what to do. That takes about three minutes. Back in the kitchen, I stare at the envelope like it might reveal a set of instructions. It's sealed, but only at the bottom where the tip of the triangle meets the envelope back. I run my finger along the underside of the crease. It wouldn't take much to open it up.

I fill the kettle with water and place it on the back of the stove. You can steam an envelope open. That's a thing, right?

While I wait for the water to boil, I take the flash drive and slip into Emilia's office. She's taken her laptop with her to Amagansett, naturally, but the giant desktop computer she uses for her graphic design work beckons. The flash drive is hot in my palm; I know it's none of my business what's on it, but . . . it feels like my business now. I take a step toward Emilia's desk. In for a penny, in for a pound. The computer's probably password-protected anyway.

It's not. I guess when you run a home office with zero employees, there isn't a big call for computer security. She probably keeps all her personal stuff on her laptop. While I wait for the flash drive icon to pop up on the desktop, my eyes rove over Emilia's document folders. They're mostly client files, sorted by project. Standard stuff. I click open a folder for *Wayfare + Ramble*, Zoe's mom's magazine. Inside are a small handful of project sub-folders that look like they date back years, to before I was even born.

The *USB DISK* icon pops up on the desktop, and I close out of Emilia's documents. I double-click, not sure what I'm hoping—or not hoping—to find. There are two folders, labeled *CTdocs* and *CTphotos*. *CT* is presumably Caden Talbot; seems fairly self-explanatory if not very creative. I open the photo folder first.

Inside is a list of fifteen or so images with generic file names like *IMG_2252.JPG*. I click to open the photo at the top of the list.

It's a candid shot of a beautiful African American girl, eyes shut and mouth flung open in laughter. She's Caden's age, give or take. Maybe a little older. And she's definitely not Zoe. Her hair is natural and long and tied back in a red and orange scarf.

I click open the second photo. In this one, Caden and the same girl are together, leaning toward each other across a table in a dimly lit coffee shop. Caden's taking the photo; you can see his arm extended to hold out the phone. The photo has to be recent—Caden looks like himself, and besides, Martina's podcast said he and Zoe had been together since the summer after ninth grade. If this was taken any time in the last five years, it was taken while he was with Zoe.

I scroll through file information on the remaining images. It's consistent throughout. *Created: Saturday, November 30, at 3:46 P.M. Last opened: Saturday, January 4, at 11:48 P.M.* These are from last year—from exactly a month before Zoe vanished. Last opened four days after she disappeared. I click rapidly through the remaining photos. They're all shots of the same girl, either alone or with Caden. They're not explicitly romantic—no kissing, no bodies intertwined—but there's something about the pictures that is indisputably *intimate*. I try to imagine why Caden would leave this in the stable for Zoe to find, in the nightstand drawer directly below the card addressed to her, but I come up empty.

I navigate to the other folder, *CTdocs*. Before I can explore its contents, a shrill whistling sounds from the front of the house. My back stiffens, then I burst out laughing. The tea-kettle.

Inside the kitchen, I hold the envelope over the steam. This works in the movies. At first, nothing happens, and I move the envelope closer to the kettle mouth. After ten seconds, twenty, the paper wrinkles. The envelope comes undone.

I don't stop to wonder if it worked because the envelope was only sealed at the tip, or if it was because it was sealed so long ago—presumably six months, if it lines up with Zoe's disappearance. I just slide out the card and place the envelope gingerly on the countertop.

The card is made of thick, textured cream paper. *I'm sorry* is embossed across its front in rose-gold script.

Inside, I find the following message:

> If you're reading this, you came home, or you want to. I'm so sorry, Zoe. I promise I'll explain everything.
> —C

Hands trembling, I pull out my phone and take pictures of the inside and outside of the card, then the envelope front. Then I return the card to its place and seal it back up. The night we hung out in the stable, Caden told me he thinks Zoe might still be alive. Leaving a note for her makes sense. Of course she'd know about his spot in the unused stall. Maybe he's been hoping, all these months, that she'd come home and find it.

Unless he left the card for someone else to find. Someone who agrees with Martina's "boyfriend theory," who thinks Caden knows something about Zoe's disappearance. Maybe even had something to do with it. Leaving a note for Zoe would be pretty clever, if you had something to hide.

Back in the office, I return to the *CTdocs* folder. Inside is just one file, a Word document. I open it.

The text inside looks like it's been cut and pasted from a series of emails between two accounts: *ThurGoldMarshall@ gmail.com* and *IdaBeWise@gmail.com*, with dates ranging from August 20 to November 28 of last year. They're clearly aliases, spins on the names of important historical figures. Someone didn't want to use their school or personal accounts. The emails range from quick notes to make plans to intense academic discussions to impassioned letters between two people who want to be together—by October and November, they're a hot jumble of feelings. *I think I'm falling for you. I don't know what to do. I can't see you. I need to see you. I hate myself. I need to figure this out.*

The emails aren't signed, and they never use their names. It's clearly intentional, to preserve anonymity. But I can only assume that IdaBeWise is the girl from the photos and ThurGoldMarshall is Caden.

I rummage through Emilia's desk for a flash drive. There's an opened three-pack in the back of the top drawer, resting next to a stack of old photo prints bound together with a fraying rubber band. In the first photo, Emilia barely looks older than me. Her hair is cropped into a pixie cut that surprisingly suits her, and she has her arm wrapped around a friend with dark, waist-length hair who looks about ten years older and vaguely familiar, although I can't place her. The two women are beaming.

I put Emilia's photos back where I found them and turn my attention to the two flash drives still in the pack. With a tiny prayer I'm not going to get fired for this, I slip one out. Of all the brainless, invasive things I'm doing this afternoon, this seems like the least of my sins, but I'm still stealing from my employer. I pause, quickly calculating how long it would take me to walk to the CVS in town, buy a flash drive of my own, and get back to Clovelly Cottage. Not that long; forty-five minutes round-trip if I hustle. But I don't have any idea what time the Talbots are due home. It's already late afternoon; they could come back anytime. I slip Emilia's drive into an unused port and copy the contents of both folders over.

I'm too late anyway. Halfway through the copse of trees, envelope and original flash drive clutched in my hands and visions of the unopened Coke can I left sitting on top of the mini-fridge dancing in front of my eyes, I hear voices and a car door slam. Caden and Mrs. Talbot are home. *Fuck me.* I spin on my heel and dart back the way I came, back across the deck and into the safety of the pool house. My heart is hammering, a wild bird in my chest. I am epically, epically screwed.

Unless Caden doesn't go into the stable tonight. Unless he goes to the "servants' wing" to read, or has a hankering to watch *Cabin in the Woods* or *The Ring*, or does some yard work, or does any of the other things he does around Windermere aside from hanging out in the stable with Pike and Jackie O. As long as he doesn't check his stall tonight, I can get up super early tomorrow, while the Talbots are still sleeping, before Emilia and Tom come home, and return the flash drive and envelope to the exact spot where I found them.

I set my alarm for 4:00 a.m. Caden will never have to know.

17

THEN

July

Herron Mills, NY

MY ALARM DOESN'T WAKE ME.

Sirens do.

At two forty-five, I shove my feet into my sneakers and run out to the road along with the rest of Linden Lane. I can smell smoke; I choke on it. It's close, coming over the tree line. Coming from Windermere.

Three fire trucks crowd the street, along with an ambulance and two police cars. The neighbors are everywhere, milling. I look around for Caden, but I can't find him.

"What's happening?" I ask a woman I know I've seen before. It takes me a moment to place her as Mrs. Cooper, Claudia's mom, without all her black eye makeup.

"The stable at Windermere," she tells me. "Someone burned it to the ground."

PART III:

A Fire

Late last night when we were all in bed
Old Lady Leary lit a lantern in the shed
When the cow kicked it over, she winked her eye and said:
There'll be a hot time in the old town tonight
Fire, Fire, Fire!

—Traditional children's song

18

September

Herron Mills, NY

"WE'RE RECORDING."

"Thanks, I got it."

"Just making sure."

"Your last episode got a lot of play." It's not exactly a compliment, not exactly an accusation. Martina makes an active choice to ignore the subtext in Caden's words and just press on. She's waited a long time for this interview. Months. And she knows this is the only shot she's going to get.

"Eighteen thousand downloads and counting," she says. "People wanted to hear Anna speak." Martina is glad Caden can't see her cheek twitch. *Most* people wanted to hear Anna. Except for Aster, who's still not talking to her, and presumably the entire Spanos family. This is her chance to redeem herself in her best friend's eyes. Caden knows more than he's been letting on, more than he told police. She *knows* he does. If she can get him to reveal something on the record that could move the investigation forward, Aster will have to forgive her.

On the other end of the line, Caden grunts. Martina tries to picture him in his dorm room at Yale. Or maybe he lives in a house off campus. She doesn't really know much about his life, now that he's gone again from Herron Mills, moving on into his junior year, his regular life falling back into place like none of this is happening. Or maybe that's unfair. Maybe Caden is as fixated as she is, as hell-bent on learning the truth. But she doubts it.

For her part, Martina is closed inside her bedroom closet. It's not the ideal setup, with Mami downstairs and liable to interrupt her at any time, but it's Saturday, and recording at home was the easiest option. At least the sound quality inside the closet is pretty great.

"I agreed to speak with you about Anna Cicconi," Caden says. "You had some questions?"

Caden has made it very explicit to Martina that he will discuss Anna and only Anna during this interview. Not Zoe. Still, after all this time, not Zoe. And even though Martina is desperate to ask about what was happening between Zoe and Caden last winter—all the things she and Anna uncovered over the summer, after the first four episodes of the podcast had already aired—Martina will respect Caden's stipulations. At least until the end of the interview, after she's already gotten the tape she came for. Anything else is just a bonus.

She knows Caden only—finally—agreed to this interview because of two things. One, the autopsy results have led to (as of yet unsubstantiated) talk of Anna's legal team filing a motion to dismiss the charges against her. And Martina suspects that Caden is as conflicted about Anna's possible involvement in Zoe's death as she is. That, coupled with the fact that people are actually listening to *Missing Zoe*, spurred Caden to finally respond to her interview request. Episode Five aired on Tuesday; she doesn't have a lot of time to get Episode Six together to meet her posting schedule. But whatever she can get from Caden today, even if it's only a little, will entice people to press play.

"Let's start with the fire. Can you tell us what happened early in the morning of Monday, July sixth?"

"Okay. Well, Mom and I had been in the city that weekend, visiting family friends. We'd only been home for a few hours."

"Your friends on the Upper West Side? The same friends you were visiting the night Zoe disappeared?"

There's a slight pause before Caden speaks. "I don't know why that matters, but yes, the same friends. Doreen is a close friend of my mom's from childhood. We visit them frequently."

"Okay, so you were in the city with Doreen and her family for the Fourth of July, and you drove home that Sunday?" Martina presses her head back into the soft fabric of the many vintage dresses hanging behind her.

"We left the city in the early afternoon. Traffic was terrible, holiday weekend. We got home around four thirty or five, I don't remember exactly."

"And the stable was fine that evening?"

"I didn't go inside that night, but Mom did. She took Jackie O. out for a ride soon after we got home. That's one of her horses."

"And she didn't mention anything concerning to you? No electrical problems, nothing like that?" Two and a half months later, and Martina knows charges were never filed against anyone in connection to the stable fire. She has reason to believe the fire was no electrical accident, no accident at all. But Caden doesn't know what she knows. Whatever Caden tells her now, she's willing to bet it won't be the whole truth.

"She didn't, but it wouldn't be like my mother to notice if the wiring was on the fritz. She's very devoted to her horses, but she doesn't maintain the stable herself."

"And who does that?"

"Charlie Anderson. He runs an equestrian care business on the East End. He'd been out that afternoon, tending to the horses and doing some landscaping for us. The police spoke to him right after the fire. He wasn't involved."

"You're certain?"

"Completely. No stable, no business for Charlie. We're boarding the horses in Pine Neck until we get the stable rebuilt. The first contractor fell through, and now that I'm back on campus, it's slow going."

"So Charlie didn't set the fire on purpose, but could it have been an accident? He was the last person known to be in the Windermere stable, aside from your mother." Martina doesn't really think Charlie was involved, but she wonders about Mrs. Talbot. How much she might have known about her son and his romantic relationships. What she might have seen—or seen missing—from Caden's hiding spot. How deep her love for her son's fiancée might have run.

"Unlikely. Charlie was working at Windermere between noon and three that afternoon, give or take. The fire didn't start until the middle of the night. By the time Kyra noticed the flames and called the police—she's our neighbor at Magnolia House next door—it had burned almost entirely to the ground."

"The fire trucks came around two thirty?"

"About that. That's almost twelve hours after Charlie left. If there was an electrical short, it would have been from a light my mom left on, not Charlie. But that wasn't what started the fire."

"You think it was arson?" Martina picks up a gray cardigan sweater that has fallen to the closet floor and fiddles absently with its buttons.

"Someone opened the stable doors and let out the horses. It was most definitely arson."

For once, Martina and Caden are on exactly the same page. "But the police didn't agree?"

"By the time the fire was out, there wasn't much of the stable left to inspect. We keep a simple wooden latch on the doors; it opens with slight pressure from inside. It's specifically designed so animals won't be trapped in case of an emergency. In theory, the horses could have broken through their stalls and let themselves out, but they didn't."

"How do you know?" Martina knows the answer already, but she needs Caden to say it for the podcast. It'll make a great sound bite.

"They weren't panicked when Arvin and Jeffrey found them two houses over, at Seacrest. They were just grazing on their garden. There was no smoke on their fur. No burns, no wood splinters. They were never anywhere near that fire."

"But the police didn't see this as compelling evidence of

arson?" To Martina, as to Caden, it seems clear enough. It's the identity of the arsonist that remains a mystery.

"I guess not. The problem was, there was no evidence anyone had been on the Windermere property that night. No fire starters or accelerants found at the scene, although that doesn't mean they weren't used. Nothing to point to anything or anyone being involved. The stable and everything in it was completely destroyed; it's a miracle the fire didn't spread to the trees. They just didn't have any leads to investigate."

"So let's talk about Anna. She was there that night?"

"I didn't see her, but a couple of the neighbors remember speaking to her. Everyone on Linden Lane was out in the street, so it's no surprise she was there."

"But you found her behavior strange?" Martina knows perfectly well why Anna's behavior toward Caden changed after that night. It had nothing to do with the fire, not specifically. It was because of what Anna found inside the stable earlier that day. As far as she knows, Caden is still unaware that Anna discovered the card and flash drive. If they'd been inside the stall where they should have been that night, they would have burned along with everything else.

"It's not how Anna was acting that night. It's how she started acting in the weeks after the fire."

"How's that?" Martina drops the cardigan back to the floor and leans forward.

"It's hard to explain. Anna and I weren't close exactly, but we'd gotten to know each other a little that summer. I was pretty tethered to Windermere, looking after my mom, so Anna would come over sometimes. We'd just watched a movie together earlier that week. And she'd been inside the stable before."

"So she had access?"

"Well, as I mentioned, the stable wasn't locked. Technically anyone with access to Windermere had access to the stable. You'd have to get through the entry gate out front, which has a security system, or break in through the hedge, I guess. But I'd shown Anna a shortcut through the trees between Clovelly Cottage and Windermere. So she knew how to get onto the grounds without going through the gate."

"I see."

"We'd made tentative plans to meet up that week, after Mom and I got back from the city. But after the fire, Anna started avoiding me, making excuses for why she couldn't hang out. That was the first strange thing."

"And there was more? Behavior that seemed strange?" Martina is dying to hear Caden's take. To understand how this escalated to the point where Anna confessed to manslaughter and concealing Zoe's body.

"When we did see each other, she started acting . . . weird. Describing in vivid detail places in Herron Mills she swore she'd never been. Asking a lot of questions about Zoe."

"Maybe she was curious, like everyone else."

"It wasn't just curiosity. It was like she knew Zoe, or thought she did. She was trying to connect dots that just weren't there."

"So you don't think Anna knew Zoe. That Anna was there the night Zoe died."

"I don't know. I did believe it at the time. I told Anna she had to go to the police, to tell them what she knew. When she confessed, it made sense. She'd convinced me. She knew too much about Zoe, about us. But now that the autopsy results have come back, now that we know Zoe didn't fall from the balcony, now it's all starting to sound a bit absurd. People kept telling her she looked like Zoe. This whole town was trying to solve the mystery of what happened. I think she became obsessed with the idea of some connection between them that just wasn't there."

Martina takes a deep breath. This might go south real fast, but if it does, she has what she needs. "I want to go back a minute, to something you said earlier."

"Okay?"

"For a person on foot, it wouldn't be hard to get onto the Windermere grounds through a break in the hedge, or from one of the surrounding properties."

"Yeah, it's not exactly high security. All the houses around here are like that."

"And the night Zoe disappeared, no one was home at Windermere."

"Right . . ."

"So why didn't you tell police you found evidence of someone drinking in the Windermere stable when you got home from the city on the afternoon of January first?"

"What the—?"

"After Zoe's body was found last month, that's when you told police what you discovered back in January. That someone had been in the stable while you were in the city. You found an empty whiskey bottle and several empty bottles of beer. But instead of telling police, you disposed of the bottles."

"I obviously didn't think they had anything to do with Zoe." Caden's voice is thin.

"The police could have used a print kit, found out who

was in the stable that night. But instead, you threw the bottles away."

"If this doesn't have anything to do with Anna—"

"But I think it does. Because here's my question. Who do you think was drinking in the stable that night? Was it Zoe? Anna? Were you there?"

"I was in the city, as you know. I have no idea who was drinking in the stable that night. As you've just established, literally anyone on foot could have gotten in."

"A suspect pool that could have been significantly narrowed if you'd have told police about the bottles right away."

"We didn't have any reason to believe Zoe had been anywhere near Windermere that night. Not until Anna confessed to being there with her. Why would I think some empty bottles in the stable had anything to do with Zoe or her disappearance?"

"Maybe because Zoe Spanos was your fiancée. Maybe because she was at Windermere all the time, and knew you kept whiskey in the stable."

"Zoe didn't drink. She was on antianxiety meds, as has, at this point, been well-publicized. Zoe drinking alone or with anyone else in the stable was not a remote possibility in my mind."

"Did Zoe know you were falling for someone else? Did she know about Tiana?"

There's no sound on the other end of the line. Martina stares at her phone screen and waits for confirmation. Caden has ended the call.

19

THEN

July

Herron Mills, NY

AT SOME POINT I go back to bed, but I can't really sleep. When my alarm rings at four, I stare blankly at my phone. There's nowhere to return the pilfered items to. The stable is gone.

My brain cycles into overdrive, the possibilities tumbling around like wet towels in the dryer. Caden going into the stable last night, finding his things missing. Caden starting the fire. Someone else—who?—who knew about Caden's hiding spot, what I took. The mystery girl from the photos, whoever she is. Mrs. Talbot, maybe. Or Zoe, if she's out there.

The timing can't be a coincidence. Whoever set that fire knew that someone had been in the stable. The fire was either a message for me to back off, or an attempt to cover up what I'd done. *Stop digging.*

It hits me that one way or the other, the fire starter probably doesn't know it was me. They didn't target me directly; the fire sent a message that would reach anyone who took the flash drive.

By the time the sun comes up, I'm exhausted and no closer to any answers. Caden seems like the most likely candidate; he definitely knew what he had hidden. The card suggests he didn't have anything to do with Zoe's disappearance, that he was waiting for her to come home. But he left the flash drive there too. And what's on it definitely doesn't make him look good. He was engaged to Zoe, but he wanted to be with someone else. That's motive.

A sinister voice at the back of my head says Caden could have staged the scene in the stall. That the card wasn't ever there for Zoe to find. But then my mind gutters out when I try to unravel who he was staging it for. Much as I don't want to believe it, Caden might be responsible for Zoe's disappearance—or even death.

I make myself take a shower, apply aloe, make breakfast. Tom and Emilia will be back sometime this afternoon. Paisley returns tonight. And then tomorrow morning, it's back to business as usual at Clovelly Cottage. If I'm going to do anything with what I found, it has to be today.

At a quarter till eleven, I set off on foot toward Jenkins' Creamery, taking the quicker way into town, past Windermere. The estate looks quiet, at least from the outside. Nothing lingers from last night's commotion, and there's no view of whatever remains of the stable from the road. I pause briefly at the entry gate, but then I keep going. I don't want to see Caden. I don't know what I'd say.

When I arrive at the ice-cream shop, they're just opening up. To my disappointment, it's not Martina behind the counter, or her dad. The girl in the white apron is blond and unfamiliar.

"What can I get for you?" she asks with a sweet smile.

"I'm actually looking for Martina. Is she in today?"

"Martina!" she calls into the back. "Visitor."

A minute later, Martina emerges from the back of the shop, white apron draped over what looks like another vintage dress, green this time.

"Anna, right?"

"Good memory. You got a sec?"

We take the table in the shop's front window, which is far enough away from the counter to keep the blond girl out of earshot as long as we keep our voices down. I pull out the card and original flash drive and set them on the table between us.

"Zoe?" she whispers, reading the envelope's inscription.

"I know we don't really know each other," I whisper back, "but I've been listening to your podcast. And you're the only person I know around here who might be able to help me."

Twenty minutes later, I've filled Martina in on everything I can think to tell her about how I got the job with the Bellamys, my budding friendship with Caden, finding the card and flash drive, and the fire last night. She's heard about the fire already; I'm sure the whole town knows by now.

"Mrs. Talbot would let Zoe take the horses out sometimes," I add. "So she must have been pretty familiar with the Windermere stable. It makes sense that Caden would leave a message for Zoe there."

"How do you know that?" Martina asks. "About Zoe and the horses?"

"It was in your podcast," I say. "Wasn't it?"

Martina gives me a funny look. "I don't think so."

I shrug. "Or maybe I read it online." But I really can't remember. I touch my fingertips to my temples. It's like it just arrived in my brain, sourceless. Or like it's been stored there for months.

"I need to get back to work," Martina says when the blond girl gives us the hairy eyeball for the third time. "No special privileges for the owner's kid."

"Right, sure. Do you think you can do anything with these? I made copies, but it's not like I can return the originals now." A part of me says I should take what I found to the police, but I was trespassing. I stole this stuff. Can they do anything with illegally obtained evidence? Even if they could, I'm not sure I want them to. Not until I know more, not until I'm *sure* Caden had something to do with Zoe's disappearance. Because if he didn't, whatever happens to him next will be on me. And that's not a mistake I could live with.

She slips them into her apron pocket and stands, pushing back her chair. "I'm not exactly *CSI*, but I'll check them out. I might recognize the girl, or be able to figure out who she is. Give me your number; I'll text you."

We exchange numbers, and I slip my phone back into my pocket. "Just promise me one thing."

"What's that?" she asks.

"We keep this between the two of us. No podcast, no throwing shade at Caden unless we uncover something real. And if we do, we go to the police."

Martina nods. "Agreed. This stays between us."

"And just avoid Caden for now," I repeat. "No matter what

you find. Either he already knows his stuff is missing and burned down the stable to send a message . . ."

". . . or he has no idea it ever went missing and thinks his stuff burned in the fire." Martina's eyes flash as she finishes my sentence.

"Exactly. I really want to believe he's innocent. But if he did burn the stable down, he might be . . . dangerous." The word sounds weird in my ears, but I know it could be true.

"Yeah, I doubt Caden Talbot's villainous capabilities, but I agree, safety first. And what I don't doubt is that boy's ability to harbor secrets. I knew he was hiding something." She narrows her eyes and reaches back to tighten her long brown ponytail. "I'll text you. Soon as I find something."

"Are you going to buy anything?" the blond girl asks when Martina has vanished again into the back and I'm still standing at our window table. It's not like they've had a flood of customers in the twenty minutes I've been here; I'd feel worse if she'd been doing anything aside from standing behind the counter and flipping through her phone while Martina and I were talking, but I do probably owe them a sale.

"Coffee," I say. "With sugar."

On Tuesday morning, it's like the holiday weekend never happened at Clovelly Cottage. Tom is already en route to the city by the time I wake up, and Emilia's usual breakfast spread is laid out on the soapstone countertop. The Paulson-Gosses got back with Paisley late last night, and this morning she's bright eyed, tanner than ever, and ready for the beach.

We post up at our usual spot, me underneath the Bellamys' red-and-white striped umbrella—layered in aloe, then sunscreen, then a T-shirt—and Paisley splashing around in the water.

"You're burned," she comments when she comes into the shade for a snack break. I pass her the bag of pretzels.

"Red like a lobster," I agree. "I spent too long in the sun on Saturday."

"What were you doing?"

"My friend Kaylee came to visit from Brooklyn, and we went to a party."

"Where?"

I smile. It's like twenty questions with this kid. "Out on Montauk. Remember Max the penguin expert?"

The corners of Paisley's lips tug down in a frown. "Yeah?"

"Well, he invited us. And you were right, he's not very nice."

"You went to a party with Max?"

"And a bunch of his friends. It wasn't very fun. I'd rather be here with you."

Wordlessly, Paisley hands the pretzels back to me and retrieves Emilia's iPad from our beach bag. I don't know how she can use it through the pink waterproof casing, but she doesn't seem to have any trouble. She opens up a game and starts playing.

"Hey, Paisley?"

The iPad makes a series of *pings* and *whirrs*. She doesn't respond.

"Paisley?"

"I'm playing Fruit Ninja."

"I can see that. Paisley?"

"Mmm?"

"Why don't you like Max Adler?"

Paisley keeps slicing pineapples and watermelons. Without looking up from her game, she says, "There was a fire at Windermere."

I sigh. Not what I asked, but if she needs to talk about the fire, I'm here for that.

"Yeah, there was."

"Mom said the stable burned down, but the horses are okay."

"That's right. The horses got out, they're fine. Fortunately, the fire didn't spread. It was scary, but no one was hurt."

"Did you see it?" she asks.

"I just saw some smoke over the trees. The firefighters were already working to put it out by the time I woke up."

Paisley nods. "It's creepy over there. I'm glad the stable is gone."

I try to get her to open up, say more, but after that, she shuts down entirely. I stretch out on the beach towel and close my eyes. With Paisley not talking to me, my mind kicks into motion. I try to imagine why Caden hid the flash drive in the stable in the first place. Zoe must have already seen what was on it, or found out about the girl from the photos. That's why he wrote that apology card. Maybe they fought last December. Maybe Zoe ran after discovering her fiancé wanted to be with someone else. Or maybe Caden did something to Zoe. . . .

I push that thought away, turn to the mystery girl from the pictures. "IdaBeWise." She must have known all about Zoe, resented Zoe for keeping her and Caden apart. Caden was scared to end things with Zoe, but he loved this other girl. Maybe enough to protect her.

"Anna?"

My head jerks up from the beach towel. Paisley is looking at me like this isn't the first time she's said my name.

"We're supposed to meet Mom in the pickup area in five minutes."

I wince and push myself up. "Don't tell your mom I lost track of time, okay?"

Paisley nods solemnly.

By the time we're waiting for Emilia to pick us up, neither Paisley or I have much to say. Her fear of Windermere seems to have started when the place fell into disrepair. I can't really blame her; it does resemble a haunted mansion. But I wonder also if it's grounded in something more real, more menacing. Caden lied to me about his relationship with Zoe. He lied to everyone, including the police. What else is Windermere keeping buried?

THEN

July

Herron Mills, NY

Find anything?

Hello to you too.

She can't actually be pissed. Martina doesn't strike me as the pleasantries type. Before I can type anything back, another text pops up on my screen.

Haha. Find anything?

Ran all sixteen photos through a reverse
Google Image search. No luck.

So what does that mean?

None of these photos have been posted
online, so there's nothing for Google to
match them to.

Crap. Of course not. If Caden and "IdaBeWise" were doing even the bare minimum to keep things on the down low, they definitely wouldn't have been posting their personal photos on Facebook.

OK, now what?

Now I keep digging.

I manage to avoid Caden for most of the week. I send him a few texts, deciding it would be much weirder if I didn't check in after the fire, make sure he and his mom are doing okay, but in the evenings I tell him I'm tired, or that Emilia has me doing some extra stuff around Clovelly Cottage. I can't tell if he's buying it or not. Every so often, as Paisley and I are exploring the Working Waterfront at the Children's Maritime Museum or escaping into the air-conditioning for two frosty hours at the Herron Mills movie theater, I start to miss him.

Maybe there's a perfectly logical explanation for what I found in the stable.

Maybe he had nothing to do with the fire.

But probably not.

By Saturday night, I'm going a little stir-crazy. Kaylee hasn't responded to any of my texts since the Fourth, I'm about to give up on ever hearing back from Starr, I've already talked to my mom twice in three days, and there's nothing new to sketch. Would it be weird to text Martina just to see if she wants to hang out?

I'm holding my phone, composing a totally non-desperate-sounding message in my head, when the screen lights up.

Have you seen the windmills yet?

Caden. I press my lips between my teeth.

Only in passing.

Come with me on a little stroll?

It's eight fifteen. I've never seen him leave Windermere this late. Much as I'm sure walking off with Caden into the night is a bad idea, I'm also a little curious and a lot bored. And the illogical part of my brain doesn't want to believe he's a bad person, despite the photo evidence.

Your mom won't mind?

Doreen's here with her tonight.
She'll be okay.

I don't ask who Doreen is. A nurse or a friend. Either way, my boredom has already gotten the better of me, as has the voice that says I need to put in some face time with Caden sooner or later, otherwise he'll definitely know something's up. I'm going.

Ten minutes later, we're leaving Linden Lane, walking toward town. The sun is rapidly sinking, the warm summer dark settling in. When we've walked a ways down Main Street, he motions for us to turn right, just past the marina. Then we take a left onto a street I haven't explored before with Paisley.

"This way. We'll cut through Parrish Park."

"Parrish Park?"

"I'm surprised Paisley hasn't taken you there yet. Part of the lake's roped off for swimming, and there's a lot more shade than at the beach." I catch him casting a wayward glance at my arms, which are still noticeably red under the yellow streetlamp light, and starting to peel.

"Little brat," I laugh. "She's been holding out on me."

"The Arling Windmill's right on the other side of the park. Technically I think it's on park grounds. If you're on foot, you can cut straight through."

As we walk, he gives me the post-fire updates. Mrs. Talbot has been upset all week, the trauma aggravating what Caden refers to as her positive symptoms, which involve scattered thoughts and the occasional hallucination. There doesn't seem to be anything positive about either of those things, but Caden explains that the psychotic behaviors associated with schizophrenia are classified in this way. Hence, the presence of Doreen—who turns out to be the childhood friend they'd been visiting in the city over the Fourth—for the weekend.

Again, I wonder if Caden could have really set the fire. He would have to have anticipated its impact on his mom's health, likewise the absence of her horses, who Caden says are being temporarily boarded at a stable fifteen minutes north. I wonder fleetingly if Mrs. Talbot could have set the fire herself during a hallucinatory break from reality, then feel immediately guilty for assuming things about her illness I can't possibly know.

But if I rule out the Talbots, that doesn't leave much of a suspect pool.

Caden's acting remarkably normal around me. He's not holding anything back in his description of the fire's aftermath, nor is he asking me leading questions or doing anything to signal he suspects me of snooping or theft. Either he didn't set the fire, or he's a very good liar. Either he doesn't have any idea I found the flash drive, or he's a very good liar.

Which he must be. Considering he had this whole town—and maybe even Zoe herself—fooled about his devotion.

True, he wasn't technically cheating if I trust the emails; he cared enough for Zoe to tell the mystery girl they had to wait until he figured things out. That's respectable, to a point. But if he finally got up the nerve to break up with Zoe over winter break, and things went badly . . . I cast a sideways glance at Caden. I wonder where the girl from the photos is now. Maybe she's just collateral damage in this whole mess. Or maybe when Caden wouldn't step up and end things with Zoe, "Ida" took matters into her own hands. . . .

Both scenarios make my stomach twist.

"Honestly," Caden says as we enter the park, both of us willfully ignoring the PARRISH PARK CLOSED AFTER SUNDOWN sign, "I know this might sound a little strange, but it's a bit of a relief."

"What is?" I ask, digging my flashlight out of my bag and

shining it on the walkway in front of our feet. Caden opens the flashlight app on his phone.

"The fire. It's a giant inconvenience, having to board the horses and contract someone to rebuild, but Mom's already doing better with Doreen here. Things will get back to normal."

"Sure. But how is that a relief?" I shine the beam around, trying to get a sense of my surroundings. To our right is a tall row of trees; beyond them, the road outside the park. To our left is a grassy bank leading down to a lake so huge I'm shocked I didn't know it was here. There's a lifeguard stand, and a roped-off swimming area with a sandy strip of beach, and beyond that, what looks like miles and miles of inky water and sky.

"I was keeping some bad memories inside those walls," Caden says. "With the stable gone, it feels like a clean slate."

I swallow. Caden thinks the card and flash drive burned with the stable. That must be what he means by "bad memories" and "clean slate." He has no idea that I—or anyone— took them from his hiding spot. Unless he's testing me, trying to gauge my reaction.

The path takes us away from the lake and through a stretch of leafy bushes. If it's the former, he's probably not an arsonist, but it doesn't answer my questions about why those things were hidden there in the first place. I keep my face neutral.

"I present to you," he says, voice suddenly light, "the Arling Windmill." The path has spit us out on the other side of the bushes, and the windmill stands suddenly before us. "We'll have to come back in the daytime if you want to look inside, but considering it's haunted, the best way to see it is really at night."

"Haunted?" I squeak, voice pitching up in spite of myself.

"Oh yeah, you haven't heard the local legend?"

I shine my flashlight beam across the front of the windmill. Its base is stone, but most of its body is shrouded in the same wooden shingles that cover Windermere and a lot of the older buildings in Herron Mills. Several windows are cut into the sides. At its top, of course, are four windmill blades. They're completely still in the windless night.

"I have a feeling you're going to tell me," I say.

Caden's face breaks into a mischievous grin, and I mentally slap myself. *Off-limits, Anna. Probably still in love with someone else. Possibly dangerous. Why can't you wrap your head around that?*

"Well, the Arling Windmill was built sometime in the mid-eighteen hundreds. I'm sure Google can give you an exact date. But for the first hundred-ish years of its existence, it was located about twenty miles from here, on the Arling estate. The windmill was restored and relocated to Herron Mills in the nineteen fifties or sixties, after the death of the last surviving Long Island Arling."

"And that makes it haunted? That's not a very good ghost story."

"Patience, young Anna. That's just the history. I'm getting to the ghost."

I cross my arms over my chest and try to look tough. I'm failing miserably, judging by the amused expression on Caden's face.

"This windmill used to be the playhouse for young Dorothea Arling, known to her family as Dot. When Dot was a wee child of six, she tripped on the windmill steps and broke her neck. Now"—Caden raises his phone for dramatic effect, shining the flashlight beam on the windmill's uppermost window—"passersby report seeing the sallow face of a little towheaded lass in the windows at night, especially in July, the month Dot died."

"Shut up," I say, but I can't take my eyes off the window glass.

"Fine, I don't know what month she died, but the rest is true. People have been saying they've seen her face in the window for years." He drops the beam back to the ground.

"Have you ever seen her?" I ask.

"Nah, I don't believe any of that stuff."

"Guess that's how you can watch so many scary movies."

"Hmm. Never really thought about it, but you might be right, Anna Cicconi."

Back on Linden Lane, Caden and I part ways with a wave. The Arling Windmill is still in my head as I walk down the drive toward Clovelly Cottage, then round the corner of the house toward the pool deck. It's a horrible story, however much is true. I can't unsee the image of a tiny blond girl tumbling down the steps to her death. Her broken body at the base of the stairs, the spectral gleam of her face in the grubby windmill window. I shove my hands deep into my pockets.

When I get to the deck, I'm walking fast, eager to get inside the pool house and close the door behind me. But the broad shape of a body, blacked out in silhouette against the bedroom light I must have left on, stops me in my tracks.

"Anna."

It's a woman's voice, but not one I can easily place. The breeze tugs at her dress, or maybe it's a nightgown, and the fabric billows out, making her appear oddly shapeless. Ghostly.

I press my lips between my teeth, try to shake myself free from Caden's silly ghost stories.

"Yes?" I can't keep the tremble out of my voice.

She takes a step toward me, out of the light. I squint.

"I'm glad you're home. I'd like the two of us to have a chat."

She keeps walking forward. Two steps, three. I take a step back, feel for my phone in my pocket. When there's about four feet between us, she comes into focus in the dark. Meredith Talbot, barefoot and wearing a nightgown that looks too hot and scratchy for summer.

She must have seen me with Caden, at the stable or in the film room. She knows I haven't been staying away from Windermere like she asked. But when she comes to a stop in front of me, her body uncomfortably close to mine, it's not Windermere she wants to talk about.

"You were seen in town with the Jenkins girl," she says, a note of accusation in her voice. *You were seen*. Like I've violated some social code by hanging out with Martina. Someone must have spotted us at the ice-cream shop. My breath hitches. What had I been thinking, sitting in that front window? Anyone could have seen the flash drive on the table between us. Possibly even overheard our conversation. I press my lips together and wait for Mrs. Talbot to reveal her hand.

"I don't know what you think you know," she continues, "about my son. Martina Jenkins has already caused enough trouble with her podcast, pointing the finger at Caden. It's irresponsible, implicating someone without any evidence. If that girl wants to be a journalist, she has a lot to learn. Preferably without dragging our family through the mud in the process."

I breathe out. If she knew I had the flash drive, she would have said so by now. Looks like I'm just guilty by association, wrapped up in this bone Mrs. Talbot has to pick—somewhat understandably—with Martina.

She narrows her eyes at me. "We've been through enough," she says after a beat, when I'm still silent. "Don't think I don't know what you're up to. Befriending Caden, earning my son's trust. Then running off and spilling . . . whatever he's told you . . . to the Jenkins girl."

Whatever he's told you. So Mrs. Talbot knows that her son has something to hide. But she's not going to spell it out for me because she doesn't know how much I know. I breathe a little deeper.

Maybe she just means Caden's engagement to Zoe, but I doubt it. If Herron Mills found out they were engaged, it would stir up some gossip, but it wouldn't be the end of the world. But if everyone knew about "IdaBeWise," how Caden was falling for someone else, looking for a way out of his relationship with Zoe right before she disappeared? Mrs. Talbot glares down at me, and there's something behind the flash of scorn in her eyes. Fear.

Caden's told me how much his mom loved Zoe. How close they were. But as much love as she had for her son's fiancée, it's clear that the person she'll do anything to protect is Caden. I wish I could tell her that I don't want Caden slandered either, that that's exactly why I've been talking to Martina and not the police. At least until we know more.

"I should go inside," I say carefully. I'm not planning to make any promises tonight that I can't keep. "Do you need help getting back to Windermere?" Aside from the fact that she's over here barefoot in her nightgown, she seems perfectly coherent—no evidence of the positive symptoms Caden mentioned earlier. But still, I can't just leave her out here.

"I'm fine," she snaps. "I'm not a child."

"Of course not," I mumble, stepping around her and toward the door. I wonder if Doreen and Caden have noticed she's missing by now and resolve to shoot Caden a quick text as soon as she leaves.

"Good night, Mrs. Talbot." I step inside and slide the pool house door closed.

Hours after Mrs. Talbot is back at Windermere—Caden apologized profusely, but I doubt he'd be so apologetic if he knew the whole story—I'm still wide awake. Around two o'clock, I give up and get dressed. My feet take me away from Clovelly Cottage, deeper into residential Herron Mills. The village may be small, but if tonight's excursion to the windmill taught me anything, it's that Herron Mills is hiding secrets I haven't yet uncovered.

I've gone a couple miles when I arrive at a house that makes me stop short. I'm not sure why; it's huge, set far back from the road, and shrouded in nighttime quiet. Which is to say, it's just like every other house I've passed tonight. But there's something so familiar about this place. Forty-Five Crescent Circle. I've been here before.

I close my eyes. My feet are still planted on the sidewalk, but my mind is in a room that feels warm and damp and smells earthy like a greenhouse. I breathe in deep, willing my memory to take over. To show me whatever it is this house is stirring up.

With my mind's eye, I look around. I'm standing inside a glassed-in pool at the back of the house. There's lush vegetation on all sides like some kind of enchanted tropical forest. The floor is an expanse of terra-cotta tile. Emerald-green vines crawl up bronze poles, and fuchsia and buttery yellow blooms spill from scores of hanging planters. Wisps of steam rise from the water, and a small waterfall trickles down a stone wall into the pool.

Eyes still closed, I look slowly to my left. Stretched out on lounge chairs are three girls in brightly colored bathing suits, drinking pink cocktails. Two of the girls look a lot like me.

I gasp, eyes flying open.

I'm back on the sidewalk, staring at the house in front of me. The air feels hot and thick with steam, a lingering thread of memory invading the present. My legs are weak from too much walking, too much sun, not enough sleep. I slump down in the grass in front of the entry gate and press my forehead into my hands.

I close my eyes, try to picture the girls again. See their faces. But this time, the memory is gone.

THEN
July

Herron Mills, NY

JULY SWELTERS. As the days tick by, a salty film descends upon everything and everyone in Herron Mills, making our skin itch and armpits sweat and drawing us like hungry gulls toward the ocean. Unlike in the city, there's no sickly sweet garbage smell on Tuesdays or persistent cry of the Mr. Softee truck to break up the summer air. My days are a constant cycle of sunshine and beach salt and my nights a retreat into cool showers and air-conditioning.

I mostly avoid Caden for the next few days, finding it hard to strike the balance between keeping up appearances and accepting that he's dishonest at best and dangerous at worst.

On Wednesday, he texts me just as we're wrapping up dinner. I excuse myself into the pool house.

> You're acting weird.

> > Huh?

> Don't tell me Emilia has you
> doing chores again at night. Do
> you have a secret boyfriend,
> Anna Cicconi?

The irony. I think fast.

> > Haha. The nonstop pace of the job is just
> > getting to me. I was embarrassed to say I
> > was going to sleep at 9:00. 🤣

> Well if you can make it up past your
> bedtime, we could do movie night
> again?

I can't put him off much longer. My fingers hover over the screen.

> > Sure thing. Meet you out back at 7:30?

I put down the phone, then pick it right back up. I need to talk to Kaylee.

"Hey." Kaylee's voice is flat. I'm surprised she even picked up, given the fact that two very short texts are all I've gotten out of her since she went back to Brooklyn.

"If it makes you feel any better," I say, "that Max guy hasn't sent me a single text since we left his terrible party. He's clearly no longer into me."

"Max who?"

"Ha-ha."

"Dude, it's fine. Ian and I are back on again anyway."

Ah. So that's why Kaylee's been MIA. I am not Ian Nussbaum's biggest fan, mainly due to his inability to stay committed to Kaylee for more than two months at a time, but I have to admit I'm relieved her silence has been Ian related, not Anna related.

"Oh yeah? Tell me what's new with Ian."

As Kaylee fills me in on Ian's latest million-dollar idea—a Meetup-style app for video gamers that would also bring you chips and beer—which actually sounds moderately interesting, and their plan to look for an apartment together in the fall, which sounds like a recipe for heartbreak and financial disaster rolled into one, my mind keeps cycling back to Fourth of July weekend. While I'm thrilled to hear that Kaylee is over it, I'm not sure I am.

To clarify, I am 100 percent over Max Adler, not that there was anything to get over in the first place. But Kaylee's uncharacteristic ability to find her way to Bridgehampton unassisted; her snappy familiarity with the layout of the liquor store; her friend Becca that I could swear we don't know from Brooklyn; her complete lack of questions about Herron Mills or the Hamptons in general? Maybe I'm over-thinking things. Probably I am. But Saturday night's strange memory, or whatever that was, has stayed with me. I think Kaylee might have been the third girl drinking cocktails at that glassed-in pool . . . Zoe, Kaylee, and me.

"Do you know a girl named Zoe Spanos?" I interrupt.

"Who?"

"Zoe Spanos. I think we might have partied with her last year, maybe over the summer or winter break?"

"Doesn't ring a bell. She one of Mike's friends?"

"No, she's from here. From Herron Mills," I clarify.

"Girl, are you on that again?" Kaylee asks. "I told you I've never been out there before. Your digs are posh as shit. I think I'd remember."

"Yeah, I know. I just thought . . . this Zoe girl, she looks a lot like me. Do you remember anyone like that?"

"A girl who looks just like you? Definitely not."

"Forget it," I sigh. My brain has been doing undeniably weird things all summer. What I said to Caden wasn't a total lie—this job *is* all-consuming. Save for the not-so-restful break over the Fourth, I haven't had a day off since I got here. I don't get weekends. Paisley's wonderful, and the Bellamys are great employers, but taking care of an eight-year-old is exhausting, and the constant string of workdays combined with too much sun and too many unsolved mysteries is starting to make my head swim.

I hang up with Kaylee, satisfied everything is back to normal between us, and change out of my dinner dress (one of my new ones, with pockets) and back into regular clothes before meeting up with Caden.

I still have a few minutes, so I head into the main house

kitchen to poke around for movie snacks. I'm filling a Tupperware from a giant bag of rosemary olive oil popcorn when the Bellamys' landline rings. It's a 212 number, someone calling from Manhattan. Maybe Tom. I can hear Emilia upstairs with Paisley, so I pick up the phone.

"Bellamy residence."

"Yeah, is Tom there?" a male voice asks. He sounds like he's in a rush.

"He's in the city during the week," I supply. "Do you have his cell?"

There's a pause on the other end. "Is this Emilia?"

"No, this is Anna. The nanny."

Another pause. "And you're sure he's not there? Because he left the office early today."

"Oh. I . . . I don't know. I mean, no, he's not here."

The line goes dead.

I file that away under 1,000 percent not my business and pop the lid on the Tupperware.

When I come out on the other side of the trees between the two estates, I'm not prepared for the complete wreckage of the stable in front of me. I wasn't expecting to see a brand new stable already erected in its place, but the scene looks basically untouched since the night of the fire. The ground is littered with ashes and charred slats of wood, and the surrounding grass is burned away. The rest of the lawn is still nicely mown, but the gaping, blackened eyesore in the back of the property kind of steals the stage.

"I'm getting a contractor out here next week," Caden says.

"I hope. As you might find unsurprising by now, Mom's been difficult about the process. She wants her horses back, but the idea of letting multiple people onto the property to work isn't easy for her. It's going to take some cajoling."

"Right." I look up, and there she is—Meredith Talbot, darkening an upstairs window. She looks none too pleased to see me standing in the backyard with her son. I raise my hand in an apologetic wave.

"She really doesn't like me," I say to Caden.

"She doesn't like new people, full stop. The fact that you look like Zoe doesn't help, but if it makes you feel any better, she wouldn't have liked you anyway."

"Thanks . . . I guess." We both laugh.

Caden leans back and blows a kiss up to his mother, who gives him a small smile before retreating from the window, back into Windermere.

"I wanted to ask you about something," I say as we walk across the lawn, toward the back patio. "It's about this place I remembered the other night."

"A place in Herron Mills?" Caden asks.

"I don't know. That's what I'm trying to find out."

"Okay, shoot."

We sit at the patio table, and I describe the glassed-in pool with the crawling vines and muggy greenhouse air. Jake pushes through the back door and flops at Caden's feet, tail twitching excitedly. I leave Zoe and Kaylee out of my description, focusing only on the setting. As I talk, I watch Caden's mouth shift into a frown.

When I'm done, he's stone silent.

"Does that . . . sound familiar to you at all?"

"When is this memory from?" Caden asks. There's a hard edge to his voice.

"I'm not sure," I admit. "This is going to sound a little woo-woo, but it kind of came to me all of a sudden, while I was out walking in town the other night. So I'm not even sure it's real." But as the words spill out of my mouth, I know they're not true. The glassed-in pool is very real. I can tell from the fixed way Caden is staring at me.

"The pool you're describing belongs to the Spanos family," he says finally. My heart stops. "George is a landscape architect; he had it custom designed. It's certainly not the only glassed-in pool in the world, but it's the only one around here with terra-cotta tiling and a waterfall and a jungle of tropical vegetation." He leans forward on the patio chair, places his elbows on his knees. "When were you there, Anna?"

My mind is reeling. Of course it would be her house; I shouldn't have said anything to Caden. But in my heart of hearts, I had expected him to tell me he'd never seen a pool like that. That my brain had cooked it up.

"I don't know," I splutter. "I've never been to Zoe's house."

"So you're telling me a perfectly formed image of their pool just . . . came to you? Right down to the tiling and types of flowers?"

"Maybe I saw a picture somewhere?" I suggest. Over the past month, I've tapped Google dry for every scrap of information about Zoe I can find. Maybe my memory wasn't a memory at all. I'd gotten too much sun, and I'd been awake for over twenty hours. Maybe what I saw was just exhaustion combined with stuff I found online. I tell myself it's possible.

Out loud, I say, "Mrs. Spanos is a magazine editor, right? Did they ever do a photo shoot of their house?"

"How do you know what Joan does?" There's more than a hint of suspicion in Caden's voice.

I know this one. "It was in Martina's podcast. The village historian said she worked at a travel magazine. If they ran a spread, I might have seen it online."

"I guess . . ."

"I googled Herron Mills when I was interviewing for the job," I hedge. "I looked at a bunch of blogs and articles."

Caden sits back in his chair. "Maybe," he says. "There could have been a profile. There are profiles of homes in the Hamptons all the time."

"I swear I've never been there," I backpedal. "I shouldn't have called it a memory. I've never even met anyone in the Spanos family except Aster. And I just ran into her that one time outside Jenkins' Creamery."

"It's weird, Anna. You described how it felt. How it smells in there. And you were dead-on."

"I have an overactive imagination. When I was little, my mom said I was either going to grow up to be a writer or an inventor. She wasn't far off—maybe that's why I'm always sketching. Usually I channel all that imaginative stuff into my drawings. I should keep it on paper where it belongs." I'm rambling. And Caden's looking at me like he's not sure what to make of my story. Not sure what to make of me.

"Huh," he says finally. "Stranger and stranger." He shoves himself back from the patio table and stands up. "Now are we going to watch that movie?"

❧ ☙ ❧

When I start my walk back to Clovelly Cottage at ten thirty, I have a new message from Martina waiting.

> Going through the Yale student directory online. It's painful. 😭

I attempt to shine my flashlight on the ground in front of me with one hand and text with the other. It's slow going, but the distraction from my intensely awkward evening with Caden is welcome. We basically didn't talk through the whole movie, some B horror flick from the eighties. And then I left as soon as it was over.

> Painful how?

The three dots hover while Martina types.

> It's not just a listing. You have to search by combinations of at least three letters. Then I'm typing names of the female students who come up into Google and running an image search to see if any match Ida's. Who's obviously not really Ida.

> Crap, I'm sorry.

> Did you know A names are the most common? I might switch to U or X soon.

There must be computers at the library,
right? I could go after work tomorrow
and help.

Library closes at 4, but thanks. I sent a
couple of the Ida photos to my friend's
sister. She's a sophomore at Yale. She
didn't recognize her, but she'll ask
around discreetly.

Are you sure Ida's a Yale student?

No. But it's our most likely bet. She's
definitely not from around here, and
where else was Caden spending all his
time?

She could be a local from New Haven.

Let's hope she's not. Then we're really
screwed. I've already checked out her
Gmail account. It's registered to Ida B.
Wells, naturally. So, dead end there.

Right. Thanks, Martina. 😊

Sure, I'll keep you posted.

I cross the lawn to the pool house and step inside. My
shoulders unclench the moment the door slides shut behind

me. I didn't realize how tense I was. I flop down on my bed and try to make sense of tonight. The glassed-in pool is part of Zoe's house. That was probably Zoe's house I was standing in front of the other night. It was on a street called Crescent Circle, but I can't remember the exact address. I should have written it down.

I grab my phone. It only takes a minute of searching online to confirm my suspicions: Forty-Five Crescent Circle belongs to George and Joan Spanos.

Maybe I saw the pool in a magazine spread, but I seriously doubt it. It was a memory. Somehow, I've been there before.

With Zoe.

22

July

Herron Mills, NY

"THREE CALLS IN two weeks? Is something wrong?"

I can hear myself inwardly groan. I can't win. I'm either calling my mom not enough or too much. But today's call isn't just a mother-daughter check-in. Today's call has a specific purpose.

"This a bad time?" I ask.

"Of course not, sweetie. What's up?"

"I need to ask you about Herron Mills."

There's a long pause on Mom's end of the line.

"There are these things I remember," I press on. "Like, the first week I was out here, I could swear I'd been to this exact beach before. It's not like the city beaches; it's narrow but really nice? And there's an ice-cream shop with an elaborate chalkboard menu." As I tick off my eerie moments of nostalgia, even I have to admit, they sound a little thin.

"Anna."

"And I remembered this glassed-in pool. . . ."

"Anna," Mom repeats. "That sounds a lot like Stone Harbor."

I stop. "Where?"

"Stone Harbor? It's on the Jersey shore. When your dad and I were together, we used to take you on trips there in the summer. There was a really nice beach. And you loved the ice-cream shop. The hotel where we stayed, it had an indoor pool."

"With vines and stuff?" My heart sinks a little in my chest.

"There were planters, yes. Lots of vines and flowers. You called it 'the tropical rain forest'; I don't know how you even knew what a rain forest looked like." My heart sinks a little deeper.

"And we never came here? To Herron Mills?"

Mom's snort is so loud I almost pull the phone away from my ear.

"To *the Hamptons*? Lord, no. Your father was far too cheap for that."

Paisley and I spend Tuesday morning at Parrish Lake, our second trip there since Caden clued me in to its shade. In the afternoon, I promise Paisley ice cream if she'll hang out with me at the library for a couple hours. Turns out, she loves the children's room, so it's a win-win.

I spend the first few minutes poking around the Yale student directory, randomly searching the Rs, figuring Martina probably hasn't gotten that far in the alphabet yet. She was right; it's a giant pain. You have to enter combinations of at least three letters to pull up anyone's directory listing, so I start with *Raa*, then *Rab*, then *Rac*, and so on. Muriel Raab. Rabia Sadik. Rachel Paulson. Then transfer the names over to Google, run an image search, look for anyone who looks like "Ida" from the photos. I give up pretty fast.

That's not the reason I'm here anyway. I close out of the Yale directory and type a new name into Google:

John R. Cicconi. My father.

The same old results come up; this is not a new game. But it's been a while since I tried to find him. When I went into high school, I made myself a promise: No more moping around about the father who clearly doesn't give a rat's ass about me. No more fantasizing about the day he'll come home, all rich and handsome, and sweep Mom and me away to a nice house in the suburbs. No more fantasizing he'll come back at all.

But for the first time in years, I feel the burning need to talk to him. I just want him to back Mom up, to hear him say, *You're remembering Stone Harbor. It's still vivid for you because those were the last good times we had together as a family. You're searching for that link, and you're just a little mixed up.* I can hear his rough, soft voice in my ear. The voice I haven't heard in years. I can see it: the two beach towns shifting and merging in my memory. That would explain a lot. But it doesn't explain my precise memory of the glassed-in pool, the way Caden was sure it was Zoe's house I was describing. How when I think about that pool, it's Zoe and Kaylee I see.

It doesn't matter, though. Google turns up nothing new, nothing that might point me toward where he's living now, what he's been up to for the last twelve years. Mom either doesn't know or wishes she doesn't. She firmly refuses to talk about him. If I had a city, or even a state, I might be able to track him down. But I have no idea. My father stopped wanting to be my father a long time ago. He doesn't want to be found.

I'm out the library doors and halfway to the sidewalk before I remember Paisley's still reading inside.

That night, Martina texts me.

> News, but I'm working until 10.
> Meet me in front of the shop?

When I walk up at a few minutes of, Martina's inside, placing chairs on top of tables. The blond girl from before waves goodbye and pushes through the door.

"We're closed," she says when she sees me perched on a bench out front.

"Just waiting for Martina."

She nods, then unlocks her car and slips inside.

A few minutes later, Martina's sitting next to me, grinning.

"I found her," she says. "Tiana Percy, Yale rising senior. She's one year ahead of Caden." She holds out her phone, and I scroll through the public photos of Tiana. It's definitely the same girl.

"How'd you find her?"

"My friend's sister's friend recognized her from around campus. She couldn't remember her last name, but once I could search for Tiana in the directory, I found her pretty fast.

But the only thing I could find connecting her to Caden was a group photo from the African American Studies Department's website." She takes her phone back and pulls it up.

I hold the screen close and squint down at the group shot, a bunch of students gathered behind a seminar table and smiling. "They're not even standing together."

"No, but it proves they know each other. Tiana Percy is our Ida."

"Okay." I hand Martina's phone back. "But where do we go from here?"

"I emailed her, said I was doing an article for my high school paper about organizations for students of color on Ivy League campuses. She's the head of Yale's Black Women's Coalition, so it adds up."

"Think she'll bite?"

Martina shrugs. "It's only been a few hours. My school account's Martina Jenkins, not Martina Green, and I am the EIC of my high school paper. She wouldn't connect me to the podcast unless she really does her research."

"And if she does?"

"Then I'll keep digging on my own. See what else I can turn up."

"Thanks, Martina." I shove my hands in my hoodie pockets. Despite how hot it's been during the day, it's cool at night close to the water.

A pair of headlights flash momentarily, then dim as a car pulls into the space on the street in front of us. Martina stands and gives the driver a wave.

"That's my ride." She slides her phone into her dress pocket.

"Hey, Martina?" I ask, standing up too. "I know you've got

lots of friends here already, but to be honest, Caden's the only person I'm really friendly with, and . . ."

"Things are a touch weird right now?"

"To say the least. I don't want to be a third wheel, but if you and Aster ever want to do something in the evenings, I'm free after dinner."

"Sure." Martina grins. "We're hanging out on Friday. You should come along. I'll text you when I know the plan."

"That would be great." As Martina rounds the car to the passenger's side, I smile wide and make a silent wish that plan involves hanging out at Aster's. I need to get inside those walls. See the pool for myself.

Alone again on the bench in front of the closed shop, silence settles all around me. Up the block, an awning rustles. One car drives by. It's never this quiet in the city. It's almost oppressive. *You are alone. You are alone.* I open up Messenger, and my unanswered notes to Starr glare up at me. I type out one more.

> Did you know I'm in the Hamptons for the summer? Do you even care?

23

July

Herron Mills, NY

IT'S POURING ON Friday, so we eat dinner in the Bellamys' dining room instead of out on the pool deck. Mary's stretched beyond her typical Mediterranean repertoire, and I'm pretty sure this isn't what pad thai is supposed to taste like, but I eat it anyway to be polite. Tom seems distracted, constantly checking his phone, so I don't feel too bad checking mine when Martina texts with an offer to hang out at Aster's tonight.

> Bring your swimsuit. There's an
> indoor pool; it's fun in the rain.

It's almost too perfect. I can't keep the grin off my face. "Plans tonight?" Emilia asks.

"Oh, sorry." I tuck my phone away. "Yeah. Yes. I'm meeting up with a couple girls from town, Martina and Aster."

"Aster Spanos?" Tom asks, joining the dinner conversation for the first time tonight. He sets his phone down on the table.

"I introduced them," Paisley says. She turns to me. "I can't believe you're hanging out without me!" She's teasing, but maybe also a little hurt.

Emilia laughs and says something about the unfairness of childhood. She's talking to Paisley, but her eyes stay trained on me. The back of my neck itches.

"Please give Joan my best," she says softly when Paisley has excused herself to watch TV inside and Tom is on his phone again. Her voice is tight, and I know I've stepped into something best avoided. I promise to say "hi," even though I know I won't.

At seven fifteen, Martina's mom's car is pulled up outside the Clovelly Cottage gates, and I'm hurrying down the drive, umbrella barely putting up a fight against the steady, lukewarm downpour. I slide into the backseat and try not to create a puddle on the floor of their nice car.

Martina's mom, a quiet woman who keeps the soundtrack of soft instrumental music at a barely discernible volume and drives at two miles below the speed limit, drops us off with instructions to call her for a ride back no later than ten thirty.

Outside the car, my breath catches. We're standing in front of the house from the other night, just like I knew we would be. The internet may have already confirmed the address, but being here again makes it feel that much more real. *I know this place.*

Martina punches in the security code and beckons me to follow. "She never lets me borrow the car," she complains as we make our way up the driveway. "It would be so much easier, but she's a total control freak."

We had a car until last fall, when it unceremoniously died on us after fourteen years and over two hundred thousand miles. Just in time for me to get my license. Mom wants to replace it, but she hasn't saved up enough yet. For a few short months, though, I had wheels. I used to drive that little junker five blocks to Kaylee's even though I could walk faster than I could park it, just because I could. Parents out here are so *involved*.

As we near the Spanoses' front door, I try to take in every detail through the waning light and still-pouring rain. The house—Maple Grove, Martina tells me, for the many maple trees surrounding the back of the property—is modern and huge, like a lot of homes out here. One minute it's familiar, the next it's a trick of the light. We step onto the porch, below the overhang, and take down our umbrellas.

"You didn't tell her anything, right?" I whisper to Martina. "About Tiana Percy?" Again I wonder what Tiana might be capable of. What she might have done to make Zoe go away . . .

"Not a thing," Martina whispers back, touching the pad of her thumb and index finger together and running them across her lips like a zipper. "It's a little weird keeping it hidden, but there's no point in upsetting them yet, not until we find out more."

Aster greets us at the door wearing a red and teal sarong. A little white dog runs circles around her feet.

"This is Julia Child," she says. "Zoe named her."

I squat down to offer Julia Child my hand to sniff, but she

completes her laps around Aster and runs off into the back of the house without even acknowledging my presence.

"She's nine and still a total energy ball," Aster says. "Don't take it personally."

We make our way through the house and into the kitchen, and to my disappointment or relief, nothing looks particularly familiar. It's a nice house with nice stuff, but there are no chilly tendrils of memory reaching out to grab me like the other night. The possibility that I was just confusing Herron Mills and my recent deep dive into Zoe's life with some memories of childhood vacations dances at the back of my mind.

In the kitchen, Aster and Martina flutter around collecting cups, straws, and a pitcher of something that looks like lemonade. I'm instructed to grab a tote bag filled with snacks, and then we head through a large red-stone archway connecting the kitchen to an airy breakfast nook, which then leads out to the pool. When we step through the sliding glass doors, I stop doubting myself. I may not have Kaylee's steel trap memory, but the pool is unmistakable.

I press my lips between my teeth and try to keep the mix of shock and validation off my face. Maybe there was a similar glassed-in pool at the hotel in Stone Harbor. But *this* is the pool that's been tugging at the edges of my memory, telling me to pay attention.

I'm so focused on keeping my expression neutral that I don't realize I've stopped walking. My feet are glued to the terra-cotta tiles, my eyes roving all around, taking in the lush vines, the pink and orange and yellow blooms, the delicate waterfall—all the details I knew I'd find. The dog scampers in through the sliding glass doors and brushes past my legs in a blur of white, yapping at something only she can see in the air in front of her.

"What's out there, Belle?" I squat down and extend my hand toward her again.

Aster turns slowly to face me. "What did you call her?"

Choosing that moment to acknowledge my existence, the dog nuzzles her little pink and white snout into my hand. I look up. "Um. Julia Child, right?"

"Right," she says, face tilted slightly to the side. "I thought . . ."

Aster trails off, and Martina clears her throat, saving us from the awkwardness. "Pretty amazing, right?" She gestures with her chin around the space.

"It's gorgeous," I say, straightening up. "I thought the Bellamys' pool was impressive, but this is something else. . . ."

"My dad's in landscaping," Aster says. She's slipped out of her sarong and stands at a glass-topped table in a black tankini, filling three plastic, pineapple-shaped cups from the lemonade pitcher. I force my legs to work again, to carry me over to where she's standing so I can unload the snacks onto the table. Martina slips her dress over her head, revealing a blue and white polka dot one-piece with a little skirt that's either actually vintage or styled to look that way.

"He worked with another architect who specializes in glass to design the pool when we moved in," Aster continues. "I'm sure he'll find his way down here at some point tonight. He'll talk your ear off about it if you let him. Lemon Spritz?"

She holds a pineapple cup out toward me, and I accept.

"It's a mocktail," Martina clarifies before I can place the pink-and-white paper straw between my lips. "So don't get too excited."

"I don't really drink," I say. "Or I'm trying not to. So this is perfect."

We walk over to the lounge chairs at the edge of the pool and settle in. "This pool is like something out of a magazine," I say, fishing.

Aster laughs. "Well, between landscape architect Dad and magazine editor Mom, you could say they're a little obsessed with aesthetics."

"Did her magazine ever run a profile?" I ask.

"I don't think so," Aster says. "They probably should."

"Mrs. Spanos is something else," Martina adds. "She had kind of major shoulder surgery last fall, and she took like one day off work."

"Not even that," Aster says. "She was working from her hospital bed."

"Your parents sound like the Bellamys. Aside from the Fourth, I haven't seen them take a day off all summer."

Martina shrugs. "That's how it is out here. When people hear 'Hamptons,' they think bougie vacation spot. But everyone's a workaholic."

I slip out of my damp cutoffs and T-shirt and hang them on the back of the chair, not that they have much hope of drying out with the humidity in here. As the sun fades out and rain streams in silver rivulets down the outsides of the glass walls, it hits that for the first time this summer, I don't have to worry about sunscreen.

Martina and Aster start chatting about some kids in their class, and I take a sip of my mocktail. The bite of the lemonade and fizz of the seltzer taste familiar too, somehow, like a memory on my tongue. Before I know it, I've drained the whole cup.

"They're good, right?" Aster asks, drawing me into their conversation. "The Lemon Spritz is a George Spanos specialty."

"Did I hear my name?" We all turn our heads to look back to the sliding glass doors, where a bearded, thick-waisted man in his late forties now stands. He's wearing plaid golf shorts and a lime green polo shirt. Julia Child lets out a series of excited yaps and scrambles from beneath Aster's lounger. While he leans down to scoop her up, I hurry to twist my hair behind my head and loop it into a messy bun with the elastic on my wrist. There's no need for sunglasses, but I slip on the pair from my bag anyway. This is Zoe's dad. The last thing he needs is to find a ghost in his backyard.

"Hey, Dad." Aster pushes up from her lounge chair and walks back to the snack table. "This is Martina's friend, Anna," she says, motioning toward me with her chin and filling a bowl with rosemary and parmesan popcorn.

Mr. Spanos squints at me. Despite my efforts to minimize the Zoe-factor, I know the resemblance is still there, that he's registering it now. I start to ramble, my usual spiel about nannying for Paisley, and how much I'm enjoying Herron Mills, and where I'm going to college in the fall. His face relaxes a little. I'm sure my verbal deluge has done wonders to set me apart from his star student daughter.

When he retreats into the living room to watch a movie with his wife, I keep my sunglasses on. A few minutes later, we're treated to a check-in from Mrs. Spanos, who I definitely recognize from somewhere. I've probably seen her around town. The thought that her hair looks different pops into my head. Not that I have any idea what it looked like before. Then at nine, Mr. Spanos peeks in again.

"They're extra hovery tonight," Martina observes. "Not that they're not always a bit . . ."

"Overprotective?" Aster laughs. "Always were on the helicopter side, but it's gotten a lot worse since . . . January." Her voice drops.

"It's me," I blurt out. "I know it's weird how we look alike." I tell them about Paisley, and how Emilia let her pick her summer nanny.

Martina snorts. "That's hilarious."

"And totally fitting," Aster adds. "Paisley adored Zoe. *Adores*."

We're all quiet for a moment, letting Aster's slip of the tongue linger on the air. It's morbid to think about, but Aster's put a voice to the question no one seems to want to ask: After nearly seven months, could Zoe really, possibly still be alive?

"I miss her every minute," Aster says after a beat. "I thought it would fade eventually. But I don't think it ever will."

Martina reaches out from her lounger and slips her hand into her friend's. Feeling like a third wheel, I get up to refill my Lemon Spritz. In a minute, Aster clears her throat.

"I should have warned them about the doppelgänger effect," she says. "It's my bad." I can feel her eyes lingering on the back of my head.

"It's less pronounced with her hair up," Martina observes.

"Do you think I should cut it?"

"Because of Zoe?" Aster asks. "Definitely not. That's like . . . letting the weirdness win."

"I think it looks good long," Martina agrees.

"Me too," I sigh. "I'm just ready for all the weirdness to go away."

While Martina calls her mom to request a pickup at a few minutes before the appointed time, I slip back into my still-damp shorts and top and Aster points me toward the hall bathroom so I can pee before we go. Halfway there, I sense a pair of eyes on me.

"Anna."

I spin around. Out of the shadows of what must be their living room, Mr. Spanos steps into the brightness of the hall. He's taller than I realized, and his beard needs a trim. Something feral and hungry dances in his eyes, which fix on me like steel clamps for a moment that stretches on for days. I'm an animal, snared.

"I just wanted to say what a pleasure it was to meet you," he says finally, but his friendly words hold a challenge, something quivering beneath the surface. I'm frozen in my tracks, but my whole body is shaking. He doesn't seem to notice. His gaze is still trained squarely on my face. "What did you say your last name was?"

"I didn't," I say quickly, my voice a thin rasp. "It's Cicconi."

His shoulders drop then, like those of a marionette whose strings have been clipped, and he leans heavily to the side, full weight pressed against a closed closet door. "You should leave." His voice is soft, but there's no kindness in the words. His grief is right there, shimmering.

"I'm sorry." I'm not even sure what I'm apologizing for. A father's suffering? Or my resemblance to his missing daughter? "We're waiting for Martina's mom. I was just . . ." I gesture weakly toward the bathroom, arm trembling.

"Of course," he says, recovering himself.

I feel his eyes on me the whole way down the hall.

Inside the bathroom, I slump on the edge of the tub and try to stop shaking. His daughter is gone, and here I am, standing in his house, breathing Zoe's air. *So thoughtless.* I wrap my arms tight around my waist. There was something more than grief in the way he looked at me. Blame or pure, unfiltered rage. I have the itchy feeling that if I had just looked closer, I might have seen what's bottled up inside his chest.

I press my fists into my eyes, trying to force my brain into submission. It refuses. Then I lean over and hang my head between my knees, hair spilling out of its topknot and dusting the floor in a thick black curtain. I can't stop seeing the hard outline of his face.

Deep breath in, deep breath out. Maybe I'm reading him wrong. Maybe it was only grief, after all, bubbling to the surface in all its ugly trappings—grief like a gaping wound for a daughter who is gone and likely not coming home again. I feel immediately guilty for making something sinister out of this man's pain.

I let myself wonder what it would be like to have parents who were so present. Helicopter parents, Aster called them. My mind wanders briefly to the second episode of Martina's podcast, to her conversation with Aster's friend from swim team. How she'd been disgusted with people on Reddit for criticizing the Spanoses' parenting skills, accusing them of a lack of vigilance. Now that I've met them, it's clear they're the opposite of inattentive. I can't even get a geographical region for my dad, let alone an email or phone number. And much as Mom complained about me going away this summer, it's not like we'd actually see much of each other if I was home. Not with her two jobs and irregular schedule. I can't even imagine having parents hanging out at home, supervising on a Friday night.

It's kind of nice how much they care. That's the important thing.

I make myself get up and actually pee and get ready to leave. By the time Martina's mom texts that she's out front, I'm calm again, convinced Mr. Spanos wasn't actually as scary as he seemed. The creeped-out feeling has been replaced by a new kind of nostalgia, something distinct from the flashes of memory I've been experiencing all summer. This is more like a longing for a childhood different from my own. Zoe's childhood, maybe, or Martina's. A childhood with money and two parents who won't let you borrow the car because they're worried about you. Who won't let you out of their sight because they love you that much.

But Zoe vanished anyway, I remind myself, and my stomach coils into a tight knot.

24

September

Herron Mills, NY

MARTINA REFRESHES HER screen every two minutes, but no new updates have posted since early afternoon. This is all she's going to get. Tiana Percy coming forward was a hot story for an hour this morning, but it's already faded into the background. Martina should be solving the SAT practice problems she promised Dad she'd do tonight, or struggling through the Spanish homework that might come a bit easier if Mami had ever spoken Spanish with her growing up. Instead Martina presses play on the video clip one more time. The words BREAKING NEWS fill the screen in silver block letters.

"New information has emerged today in the ongoing Zoe Spanos homicide investigation," a too perky newscaster says from behind the desk. "Yale University senior Tiana Percy has come forward as an alibi witness for Caden Talbot, boyfriend of slain Herron Mills teen Zoe Spanos. Miss Spanos disappeared from Herron Mills on her way to a house party last New Year's Eve, and her body was recovered from nearby Parrish Lake in August. Mr. Talbot was previously identified as a person of interest in the investigation and has been cooperating with police."

Photos of Zoe, Caden, and Tiana fill the screen as the newscaster continues.

"Ms. Percy spoke voluntarily with the Herron Mills PD this morning after a high school friend posted a series of photos online, placing her with Caden Talbot at a New Year's Eve party in Westchester during the window police have identified for Zoe's death. Ms. Percy was unwilling to comment on the nature of her relationship with classmate Caden Talbot, but says she was aware of Mr. Talbot's relationship with Miss Spanos."

Martina slumps back in her desk chair. She has to admit, she never "liked" Caden for Zoe's killer, to borrow a term from police-speak. But until now, those hours after 10:30 p.m. had remained unaccounted for. With Tiana proving Caden's whereabouts, at her side in her Westchester hometown, Caden's innocence has been verified. Tiana was able to pull up tons of photos from the party, all of which she'd been saving on her phone. They hadn't been shared anywhere online, at Caden's request. But Tiana's photos can be matched to others from that same party, posted online by Tiana's friends, placing Caden in Rye, NY, between the hours of 11:45 p.m. and 3:00 a.m.

It's a two-hour drive from Rye to Herron Mills under the

best of circumstances. Caden definitely wasn't with Zoe at the White Sand Marina when the last GPS activity registered on her phone. He couldn't have had anything to do with the purchase of the Greyhound ticket, at least not in person. He couldn't have made it out to Herron Mills and back to the Upper West Side by six thirty, when he was seen by Doreen Winn-Carey on her living room couch.

Neither Caden Talbot nor Tiana Percy were responsible for Zoe's death.

Martina pulls up Aster's number, fires off a text.

> Hi. I'm around, if you want to talk?
>
> Miss you.

Martina doesn't expect a reply.

"I hear you got Caden to talk." Anna sounds excited today. Energized. Martina hates to be the one to burst her bubble.

"Yes and no," she says, exhaustion evident in her voice. It's Friday, the day after Tiana came forward, the end of a long week. Martina's in Miss Fox-Rigg's chemistry lab again, staring out the window into sheets of driving rain. The storm's going to mess up the tape, but it doesn't matter. She's not planning to air this interview; this is just a chance for them to talk.

Episode Six went live on Tuesday to thirty thousand downloads and counting. She'd been right; people wanted to hear Caden speak. Even if what she ultimately aired was all about Anna and a two-month-old, unsolved stable fire. It had been too much to hope Caden would actually open up about his relationship with Zoe—or Tiana.

"Yes and no?" Anna repeats Martina's words back to her. "What does that mean?"

"I got my interview," Martina says. "But he wouldn't go on the record about the night of Zoe's disappearance. Not that I expected he would."

Anna sighs. "Thanks for getting me that address, by the way."

"No problem. Any response?"

"Not yet. I'm not giving up, though."

"I hope you hear back," Martina says. "Keep me posted?"

Anna steers the conversation back to Caden. "Did you ask him about the empties in the stable? Did he say anything privately?" Her voice is so eager. Martina gets it. Caden may have a solid alibi now, but it doesn't change the fact that *he knows something*. And now that he's been cleared in the investigation, it's unlikely the police will talk to him again.

Martina scrubs her hand across her eyes. She is slowly beginning to fit the pieces together, understand how this all led to the charges against Anna. When Zoe's body was found in August, Caden was brought back in to speak with the Herron Mills PD. They reinterviewed everyone they'd previously talked to regarding Zoe's case. He felt guilty or scared; something compelled him to tell the police about the bottles he'd found. She can visualize how the conversation went down. *Tell us every detail about the afternoon of January first, even if it didn't seem important at the time.* That's what police always say.

So Caden told them about the empties, how he figured some local kids had broken onto the property while he and his mom were away, how he tossed them. How he'd never tied them to Zoe because she didn't drink.

When the police interviewed Anna, she said she was drinking with Zoe at Windermere that night. She probably mentioned Caden's Glenlivet, and they got her to say they were also drinking beer. The police made sure Anna's story fit Caden's. Match point.

"I did ask," Martina says. "He told me the same thing he told police, as far as I can tell."

Anna groans, the sound reverberating through the phone line. "I don't believe him," she says. "Caden knows who was drinking in the stable that night—he has to. How many people knew he kept whiskey hidden there? They made me think it was me . . . but it wasn't. I'm sure of that now."

Martina wishes she could be that certain. She wants to believe Anna unequivocally. But Zoe's killer wasn't Tiana. It wasn't Caden. The suspect pool is getting smaller and smaller, and no one's coming forward to provide an alibi witness for Anna Cicconi.

25

THEN

July

Herron Mills, NY

THE WEEKEND ROLLS into the new week with nonstop rain, a new baking project with Paisley (peppermint brownies this time), a Disney movie marathon, and finally sunshine and back to the beach on Tuesday. Martina still hasn't heard from Tiana Percy, and at this point, we're both starting to give up hope. Maybe she figured out who Martina was. Maybe I should have been the one to email her. Maybe she doesn't check her university account over the summer.

With the Zoe-Caden-Tiana triangle still a mystery, and all my little memory fragments of Herron Mills and Zoe still refusing to coalesce into a real, tangible piece of my very recent past that I can grasp onto, July in Herron Mills barrels on. On Wednesday, Emilia gives me permission to take Paisley into the city on a day trip, something Paisley has been asking for nearly since I arrived. Second to the Zoe-factor, clearly the New York City appeal was my other big draw.

We take the train back Wednesday evening, exhausted and stuffed with pierogi from Veselka and way too much fro-yo from 16 Handles (Green Tea Vanilla for me and something called Cake Cake Cake Batter with about ten toppings for Paisley). The instant we clamber into Emilia's car at Bridge-hampton, she says she wants "a moment of my time" when we get home, which can't be good. I spend the ten-minute ride sweating, racking my brain for ways I might have messed up with Paisley, then wondering if, after all this time, the Bellamys checked my references and didn't like what they found.

Fortunately, Paisley fills the air in the car with a detailed rendition of the day's events: late morning picnic in Central Park with bagels and lox from Zabar's, followed by the Let's Dance! and Art, Artists, and You exhibits at the Children's Museum of Manhattan, then downtown for a Meet the Residents tour at the LES Tenement Museum, which I'd worried might appeal more to me than Paisley, but was the runaway hit of the day, second only to dessert.

When we step through the front door at Clovelly Cottage, the first thing I see is flowers. Lots and lots of flowers—four huge bouquets on the white marble table in the entry hall, bursting with purple irises, red poppies, bright yellow sunflowers, and a whole host of blooms I don't recognize by name. It looks like someone got married in here today and the happy couple left all the floral arrangements behind.

"Wow," Paisley says.

"These are beautiful, Emilia. Are you hosting another event?"

"Actually, Anna," she replies, voice tight, "these are for you."

Emilia sends Paisley upstairs to get ready for bed, to a chorus of protests. I promise to run up to say good night once I'm done talking to Emilia, a rarity since it's far past the regular Clovelly Cottage dinnertime—and Paisley's bedtime. She vanishes up the stairs.

"A young man named Max Adler stopped by while you were out today," Emilia says. "You know you're perfectly welcome to go out or have guests over outside work hours, but he arrived with two other friends, who he seemed to have recruited to carry floral arrangements, right in the middle of a client call. It was disruptive."

"I'm so sorry," I say, heat flooding my cheeks. "I had no idea he was coming over. I barely know the guy, and I haven't heard from him in weeks. I don't know how he even found me here."

Emilia's face softens. "Men will go to great lengths in their pursuit of a beautiful woman." She gives me a small smile.

"I'm really sorry," I repeat. "Honestly, after the way we left things, I never thought I'd hear from him again. I'll let him know he can't show up here unannounced like that."

"I overreacted," Emilia says, eyes drifting up the stairs after Paisley. She lowers her voice. "I'm the one who should be apologizing. Things have been . . . difficult . . . with Tom this summer. The flowers touched a nerve."

I swallow, mind retracing Tom's sometimes furtive behavior over the past few weeks. I've been so focused on other things, I haven't given Tom a lot of thought, but looking at Emilia's pained face, it hits me that maybe something is going on between him and Joan Spanos. Emilia has acted a little strange every time the topic of Zoe's mom has come up. Maybe I should have told her about seeing Tom's car when he said he was at the office late that first week, and about the person who called looking for him the other night.

"Is something going on with Mrs. Spanos?" I ask, heat crawling up my neck.

"With Tom and Joan?" Emilia bursts out laughing. I slip my foot out of my sandal and scratch my big toe against my ankle. I'm not sure what's so funny. "No, honey," Emilia says, recovering herself. "When I was just a couple years older than you—this was years before I met Tom—I had my first graphic design internship at Joan's magazine. She and I were involved for a bit. I guess you could say Joan was my first love. She was separated from her husband at the time, but they got back together, and Joan and I fell out of touch."

"Oh!" My mind flashes to the photo I found in the back of Emilia's desk when I was rooting around for flash drives. Emilia was young; she had her arm wrapped around an older woman with dark, waist-length hair. Joan Spanos—*that's* why she looked so familiar the other night.

"Anyway, that's ancient history," Emilia says after a minute. "Tom's not . . . it's not an affair. At first, I thought he was seeing someone else. We fought about it over the Fourth. But it's not that. Work has been hard; the company's struggling. The partners reduced his client load by half at the start of the summer. He was too embarrassed to tell me." She sighs and runs a hand along the marble tabletop.

"I didn't realize," I say after a minute. So that's why Tom's been avoiding the office. "You thought the flowers were from him?"

She straightens back up. "It was silly of me to get upset. As I'm sure you're already figuring out, relationships are rarely easy."

"Can I ask you something?" I say after a minute. "Did you recognize that guy Max today?"

Emilia frowns. "I don't think so. Not that I can recall, anyway. Why?"

"We met him at the aquarium; he works there. Paisley seemed to know him from somewhere, so I was just curious."

Emilia shakes her head back and forth, brown bob swishing. "He didn't seem familiar, but Paisley has sharp eyes." She smiles. "Now, do you want help carrying these to the pool house?"

I stare at the lavish bouquets, but all I can see is Max's face twisted into an ugly scowl when I shoved him off me on Montauk. "They look so beautiful in the entryway," I say. "Would you mind if we left them here?"

"Of course not." Emilia plucks a small white card from the center bouquet. "But you should have this."

I take a peek at the card, which reads simply: *Anna, I'm so sorry. Max.* Then I shove it in my pocket and excuse myself to go say a quick good night to Paisley, so Emilia can get on with the bedtime routine. On my way up the stairs, I text Max.

> That was quite a gesture, but you can't
> just show up at my employers' house.
> Please don't do that again.

His reply comes right away.

> Sorry about that. I only wanted
> to apologize. One bouquet for
> each week I should have called
> you. I hope you'll forgive me,
> Anna. 🌼

Typical. He doesn't call for nearly four weeks, then makes some expensive, clichéd gesture. Even if I'd been into him in the first place, I'd never go for that. Four weeks is about three and a half weeks too long. Besides, he's an ass. Before I can write back, he texts again.

> Not just for not calling. But also for
> how I acted on the Fourth. It was
> unacceptable, and I'm sorry.

> Consider your apology accepted, but I
> don't think we're a good fit. Night, Max.

I press send to get him off my back, then switch my phone to silent. I make my way to Paisley's bedroom, a pretty peach room at the end of the second-floor hallway, on the side of Clovelly Cottage facing Windermere. We've played in here a few times, but I haven't spent a lot of time on the second floor. It's a few minutes before nine, and Paisley is changed into a nightgown. On a regular night, Emilia would already have her tucked into bed. I find her seated on a little stool at the room's south-facing window, peering at the night sky through a telescope.

"I forgot you were into astronomy."

She turns and shrugs. "We only hang out during the day. But now you can take a turn."

I survey the several astronomy guides for kids spread open on a round play table near the window. Tacked to a cork board on the wall behind it is a big checklist of constellations, planets, moon stages, and their corresponding observation dates.

"It's really clear tonight," she says. "You can see Virgo. She's the maiden. And Leo, the lion."

Paisley stands up to let me take a look. After a quick, fruitless search for the stars she's describing, I tilt the telescope gently down, toward Windermere. At first, I can't tell what I'm seeing. The estate itself is too far toward the road to get a good look from this vantage point, but as I adjust the lens, my view focuses in on the riding pen—and a clear shot of the charred patch of earth where the stable used to be.

I return the telescope to its skyward-facing position.

"Do you ever look next door?" I ask Paisley. "At Windermere?"

She scrunches her nose at me. "That would be snooping."

I shrug. "I'd be curious, that's all."

"I have to brush my teeth," she says, hurrying suddenly into the hall and toward the bathroom. Clearly this conversation is a nonstarter.

I'm left alone in her bedroom. Maybe Paisley's a better person than I am. But if I were an eight-year-old with a clear view of the neighbors' backyard, I'd never be able to tear my eyes away.

Back in the pool house, I lie on top of the sheets and stare at the ceiling. I click my phone on out of habit, not even sure what I want. Information. Validation. Something *real*.

In Messenger, I avoid my one-sided exchange with Starr and scroll instead through old conversations with Kaylee, Mike, some girls from school I haven't thought about since graduation. There's no one I want to talk to. Bored, I click over to Requests to see if anyone new has found me lately.

My heart freezes in my chest.

Buried beneath a string of *hi*'s and *sup*'s and *hey beautiful*'s from guys I don't know are two requests dated 12/10 and 12/28.

The messages are from Zoe Spanos.

PART IV:

A Body

You're a story, but that doesn't make you any less true.

—Melissa Albert, *The Hazel Wood*

26

NOW

September

Herron Mills, NY

"IT'S CALLED A pretrial motion to dismiss. They filed it yesterday on the grounds of police misconduct. I shouldn't have been interrogated for hours without a recording, or before my mother arrived. And of course my confession was inconsistent with the autopsy results, which should help my case." Anna's voice is alive today; there's none of the dull flatness Martina has become used to.

"So what happens now?" It's almost five on Saturday afternoon. Martina is positioned in her bedroom closet again, talking to Anna when she should be doing about five other things. She's supposed to take the SATs next weekend, but Mami and Dad don't know she's already rescheduled for the November exam date. This is more important than some test she's going to bomb anyway.

"We hope the judge agrees to dismiss the case. But a lot can still happen."

"Such as?"

"Well, the prosecution will probably file a response contesting our motion. My lawyers said it's almost guaranteed that will happen, so I'm ready for it. Then the judge sets a date for both sides to appear in court and argue our positions."

"And then she decides whether or not to grant the motion?"

"Right. If she denies it, we're back to where we started. Either I agree to a plea, or we go to trial. But if she grants it, the charges against me will be dismissed. I get to go home." Martina's not sure, but she thinks the strain she hears in Anna's voice might be tears.

"How long will you have to wait?" she asks softly.

"I'm not sure. I think the prosecution has to respond pretty fast, but then it depends on the judge's schedule and what date gets set."

Martina exhales slowly through her teeth. Zoe's family is going to be livid. She can already envision the holes Aster's eyes will bore into her skull at school on Monday. But if Anna is innocent, this is good news. The best she could have hoped for. Martina decides to focus on that.

And she has some news for Anna—news she's pretty sure hasn't gotten to Anna's legal team yet. She's been debating whether or not to say anything since the second they got on the phone, but in this moment, it seems right. She has to tell her.

"Want to hear something potentially exciting?"

"Always," Anna says.

"This morning, I was working at the shop, and Emilia

brought Paisley in around the end of my shift."

"Okay . . . ," Anna says slowly, and it strikes Martina that the mention of Anna's former employers must not be easy. While it's hardly the worst part of all of this, Anna lost her summer job along with everything else.

"Bear with me," she says. "While they were eating their ice cream, Emilia got a call. It sounded like she was talking to her husband."

"Tom?"

"Right, Tom. So she tells him that they're at Jenkins', and that she took Paisley here as a reward for—get this—speaking with the detectives this morning."

"About what?" Anna's voice pitches up. "Did she say?"

"Not specifically," Martina says, "but what aside from your case could Paisley Bellamy possibly need to speak to detectives about? Maybe they were giving a character statement."

"Maybe," Anna muses. "I'll ask. If the case does go to trial, maybe my lawyers want Emilia and Paisley to speak as witnesses on my behalf. I'm not really sure how all that works."

"Me either," Martina admits. "But this is a good thing, Anna. It has to be. Things are happening, finally."

"I just want to go home," Anna says, her voice small. "I don't even care anymore if I never find out what really happened. I'm so tired."

"I know," Martina says, although she doesn't, not at all. She doesn't have any idea how Anna must feel, locked up in juvie week after week. And while Anna might be too tired to care about the truth, Martina isn't. The need to know burns inside her, intense and center-of-the-sun hot. She's so close to the truth, she can taste it, molten lava scorching her tongue.

THEN

August

Herron Mills, NY

OVER THE PAST three days, I've reread Zoe's messages so many times I've lost track.

12/10: Hi. I tried to add you, but it looks like we don't have any mutual friends. I know this is random, but there's something I'd really like to talk to you about. I'm in Providence, at school, but I'm going to be home over winter break soon, and you're in Brooklyn, right? I could come out there or you could come to Herron Mills. Message me back?

12/28: Hey Anna. I don't know if you saw my last message. Anyway I'm home now. If you take the LIRR to Bridgehampton, I'll come pick you up. I'd be happy to pay for your ticket. There's some stuff I think you should know,

and I'm not trying to be cryptic, it's just better if we talk in person. I'm at
631-959-4095 if you want to give me a call.

When I read her messages one way, she's writing to a
girl she knows. When I read them again, she's talking to a
stranger. I read them so many times I can recite Zoe's words
in my sleep.

On Saturday night, I'm alone in the pool house, Zoe's
messages open on my screen. I look away, but the words
dance along the bedroom wall. She gave me her number.
I didn't respond to her on Messenger, but I could have
called her. I don't remember doing it, but then again, I don't
remember reading these messages before either. And Messenger shows that I did. I click over to my call log, but I
already know I won't find anything there. I've only had this
phone since June.

A persistent voice inside my head says I called Zoe in
December. That three days later, I came to Herron Mills like
she asked.

And then she disappeared.

I stare at her messages one more time. Then I write back.

8/1: Zoe? Hello?

In the two weeks that have passed since my last awkward
movie night with Caden, we've texted some, but I've only
seen him a couple times around the neighborhood when I've
been out with Paisley, and neither of us has suggested making another plan to hang out. Charlie's come and gone from

Windermere a few times over the past week, although as far as I can tell he's only gotten as far as replanting the grass in the backyard. The ruins of the stable remain untouched. Not that I've been spying. Much.

On Sunday, four days after I discovered Zoe's messages on my phone, I sit alone in the pool house for what seems like the hundredth evening in a row. Dinner's over and there's still so much night left. I think about texting Martina, but I basically invited myself along last weekend. I should probably wait for her or Aster to invite me next time.

Finally, I pull up my last messages with Caden and fire off a text. It's clear that things have shifted between us, but only I know why. If Caden thinks I got weirded out by his mom or lost interest in his friendship or even that I had something to do with the fire, he's kept his thoughts to himself.

Over the past four days, my mind has been churning, Zoe's messages triggering more and more fragments of memories that don't fit together. There's the indoor pool at Zoe's house, but it's not just that. I've been remembering specific details *about Zoe*. I've scratched the surface of something; I just need a little more information to connect the dots. And I think Caden can help.

Hey. Long time.

I stare at Caden's reply, then start typing.

Yeah, I know. Just busy. You want to come over and hang?

Can't really leave, as per usual. But you
can come over here. Come around front,
you can see the work I've done on the
pond.

A few minutes later, I'm waiting for Caden to let me in at
the front gate. It hits me that this might be the last time he
invites me over to Windermere. After everything I'm about to
ask, he'll probably give me a wide berth. But I can't help it. I
need answers. Caden has them.

It's only a little after seven, and the sun is still bright in the
sky. Caden gives me a tour of the renovated pond, which he
says is ready for fish again. The overgrowth has been cleared
away, revealing a pretty stone rim around the edge. He explains
that the whole thing had to be drained, the liner and skimmer
pump replaced, and so on. Honestly, compared to the shape
of the estate's interior, fixing up the koi pond seems a bit
like putting lipstick on a pig, but with Mrs. Talbot's health—
and indoor aviary—I can see why he would want to focus his
energy on an attainable goal.

I plop down in the grass and hug my knees to my chest.
Tonight, I'm wearing my hair down, and my sunglasses are
propped on top of my head. The Zoe-factor is in full effect,
and somehow that feels fitting.

"I don't know how to explain this really," I say, "so I'm just
going to dive in. I need to ask you a couple questions about
Zoe."

Caden frowns and joins me in the grass. "You're not recording this for Martina, are you?" He narrows his eyes as if I
might be concealing a wire under my clothes.

"What? No. It's just, over the last few days, I've remembered some things. At least, I think they're memories. That's why I need your help."

"Things about Zoe?" His voice is filled with skepticism. "Like the pool?"

"I know it sounds crazy," I say, then stop. Probably using that word around a kid with a mentally ill parent isn't cool. "What I mean is, I know it sounds impossible or really strange, but Zoe and I . . . I think we knew each other." I take a deep breath and continue.

"The first week I was here, Paisley and I went to Jenkins' Creamery, and they had this featured flavor, Chocolate Caramel Popcorn. I don't even like caramel usually, but I *had* to order it. And then it hit me, all these weeks later—that was Zoe's favorite flavor. That's why I remembered it."

Caden's mouth is hanging slightly open.

"I'm right, aren't I?" I press. My heart is a wild animal in my chest. This is it. Caden's going to help me solve this thing.

He nods, then swallows. "She always ordered it. Never wanted to try anything else."

"Her favorite color," I go on. "It's gold. She'll go for yellow as a compromise, but she loves gold best."

"Gold looks really great with her complexion," Caden says. "She'd always say it made her feel . . ."

". . . like a princess," I finish for him. Because somehow, I know. I remember. She told me that too. We *did* meet up in December. Maybe we even knew each other from before. This is not just in my head.

"Holy shit," Caden says. The look on his face isn't surprise. It's something between shock and horror.

"She loved all kinds of animals," I continue, confidence growing. "She was great with them. But she was terrified of thunderstorms. Like, drenched in sweat, full-on anxiety attack, terrified. There was this one closet on the first floor of her house, right between the bathroom and the living room, where she'd go during storms. There was a light in there, and all the coats, they'd muffle the sound."

"Astraphobia," Caden says softly. "She worried about storms at sea, didn't want the phobia to hold her back from participating in marine research trips. We talked about it a lot."

I nod. There's no way my brain could have cooked that up. It's so specific. It *has* to be a memory. Which means this last one is too. "And her favorite poem—*our* favorite poem—was Tennyson's 'The Lady of Shalott.' I've loved it since childhood, ever since I saw *Anne of Green Gables*. Anne tries to act out the poem and almost drowns in the lake."

Caden's eyes pop.

"I know it sounds morbid," I continue, "but she gets rescued by her arch-nemesis, Gilbert Blythe. I think Zoe and I used to recite the poem together, our favorite stanzas, just like Anne did. The poem is the most beautiful tragedy. And it was ours."

For a moment, we're both silent. All the pieces that have been shifting and crossing like shadows in my mind are taking full, vibrant form. These memories are real; Caden's confirmed it. In a way I still can't account for, Zoe was a part of my life.

Then, Caden asks the question I've known would be coming. "How do you know all this, Anna?"

I'm silent because I don't know what to say. Fact: Zoe

messaged me in December, before she disappeared. Fact: I know things about her life that only a friend would know.

After that, it all gets blurry.

"Is this some sick kind of joke?" Caden is saying. "Is this coming from Paisley?"

"No," I say, my voice insistent. "I promise it's not that."

"Because you look a lot like her," he says, "as you know. You sure you're not just . . . a little fixated? No one would blame you for being curious. But this, whatever this is with the pool and now all these supposed memories about Zoe, it isn't healthy. You need to drop it."

My breath catches because a part of me knows he's right. Everything about this feels very, very not healthy. Almost dangerous. But . . . "I swear to god," I say. "I'm not making this up."

For a moment, Caden looks like he wants to scream at me. But when he speaks again, his voice is calm. "Before, you told me you used to party a lot. Black out. Did that happen often?"

"More than it should have."

"Did it happen on New Year's?"

I don't say anything. I can see something happening behind Caden's eyes. There's some kind of calculus at work, variables shifting, a formula taking shape. I shove myself up off the grass.

"I should go."

Caden gets up too. "I think maybe you should." There's a hard edge to his voice, a meanness there.

"Look, I'm not lying to you," I say, suddenly defensive. After all, he's the one who's been lying to everyone about his supposedly perfect relationship with Zoe while he was trying to get up the nerve to leave her for Tiana. "These memories are real."

"If you know something about where she is," Caden says, jaw twitching, "you need to tell someone, Anna. You need to tell the police."

"I don't." I take a step back. My heart is beating wild again. "I swear."

Caden gives me a hard stare. I try to hold his gaze, but it's piercing right through me.

"I think you should stay away from Windermere for a while," he says.

My eyes fly automatically to the house, to the ravens gathered once more on the third-floor balcony rail. A window opens, and for a moment the sky in front of Windermere is a cloud of black feathers. Then, the birds reconvene in a nearby tree, revealing the thin face of Mrs. Talbot at the window. Her words from Tom's party, which seems a million years ago now, come flooding back to me: *I won't expect to see you at Windermere again. We don't need anything . . . stirred up.*

I turn and run.

28

August

Herron Mills, NY

MY DREAMS ARE filled with a crackling, hissing static I can't switch off. Even when I wake, it's like a swarm of angry bees has taken up residence in my head and won't leave. Mercifully, Paisley has a Monday morning playdate with Raychel, so I get a few hours to myself. I float aimlessly in the Bellamys' pool, trying to clear my head, decompress. I need to get it together. I need to snap out of this, whatever *this* is. I dive under, let the water swirl around my body in a cool embrace. I imagine the bees swarming out of my ears, my nose, my mouth, drowning on the slick navy tile below.

When I float back to the surface, they're louder than ever.

I can't focus. My skin itches where my sunburn faded weeks ago. The thought of food makes my stomach heave. When

Elizabeth drops Paisley off in the early afternoon, I take her to Jenkins' and chew ice cubes while she eats. We go to a movie we've already seen twice, and in the dark theater, my mind wanders to rooms filled with murky water and girls in gold dresses tumbling through blackness. When the movie ends, I sit frozen in the theater seat until Paisley shakes my hand.

"Anna, it's time to go."

I forgot where we were. I forgot about Paisley altogether. I can't trust myself with her. I can barely hold two thoughts in my head at once.

Zoe and I were friends. I blacked out on New Year's Eve.

Monday's dreams are more static. When I wake on Tuesday, I'm not sure I've slept at all. In the bathroom mirror, dark rings bloom beneath my eyes like heavy storm clouds. I try to cover them up, but the concealer only succeeds in making me look like a ghost who lost a bar fight. The bees prod me into the kitchen, where Emilia has the local news switched on. I fill a bowl with fruit I know I won't eat while a reporter announces that swimming and fishing have been prohibited in Parrish Lake until further notice.

"They found toxic algae," Paisley says through a mouthful of cereal. "I want to see."

I nod. Parrish Lake. I can do this. "Okay. I don't know how much we'll be able to see, but we can walk over after breakfast and check it out." The bees hum louder in my ears.

Most of Herron Mills seems to have the same idea. Anyone who isn't working is gathered on the shore, watching a crew of park staffers thread across the water on small boats. It's hot out, but I can't stop shivering. Some boaters are pouring something that looks like cat litter from large bags into the lake, while others skim the surface with nets and collect ropes of greenish-brown algae from the bottom with long, sturdy rakes. Paisley spots Martina further down in the crowd and tugs me over to join her.

"It's a fish-safe chemical herbicide," she says, barely glancing up from her phone to greet us. "I already asked." I look at her screen, which is open to the notes app. The words dance like tiny insects in the sun. I think about ants, frying beneath a magnifying glass, and shiver again. Martina keeps typing, then finally drops her phone to her side.

"Fascinating stuff?" My voice sounds strangely high-pitched and strained through the bees' persistent drone.

She shrugs. "School starts back up in a few weeks. I need to go into the semester with a few ideas for the paper."

I nod vigorously, and her face bobs up and down, up and down.

For the first time, Martina looks straight at me. "Are you okay? You look a little . . . sallow."

"I'm fine," I say quickly. "Just didn't sleep right."

Martina starts to say something else, but before she can get the words out, Paisley is tugging on her dress pocket. "Tell me what happened." She cranes her neck to get a better view through the crowd of adults. "On TV, they said that fish died."

"Yeah," Martina says, attention turning to Paisley. "There was a big fish kill over the weekend, and they did some testing. Looks like there's some new plant life in one part of the lake, and it's toxic to fish. Might also be harmful to humans and pets. They didn't find any in the swimming area, but to be safe, they're doing full-scale algae control this week before they open the lake back up for use."

"Wow," Paisley says, impressed. I wrap one arm around my waist. I can't tell if I'm hungry or nauseous. I forced down a few bites at dinner last night, to be polite, but I can't remember the last full meal I ate. It must have been dinner on Sunday, before Caden told me to stay away from Windermere. My stomach heaves, then settles into a tight, painful knot.

Martina squats down next to Paisley and points toward a park attendant standing on the shore a few feet in front of us, directing one of the boats out further into the lake. "Paula Aimes, Herron Mills Parks Director. Extremely helpful."

I let my eyes travel out across the lake. Toward the center of the water, closer to the bank that faces the Arling Windmill than the shallow, roped-off swimming area, a woman with one of the long rakes is speaking into a walkie-talkie. She's much too far out for me to hear what she's saying, but in the other boats, I can see people lifting their walkies to their ears, then the boats start motoring toward her. Someone in the first boat to arrive raises what looks like a massive spotlight and shines it down into the water below.

Paula Aimes's walkie crackles to life on the shore in front of us, and suddenly the bees are silent. "Hey, Paula, I think we've got something out here. Looks like a small boat sunk to the bottom. It's about ten yards down, give or take, so we're going to need to bring in a diver."

The crowd takes up the buzzing the bees left behind. I hear murmurs of "Catherine Hunt's missing motorboat" and "Do you think she tried to take it out on the lake" and "Zoe" and "Zoe" and "Zoe."

My eyes latch on to the water's bright surface. My ears blot the voices out. The memory comes in a dark, airless rush: *Me pitching to my knees on the shore, the water black and greedy in front of me. The cold whip of the wind across my cheeks, the sickening heave of too much whiskey mixed with god knows what else in the pit of my stomach. Kaylee's scream shrill in my ears, her hands grasping at my arms, dragging me back.*

Zoe's body in the water. Sinking down, down.

"Anna?" Paisley's looking up at me. I force myself to smile, tell her it's fine. We're fine.

When the police arrive, we're all instructed to leave, go home, clear out. We make our way toward the park exit along with everyone else, Martina talking a mile a minute, Paisley clutching both our hands.

"We don't know what they'll find," I assure Paisley, my voice a pale impression of normal. "That spotlight can't work very well on a bright day like this. It could be anything on the lake bottom, just a big rock."

But it's not a rock. I know it, deep in the hollows of my gut. She's down there. Zoe's down there, in that boat. My legs sway beneath me, and Martina clutches my arm to keep me from falling.

"I'm walking you home," she says. "You look sick."

"I'm fine," I mumble, but I'm not. I can't keep the truth compartmentalized any longer: Zoe messaged me in December. She gave me her number. Told me things about her life. On New Year's Eve, she disappeared. On New Year's Eve, I blacked out. . . .

"I'll take Paisley in to Mrs. Bellamy and explain you're not feeling well. You need to get some sleep."

I nod weakly. Paisley squeezes my hand and says she hopes I feel better soon. We keep walking until we get to Clovelly

Cottage, and Martina sends me around back to the pool house while she and Paisley go up to the front.

Somehow, I get inside. When I'm alone, I pull out my phone with trembling hands.

"You need to tell me the truth about New Year's," I say when Kaylee picks up.

There's a long pause on the other end of the line.

"I'm starting to remember," I press. "Something bad . . ." I lean all my weight against the back of the pool house door. My legs are liquid beneath me.

"Anna," she says finally. "We should talk about New Year's. But not on the phone."

"You need to tell me," I say again. "We came out to Herron Mills, you and me. What happened to Zoe?"

"Look." She sounds like a mother reasoning with a disobedient toddler. "I looked up that Zoe Spanos girl. *We didn't know her.*"

Kaylee's voice is insistent. But Kaylee is lying.

"I can handle it, Kay. We were together, you and me. She *died* that night."

On the other end of the line, Kaylee lets out a deep, jagged breath. She's protecting me, but I know. Contained in that sound are all the things she doesn't want to tell me. "Come home, Anna. So we can really talk."

I end the call without saying goodbye. The dark thoughts that have been haunting me all summer dance across the pool house walls in one violent vignette after the next.

Paisley floating facedown in the ocean, blond hair framing her small head like a halo.

Ravens on the Windermere balcony rail. Everything tilting. Falling.

Paisley's broken body slumped across the backseat of the car. Dark water rushing in.

A girl, falling, body twisting in a long white party dress with a pale yellow sash. Her face frozen in terror. My face. Zoe's.

Falling again. The balcony rail disintegrating beneath me. Beneath us.

Shapes in the dark water. Nighttime seeping over the surf. Bodies made faceless in the near-dark.

Kaylee's scream shrill in my ears, her hands grasping at my arms, dragging me back.

Zoe's body in the water. Sinking down, down.

And then I know. This isn't my mind playing tricks on me. This is guilt beating against my skull, forcing itself out. My brain trying to show me the truth about Zoe. About what I did.

In Brooklyn, I was able to keep it at bay for a while. Drown the truth in booze, pot, pills. But not here. Not anymore.

I collapse on the bed, on top of the covers, and press my face into the cool white pillow, willing sleep to come.

PARTIAL TRANSCRIPT OF *MISSING ZOE*
EPISODE SEVEN: MAX FACTOR

[*MISSING ZOE* INSTRUMENTAL THEME]

MARTINA GREEN: In our second segment, we'll hear from another acquaintance of Max Adler's. Mr. Adler was brought in by the Herron Mills PD this past Sunday, September twenty-seventh, for questioning. This follows my own observation that Anna Cicconi's former employers, the Bellamys, spoke with Herron Mills detectives on Saturday the twenty-sixth, however the Bellamy family could not be reached for confirmation or comment.

Getting back to what we know for sure, Mr. Adler is not under arrest at this time, but police are calling him a new person of interest in the Zoe Spanos investigation. While charges against Anna Cicconi have not been dropped, Judge Castera is considering a pretrial motion filed by the defense to dismiss both the charges of second-degree manslaughter and concealment of a corpse brought against Miss Cicconi. If that happens, this case could be reopened as a homicide investigation.

To get the inside scoop on Max Adler, I spoke yesterday with Michelle Heath, a third-year student in the marine biology program at Brown University.

MICHELLE HEATH: Sure, I know Max. He graduated last year, but he was a pretty big presence in the bio department when he was here.

MARTINA GREEN: Can you tell us what you mean by "a pretty big presence"?

MICHELLE HEATH: Max has a big personality. He wasn't the top student in the ecology and evolutionary bio program, but he probably could have been if he scaled the partying back a couple notches. He's charming and easy on the eyes. I'd say most every straight, female biology major knew who Max was.

MARTINA GREEN: Going back to last fall—the fall of his senior year. Was Max dating anyone?

MICHELLE HEATH: Not that I'm aware of. He was dating this girl Maxine when I was a first-year, which I only remember because they were Max and Maxine. But they broke up a long time ago. I heard rumors about him hooking up with a couple girls that fall, but I don't really know. I think he was holding out for Zoe.

MARTINA GREEN: Can you clarify for our listeners that the Zoe in question is Zoe Spanos?

MICHELLE HEATH: That's right. Max had it bad for Zoe, it was pretty obvious. I wasn't super close with her, but we had a lab together that fall. This one time toward the end of the semester, she was getting all these texts during lab. We were partnered up, and she kept stopping to check her phone. It was annoying. She apologized, saying Max wouldn't stop texting her.

MARTINA GREEN: And you're certain the texts were from Max Adler?

MICHELLE HEATH: Completely. She showed me her screen; there was a whole string of texts asking her to meet up with him that night.

MARTINA GREEN: Do you remember when this was specifically?

MICHELLE HEATH: Early December, I think. It was right before winter break.

MARTINA GREEN: Do you know if Zoe did meet up with Max? Did she tell you anything else about the nature of their relationship?

MICHELLE HEATH: No, sorry. Like I said, we were just bio friends. I knew she had a boyfriend from home; probably, Max was trying to get Zoe to break up with him. But I'm just guessing.

MARTINA GREEN: Listeners, while the exact nature of Max Adler's relationship with Zoe Spanos remains unclear, what we know for sure is this: They knew each other from Brown and were close enough that they had exchanged phone numbers. We know also that the Herron Mills PD found reason to bring Mr. Adler in for questioning this weekend. I hope to bring you further updates on this development next week.

I had planned to conclude this episode with a follow-up conversation with Anna Cicconi, but her legal team is not permitting further interviews while her pretrial motion is pending. I did speak with Anna off the record on Saturday, and she expressed her enthusiasm that *Missing Zoe* has gained so many listeners since we spoke earlier this month. In fact,

Episode Six reached a record sixty thousand downloads, which is all thanks to you.

Please keep listening. I'm Martina Green, and I'll be back next week with more *Missing Zoe*.

[CODA TO *MISSING ZOE* INSTRUMENTAL THEME]

29

August

Herron Mills, NY

WHEN I WAKE UP, it's dark. A full moon glows outside the window. I'm not sure how long I've been sleeping. On the nightstand are two cold pieces of toast and a glass of orange juice. It looks like I drank half of it, but I don't remember that. I don't remember Emilia coming to check on me either, but she must have. Next to the plate is a note:

Sleep as long as you need to. Please call if you need anything. -Emilia.

I force myself to sit up and take a couple wooden bites of toast. I feel hungry, but my stomach clenches, and I push the plate aside, afraid I won't be able to keep it down. I search my pockets for my phone, then my bag. My legs feel like rubber bands; my mouth tastes like chalk. Finally I find it plugged into the charger in the pool house kitchen. Emilia must have done that too.

I lean heavily against the counter and navigate to the news, dreading what I know I'll find, but needing to see it anyway.

George Spanos of Herron Mills, NY, was seen entering the town morgue at 3:47 p.m. on Monday. Local officials confirm he was called in to identify the body of a young woman found in Parrish Lake. Earlier this morning, Parks Director Paula Aimes alerted police to the presence of a small motorboat submerged toward the center of the lake, which was discovered by her staff during algae cleanup efforts. When it was raised to the surface, a young woman's body was found in the bed of the motorboat, enclosed beneath a tarp.

While officials have not yet confirmed the identity of the body, the disappearance of nineteen-year-old Zoe Spanos from Herron Mills last December 31 is at the forefront of local residents' minds. A small motorboat belonging to Catherine Hunt, also of Herron Mills, was reported missing that same night, and police have long suspected the two events may be connected. . . .

I stumble into the bathroom and lose my two bites of toast into the toilet bowl.

When I crawl back into bed, I'm afraid to close my eyes. The bees are back, swirling around the inside of my skull until all I can hear is a dull, ringing wail. Three days after she messaged me, Zoe disappeared. And now, a boat. A body.

In my mind, I'm on the balcony at Windermere again. It's

winter; fat flakes swirl all around, and on the railing a white ribbon of snow is starting to gather. The night is cold and crisp; the house lights are out, but up above, a round moon glows through the treetops, and the sky is dotted with stars. Zoe's there, in a gold dress with a billowy taffeta skirt. Her hair is twisted up in a high knot; she looks like a ballerina.

Kaylee's there too, huddled into her puffy winter coat and clutching a highball glass. She raises her glass toward me in a toast, and it sparkles golden in the moonlight. Then she drains it in one gulp before slipping through the door, into Windermere.

I look down at myself. I'm wearing my ugly brown winter boots and the navy peacoat I've had since tenth grade. Beneath my coat is a party dress.

"Aren't you cold?" I ask Zoe. Kaylee and I are all bundled up, but she's only wearing a summery dress. Zoe laughs, the sound a shower of stardust in the night.

"Dance with me, Anna." She twirls once, twice, her slippers making delicate circles in the snow. Then she reaches out, and I take her hands in mine, one arm crossed over the other in a long X. She's laughing, and then I'm laughing, and we're both twirling, ballerinas in the crisp winter night. We spin and spin, and then I feel my feet slipping on the snow.

"Anna!" she screams, and her hands slip out of mine, two birds bursting into flight. And then Zoe, too, is flying, the backs of her knees glancing off the balcony rail, her gold dress soaring into the moonlit night, and I'm falling back, back, onto the balcony, my back striking the ground, then my head, and everything fading into blackness.

I squeeze my eyes shut, press my fists into the lids until I see stars. It would be so easy to dismiss everything I just saw as the work of my overactive imagination.

But I can't.

The sun is streaming bright and hot through the pool house windows. It's late. My phone is buzzing on the kitchen counter, a text message reminder. Something tells me it's been buzzing for a while. I drag myself out of bed and into the bathroom, where I stick my head under the faucet and gulp mouthfuls of cold water. I can't get enough. I drink and drink until my stomach hurts. My phone buzzes again, drawing me into the kitchen. The texts are from Caden.

> You probably know already,
> Zoe's dad identified her body.

> I'm leaving the police station now.

> This text is a courtesy, Anna. The police
> are going to be coming to Clovelly
> Cottage this afternoon.

> I don't understand it, but I know
> you know something. You need
> to talk to the police.

I close out of the texts and look at the time. 1:20 p.m. I've been sleeping for over twenty-four hours. I can't believe Emilia let me sleep so long. My chest tightens with a fresh rush of guilt.

In the bedroom, I grab my sketchbook and watercolor

pencils from the table. Then I flip through to a clean page and begin to draw, letting my memory guide me.

My hand flies across the paper in confident, bold strokes. It's a sketch of the famous Waterhouse painting of the Lady of Shalott, a painting I've copied dozens of times before. I don't even need to look at the original; I can copy it from memory. But instead of Waterhouse's red-haired lady, the woman in the boat is Zoe. My watercolors capture her raven hair, olive skin, the boat her watery grave.

I breathe.

For the first time in days, everything is perfectly, brilliantly clear. I've been moving through a dense gray fog, and suddenly the sun is out. I understand it now—what my brain's been trying to tell me.

Caden's already notified the police. No sense in waiting for them to come here, to the Bellamys' front door. I still feel nauseous and a little unsteady, but the bees are gone. I set my pencil down and tuck the sketchbook away. With a grim, fixed determination, I turn on the shower and pull a red tank top and a clean pair of cutoffs out of my drawer. I'm going to get ready. And then I'm going down to the station myself.

PARTIAL TRANSCRIPT OF *MISSING ZOE*
EPISODE EIGHT: THROUGH A TELESCOPE LENS

[ELECTRONIC BACKGROUND MUSIC]

YOUNG MALE VOICE: . . . a couple days after Christmas, she starts texting me. Wants to know if I want to hang out over break. . . . Then sometime midafternoon on New Year's, she asks if I want to come out to Herron Mills for a party at this guy Jacob Trainer's house.

[END BACKGROUND MUSIC]

MARTINA GREEN: Thanks for tuning in to the eighth episode of *Missing Zoe*. Today is Tuesday, October sixth, and it's been two months and two days since Zoe's body was found in Parrish Lake. Her death remains unsolved, and we're still missing Zoe.

[*MISSING ZOE* INSTRUMENTAL THEME]

MARTINA GREEN: I'm going to cut right to the chase today. As you know if you've been following the action in the past week, Max Adler of Montauk, New York, was brought in for questioning in the Zoe Spanos case, identified as a person of interest by the Herron Mills PD, and then released without charge. I caught up with Mr. Adler over the weekend at his family's home in Montauk, and I'm pleased to bring that interview to you today.

MAX ADLER: There's a lot of misinformation out there, and I've seen a bunch about myself this week. To be perfectly honest, I don't trust the mainstream media. But people are listening to your podcast, and I want to clear some things up.

MARTINA GREEN: Thanks for agreeing to speak with me, Max. Why don't you go ahead and tell us what happened with police this past weekend.

MAX ADLER: Right. I got called into the station on Sunday morning. I agreed to go voluntarily; I was never arrested. Detectives Holloway and Massey said they had some questions about the night Zoe Spanos disappeared, following a conversation they'd had with the kid Anna had been babysitting this summer.

MARTINA GREEN: Did they tell you the content of that conversation?

MAX ADLER: They did. Seems she saw me through her bedroom window on New Year's Eve; I guess the girl has a telescope in her room. The Bellamys live next door to the Talbots—Caden Talbot is the guy Zoe had been dating, as everyone knows. Apparently fireworks woke the kid up after she'd gone to bed that night. She went to the window to look and saw Zoe and me entering the stable, then me leaving alone.

MARTINA GREEN: And is that true? Were you and Zoe at the Talbot estate on New Year's Eve?

MAX ADLER: Yeah, we were there for about an hour that night.

MARTINA GREEN: Can you tell us what you told police?

MAX ADLER: Here's the deal. Zoe and I know—um, knew—each other from bio at Brown. I was two years ahead of her, and I had a girlfriend when she was a first-year. But then last year, I was single, and Zoe and I kept running into each other around the department. I finally convinced her to go out for a coffee with me, and she told me she was having a rough time at home. Stuff with her dad, although she didn't say what. Things weren't great with her boyfriend either. He'd been distant since the summer, she thought they were drifting apart.

Naturally I figured she was opening up to me about this for a reason. I thought she was interested. I asked her out a few times, and she kept saying not right now—but it wasn't a hard no. I didn't push, but I figured she was waiting to see how things played out with her boyfriend. I respected that. Then after Thanksgiving, she came back to campus and called me, super upset. She asked me to meet her in the library, so I went. Said while she was home over Thanksgiving, she'd found these pictures and emails on Caden's computer. He was in love with another girl.

MARTINA GREEN: Zoe knew about Tiana Percy?

MAX ADLER: Tiana, right. She was in the news recently, provided Caden's alibi for New Year's Eve. Anyway, Zoe came to me about this, right? I figure she wants revenge at the very least, or even better, she's ready to move on.

MARTINA GREEN: And then what happened?

MAX ADLER: Nothing. She tells me she shouldn't have said anything, and she has to leave. She barely talks to me again until it's almost winter break, and then the weekend before break starts, I hear she's at Yale visiting Caden. So I figure they worked things out, whatever.

MARTINA GREEN: Did you see her again before the semester ended?

MAX ADLER: Just once in the lab. But then, a couple days after Christmas, she starts texting me. Wants to know if I want to hang out over break. I say sure, but she drags her feet on making a plan. Then sometime midafternoon on New Year's, she asks if I want to come out to Herron Mills for a party at this guy Jacob Trainer's house. Turns out Jacob and I have a couple friends in common from baseball back in high school, so I say sure, I'll go. I had plans in Montauk, but I ditch them for her.

MARTINA GREEN: Did Zoe ask you to meet her at the party?

MAX ADLER: No, she wanted to pre-party before we went over. Told me to meet her at Windermere and gave me the address. I thought it was her house; I didn't know it was Caden's. She met me at the front gate and took me around back to the stable. The Bellamy girl must have watched us walking inside.

MARTINA GREEN: And when was this?

MAX ADLER: Early. Nine thirty maybe?

MARTINA GREEN: Okay. What happened once you got to the stable?

MAX ADLER: Like I said, Zoe wanted to pre-party before we went out. I'd brought a six-pack, but she had an open bottle of whiskey in the stable, and judging from how she was acting when I got there, she was already a couple shots in when I arrived.

MARTINA GREEN: And how was Zoe acting?

MAX ADLER: She was all over me. Kissing me, running her hands all over my chest. It was cool at first, we made out for a while. I offered her a beer, but she said she was going to stick with whiskey. Judging by how emotional she got, I don't think she was much of a drinker.

MARTINA GREEN: Do you know how much she drank that night?

MAX ADLER: The bottle was almost empty when I got there. But I don't know how much she'd already had. I stayed long enough to drink a beer and part of a second before she really started flipping out. She kept running her fingers along her neck. She wasn't wearing that necklace she always has on—the little gold chain with her initials on it?—and it was like she kept reaching for it, but it wasn't there. Things got real weird when she started crying and kind of writhing around on the stable floor, moaning about Caden and Tiana. That shit killed the mood real fast.

MARTINA GREEN: Did she say anything specific that you remember?

MAX ADLER: She wasn't making a whole lot of sense, but she said something about being in Caden's stable, drinking his whiskey, and then I put two and two together. She had a flash drive in her fist she kept waving around, and eventually she threw it against one of the stall doors. She was a mess.

MARTINA GREEN: And what did you do?

MAX ADLER: I tried to get her to stop crying, said I'd drive her home. But she told me to leave. I didn't want to leave her like that, but she was screaming "get the hell out" and "leave me alone." Finally, I just left her there.

MARTINA GREEN: You left Zoe in the stable?

MAX ADLER: I know it sounds like a dick move, but believe me, she wanted me gone. I think she wanted to hook up with someone under Caden's roof—a kind of "fuck you," you know? And then she changed her mind. So I left.

MARTINA GREEN: And that's when you were seen again, from the Bellamys' house?

MAX ADLER: Must've been. It was probably around ten thirty, and yeah, there were fireworks going off nearby and a bunch of people partying on the beach. It was loud, normal stuff for New Year's. I left the stable and walked around the side of the house, back to the front where I'd left my car. Zoe must've walked; there weren't any other cars parked on the street out front. Then I drove to Trainer's place. I figured since I'd come all the way out to Herron Mills, I might as well hit up the party. And thank god I did, cause lots of people saw me that night. The police had already looked through a bunch of photos; I was in a few, and I had a bunch of alibi witnesses.

MARTINA GREEN: Did you hear from Zoe at all after you left Windermere?

MAX ADLER: Nope. Honestly, I wasn't that worried. I just figured she'd walked home and was sleeping it off. It wasn't until a couple days later that I heard on the news she was missing.

MARTINA GREEN: And why didn't you go to the police then? You could have helped put a few pieces together months ago.

MAX ADLER: I know, okay? It wasn't my finest hour. But honestly, I knew her disappearance didn't have anything to do with me. She was drunk and upset when I left the stable, sure, but she was fine. I was trying to graduate from Brown. I didn't want to get tangled up in a missing-persons investigation. I don't know what happened that night any more than anyone else.

MARTINA GREEN: And you didn't try to get in touch with her at all?

MAX ADLER: Look, I know this doesn't make me sound great, but no. I didn't. She was a hot mess; it was kind of a turnoff. Maybe I should have checked in with her, sure, but I didn't have anything to do with Zoe winding up at the bottom of Parrish Lake. Walking away when a girl tells you to leave her alone isn't a crime. The police agreed.

MARTINA GREEN: The day after Zoe's body was found, Caden Talbot told police that he'd discovered an empty bottle of whiskey and two empty beer bottles in the stable on January first. Presumably those belonged to you and Zoe?

MAX ADLER: The whiskey was technically Caden's, from what Zoe was saying, but yeah, the two beer bottles would have been mine.

MARTINA GREEN: And it was just you and Zoe pre-partying in the stable. Anna Cicconi wasn't with you?

MAX ADLER: No way. I met Anna for the first time this summer, when she came to the aquarium where I work. She definitely wasn't drinking with us that night.

MARTINA GREEN: And what about Kaylee Harrison?

MAX ADLER: Kaylee . . .

MARTINA GREEN: Anna's friend from Brooklyn who she said in her August fifth confession was with her at Windermere the night Zoe disappeared?

MAX ADLER: Oh right, I've met Kaylee. Anna brought her to a party over the summer. But no, she wasn't there that night. I only met Kaylee once, this July. Unless Zoe invited someone else over after I left, it was definitely just Zoe and me drinking in the stable. Those were our bottles Caden found.

MARTINA GREEN: Thanks, Max.

[SOFT ELECTRONIC MUSIC PLAYS IN THE BACKGROUND]

Okay listeners, it's go time. *Missing Zoe* reached eighty thousand of you last episode. That's huge. That means there are a lot of you tuning in—people who want justice for Zoe, who know that justice doesn't happen without the whole truth. And now it's my turn to ask you a favor. If you have any information about the night of December thirty-first or morning of January first that might help police uncover what happened to Zoe Spanos after Max Adler left her alone in the Windermere stable, this is the time to come forward. Even if it's a detail that seems insignificant.

With the information we know now, the likelihood that Anna Cicconi was even in Herron Mills the night Zoe died is very, very slim. Anna's pretrial motion to dismiss the charges against her is still pending review by the court. If anyone has information that could help prevent the wrongful conviction and imprisonment of an innocent girl, this is the time to step up. Anna needs you. It's your responsibility to help. You can reach an anonymous tip line established by the Spanos family at 631-958-2757, or you can contact the Herron Mills PD directly.

[END BACKGROUND MUSIC]

Next up, I'll be speaking to criminal defense attorney Katarina Wall. Ms. Wall does not represent Anna Cicconi, but she'll be able to provide a general overview of the legal procedures involved in pretrial motions to dismiss in New York State. . . .

October

Herron Mills, NY

IT'S LATE. The night sky swirls with the first inky ribbons of autumn-crisped air as Martina and Aster make their way through the girl-sized gaps in the unkempt privacy hedge that has long ceased to effectively partition Windermere from Linden Lane. A wayward branch reaches out to snare Martina's hair in its grasp, and she pauses a second to free her ponytail, yank it back into place.

Martina's mind travels to the olive branch she extended to Aster tonight when she invited her to come along. Things have been frosty verging on arctic between the two girls since Martina aired her interview with Anna three weeks ago. There was a momentary thaw when it looked like Max Adler might be a real suspect—a new arrest to give the Spanos family hope while Anna's story disintegrated between their fingers—but with no arrest made and Max's role crystalizing in the public eye (an asshole, for sure, but not a killer), the glares Aster shoots Martina at school have become pure ice again.

Aster walks ten steps ahead of Martina, her pace quick and sure-footed. Martina has barely extracted herself from the privacy hedge, but Aster is halfway down the drive, veering right to skirt the porch, her body swallowed by shadow as she rounds the side of the estate.

Martina picks up her pace. Her friend knows the Windermere grounds well, has spent afternoons here with Zoe and Caden, others babysitting Paisley. But this place—made even more gothic, more ghostly in the cold October moonlight— is uncharted ground for Martina. She stops a moment to tip her head back, straight up to the third-floor balcony that has loomed with infamy in her mind's eye since August. It juts out against the sky, a stone jaw missing a few teeth at the rails. No bird-boned girl could survive a fall from such a height. *But no*, Martina reminds herself, pressing on down the drive, after Aster, *no one fell from Windermere.*

To sort story from reality. Fact from fabrication. That's why Martina is here tonight, at least she hopes. She's here for Anna, mostly. She's spent weeks torn between Anna's potential guilt and innocence, but now Martina is sure. Anna didn't kill Zoe, accidentally or otherwise. But someone did. She hurries quietly around the side of the estate, into the backyard where the weeds reach up to snag her tights like bony fingers in the moonlight. She shivers.

Aster is already at the back of the property, feet planted in the soot where the stable doors used to be. Their destination.

The ruined ground the keeper of Zoe's secrets. Because after Max left Zoe alone that night, something happened. Her story continued, then ended somewhere between the Windermere stable and Parrish Lake. The rational part of Martina's brain says it's too late to find anything here, that the police missed their chance at answers when Caden threw away the empties he found, when Max failed to report his story back when it could have been of any use, before the stable burned to the ground three months ago.

But a small, insistent tug in her gut says she has to look for herself. For Anna. And that bringing Aster with her tonight, including her in this longest of long-shot attempts at finding something, *anything* police missed in the ruins of the Windermere stable, might be the only chance she has of winning her friend's forgiveness. Because if they find something tonight—a scrap of information, a shred of a clue—maybe, just maybe, Aster will begin to thaw the hard wall of ice she's raised between them.

Martina steals one glance back at Windermere, eyes traveling up to the second floor. The windows are dark. Caden is all the way across the Long Island Sound, in New Haven, but Mrs. Talbot is inside, hopefully sleeping deeply. Martina feels bad about snooping around out here without permission, but she knows enough about Caden's mom's desire for privacy to know that asking would have gotten her nowhere. So.

"See anything?" she stage-whispers to Aster as she steps across a charred beam, into the soot.

Aster stays where she is. She hooks her thumbs into her jeans pockets and shrugs. "What's to see?" she asks, not even attempting to whisper. Martina flinches, but they're far enough out on the property that there's no way Mrs. Talbot could hear them through closed windows. Hopefully.

"It's just a bunch of burned-up wood and charred metal," Aster continues. "If there was ever anything to find, it burned with the stable."

Martina presses her lips between her teeth. Aster's not wrong, probably, but she had been hoping that once they got here, Aster would get into the spirit of the search. Instead, her resentment toward Martina is as steely as ever.

"I'm going to start looking around." Martina tugs on a pair of latex gloves and holds another out toward Aster, who takes them soundlessly. Then she slips her phone from her jacket pocket and switches on the flashlight app, holding the beam close to the ground and hoping it won't attract any unwanted attention. Wood crumbles beneath her boots as she walks toward what used to be the far end of the stable, in the general direction of Caden's stall.

At the front of the stable, Aster sinks down onto a plank of what probably used to be rafter and scuffs the ground aimlessly with her foot.

Phone in one hand, Martina begins sifting through the rubble. She's not even sure what she's looking for, if she's entirely honest, which she'd rather not be. She needs to find *something*. Something that will lead to justice for Zoe, that will win her best friend back, that will compel the judge to grant Anna's pretrial motion to dismiss. It's a lot to hope for.

A wheedling voice at the back of her head says the Herron Mills PD won't thank her for meddling with what might be a crime scene, but they've shown little interest in the Windermere grounds after Max Adler spoke with them. She knows they've been out here once, about a week ago, but the visit seems to have been perfunctory. Nothing's taped off, no evidence tagged, no sign that the police plan to return. Their thinking seems to be very much in line with Aster's: Whatever evidence there was to be found here was witlessly tossed by Caden in January or sent up in flames in July. Martina knows it's a real possibility that Zoe left the stable shortly after Max that night, that whatever happened to her happened far from Windermere. But she's not ready to give up yet.

She's been on her hands and knees for less than a minute, tights and gloves thoroughly blackened with ash, when the flashlight beam catches a small glint in the rubble. The fine hairs on the back of her neck prickle. She switches her phone off and slips it back into her dress pocket. Breath hitched in the back of her throat, she glances over her shoulder. Behind her, Aster is still scuffing the toe of her shoe in the dirt, boredom glazed across her face.

Martina's pulse quickens. She won't say anything until she's sure. She scoots closer. As her fingers find the gleam in the ash, cool and delicate and familiar, a voice cuts across the lawn.

"You."

Just the one word. Both girls' heads whip around toward the source of the sound. Ten yards away but approaching fast, Mrs. Talbot is striding across the grounds in a bloodred nightgown and black riding boots. The girls' faces are snared instantly in a flood of white light from the hurricane lamp clutched in the older woman's right hand. In her left swings something else, the length of a hunting rifle. Martina stops breathing.

"Let's get out of here," Aster mutters, shoving herself to

her feet, but before she can run, Martina is next to her, clutching her wrist in her soot-smeared glove.

"Wait," she cautions, frozen by visions of Mrs. Talbot raising the rifle, firing after them as they run across the lawn toward Clovelly Cottage. "Is that *a gun?*"

But it's a parasol with a long, ornate, wooden handle, lovely if rather out of place in the moonlight. Every few steps, Mrs. Talbot presses its pointy tip into the grass like a cane.

"You," she says again, and Aster wrenches herself from Martina's grasp. "I've seen you here before." She raises the makeshift cane, points it straight at Martina. Pretty or not, she doesn't doubt it could do some damage.

"I haven't—" Martina starts to say, but before she can finish, the stick wavers. Toward Aster.

"On my property," Mrs. Talbot continues. "Trespassing, just like tonight." She stops at the threshold to the stable, as if doors still stood between them. The pointy end of the parasol trembles in the air, a foot from Aster's chest.

Martina sucks in a sharp breath. In her jacket pocket, her fingers close around her phone.

"I used to bring Paisley over here," Aster says, voice shaky. "Remember?"

"I know who you are," Mrs. Talbot says, voice slicing the night air. "Little Aster Spanos. Always tagging after Zoe. Your sister's the only reason I didn't call the cops the other times I saw you back here, snooping around. Your family's already had so much grief." Her voice softens then, and the parasol lowers slowly to the ground.

"We're very sorry," Martina says. "We were just leaving." With her free hand, she reaches slowly toward Aster's elbow, ready to guide her friend away from the stable.

Aster flinches back. "That wasn't me," she says, voice pitched high. "You've got it wrong."

"Careful there," the older woman growls. "Don't tell me what I saw." The parasol's pointy tip jabs the air.

This time, Martina flinches. Mrs. Talbot has likely endured a lifetime of people telling her what she saw or didn't see, what's reality and what's an invention of her brain. Maybe Aster didn't intend to make any hasty implications, but she needs to let this go.

The parasol jerks then, toward Martina. She lets out a small gasp, raising both hands in front of her.

"And you," Mrs. Talbot says, eyes narrowing. "You're the Jenkins girl."

"Martina," she manages to get out.

"I'm well aware." Mrs. Talbot presses her lips together in disapproval. "You've done my son no favors with your podcast. Back to stir up more trouble?"

Martina swallows, but her throat stays dry. "We're very sorry. Again. It's just, after what Max Adler told police . . . and they don't seem to be looking very hard, so we thought we'd try on our own—"

"And what did you find?" Mrs. Talbot shines the bright LED light of the hurricane lamp on Martina's raised hands. Her fingers are still wrapped around her phone, and something else, a gleam of gold in the lamplight.

Martina tries to shove it back into her jacket pocket, but Mrs. Talbot's words stop her short.

"I saw you back there, pulling it from the rubble. Is that Zoe's?"

Martina's eyes flicker to her friend. "No. It's Aster's."

In the back of her mind, the implications have been spiraling since the second her fingers closed around the gold hoop earring with the helixed twist. The last time she saw Aster wearing them was the afternoon before Martina's interview with Anna aired. Martina assumed her friend had taken the earrings off to spite her, but the flash in Aster's eyes now tells Martina she was wrong. Dead wrong.

"You don't know that," Aster says, voice high and sharp. "They're hardly one of a kind."

But Martina does know. Fear dances across Aster's face.

"Mrs. Talbot saw you," she says, not quite gently. "On the grounds, more than once. What have you been doing at Windermere?"

Aster's eyes dart between Martina and Mrs. Talbot. She takes a step back. For a moment, it looks like she's going to run, and Martina reaches out toward her friend. Aster flinches away from Martina's grasp.

"I didn't—" she starts to say, then falters.

"I'm sure the authorities will sort this out," Mrs. Talbot says. "If you weren't doing anything wrong, Aster, there's no need to worry." Her voice is brittle.

Aster freezes. Two sets of eyes are trained on her, burning through her skin. To Martina, she looks like a rabbit snared in high beams. Pure panic blooms across her face.

For a second that seems to yawn out forever, no one speaks. No one moves.

Then, lightning quick, Aster's hand shoots down into the rubble. When she straightens up, she's clutching a charred metal beam, about the length and width of her forearm.

Martina stumbles back. "What are you doing?"

"Your fucking podcast," Aster spits, taking a step forward.

Martina's eyes flicker to Mrs. Talbot, silently willing the older woman to *do something*, but Mrs. Talbot is stepping back, back, back toward the house. Away from this turn of events.

"I'm sorry," Martina mutters, although she's not sorry, not at all, just confused. Her mind whirrs. Aster came here, to the ruins of the Windermere stable, the day the interview with Anna aired. She lost her earring. And that's not the only time Mrs. Talbot has seen her on the grounds. Now Aster is threatening her. She's missing dots, or lines to connect them, can't think at all with Aster stepping toward her again, beam trembling in her hand.

"You ruined everything, Martina. Can't you see that?"

Martina can't see anything beyond the twisted piece of metal in Aster's hand. She swallows. "I ruined everything," she repeats. Her heart is pounding. She can't outrun Aster, star athlete versus wannabe journalist. All she has are her words, and they're failing her. "I should never have done the podcast. Gotten involved."

"You were getting way too close," Aster continues. "Back in July. Someone took the flash drive, and Caden's stupid apology card. It was you."

It was Anna, Martina thinks, but this is hardly the time for technicalities. "You set the fire," she says numbly.

"You can't prove that," Aster snaps, panic rising in her voice. "You need to back off. Forget what you think you found."

"I'm sorry," Martina says again. The words taste sour on her tongue. Aster may not be ready to admit it, but it's all coming into focus: Aster had been keeping tabs on the flash drive and Caden's card. When they disappeared, she set the stable on fire. What's still murky is why.

"When she confessed, I could breathe again," Aster says. "But then *you* couldn't let it go. The police believed her. Everyone believed her except you, Martina." Aster's words sing with venom and fear. Blood rushes to Martina's head, roars in her ears.

Behind her, Martina can hear Mrs. Talbot's voice, but she can't make out what the older woman is saying. She must be back at the house by now. Abandoning Martina. Saving herself. She could have left her the parasol, at least, not that Martina's sure she could have used it, even to protect herself.

Aster takes another step forward, and Martina steps back. Her foot lands on a broken beam, and her ankle rolls. First Mrs. Talbot, now her own body, betraying her. She goes down hard, wood splinters biting into her palms and tailbone cracking painfully against the dirt. The earring and her phone skid away from her, into the ash. A whimper slips through her lips, and Aster takes a step forward, two, until she's standing directly over Martina, one foot on each side of her chest.

"Let it go, Martina." It's part warning, part plea. "Promise me."

Martina's eyes fill with tears. Her best friend, petite Aster, too short for swimming and ten times as fierce because of it, is standing over her, metal beam clutched in her hand. It's shaking, hard.

"Okay," Martina says. "Okay."

Aster looks down at the rod, really seeing it for the first time. "Shit," she mutters. She flings it hard into the grass, like it might bite. Then she collapses down beside Martina, buries her face in her hands. "I'm sorry. I don't know what I was thinking. I'd never . . ."

Martina shoves herself up to a sitting position, then places her palm hesitantly on her best friend's shoulder. "Aster," she whispers. "It'll be okay. We're going to figure this out."

"Aster Spanos." A woman's voice cuts across the lawn. Both girls' heads snap up. The woman is striding purposefully toward them. "My name is Officer Gwendolyn Park with the Herron Mills PD."

"Trespassing," she can hear Mrs. Talbot say from somewhere safely across the lawn. "And now this." Martina thinks she can make out a second uniformed figure standing next to her. The older woman's words from earlier flood her ears: *Your sister's the only reason I didn't call the cops the other times I saw you back here, snooping around.* But this time, she'd made that call. Probably before she even came outside.

Thank you, thank you, Mrs. Talbot.

Very slowly, Aster struggles to her feet. She offers her hand to Martina, who takes it, allows herself to be helped up. She searches her friend's eyes, desperate for the truth, but Aster looks away.

"We have a few questions we need you girls to answer," Officer Park is saying. She approaches, shines her flashlight beam at their feet until it lands on Aster's earring. In a minute, her partner is at her side. Carefully, eyes never leaving Aster, he slips on a pair of gloves, then bends down to pluck the earring from the ash. He places it in a baggie, then turns to Martina.

"Is everything okay here?" For a moment, Martina's eyes

stray to the metal rod, where it landed in the grass. Then she turns back to the officer.

"I'm fine."

Out of the corner of her eye, Martina can see Aster exhale.

He nods. "We need you to come down to the station with us. Both of you."

Martina hears the words *voluntary interview* and *your parents* and *your cooperation* and then she stops listening as the officers guide them toward the front of Windermere, toward the car. She tries to catch Aster's eyes one more time, but Aster won't meet her gaze.

31

October

Pathways Juvenile Center,
East New York, Brooklyn

I'M AWAKE NOW.

That's not quite right. I've been awake something like sixteen hours a day—usually more—since I came to Pathways over two months ago. Minimum 1,040 hours of awakeness. But now, these past few days, it's like I'm emerging from a very long, deeply muddled dream. It's that feeling the morning after you've taken something to help you sleep. The drug's still there in your bloodstream, fuzzing the edges, padding the air between you and the bright light of morning. But you're awake. Clawing your way to the surface.

Here's what I know to be true: Something happened on New Year's Eve. Something very bad. But I was not in Herron Mills. And I did not kill Zoe Spanos.

Almost two weeks after my defense team filed the pretrial motion, five days after the prosecution filed their response, and while we're all waiting for the judge to set a date to hear our case, I'm informed that Pathways has finally granted the update to my approved-visitors list that I requested back in August. My lawyers advise against the meeting, prep me on the things I absolutely cannot say. Aubrey, my fidgety social worker, says I should do what will "best benefit my mental and emotional health and well-being." Thanks, Aubrey. Pretty sure both of those things haven't *been* very *well* for a few months now.

But this is a conversation I need to have. I've been trying to reach Zoe's dad for weeks, at his business address so Aster and Mrs. Spanos wouldn't see my letters. On Friday afternoon, the guard who always smells like sandalwood tells me that George Spanos is waiting for me. Now that my innocence has settled in my gut like a solid fact, not a shifting, bruising question, I need to see him more than ever. I let her escort me upstairs.

We're in the lounge, a cold room trying to be warm with stained orange and yellow couches and a few windows that could use a good scrub. A smattering of other inmates with their visitors perch on couch cushions and prop elbows against tabletops. Two guards lean like land-bound hawks against the wall near the door. Across a little white table, Zoe's dad stares down into his oily coffee. I've been trying to see him for weeks, but now that he's here, my stomach is doing flip-flops. I pick at the paint flaking up from the tabletop.

"I tried to come sooner," he says finally. "I got your letters, but I wasn't on your list."

"I know." I meet his eyes for a second, then look away. I

can't unsee the hungry, animal grief that welled there the one time we met, that night at his glassed-in pool. He wants to know why I confessed. I want to know why he didn't tell me the truth.

Before I can utter the words *police coercion* or *false memories* or *compromised reasoning ability* or *improper police procedure,* he says, "I knew it would only be a matter of time before you figured it out. And you deserve to know the truth."

I stop picking at the paint.

"At first, I thought you were jealous. Zoe's life—she had everything. When Aster brought you to our home in July, my heart stopped. This girl, so much like my daughter. Nanny for the family next door to her fiancé. Befriending Caden. Befriending my younger daughter. Stepping into Zoe's life."

"It wasn't—" I start to say, but he holds up his hand. *Was it like that?* Maybe that's exactly what I was doing.

"When you confessed ten days later, I thought . . . Of course you had found each other. Of course you would grow to resent her."

My heart speeds up in my chest. I force myself to meet his eyes. His pupils are wide black pools.

"I don't think . . . ," I say finally, then start again. "We never met, Zoe and me. Not like I thought we did. But she did reach out to me. In December, right before she died. She found me online, said she needed to talk to me, in person. She told me to come meet her in Herron Mills. That's why I thought . . . But I didn't. I didn't respond to her messages. I didn't go to the Hamptons last winter."

Across the table, Mr. Spanos nods, just once, a clipped, careful gesture. His coffee is getting cold.

"You know why she wanted to talk to me. Why she wanted to meet."

He sighs, a long stream of breath that seems to deflate his entire body like a punctured tire. "I think we both know the truth, Anna. I knew the minute I laid eyes on you this summer. Zoe was a smart girl. I knew she suspected, but I refused to talk to her about it. I wasn't ready to admit the truth."

"We look so much alike because we were sisters," I say slowly, watching his face. Testing the words I think he wants me to say out loud. "I'm your daughter."

Mr. Spanos nods. The skin around his eyes relaxes. "I met your mother years ago, when I was separated from my wife. She used to come to Herron Mills on vacation with her husband. John never knew, I don't think. Or maybe he did. Maybe that's why he left your mother. The thing is, Anna, I didn't know for certain until I saw you in July. Your mother never told me. When you were little, I had my suspicions, but Gloria swore you weren't mine. I hadn't seen you since you were three years old, and then, the resemblance was only starting to show. But when you stepped into my house, when you told me your name . . ."

"Why now?" I ask the man in front of me. My father. "Why didn't you say something sooner? You could have . . . you could have saved me. Cleared up this mess!"

He frowns. "I wouldn't go that far. I thought you were guilty, just like everyone else. And telling my wife, telling Aster . . . it would have torn my family apart for no reason. Not when we thought you would go to trial for Zoe's murder."

Second-degree manslaughter, I want to correct him, but I don't.

"And now?" I ask instead.

"Now things have . . . changed."

"Because you believe me? That I didn't have anything to do with Zoe's death?"

"I know you didn't," he says, and tears fill his eyes. "Beyond a shadow of a doubt."

"How?" I almost shout, and the guards snap to attention at the edges of the room. "We're going to court soon, to argue the motion. If you know something that could help my case, you have to tell me. Mr. Spanos, please."

But he's already standing, chair scraping back against the cold concrete.

The next word hitches on my tongue. Then I spit it out. *"Dad."*

He flinches. "I'm sorry, Anna. I've already said too much."

He's not going to tell me. He's going to leave me here.

4 NEW YORK: CRIME AND COURTS

Manslaughter Charges Dropped Against Brooklyn Teen As Long Island Youth Confesses To Role In Covering Up Sister's Accidental Death Last New Year's Eve

Published Oct. 11 at 12:56 p.m.

A Brooklyn teen awaiting trial in juvenile detention since her August confession to involvement in the death of Long Island resident Zoe Spanos, 19, was released on Saturday. Anna Cicconi, 17, was charged in August with second-degree manslaughter and concealment of a corpse. Cicconi's release came on the heels of the arrest and confession of Aster Spanos, also 17, younger sister of Zoe, whose body was found submerged in a boat in Herron Mills' Parrish Lake last August.

On Saturday, Judge Emanuella Castera announced that following Aster Spanos's arrest, Anna Cicconi would be released from Pathways Juvenile Center into the immediate care of her mother, Gloria Cicconi of Bay Ridge, Brooklyn. Judge Castera had been previously considering a pretrial motion filed by Cicconi's defense team to dismiss the charges against her on the grounds of police misconduct. The motion was expedited and granted on Saturday.

While full details of Aster Spanos's confession have not been released, Spanos's lawyer said in a statement this morning that "Miss Spanos has come forward, truthfully and willingly, to disclose information she knew regarding the tragic and entirely accidental death of her sister Zoe last New Year's Eve. Miss Spanos did not cause her sister's death, nor has she been charged as such. She is cooperating fully with police. The Spanos family requests the public's respect for their privacy at this deeply difficult time."

According to police, Aster Spanos was initially taken in for questioning late Thursday evening after a neighbor complained about Spanos and another teen trespassing on her property. In a follow-up interview on Friday, she disclosed information to police regarding her sister's January first death and admitted to finding and concealing her body. The rationale for Spanos's actions is not yet known.

Aster Spanos has been charged with concealment of a corpse, aka Amanda Lynn's Law, a class E felony in New York State. The crime carries up to four years in prison and a $5,000 fine. As a minor without a previous criminal record, it is unlikely that Spanos will serve the maximum sentence, if convicted.

32

October

DETECTIVE MIRA HOLLOWAY'S shift ended an hour ago, but she's still in the interview room, reviewing the tape. It's been over twenty-four hours since Aster Spanos's arrest. This is the third time the detective has watched the interview from start to finish, pen in hand. They were overeager with the Cicconi girl, everything they thought they knew dissolving to mud. But now they've been offered a second chance like manna from heaven. She should really go home, get some sleep. But she needs to reassure herself that this time, they got things exactly right. The case depends on it. Detective Holloway's job depends on it too. She presses play.

The camera lens rests on a girl with the lean muscles of a swimmer and a feathery pixie cut. She sits all the way back in a wobbly metal chair, olive skin covered in denim and soft cotton. She tugs on a long-sleeved gray shirt, bunching the sleeves in her hands.

To the girl's right sit her parents and a solemn-faced lawyer. Hollow circles line the woman's eyes. The man shaved before they came here, but he missed a few spots.

Across from the Spanos family and their lawyer, Detective Holloway sits with AD Massey, their hands propped on a thin metal table, a new addition to the room. AD Massey pushes his rolling chair two inches forward, then two inches back, then two inches forward, then two inches back.

"You can start at the beginning, Aster," Detective Holloway says gently. A small twitch in her jaw betrays how hard she's working to keep her voice free from its characteristic edge.

The girl takes in a deep breath and scratches absently at the skin where her shirt's neckline hits her collarbone. Her mother gives her leg a reassuring squeeze.

"I guess it started over Thanksgiving break, almost a year ago. Zoe was home from Brown, and things were weird with Caden. She wouldn't talk to me about it, but I could see the hurt all over her face.

"That Saturday, Caden was hanging out with friends in the city—at least that's what he told Zoe. She spent the afternoon visiting Mrs. Talbot at Windermere, which wasn't unusual. They were really close. But when Zoe came home that night, she was in tears. She locked herself in her room and wouldn't talk to me. The next morning, she went back to Brown."

"We weren't aware—" Joan Spanos starts to say, but AD Massey silences her with a raised hand.

"This is Miss Spanos's statement," he says. "We need to hear only from her."

George Spanos takes his wife's hand in his, and they both nod at the detectives across the table.

"What happened after Zoe returned to Brown?" Detective Holloway asks.

Aster sighs softly. "I snooped around her bedroom. She'd taken her computer, obviously, but I found some flash drives in her desk drawer. On one, there was a series of photos of Caden with this pretty girl I didn't recognize, and also a bunch of emails that had been cut and pasted into a Word doc. The photos were all saved with Saturday's date, and the most recent email was dated November twenty-eighth, Thanksgiving Day. So it was all really recent, and I figured that must have been what made Zoe cry."

"Did you tell your sister what you'd found? Could she confirm your suspicion?" Detective Holloway asks.

"Not directly, no. Like I said, she wouldn't talk to me about it, which is how I knew something was wrong in the first place. She must have pulled the photos and emails from Caden's laptop while she was visiting Mrs. Talbot. If I hadn't found the flash drive in her desk, none of this would have happened." Aster's chin quivers, and her voice catches. Her mom squeezes her leg again. "If I could go back, I'd never look in Zoe's room. That's what I wish, more than anything."

From two seats over, there's a loud choking sound, and George Spanos raises a tissue to cover his mouth. The lawyer busies himself with his notes.

"What happened next, Aster?" Detective Holloway asks.

"Over the next couple weeks, I tried to get Zoe to open up. Caden was hurting her, and she was just letting it happen. I never told her what I'd found because I knew that would shut

I KILLED ZOE SPANOS

the conversation down. I tried to get her to tell me herself, but she pretended like everything was fine.

"When Zoe came home for winter break, I thought maybe things would change. But Christmas came and went—nothing. If Zoe didn't want to tell me, fine, but it was increasingly clear she wasn't going to confront Caden. She always wanted to make everyone happy. And he was taking advantage of how good she was. That asshole!" Aster's voice rises, and she drops her shirtsleeves to clench the arms of the chair in her fists. "Sorry," she adds, eyes darting to her parents.

She draws in a breath, then turns back to the detectives. "The thing is, I've always looked out for Zoe. She was the best person in the world, but she didn't know how to put herself first."

"Go ahead," Detective Holloway prompts gently, keeping the conversation going.

"When Caden texted her from the city on New Year's Eve, ditching their plans for that night, she told me she needed to be alone for a while, that she was going to take a walk on the beach. She'd been crying." Tears well in Aster's eyes, and she scrubs a sleeve across them. "I couldn't let her keep doing this to herself. It just wasn't fair. So I decided to send Caden a message. Punish him."

Aster's lawyer clears his throat but doesn't stop his client from speaking. Joan's fingers dance nervously along her collarbone.

"Okay. What did you do next?" Detective Holloway asks.

"I went over to Windermere."

"Did you have access to the grounds?"

"Like permission to be there? No, but it's easy to get onto the Talbots' property," Aster replies. "All you have to do is

344

squeeze through that overgrown privacy hedge out front. They were still in the city; there was no one around."

"And where did you go once you'd entered through the hedge?"

"To the stable. Caden used this stall in the back as a kind of hideout; he kept booze there."

"You'd been inside the Talbots' stable before?"

"A couple times, when we were all still at Jefferson. I knew about his hiding spot. I would have left the flash drive in his room if I could, but I didn't have any way inside their house. So I put it right next to his whiskey, where I knew Caden would find it. It was supposed to be an anonymous warning that someone knew—he wasn't getting away with it."

"And what happened next?"

"I went home. Zoe got back a little after I did and locked herself in her room. She left for Jacob Trainer's party around nine that night, as everyone knows. I hung out with my friend Martina for a while, but she had an eleven o'clock curfew, even though it was New Year's. Her parents are strict like that. After Martina left, I couldn't sleep. I stayed up in my room watching crap on Netflix. Around one, I got this gut feeling something was wrong. I started feeling guilty about leaving the flash drive in the stable. I still wanted to punish Caden, but it was Zoe's relationship. I knew she'd be furious when she found out what I'd done.

"I wasn't going to be able to sleep anyway, so I snuck out. Borrowed our parents' car, drove over to Windermere. I could have walked, but like I said, I had this icky feeling in my gut. I wanted to get there fast." Aster takes in a shaky breath and looks at her mom. The older woman nods at her daughter, giving her tacit maternal permission to go on.

"When I got to Windermere," Aster continues, "I knew something was wrong. The stable door was open, and the light was on. I started running, but I was too late." Aster's voice catches, and she drops her face into her hands. "Zoe was on the floor, and she was so cold. She wasn't breathing. There was an empty bottle of whiskey on the floor beside her, and the flash drive was gone." She looks up, straight into the camera. "Zoe never drinks. I can't emphasize this enough. She. Never. Drinks. It never crossed my mind she'd go to the stable that night, I swear."

"But she did," AD Massey says. "What happened when Zoe arrived, Aster?"

"Don't answer that," Aster's lawyer cuts in. "My client couldn't possibly know what happened before she arrived, detectives."

"I'll rephrase," AD Massey says. He turns to Aster. "I want you to put yourself in your sister's shoes. What do you imagine happened when Zoe got to the stable?"

Aster's lawyer holds up his hand, but Aster speaks anyway. "It's okay. She went there with that Max guy, like he said she did. It makes sense. She was hurting, looking for a distraction. But then she must have seen the flash drive. It had these yellow and black polka dots; it was pretty distinct. She would have known right away that it was hers. Maybe she thought Caden had found it in her room and taken it to his hiding spot for safekeeping?"

"Could you smell alcohol on Zoe when you found her?" Detective Holloway asks.

Aster nods.

"Please answer verbally for the recording, Aster."

"Oh right. Yes, I could. There was an empty whiskey bottle right next to her." She glances at her parents again. George is staring hard at his shoes. Joan hastily swipes tears from her eyes, then takes Aster's hand. "She must have, I don't know, gotten alcohol poisoning, or overdosed on her anxiety meds?" Aster's chin quivers, and the tears pooling along the rims of her eyes spill over. Detective Holloway pushes a tissue box toward her, and she takes a fistful.

After a minute, she says, "By the time I got there, she was gone. It was just her body left on the stable floor."

The detective clears her throat and adjusts her position in her rolling chair. "Did you move Zoe's body, Aster?"

Aster nods, then says yes before they can prompt her. "I panicked. My sister was dead *because of me.* I was scared of everyone finding out—my parents, my friends, the police. All I could think was that Zoe was dead, and it was my fault. People couldn't know what I'd done."

"You didn't make your sister drink, Aster," Detective Holloway interjects. "That was her decision. Concealing a body is a felony offense in New York State. Are you sure there's nothing else you're not telling us? If you're protecting someone, we can help."

Aster's lawyer shifts in his seat. His client shakes her head back and forth. "I'm not protecting anyone," she insists.

Detective Holloway and AD Massey exchange a look. "All right," she says. "Tell us how you moved her body."

"I buzzed the entry gate open from the inside and drove the car up to the front. Then I carried Zoe around the side of the house and laid her out in the backseat. She was heavy, but I managed. I never even thought about going back and cleaning up in the stable, but I guess Caden did that for me. I just knew I had to get Zoe away from Windermere, so no one would find her. I kept thinking over and over, I can't get caught."

"What happened after you placed Zoe in the backseat of the car?"

Aster takes in another shaky breath and reaches for a fresh tissue. "I don't think I had a real plan until I got to the marina. I pulled over to the side of the road and dug out Zoe's phone. Then I bought a Greyhound ticket. I picked Asbury Park 'cause I figured it would lead people off-track. I was thinking, I'll just make it look like she ran away. For a while, I think I convinced myself that's what really happened. That Zoe made it to Philly, that she was living a new, fabulous life and laughing at all of us."

"But you knew that wasn't true, Aster," the detective says.

Aster dabs at her eyes. "It was a fantasy, but I wanted to believe it. It was a story I told myself to keep from completely falling apart."

AD Massey rubs his hand across the back of his neck and begins his back-and-forth shuffle with his rolling chair again. Detective Holloway leans forward.

"What happened after you bought the ticket, Aster?"

"After that, I turned her phone off and drove around for a while. I didn't know what I was doing, but I had to get her body out of the backseat. I wound up in Parrish Park. The gate was open; you're not supposed to be there after dark, but it was New Year's. It was totally vacant when I got there, though. It must have been close to 3:00 a.m. There was a motorboat on the shore, on the far side, by the Arling Windmill. I guess somebody had been partying there earlier, brought the boat and then left it. There were bottles and cans all over the grass; the place was kind of a mess."

Detective Holloway and AD Massey exchange a look. They're seeing that quite a few things worked out in Aster's favor. There had been footprints and tire tracks all over the place, and besides, no one had thought to look for Zoe at Parrish Park. Everything is so agonizingly clear in hindsight.

"Tell us about the motorboat," the detective says.

"It wasn't really docked, just wedged halfway on the shore, halfway in the water. When I saw it, I knew what I had to do. That's how it felt. Like this was the solution, the only way to make it all go away. I drove the car across the lawn, right up to the shore, and got her body into the boat bed. I was so nervous someone would see me, my whole body was shaking, but I did it somehow. Adrenaline, I guess."

"And how did you sink the boat, Aster?"

"I started hauling the biggest rocks I could find from the shore and putting them all around her. They looked like gravestones." Aster's voice is becoming hollow, her eyes a little vacant.

"Are you sure the rocks were from the shore of Parrish Lake?" AD Massey interrupts.

"Yeah," Aster confirms. "From the shore."

The detectives exchange another look. The rocks found in the boat bed were, indeed, from the lakeshore. Not from Windermere, as Anna had initially claimed. The truth makes Detective Holloway's skin itch. So much of Anna's story had held water. Until none of it did.

"What happened next?" she asks.

"I didn't know how heavy I had to make it for the boat to

sink, but finally I ran out of big rocks, and I knew I just had to do it. We had a tire iron in the trunk, and I swung it at the body of the boat a few times until it made a crack that looked big enough to leak."

Next to her, George puts his head in his hands. Joan holds her daughter's hand tight, but she's staring at a fixed point on the station ceiling.

"There was a weather tarp on the shore near the boat," Aster continues. "Whoever brought it out to the lake in the first place must have taken it off; I guess they'd taken the boat out earlier and then just abandoned it. Anyway, I fastened the tarp over the bed of the boat until it was totally secure. Then I started the motor, put it in the lowest gear, and shoved it off from the shore.

"At first, I didn't think it was going to sink. It got pretty far out, and my heart was beating so fast I thought it was going to explode. But then some water must have gotten in through the crack, and then more, and then the boat just went down, all at once."

For a moment, the entire room is silent. Even AD Massey has stopped rolling his chair back and forth on the linoleum.

"Is there anything else you'd like to tell us, Aster?" Detective Holloway asks.

"I know I shouldn't have taken the flash drive from Zoe's room or left it in the stable, but I could never, ever have thought that she'd find it, or that she'd drink that night. I never wanted Zoe to die. I wanted Caden to fess up, apologize. It was all *for Zoe*. Everything else was just panic. I'll never stop being sorry."

33

October

Bay Ridge, Brooklyn, NY

"YOU HAVE TO TELL ME."

I've been home for less than forty-eight hours. Mom took a couple days off work to be with me. The JusticeFund she started online covered most of my legal fees, but she can't afford to stay home and babysit me for long. For now, though, it's fine. I'm not ready to go out, face the neighbors' gawking eyes.

But now it's late, and Mom's inside watching one of her shows, and Kaylee's here, sitting with me on the fire escape. It's chilly, but not too cold to be outside. Mom made us hot chocolate—a surprisingly maternal gesture—and it feels weird to be sipping the sweet, milky stuff from thermoses instead of our usual vodka and juice. Weird but good.

Kaylee sighs and leans her head back against the brick. "I

wanted to," she says after a minute. "I tried to get you to come home so we could talk. But you went to the goddamn cops instead."

"I know."

"You have to understand, you didn't remember. For months, you didn't remember anything. We thought it was the best thing, Ian and Mike and me. To just let you forget."

"But then I did. I started to remember."

"And you got everything mixed up."

"So enlighten me, Kay. Tell me what happened on New Year's."

Kaylee takes a long, slow gulp from her thermos. Then she closes her eyes and begins to talk. I close mine too, and the night plays across the back of my eyelids like one of Caden's movies, dancing vividly across the screen at Windermere.

It's New Year's Eve. We're in Starr's apartment, and I can scarcely keep my eyes open. I drank too much, too early. I'm curled up on her worn blue couch in my party dress, and Kaylee's crouched in front of me, trying to jam my feet into the clunky winter boots I insisted on wearing out tonight, so I won't ruin my flats in the snow that will freeze onto the sidewalks in a thin crust tonight before anyone tackles the cement with shovels and rock salt in the morning.

"Come on, Anna," she says, irritation lacing her voice. "Party time."

"Mmmm . . . ," I manage.

"Everyone wants to go out on the beach. Get up, baby girl. You'll get a second wind."

She gives up on my boots and slides in next to me on the couch, then sweeps the usual tangle of hair out of my face and tucks it behind one shoulder.

"You coming?" It's Mike's voice. I blink once, twice, try to look up at him. He won't come into focus; all I see is a blur of fist bumps and chin thrusts that make Kaylee burst out laughing.

"Yeah, we're coming," she says. "Seriously, Anna, you have to wake up."

Fifteen minutes later, we're on the beach at Coney Island, huddled on the stretch of sand between the murky gray water and the creaky boardwalk planks. To our backs, beyond the boardwalk, is Luna Park, its rides shuttered and silent in the deep winter chill. It's ten o'clock, give or take. Too early to go dancing but too late to sit around inside, waiting for something to happen. Ian takes a pull from a pint of cheap whiskey, then passes the bottle to Kaylee.

The cold keeps me awake, but barely. I force myself to look around. We're not the only people out here tonight. A few yards down the beach, far enough away that they look like children under the glow of the lamps on the boardwalk, a group of guys is using the old playground equipment cemented into the sand like their own private gym, doing chin-ups on the handle bars and push-ups against a metal rail set into the ground. A few shops on the boardwalk are open, and people lick swirl cones despite the cold. There's no swimming here in the off-season, but the beach isn't closed, except in the area where we've made camp. Our stretch of sand is marked by a few red flags that whip and snap in the wind in an attempt to keep people off the wooden pier that stretches like a bony finger out into the ocean. We shouldn't be here, but who gives a fuck. The deep shadow keeps us ghosted in the night, veiled from the prying eyes of cops or drunk old men.

"I'm going polar swimming," Starr announces, pale hands and face flashing in the moonlight.

Mike snorts. "You're crazy."

"Watch me," Starr says, and starts out toward the pier.

But we don't watch her. Mike's phone rings, and he holds up a fin-ger, one sec, then walks down the beach toward the playground. Kaylee spreads out the blanket she's had wrapped around her shoulders, and she and Ian collapse back on the sand, a blur of hands and lips and tongues. I leave them to their grope-fest. Up on the boardwalk, arms resting on the rail, is a boy I recognize from around. We've hooked up before. His hair whips into his eyes, then away from his face, reminding me how cute he is. Maybe one time last fall, I stayed the night at his place. I think he was nice. I wander across the sand to the boardwalk.

"I know you." He's looking down at me. I doubt he remembers my name, but I don't remember his, so we're even. He crouches down so his face is level with mine through the railing. He holds half a joint out to me, and I take it. For a minute, we smoke in silence, passing the joint back and forth. I tell him the name of the club where we're going later, and he types it into his phone.

"Maybe I'll see you," he says, and when my lips curve up into a smile, the muscles feel tight.

"Where's Starr?" Kaylee's voice filters through the thin night air. She's close and far away at the same time. Something's wrong with me. I feel a little bit like I'm floating above the ocean and a little bit like I'm buried deep under the sand. I force my fingers to flex, and I'm not sure what I'm touching. It's soft but gritty and a little damp.

"Anna, wake up. It's time to go, and we have to find Starr." Kaylee's hand is on my shoulder, shaking me. Her voice booms in my ear as if through a megaphone.

"Not so loud," I mumble. I peel my eyes open and wait for the world to come into focus. I'm on Kaylee's blanket, sprawled on my stomach. For a moment, it's a magic carpet, and we're soaring high up in the clouds.

I try to concentrate. That joint was laced with something. I don't know what I'm on.

I get my elbows under me and push myself up halfway. Kaylee's gone. I look around until I find her, running out along the pier. "Starr!" she yells. "Holy fuck, guys!"

I shove myself to a sitting position, then to my knees. Someone's pulling me to my feet. Ian. His eyes drill holes into mine.

"Hello, Anna? You are deep in a K-hole or something."

"Am I?" I mumble. Special K. Ketamine. Maybe that's what cute guy's joint was cut with.

Kaylee's voice floats down the pier, across the sand. "This is her coat. Her dress, oh my god!"

In a minute, Mike's next to her. "Calm the fuck down, Kay."

I force myself to start walking. The ocean gleams with the dull grays of storm clouds or car doors below me as I stumble down the pier, Ian trailing behind.

When we get to the end, it all snaps into focus. Starr's coat, dress, and shoes lie discarded on the boards. Her giant satchel bag is nowhere to be found. Kaylee has her phone pressed to her ear with one hand, the other dancing nervously against her thigh. "She's not picking up. God damnit, Starr."

"She's fine," Mike insists. "She's messing with us."

"How do you figure?" Ian asks.

Mike shrugs. "Her bag's gone, right? Either she went swimming with her purse, or she brought a change of clothes. Wouldn't be the first time Starr's pulled some stunt."

We're all silent for a moment. Mike's not wrong about the satchel bag. Unless of course someone stole it. But did any of us actually see her go in the water? My legs buckle, and then I'm kneeling at the edge of the pier, staring out. The water is cloudy and impervious. It's easy to believe

Mike. To believe Starr's fine, standing on the boardwalk at our backs, laughing at us. Because if he's wrong, we're all to blame. We all heard her say she was going in, and none of us checked on her, even once. I stare hard at the water until I think I see the flash of a girl's hand break the surface, and I gasp.

"Starr!" I scream, and then Kaylee's hands are clasped tight around my wrists, and she's pulling me back from the edge.

Because there's nothing. Just greedy, murky water that foams and froths like a hungry wild thing when it hits the legs of the pier below.

"You passed out in the Lyft," Kaylee is saying. Her chin is trembling, but her voice is steady. "On the way to the club. Mike insisted we all still go, even with Starr missing. That we should all just act normal. He'd convinced us, mostly, I guess. That it was probably a joke. And if it wasn't, that calling nine-one-one would only get us in trouble. If she was out there, it was too late to save her."

She takes another slow pull from her thermos. "I called anyway, from the club bathroom. Told the dispatcher I'd seen a woman swimming off the pier. Hung up without giving her a name." She turns, looks me in the eye. "Even then, I knew. Too little, too late."

"Where was I? Where the hell was I?"

"You never made it inside the club, babe. You passed out completely in the Lyft, and then I got you into a green cab headed home."

I close my eyes again.

The cab smelled like Indian spices and old leather.

I think I remember that, but I can't be sure.

I lean my head back against the brick wall behind us. Kaylee's words swirl all around me, inside me, cutting deep. *Starr.* And I let myself remember. I remember the water, the wind slicing across my cheeks. I remember the darkness. The wet mist in the air. I remember staring out across the water, knowing deep in my bones that this was no joke, that my friend was out there somewhere. A girl's body lost beneath the waves. I remember the guilt. Because we didn't even try to help. We wanted to believe that what Mike said was true. Because the alternative was too horrible to consider.

And so I didn't consider it. I let the truth get snared in cheap whiskey and weed and whatever else. I let it lie dormant at the back of my mind for months, unacknowledged, unexamined, until I came to Herron Mills. Until I learned about Zoe. Until the two stories—girls snatched by dark water—became inexorably tangled in my mind.

I let Mike convince me that Starr moved to Orlando the next week. He said she got a job at one of the theme parks, and it started right away. And I believed him. Why would he lie about something like that?

And no one looked for her. Not all girls have a family like Zoe's. Starr had been estranged from hers since she was sixteen. Because of us, because of what we did, no one even knew she was missing.

Starr always talked about moving south, where it was warm. I missed her. I hated her for not writing back, not keeping in touch.

But mostly, I was happy for her.

Kaylee reaches out her arms, wraps them around my shoulders. I fold my head into her hair, her neck, her chest. And then I start to sob.

34

October

Herron Mills, NY

CADEN'S LATE. After school on Tuesday, Martina waits in the newer of the two coffee shops on Main, at a table near the door. She clicks her nails against her mug, an oversize ceramic bowl with a black and pink houndstooth pattern. This place is cute, but the coffee could be stronger.

She taps her phone, checks the time. He's not really that late, only a few minutes. She was early, is nervous about seeing Caden in person. Now that she's here, she just wants to get it over with.

It's been five days since Martina and Aster went to the ruins of the Windermere stable. Five days since they were brought to the station for questioning—and Martina was swiftly released after Mrs. Talbot declined to press charges for trespassing. A small mercy. Mami and Dad were still furious, of course. She's grounded until further notice, is only here right now because she lied about an after-school project. She checks her phone again. If Caden doesn't show up soon, she'll have to leave. She only has a few minutes.

Aster's arraignment was yesterday. She's grounded too, but at least she's home, not in juvie. Martina hasn't been able to reach her friend, knows she's been charged with concealing her sister's body, but not much more than that. She saw the officer collect the earring from the stable floor. She knows Aster was interviewed that night, and that she returned in the morning with her parents. That sometime after they left Windermere, Aster changed her mind about coming clean.

"Hey." Martina's head snaps up. Caden is pulling out a chair, unwrapping a scarf from around his neck, and sliding into the seat across from her. "Sorry I'm late. Took longer than I'd thought."

"No problem." Martina gives Caden a small smile. He's only home for the night. She knows she's lucky he agreed to meet her after finishing up at the station, giving a final witness statement to Holloway and Massey.

"I wanted—"

"I didn't—"

They both speak at once, then Caden laughs. "You first, Jenkins."

Martina clears her throat and takes a small sip of coffee. "I wanted to apologize. I was really frustrated last winter, with the way the investigation was going. I'm not sorry I kept bugging you for an interview, but the things I said in my 'boyfriend theory' episode, they weren't entirely responsible. I was thinking about you as a suspect, not a person."

"Thanks," Caden says. "I appreciate that."

Martina breathes and leans back in her chair. "How was, um . . . how was everything at the station?"

"You're not recording this, are you?" Caden leans forward, a small smile playing across his lips.

"Scout's honor," Martina says. "The podcast is on hold for now. I need to do some sort of final episode, but I'm . . . Honestly, I'm not ready to go there yet. All this time, I've been trying to figure things out, get justice for Zoe's family. But then . . ."

"But then the bad guy turned out to be Aster?"

"Yeah, something like that." She drains her coffee. "Can I ask you something?"

Caden nods.

"The flash drive. Why did you leave it where someone could find it?"

"How did you—?" Caden starts to ask.

"Oh right. Um, Anna found it this summer, and the card for Zoe. Right before the fire."

"Huh." Caden scrubs his hand across his eyes, then drops it to rest on the table. "Okay. Well, I found Zoe's flash drive in the stable a few days after she went missing. I thought she was angry with me, that she'd left town to punish me. Escape for a while. I really thought she'd show up by the start of the semester." He pauses, looks down at his hands. "Anyway, on my first trip home in the spring, I put it in the stall and wrote out the card. Just in case. I didn't think anyone except Zoe would go looking there. But it was probably as much a reminder for me as it was an apology for her. Because I knew if she didn't come home . . ."

For a moment, they're both silent.

"And Tiana?" Martina finally asks.

"Yeah, that never really got off the ground. After Zoe disappeared, it just got complicated. And sad. We both felt pretty guilty."

"I really am sorry," Martina says after a minute.

Caden shrugs. "Apology accepted. I think we both have some regrets. I just wish I'd gotten the chance to apologize to Zoe."

Martina stares down into her empty mug. A layer of milky foam lines the sides. "One more thing," she says, looking up. "When I do put a final episode together, I want to include memories about Zoe, from the people closest to her. Is that something you'd be interested in doing?"

Caden smiles. "Sure. That's the kind of interview about Zoe I'd be happy to do."

"Thanks." Martina smiles back, then glances at her phone. "I should get going. I'm kind of grounded for trespassing at your house last week."

Caden laughs. "I think I'm going to stay and get a coffee. Take care, Jenkins."

Martina pushes back from the table and slings her book bag over her shoulder. Then she sticks out her hand, because it feels like the right thing to do, and Caden takes it. "See you around."

35

October

Bay Ridge, Brooklyn, NY

THE LIES STARTED the moment I was born. Now that I'm home, I spend my days cleaving truth from untruth, sorting memories into the times and places they belong. I've been talking to Mom, a lot, about my early childhood. After hearing her stories, seeing the photos she kept hidden, I'm getting better at it. This face belongs here, in this year. This event happened there. In the daylight, I'm beginning to understand. Everything that got jumbled is becoming unjumbled. I can hold one piece of memory up to the light, look at it, examine it without the other memories getting in the way, churning things into the messy concoction that scrambled my brain this summer.

But I can't shake the dreams. At night, I dream I'm in Pathways, curled up on my cot. I dream I'm inside Windermere, surrounded by birds. I dream I'm in the stable, and it's burning, and I'm burning with it.

It's almost Halloween. In Bay Ridge, some of our neighbors have gone all out with their porch and lawn decorations, as they always do. There are full-scale scenes of witches and zombies, murder and mayhem. I don't look too closely. When Mom sends me out to the store, the laundromat, to Duane Reade, I keep my eyes on the sidewalk, where the crisp browns of autumn leaves have begun to scatter. I wrap my scarf twice around my neck and button my denim jacket, relishing the chill in the air.

It's autumn. I'm outside.

SUNY New Paltz let me defer my start until the spring semester, given the circumstances. My new leaf will have to wait a few months. But it's okay. I'm home in Brooklyn. I'm free.

Today, I don't have any specific errands on my agenda. I'm just walking, listening to the crunch of leaves beneath my feet, letting the familiarity of the houses and apartments I pass wash over me, letting the memories come.

This first one isn't a memory so much as a story Mom should have told me a long time ago. She said it was her secret to keep, but I think she's beginning to understand it was mine too.

Now that we can finally talk about it, Mom says she knew the second she had me. I wasn't the daughter of her husband, John. I was the product of Mom's on-again, off-again summertime affair with a mostly laid-back landscape architect with an occasional temper, who she'd met on one of many summer vacations to Herron Mills. Because we had been to Herron

Mills—John wasn't cheap, he just wasn't a very good husband. He'd spend most of their vacations ignoring her, absorbed in his work, and eventually, she found George Spanos.

There was no Stone Harbor. It was always Herron Mills.

It explains a lot about my mom's reaction when I told her about the nanny job, why she didn't want me to go. She was so afraid I'd run into George, or Zoe, who she didn't even know was missing. That they'd see, after all this time, that I was theirs. Because Mom never told anyone the truth about my paternity—not John, even when they divorced; not George; and certainly not me. To hear her tell it, we were fine on our own. We didn't need John, and we didn't need George either, who by the time my parents split, had reunited with his wife, Joan. I get that. But she still should have told me. If she had, surely none of this would have happened the way it did. . . .

After I confessed, when I swore to Mom that I knew Zoe, that we'd spent time in Herron Mills together last winter, she believed me. Of course we'd found each other again. I can understand now why Mom thought my story was real; it's the same reason it all made sense to me. It's true that I drank too much and blacked out often. It's true that the police used to bring me home. There was just enough truth to my story; it made it all seem real.

After hearing Mom's stories, here's what I know was actually real:

I'm three, and Zoe is five. Zoe is my summer friend, two years older and infinitely wiser. Her dad and my mom take us to get ice cream at Jenkins' Creamery on Main Street while my dad works. Dad is always working, laptop open on the desk in the little house we're renting, papers spread out, phone pressed to his ear. Dad is a businessman, which means he's always busy. I'm happy Mom has a friend, happy I have Zoe.

I order chocolate with sprinkles in a waffle cone that Mr. Jenkins promises won't leak, because there's hard chocolate hidden at the bottom. Zoe orders the same thing she always orders: the featured flavor in the bright blue box on the chalkboard menu, Chocolate Caramel Popcorn.

"In a cup," she insists, even though it's better in a cone. Zoe doesn't like to get ice cream on her face, prefers to eat it neatly with a plastic spoon.

Her dad laughs as we leave the ice-cream shop and turn onto Main Street. My face is already covered in chocolate, while Zoe dabs at her clean cheeks with a napkin. "My little princess," he calls her.

We're at the glassed-in pool in Zoe's backyard, stationed on the lounge chairs with the soft plum cushions. It's late afternoon, maybe four or five, the hottest part of the day. I'm wearing a bright blue bathing suit with little white stars splashed across the fabric. Zoe is wearing her yellow two-piece, her favorite. Her dad has the air-conditioning cranked up, the cool air cutting the thick mugginess in here. He's sitting on a porch swing behind us with Mom, sipping cocktails and laughing.

Zoe and I have our own cocktails: pink lemonade and fizzy water and ice. Lemon Spritz, her dad calls them. A little yellow parasol rests on the rim of Zoe's cup, but mine has a lid, so I keep my parasol on the lounge chair beside me.

Belle, Zoe's bichon frise puppy, is flopped across Zoe's feet on her lounger. I wish Belle would come visit me, but she's drawn to Zoe like a magnet, always wants to be close to her. Zoe has a way with animals like that. Even the squirrels don't run away when she goes out in the yard to sprinkle seed along the garden wall.

"Where's your mom?" I ask, and Zoe takes a long drink.

"She works in the city," she says finally. "Daddy says her job is very important, so she has to live there with my little sister for a while. I'm going to visit them at the end of the summer, but Daddy will stay here. They're 'taking a break' right now." She surrounds the words with air quotes.

"My dad has an important job too," I say. "He's very busy. That's why he can never hang out with us."

Zoe nods solemnly, and I wonder if my parents will "take a break." But they both live in the city. Where would Dad go?

All at once, the sky darkens, and a long streamer of lightning strobes across the sky above the glass ceiling. While the light is still bright in our eyes, thunder cracks, loud and very close, and Zoe screams. I stare at the sky above us, fascinated, as rain starts pelting the glass.

"It's okay," I tell Zoe, but she's already curled in a ball, her lemonade pooling on the floor beneath our chairs. Mr. Spanos snatches her up and takes her inside, promising that the storm won't hurt her, that they'll wait in the hall closet together until it passes.

Mom sits next to me on Zoe's abandoned lounger and slips her hand into mine.

"You okay, pumpkin?" she asks, and I nod.

"Why is Zoe afraid of storms? They can't get us in here."

Mom shrugs. "Lots of kids are afraid of thunder and lightning. I'm glad you're not. Hopefully it'll pass for Zoe soon."

※ ※ ※

I'm on the balcony at Windermere. It's late afternoon, late summer, the last summer my parents will vacation in Herron Mills. The day is bright and cloudless and thankfully not too hot. The Talbots are throwing one of their classic parties, an end-of-the-summer bash. Mom is sipping a glass of rosé and chatting with the wives of George's friends. My dad is downstairs, in the back, walking out where it's quiet, by the stable and riding pen, so he can take a business call without the nuisance of the party getting in the way. If Mom and George are being too obvious, flirting and chatting, my dad's not around to notice.

I'm playing with Zoe and Caden near the balcony's southeast corner. Caden is our audience, although not a very good one. He's five, like Zoe, and quickly distracted. They know each other from school, but today will be the first—and last—time Caden and I will ever meet. For fourteen years, that is. Zoe and I are standing with the balcony rail to our backs, reciting part of a poem she's taught me while Caden fidgets with his bow tie.

> *No time hath she to sport and play:*
> *A charmed web she weaves alway.*
> *A curse is on her, if she stay*
> *Her weaving, either night or day,*
> *To look down to Camelot.*
> *She knows not what the curse may be;*
> *Therefore she weaveth steadily,*
> *Therefore no other care hath she,*
> *The Lady of Shalott.*

I trip over the strange words, but Zoe knows them by heart. She learned them from TV, from something called *Anne of Green Gables*, which Mom says we can rent at home, if she can find it on Netflix or at the budget rental place near our apartment. She says I'm too young for it, but I don't care. If Zoe loves it, I'll love it too.

As soon as we finish the passage I've learned, Caden darts off, inside the house, leaving Zoe and me to entertain ourselves again.

She reaches for my hands, and then we're twirling on the balcony, arms crossed in an X, spinning and giggling, Zoe's laugh a glittering sunbeam in the summer air. I'm in a white party dress with a yellow sash, because Zoe says yellow is the prettiest color, next to gold. Zoe is wearing a ballerina dress, shimmery gold top attached to a cream tulle skirt. We wear matching pink barrettes in our raven hair. We twirl and twirl, and the sun dances like snowflakes on our skin through the lattice of the tall maples and oaks.

Two strong hands take hold of my waist, and suddenly Zoe's sitting on her bottom on the balcony while I'm being lifted up, up, up in the air. The hands dangle me over the balcony rail, and I whimper as the ground below swells and buckles.

"Tell me who her father is, Gloria."

"What the hell are you thinking?" Mom's voice is a hot whisper, the panic hovering right beneath her desire to deflect the party's attention away from us.

The ground swells again, a roiling, churning wave.

"We're just having fun." A whisper in my ear, whiskey thick on Zoe's dad's breath. "Don't be afraid, Anna."

"George, put her down. Right now." In my mother's eyes,

tears gather, then spill over. Below me, the grass surges and retreats. My whimpering gets louder.

"Just tell me the truth, Gloria. I'm her father, aren't I?"

His palms are slick with summery, boozy sweat. They begin to slip against the shimmery fabric of my dress. I squeeze my eyes shut and silently pray he'll put me down. That this will all be over soon. Then his hands slip again, and for a second, I'm falling. Everything goes out of focus as I pitch down, body twisting in a flash of yellow and white.

Then his hands tighten around my baby fat arms, and I'm dangling. I press my eyes shut and he pulls me up, back onto the balcony, back to safety and my mom's wet sobs.

After that last summer, we don't return to Windermere. We don't return to Herron Mills. Mom resolves to make things work with Dad, but two years later, he leaves for a better opportunity. Something better than us. LA, Mom tells me now. We move to a small apartment in Bay Ridge. Mom starts working one job, then two. I forget Zoe, mostly. Mostly, I forget Herron Mills. Until fourteen years later, when I'm offered a plum gig at the Bellamy estate, and bits and pieces of my early childhood start to catch at the corners of my eyes like wisps of shadows at the end of a long summer day.

Now, I'm taking one day at a time. Allowing Mom's stories and pictures to pull my memories more clearly into focus. I turn the corner onto Eighty-Second, pass by the fruit market, the house with the purple awning. Kaylee found an apartment in Queens with Ian, which is okay for now, and she's busy with community college, which is great.

No one has heard from Starr. We've retreated back into our guilty silence. Maybe she faked her death; maybe she's living a new life somewhere amazing. I looked it up. People do it more than you'd think. I need to believe it's possible, although deep down, I know the truth.

Martina and I text every day. She's going to come out to Bay Ridge to spend the weekend with us, as soon as her parents agree to let her come. Hopefully by January, when I move up to New Paltz, there will be a new podcast everyone's listening to. A new case to push the name Anna Cicconi far, far into the background.

Most nights, when I'm lying in bed and trying not to fall asleep, delaying the dreams I know will come, my mind wanders to Zoe and Aster. My sisters. The short gasps of time I got to spend with them both. Now that I understand who she was to me, I want Zoe back more than ever. She was my summer friend, and so much more we didn't realize. Our parents' secrets like a river running between us, pushing us to opposite banks, pushing us apart.

Aster was only a baby when our parents had an affair. If I ever met her when we were kids, I don't remember it. Sometimes I think of her, and my vision goes white with fury. How she let me sit in Pathways for two months. How she must have hoped my confession would stick, that she'd get to keep the real story locked inside her heart. But then I remind myself that, in the end, she did the right thing.

She's lucky. She'll be held at home until trial. I'm glad she's not in juvie, like I was, but I know things still can't be easy. I'd like to visit her, but I'm not ready yet. Someday, I will be.

After all, she's the only sister I have left.

36

October

Herron Mills, NY

I HAVE A SECRET. It's not dirty or little or some cutesy catch-phrase. It's caustic, noxious, burning me from the inside.

I killed Zoe.

And it was a terrible, terrible mistake.

It began last year, when Mom had surgery to fix a torn rotator cuff. After the procedure, her doctors prescribed this painkiller Demerol, which she only took one time, to get through a dinner party she was hosting for *Wayfare + Ramble*. In typical Mom fashion, she refused to cancel it, even though she was barely out of the hospital and Dad said she needed to rest.

Mom drank that night, some champagne, then too much red wine. I watched her stumble into the bathroom, and the running water didn't do much to block the sound of her retching over the toilet. After that, Mom shoved the Demerol to the back of the medicine cabinet and switched to Advil instead.

I wasn't trying to kill anyone, and that's the god's honest truth. Like I told the detectives, I wanted to punish Caden for breaking my sister's heart.

But there's some stuff I didn't tell: When I got to the stable that afternoon, the open bottle of whiskey was less than a quarter full. At first, I didn't pour that much Demerol in. It was the liquid stuff, smelled a little like bananas. I started with a few drops, but then, I drained the bottle. I figured Caden would come home from the city, find the flash drive, and decide he needed a drink. It was a perfect plan. He'd pour himself a glass of whiskey, and it would make him sick. Poetic justice.

But it didn't happen that way.

What I told police about getting a bad feeling in my gut that night was true. But I wasn't just feeling guilty about the flash drive. I knew I'd gone overboard. I'd poured too much Demerol in.

Of course, I was way too late. By the time I got there, she'd drained the last drop from the bottle. Demerol, whiskey, the prescription meds she took for astraphobia and generalized anxiety—the combination was deadly.

I'm sorry, Zoe. I'm so, so sorry.

When they found her body, there was so little left of her. The coroner wasn't able to confirm the presence of Demerol in her bloodstream, but I know. I killed my sister. It was a mistake, the worst mistake possible, but they never would have ruled her death an accident if I'd told the whole story.

The truth's out there now, a version of it anyway. Another tragedy for people to ogle and judge. But there are some secrets—my secrets—that Windermere will hold forever, trapped beneath the ash like spilled blood.

Acknowledgments

When I began writing *I Killed Zoe Spanos* in early 2018, two obsessions were swirling through my head: Daphne du Maurier's classic thriller *Rebecca* and the recent boom of true crime podcasts following the wildly popular *Serial*. I wanted to marry the romantic seaside intrigue of *Rebecca* with the immediacy of the podcast format. What if Rebecca de Winter had gone missing today? Once I landed on the Hamptons setting, the rest fell swiftly into place.

So many people's enthusiasm and smarts have gone into *Zoe*'s creation and publication. First thanks go to my incredible agent, Erin Harris, whose instant excitement for this book—long before it was actually a book—and intimate knowledge of the setting inspired me to dig in deep and make it real. My editors at McElderry Books were fantastic partners in ensuring every aspect of the mystery ticked and each member of the book's cast of characters became layered and compelling. To Ruta Rimas and Nicole Fiorica, my utmost gratitude for your editorial guidance and fabulous advocacy. I am truly lucky to have had both of your hands and minds on this project.

Also at McElderry and Simon & Schuster, my sincerest thanks go out to publisher Justin Chanda; publicist Audrey Gibbons; art director Debra Sfetsios-Conover and artist Levente Szabó, who so brilliantly brought Anna—or is it Zoe?—to life on the cover; Laura Bernard, who illustrated the gorgeous map of Herron Mills in exactly the way I'd envisioned the town; in-house designers Irene Metaxatos and Rebecca Syracuse, who so beautifully coordinated the design; managing editor Bridget Madsen; copyeditor Ellen Winkler; production manager Elizabeth Blake-Linn; proofreader Mandy Veloso; deputy publisher Anne Zafian; and the fantastic sales, marketing, and operations teams. My tremendous thanks for all the in-house support!

At WME, heartfelt gratitude to my fierce film and TV agent Hilary Zaizt Michael. At Folio, big thanks to the international rights team, especially Melissa Sarver White and Madeline Froyd, and to audio rights manager Kat Odom-Tomchin. At Brillstein and eOne, much appreciation to Amy Powell and Kaleb Tuttle for your creative enthusiasm. At MBC, thank you immensely to my savvy publicist Megan Beatie.

I Killed Zoe Spanos would have been a much less thrilling and much clumsier read without the keen feedback from my early readers Karen M. McManus and Osvaldo Oyola. I can't thank you enough for your time and brilliance in shining a light on the areas that needed my closest focus. And to the NovelSleuths: your support has blown me away; you rock!

I am incredibly lucky to have the most supportive family and friends a writer could hope for. To Mom, Dad, Aunt Sally, Sonia, Lissette, and Angel—you're the best. To Katie, Francie, and Winnie, you give the best snuggles (and cause the most trouble). To my ladies—you mean the world to me. To Osvaldo—you get two mentions, and with good reason. I couldn't do this without you.

Finally, to my readers. You cannot possibly know how excited I am to be sharing my third book with you. So I'm going to try to convey it here: I AM SHOUTY CAPS LEVEL EXCITED!!! Thank you for picking up my YA-*Rebecca*-in-the-Hamptons novel. I hope it was as fun and twisty to read as it was for me to write.